POWER ON!

POWER ON!

Jean J. Ryoo and Jane Margolis

Illustrated by Charis JB

The MIT Press
Cambridge, Massachusetts
London, England

This book was set in Avenir condensed by Charis JB. Printed and bound in the United States of America.
Library of Congress Cataloging-in-Publication Data

Names: Ryoo, Jean J., author. | Margolis, Jane, author. | Jackson Barrios, Charis, illustrator.
Title: Power on! / Jean J. Ryoo and Jane Margolis ; illustrated by Charis JB.
Description: Cambridge, Massachusetts : The MIT Press, [2022] | Four high school friends use computer science and other various technologies to communicate with each other and participate in protesting systemic racism, learning how students of color and females have been historically marginalized. Includes information on important computer scientists. | Includes bibliographical references.
Identifiers: LCCN 2021004740 | ISBN 9780262543255 (paperback)
Subjects: LCSH: Computer scientists–Juvenile literature. | CYAC: Computer science–Fiction. | Communication–Fiction. | Technology–Fiction. | Racism–Fiction. | Friendship–Fiction. | High schools–Fiction. | Schools–Fiction.
Classification: LCC PZ7.7.R976 Po 2022 | DDC 741.5/973–dc23
LC record available at https://lccn.loc.gov/2021004740

10   9   8   7   6   5   4   3   2   1

This book is dedicated to Robert Parris Moses (1935–2021). His leadership in the Civil Rights movement and life as an educator deeply inspired us, showing us how these efforts are one and the same.

BOB MOSES, 1964

TABLE OF CONTENTS

CHAPTER 1
THIS IS MESSED UP

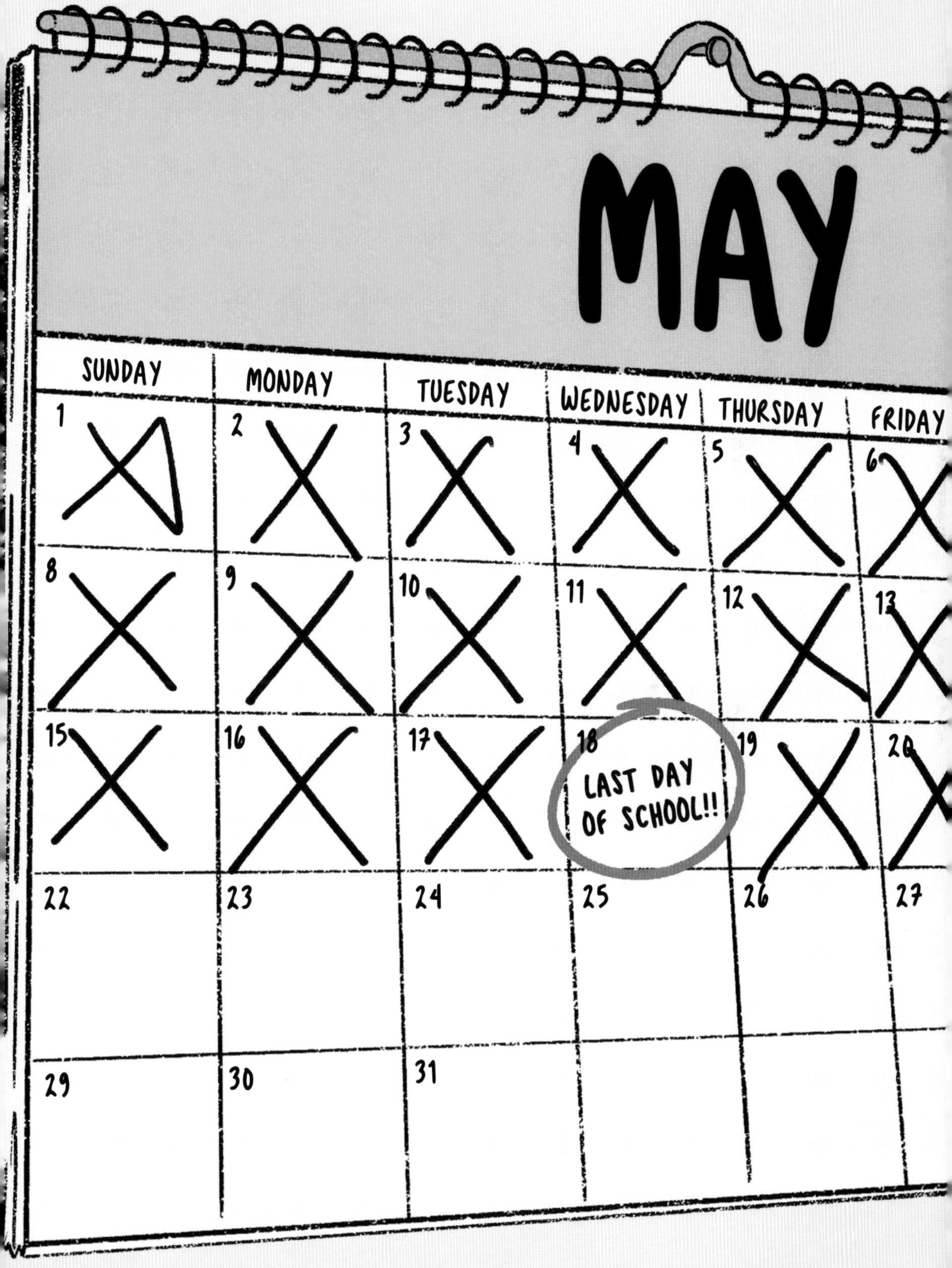

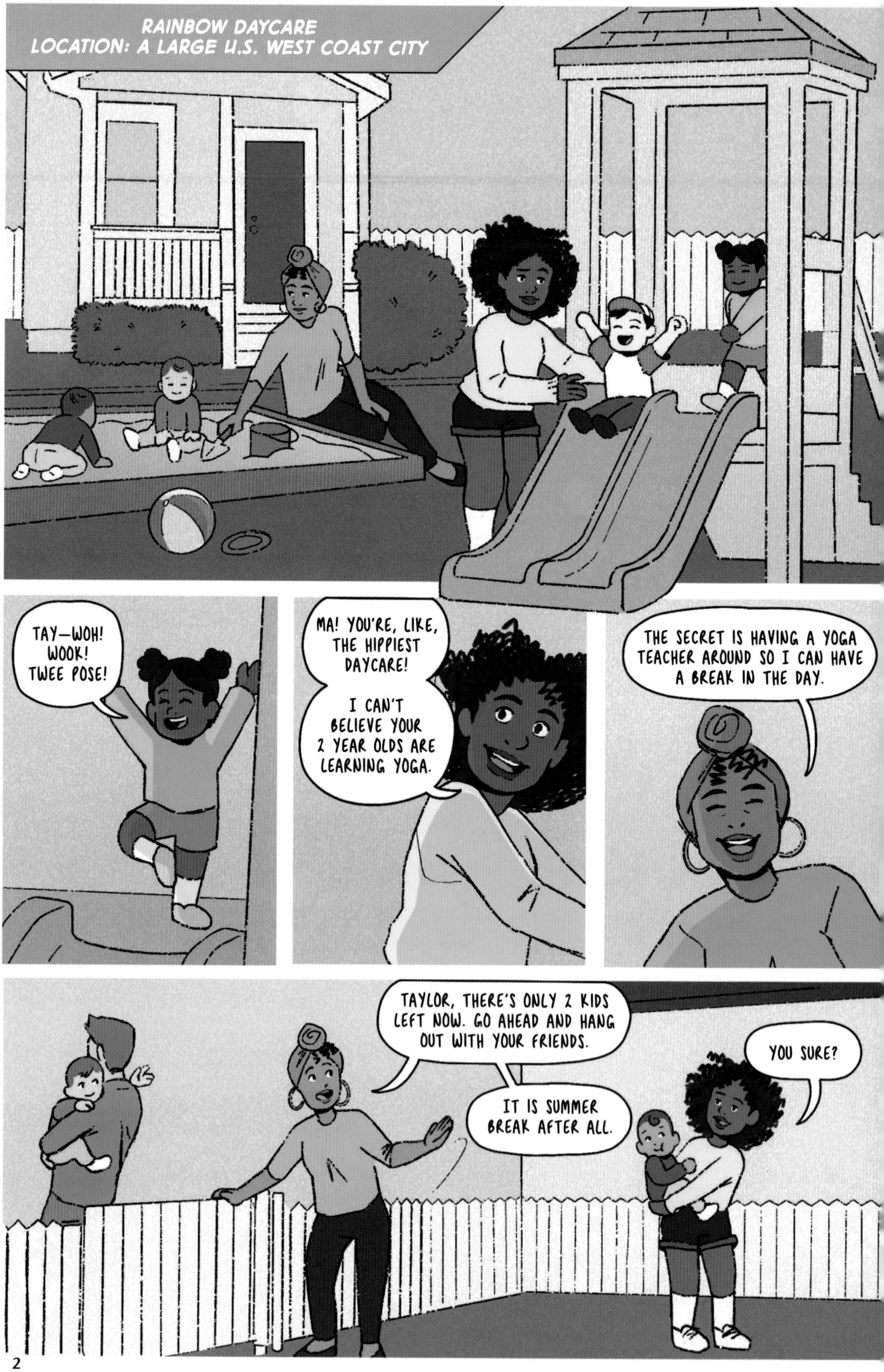
RAINBOW DAYCARE
LOCATION: A LARGE U.S. WEST COAST CITY
TAY—WOH! WOOK! TWEE POSE!
MA! YOU'RE, LIKE, THE HIPPIEST DAYCARE!
I CAN'T BELIEVE YOUR 2 YEAR OLDS ARE LEARNING YOGA.
THE SECRET IS HAVING A YOGA TEACHER AROUND SO I CAN HAVE A BREAK IN THE DAY.
TAYLOR, THERE'S ONLY 2 KIDS LEFT NOW. GO AHEAD AND HANG OUT WITH YOUR FRIENDS.
IT IS SUMMER BREAK AFTER ALL.
YOU SURE?

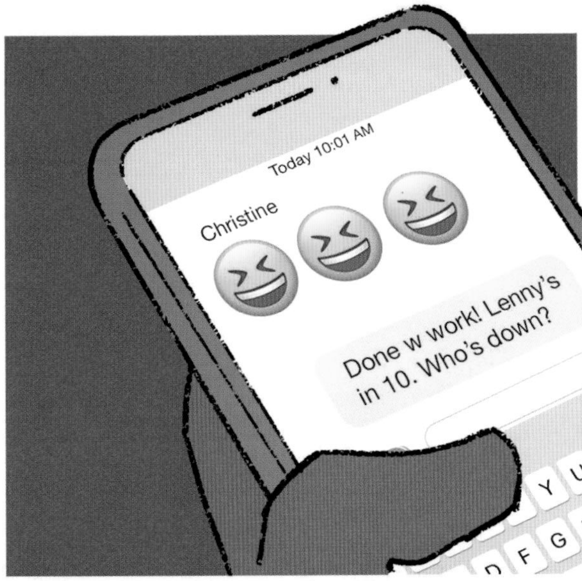
Today 10:01 AM
Christine
Done w work! Lenny's in 10. Who's down?

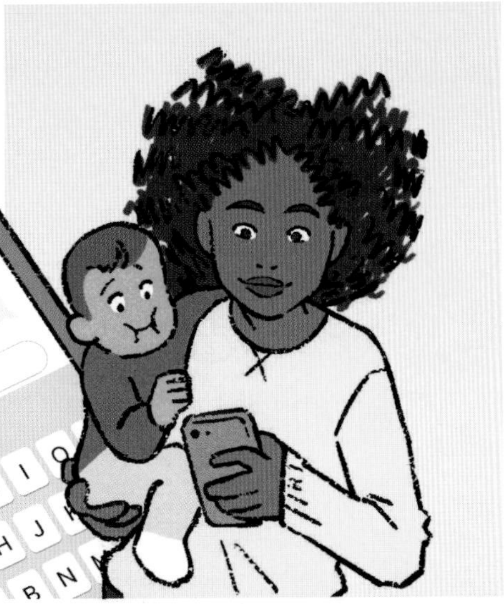

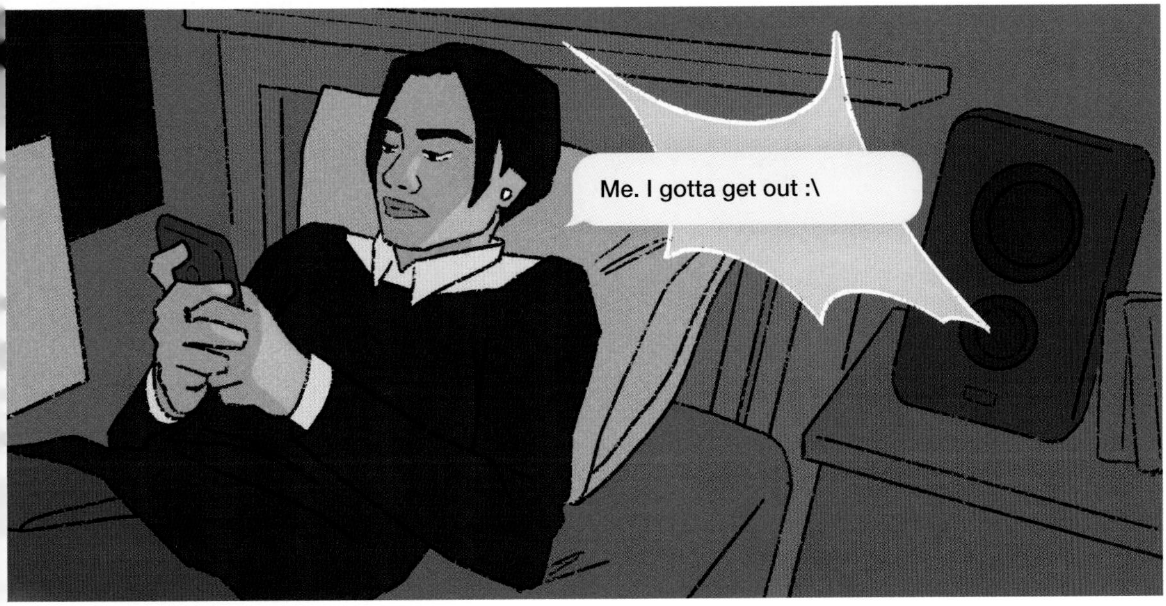
Me. I gotta get out :\

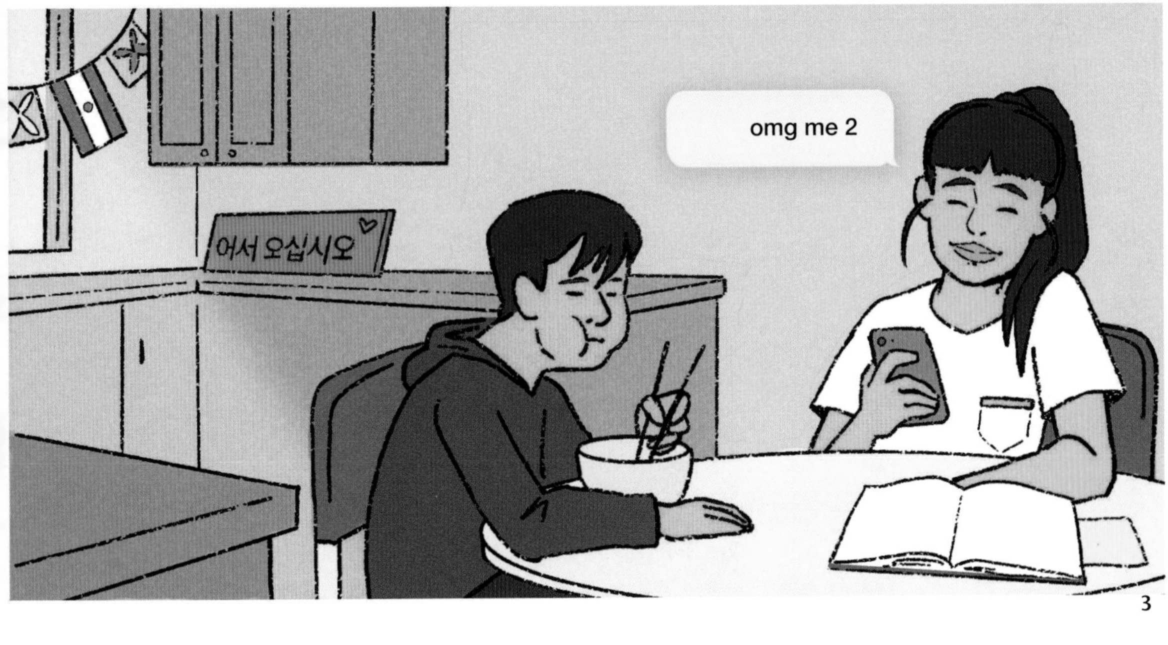
어서 오십시오
omg me 2

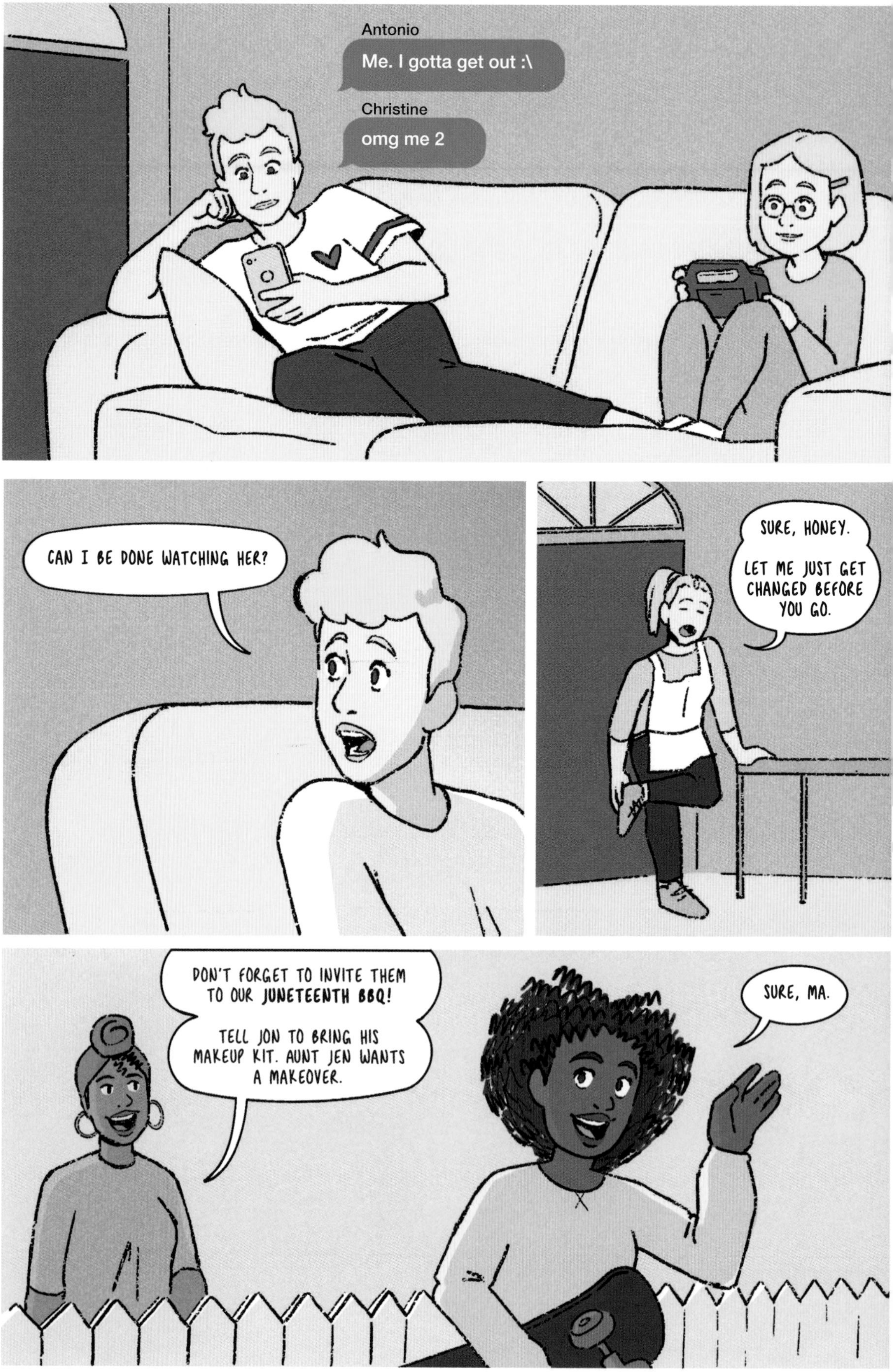
Antonio
Me. I gotta get out :\
Christine
omg me 2
CAN I BE DONE WATCHING HER?
SURE, HONEY.
LET ME JUST GET CHANGED BEFORE YOU GO.
DON'T FORGET TO INVITE THEM TO OUR JUNETEENTH BBQ!
TELL JON TO BRING HIS MAKEUP KIT. AUNT JEN WANTS A MAKEOVER.
SURE, MA.

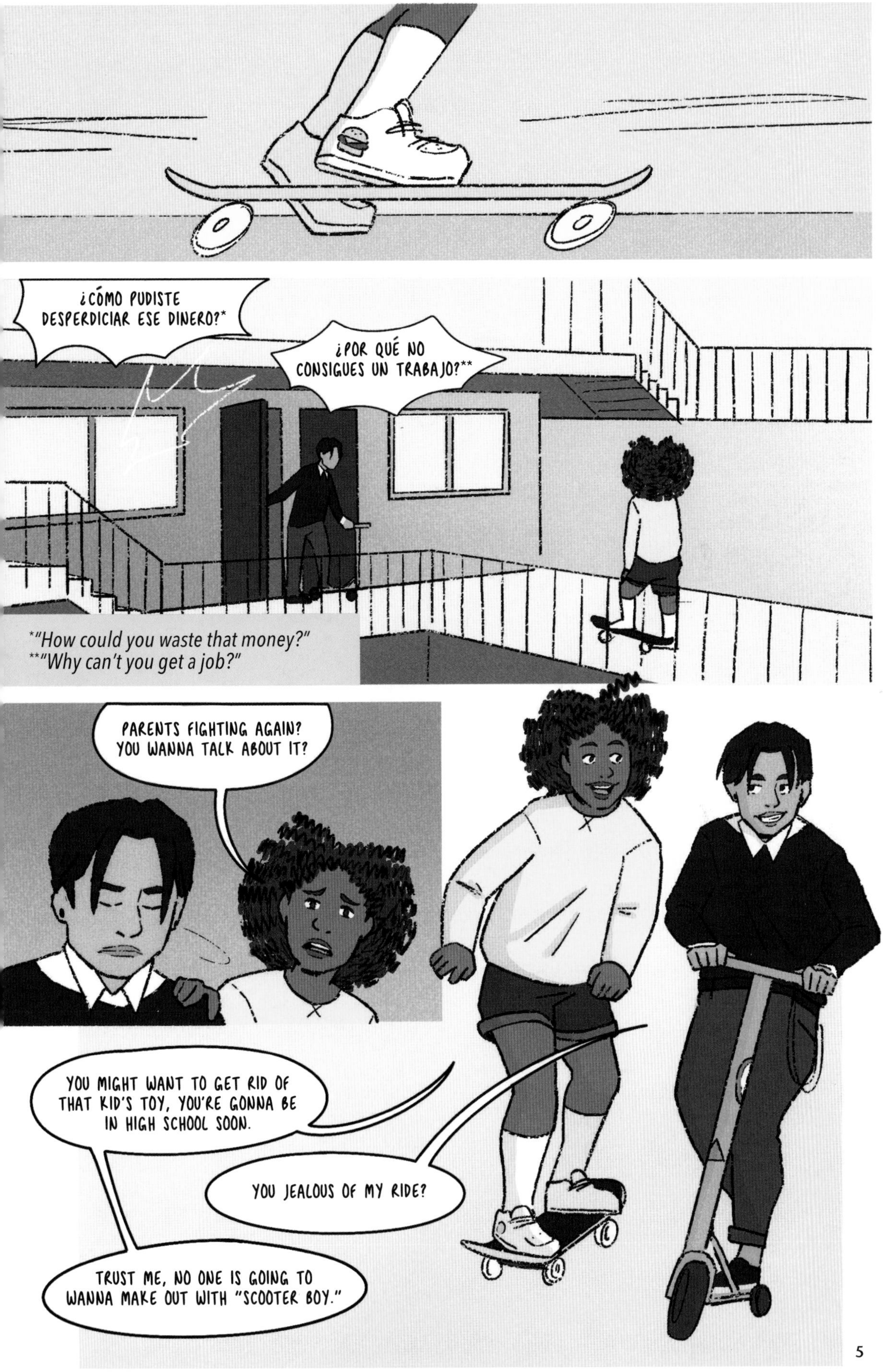
¿CÓMO PUDISTE DESPERDICIAR ESE DINERO?*
¿POR QUÉ NO CONSIGUES UN TRABAJO?**
*"How could you waste that money?"
**"Why can't you get a job?"
PARENTS FIGHTING AGAIN? YOU WANNA TALK ABOUT IT?
YOU MIGHT WANT TO GET RID OF THAT KID'S TOY, YOU'RE GONNA BE IN HIGH SCHOOL SOON.
YOU JEALOUS OF MY RIDE?
TRUST ME, NO ONE IS GOING TO WANNA MAKE OUT WITH "SCOOTER BOY."

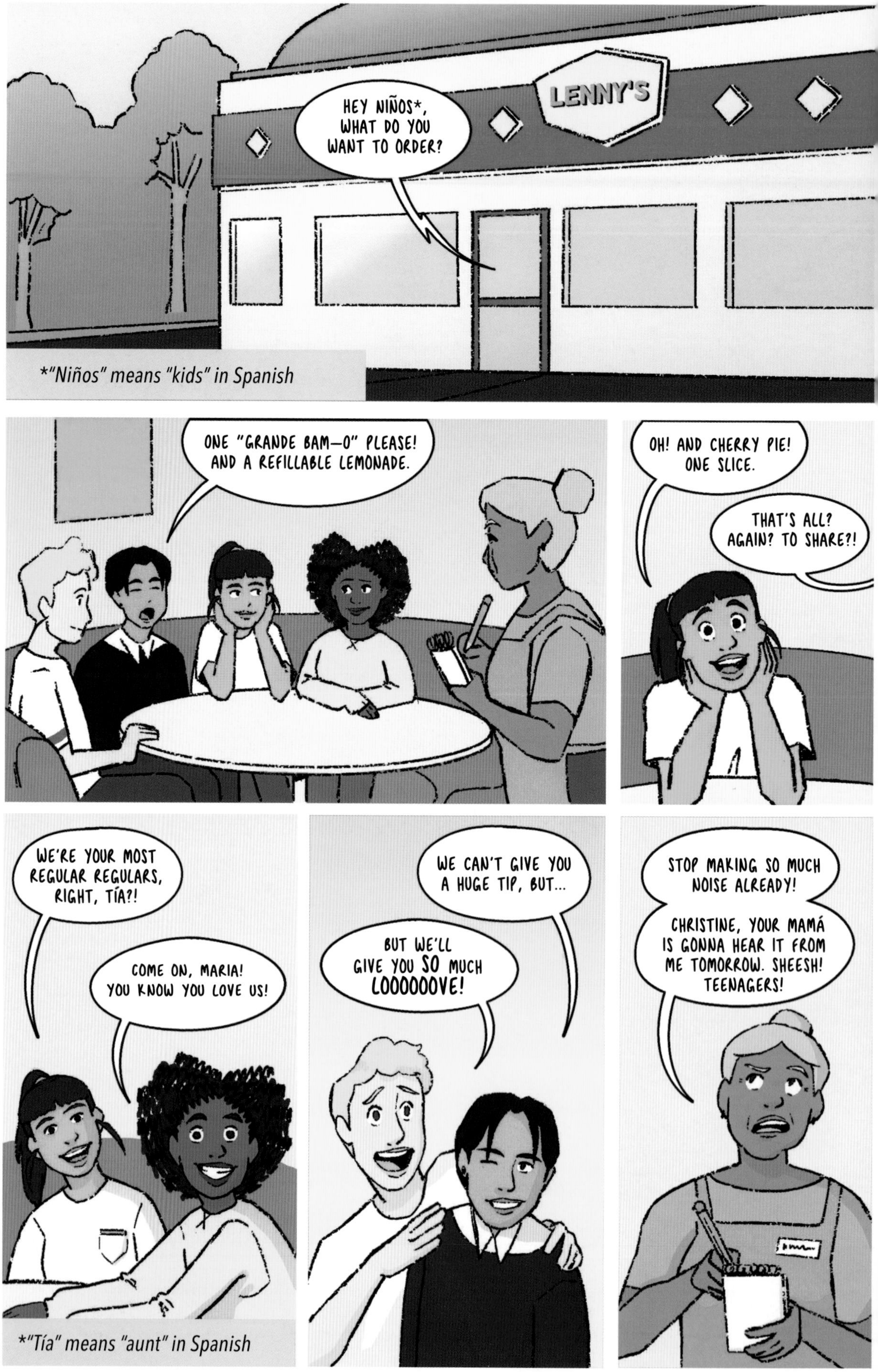
LENNY'S
HEY NIÑOS*, WHAT DO YOU WANT TO ORDER?
*"Niños" means "kids" in Spanish
ONE "GRANDE BAM—O" PLEASE! AND A REFILLABLE LEMONADE.
OH! AND CHERRY PIE! ONE SLICE.
THAT'S ALL? AGAIN? TO SHARE?!
WE'RE YOUR MOST REGULAR REGULARS, RIGHT, TÍA?!
COME ON, MARIA! YOU KNOW YOU LOVE US!
*"Tía" means "aunt" in Spanish
WE CAN'T GIVE YOU A HUGE TIP, BUT...
BUT WE'LL GIVE YOU SO MUCH LOOOOOOVE!
STOP MAKING SO MUCH NOISE ALREADY!
CHRISTINE, YOUR MAMÁ IS GONNA HEAR IT FROM ME TOMORROW. SHEESH! TEENAGERS!

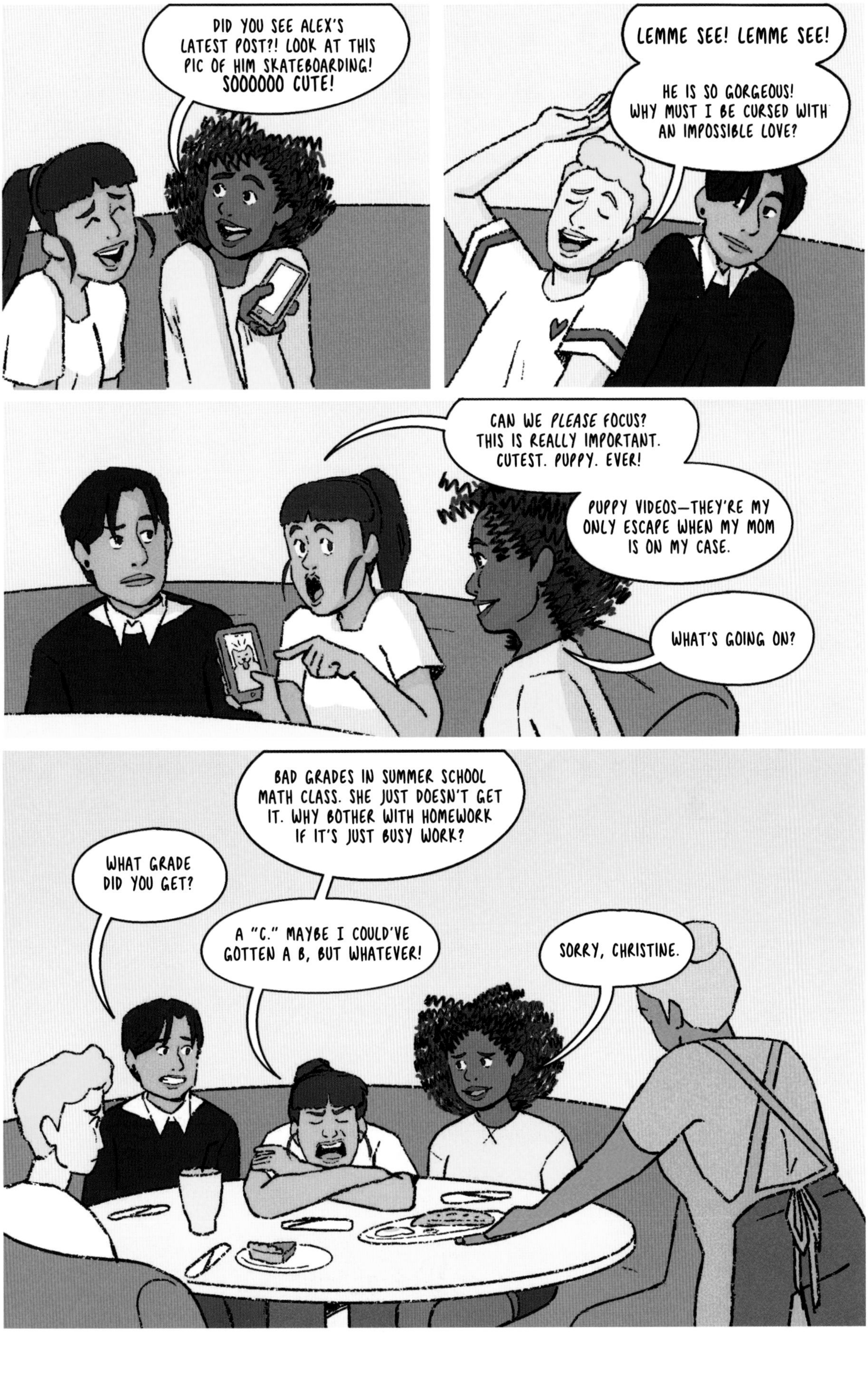
DID YOU SEE ALEX'S LATEST POST?! LOOK AT THIS PIC OF HIM SKATEBOARDING! SOOOOOO CUTE!
LEMME SEE! LEMME SEE!
HE IS SO GORGEOUS! WHY MUST I BE CURSED WITH AN IMPOSSIBLE LOVE?
CAN WE *PLEASE* FOCUS? THIS IS REALLY IMPORTANT. CUTEST. PUPPY. EVER!
PUPPY VIDEOS—THEY'RE MY ONLY ESCAPE WHEN MY MOM IS ON MY CASE.
WHAT'S GOING ON?
BAD GRADES IN SUMMER SCHOOL MATH CLASS. SHE JUST DOESN'T GET IT. WHY BOTHER WITH HOMEWORK IF IT'S JUST BUSY WORK?
WHAT GRADE DID YOU GET?
A "C." MAYBE I COULD'VE GOTTEN A B, BUT WHATEVER!
SORRY, CHRISTINE.

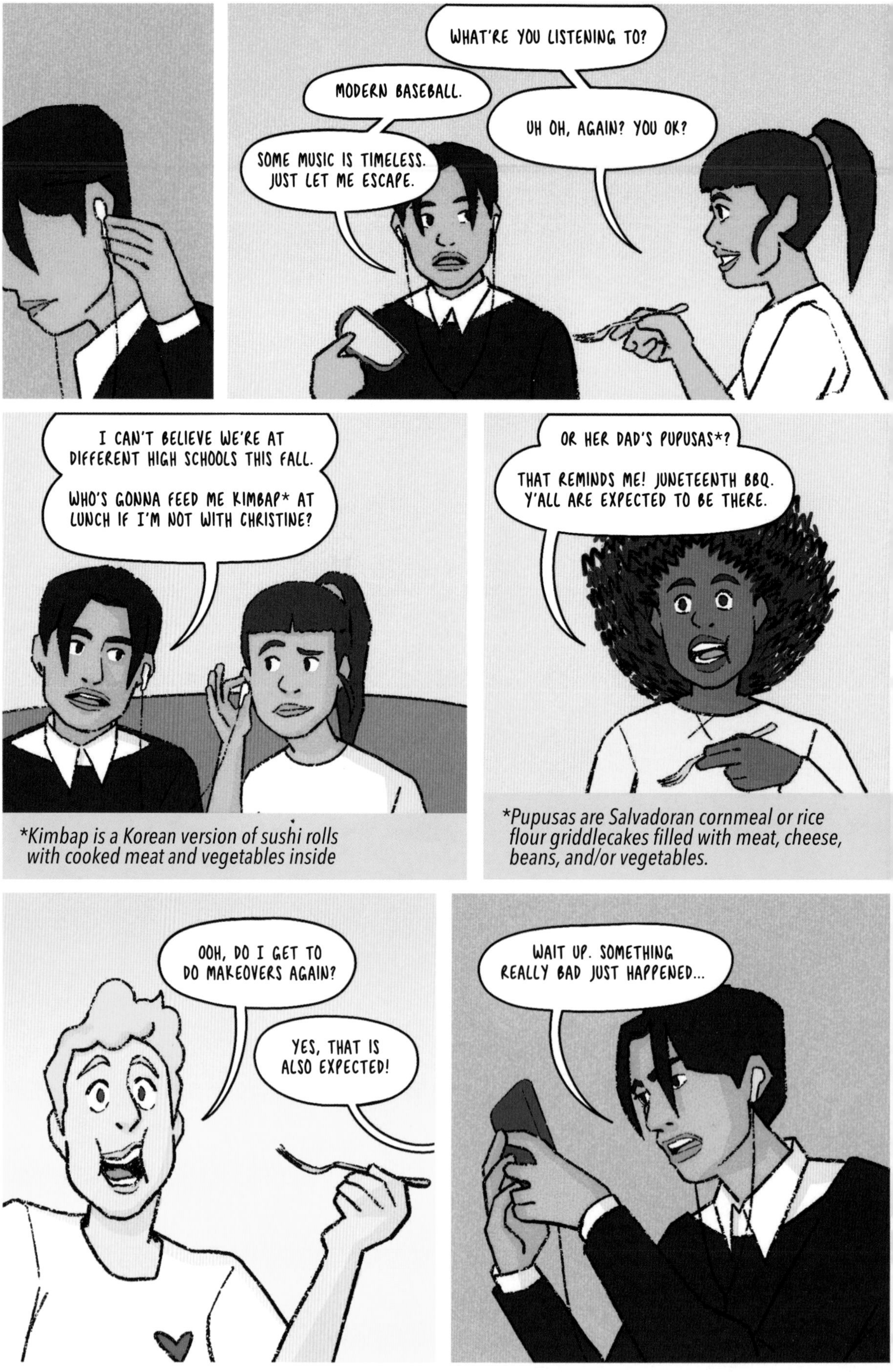
WHAT'RE YOU LISTENING TO?
MODERN BASEBALL.
UH OH, AGAIN? YOU OK?
SOME MUSIC IS TIMELESS. JUST LET ME ESCAPE.
I CAN'T BELIEVE WE'RE AT DIFFERENT HIGH SCHOOLS THIS FALL.
WHO'S GONNA FEED ME KIMBAP* AT LUNCH IF I'M NOT WITH CHRISTINE?
*Kimbap is a Korean version of sushi rolls with cooked meat and vegetables inside
OR HER DAD'S PUPUSAS*?
THAT REMINDS ME! JUNETEENTH BBQ. Y'ALL ARE EXPECTED TO BE THERE.
*Pupusas are Salvadoran cornmeal or rice flour griddlecakes filled with meat, cheese, beans, and/or vegetables.
OOH, DO I GET TO DO MAKEOVERS AGAIN?
YES, THAT IS ALSO EXPECTED!
WAIT UP. SOMETHING REALLY BAD JUST HAPPENED...

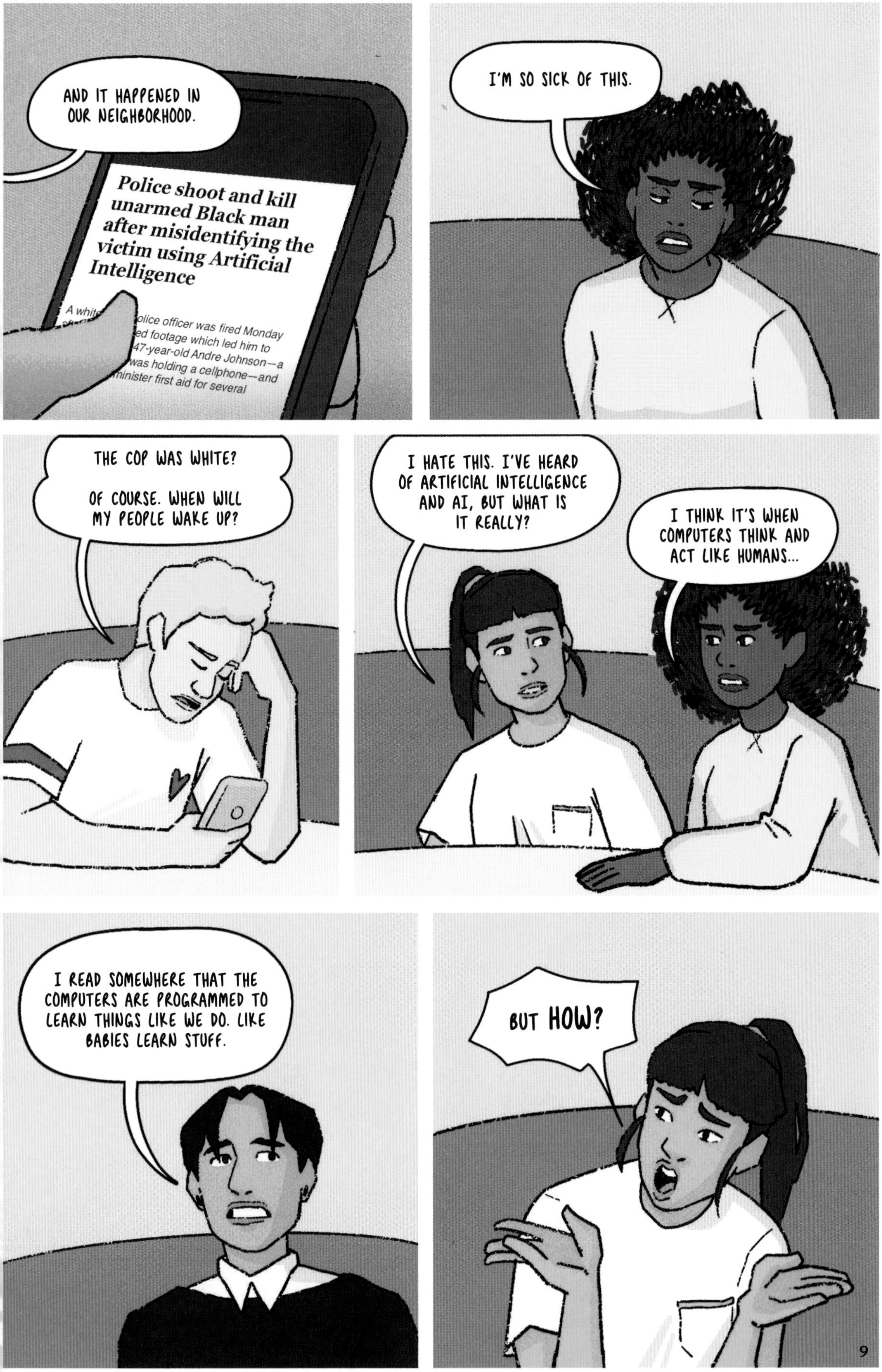

AND IT HAPPENED IN OUR NEIGHBORHOOD.
Police shoot and kill unarmed Black man after misidentifying the victim using Artificial Intelligence
I'M SO SICK OF THIS.
THE COP WAS WHITE? OF COURSE. WHEN WILL MY PEOPLE WAKE UP?
I HATE THIS. I'VE HEARD OF ARTIFICIAL INTELLIGENCE AND AI, BUT WHAT IS IT REALLY?
I THINK IT'S WHEN COMPUTERS THINK AND ACT LIKE HUMANS...
I READ SOMEWHERE THAT THE COMPUTERS ARE PROGRAMMED TO LEARN THINGS LIKE WE DO. LIKE BABIES LEARN STUFF.
BUT HOW?

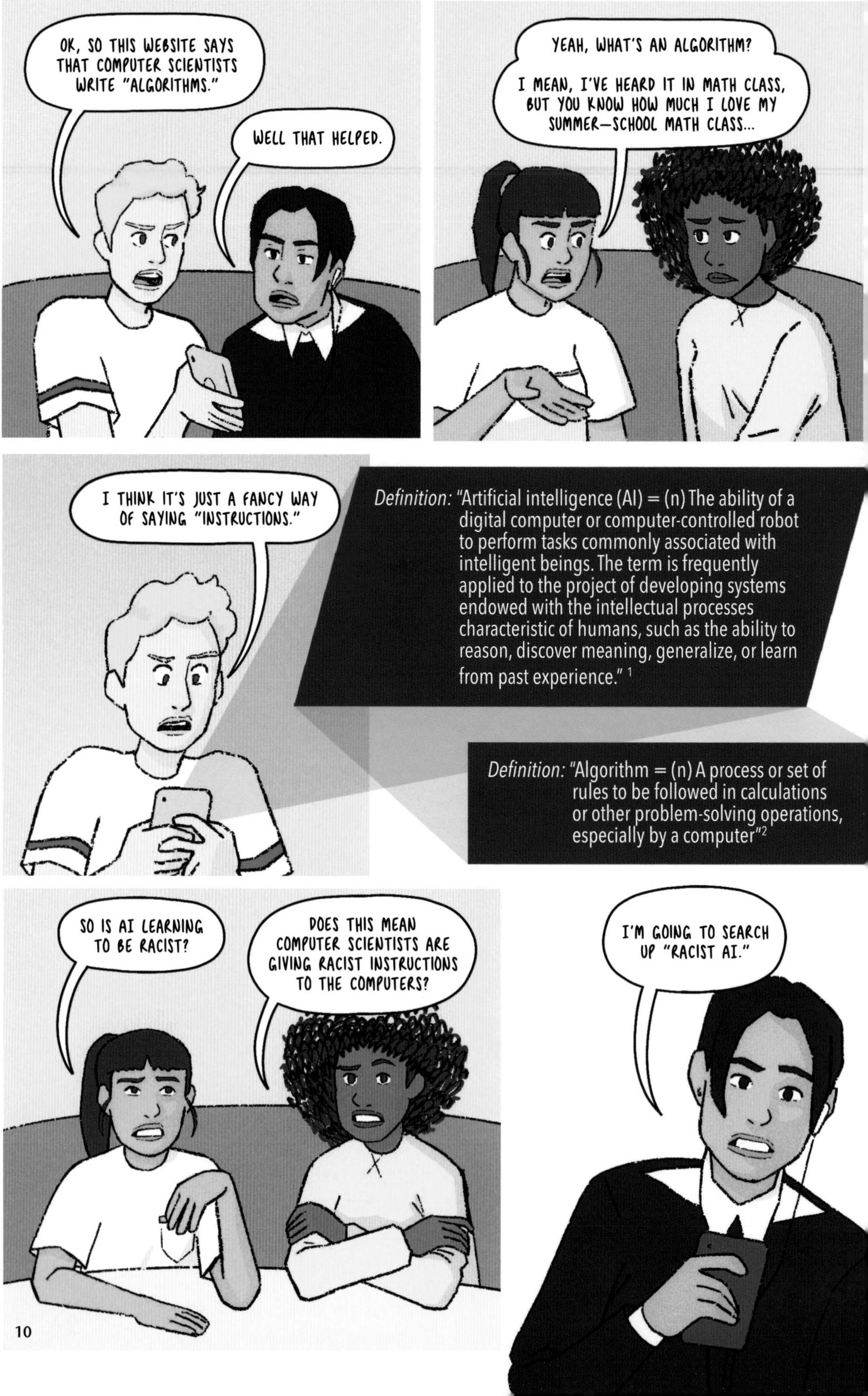
OK, SO THIS WEBSITE SAYS THAT COMPUTER SCIENTISTS WRITE "ALGORITHMS."
WELL THAT HELPED.
YEAH, WHAT'S AN ALGORITHM?
I MEAN, I'VE HEARD IT IN MATH CLASS, BUT YOU KNOW HOW MUCH I LOVE MY SUMMER—SCHOOL MATH CLASS...
I THINK IT'S JUST A FANCY WAY OF SAYING "INSTRUCTIONS."
Definition: "Artificial intelligence (AI) = (n) The ability of a digital computer or computer-controlled robot to perform tasks commonly associated with intelligent beings. The term is frequently applied to the project of developing systems endowed with the intellectual processes characteristic of humans, such as the ability to reason, discover meaning, generalize, or learn from past experience." [1]
Definition: "Algorithm = (n) A process or set of rules to be followed in calculations or other problem-solving operations, especially by a computer"[2]
SO IS AI LEARNING TO BE RACIST?
DOES THIS MEAN COMPUTER SCIENTISTS ARE GIVING RACIST INSTRUCTIONS TO THE COMPUTERS?
I'M GOING TO SEARCH UP "RACIST AI."

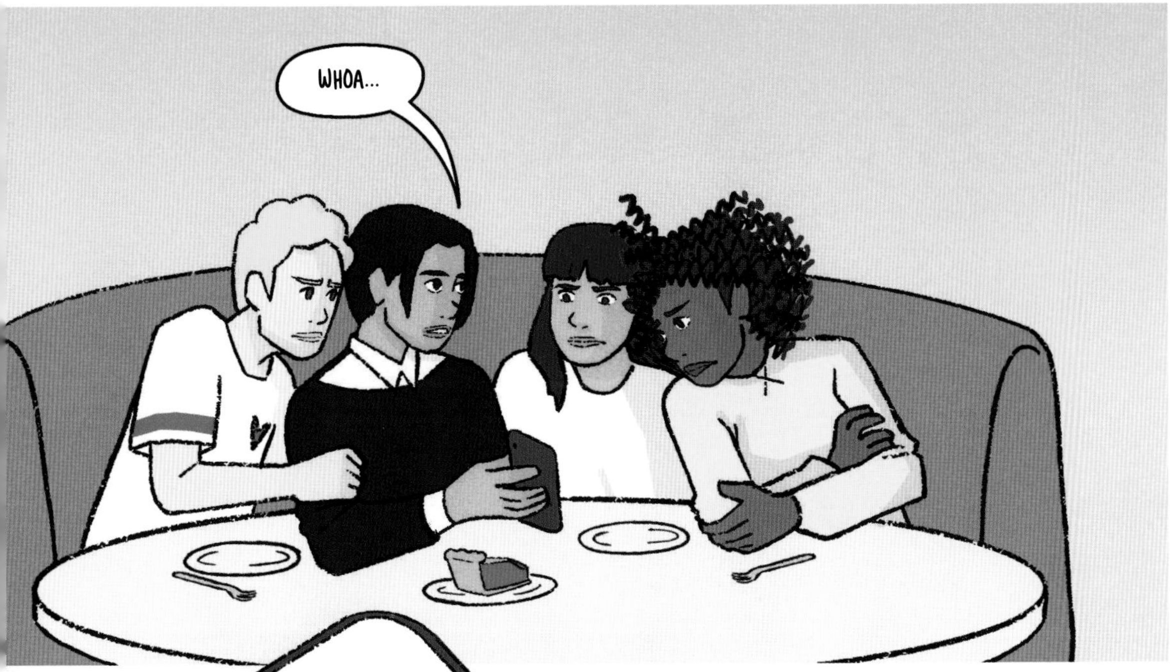
WHOA...

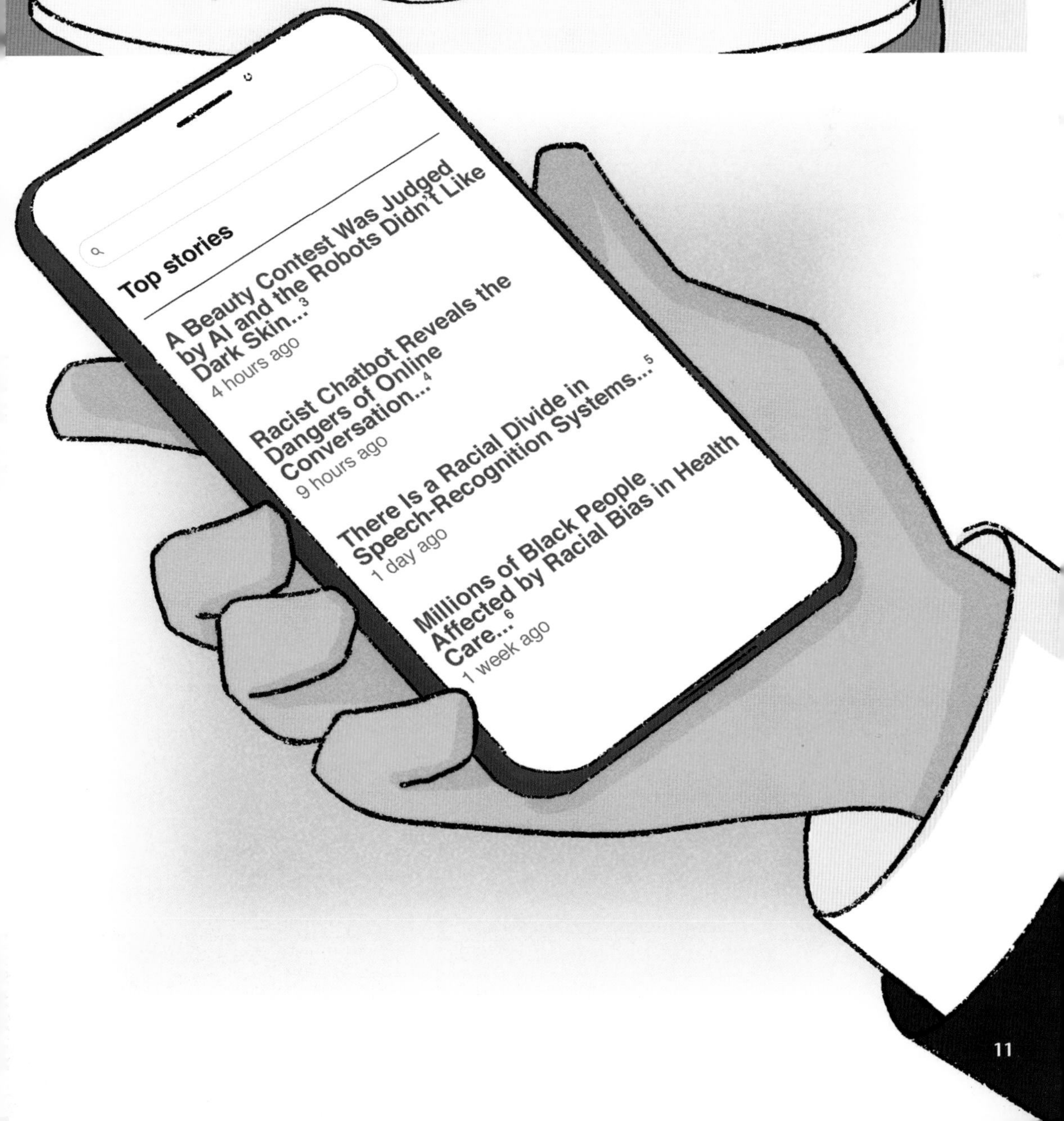
Top stories
A Beauty Contest Was Judged by AI and the Robots Didn't Like Dark Skin...[3]
4 hours ago
Racist Chatbot Reveals the Dangers of Online Conversation...[4]
9 hours ago
There Is a Racial Divide in Speech-Recognition Systems...[5]
1 day ago
Millions of Black People Affected by Racial Bias in Health Care...[6]
1 week ago

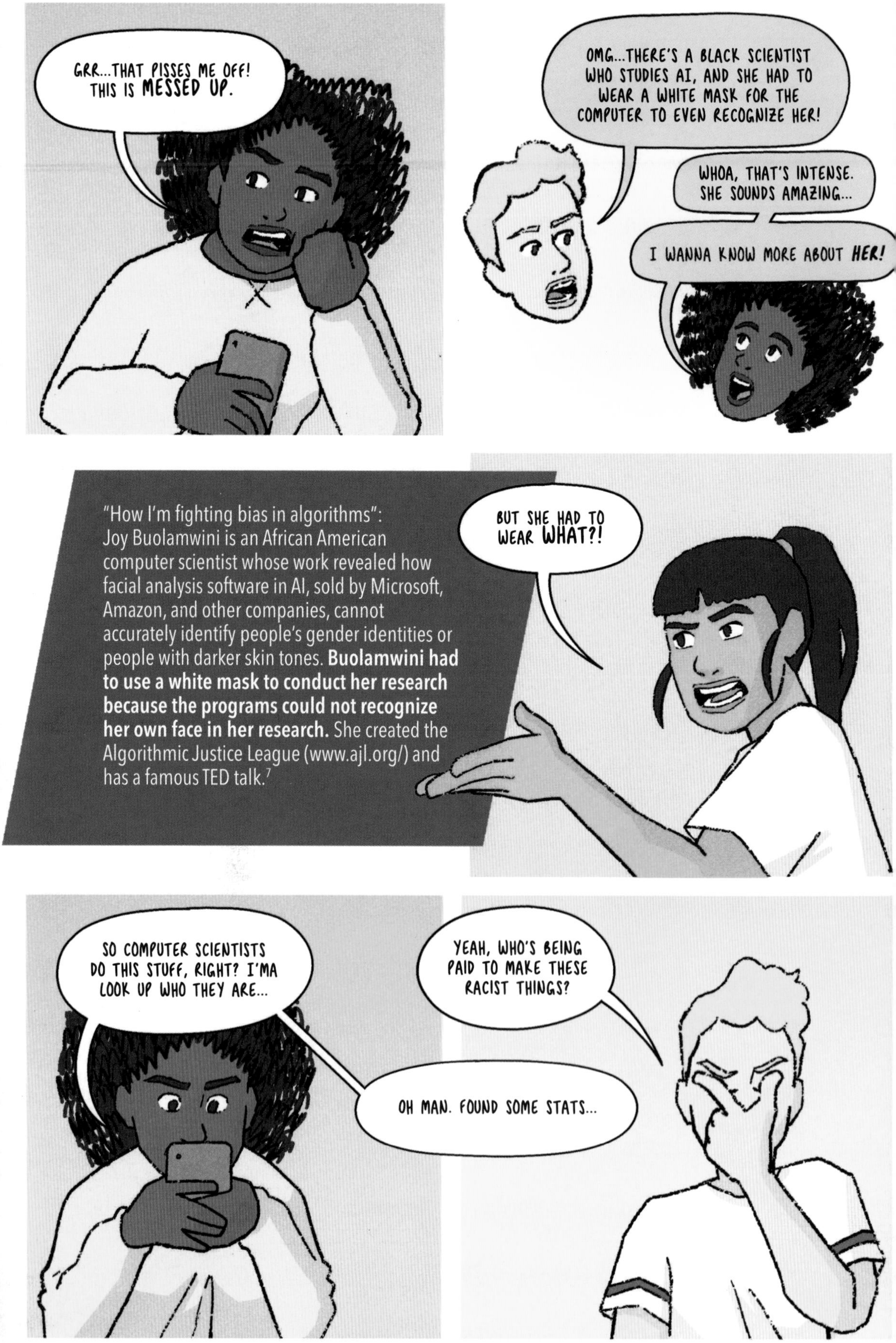
GRR...THAT PISSES ME OFF! THIS IS MESSED UP.
OMG...THERE'S A BLACK SCIENTIST WHO STUDIES AI, AND SHE HAD TO WEAR A WHITE MASK FOR THE COMPUTER TO EVEN RECOGNIZE HER!
WHOA, THAT'S INTENSE. SHE SOUNDS AMAZING...
I WANNA KNOW MORE ABOUT HER!
"How I'm fighting bias in algorithms": Joy Buolamwini is an African American computer scientist whose work revealed how facial analysis software in AI, sold by Microsoft, Amazon, and other companies, cannot accurately identify people's gender identities or people with darker skin tones. **Buolamwini had to use a white mask to conduct her research because the programs could not recognize her own face in her research.** She created the Algorithmic Justice League (www.ajl.org/) and has a famous TED talk.[7]
BUT SHE HAD TO WEAR WHAT?!
SO COMPUTER SCIENTISTS DO THIS STUFF, RIGHT? I'MA LOOK UP WHO THEY ARE...
YEAH, WHO'S BEING PAID TO MAKE THESE RACIST THINGS?
OH MAN. FOUND SOME STATS...

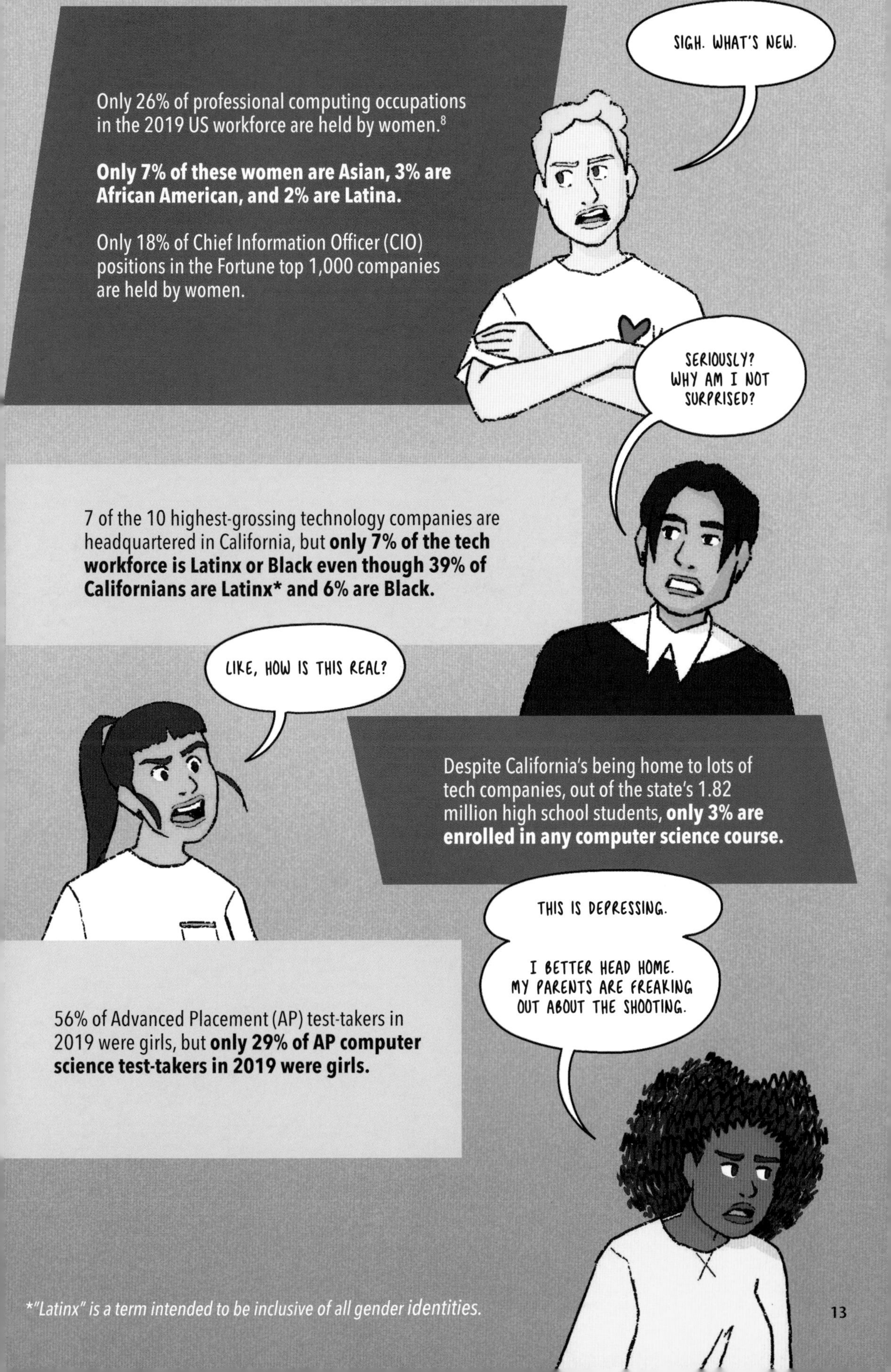
Only 26% of professional computing occupations in the 2019 US workforce are held by women.[8]
Only 7% of these women are Asian, 3% are African American, and 2% are Latina.
Only 18% of Chief Information Officer (CIO) positions in the Fortune top 1,000 companies are held by women.
SIGH. WHAT'S NEW.
SERIOUSLY? WHY AM I NOT SURPRISED?
7 of the 10 highest-grossing technology companies are headquartered in California, but **only 7% of the tech workforce is Latinx or Black even though 39% of Californians are Latinx* and 6% are Black.**
LIKE, HOW IS THIS REAL?
Despite California's being home to lots of tech companies, out of the state's 1.82 million high school students, **only 3% are enrolled in any computer science course.**
THIS IS DEPRESSING.
I BETTER HEAD HOME. MY PARENTS ARE FREAKING OUT ABOUT THE SHOOTING.
56% of Advanced Placement (AP) test-takers in 2019 were girls, but **only 29% of AP computer science test-takers in 2019 were girls.**

"Latinx" is a term intended to be inclusive of all gender identities.

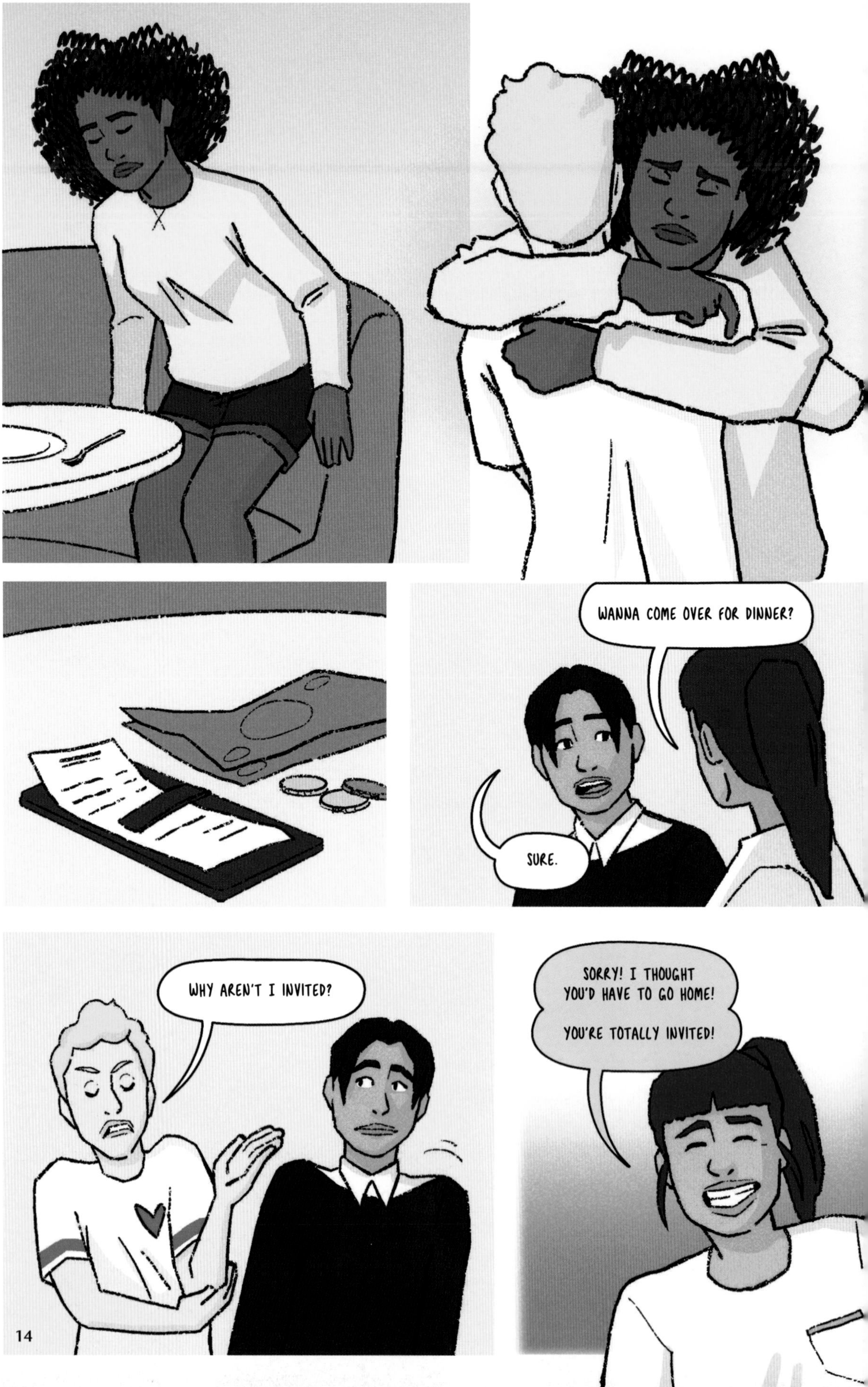
WANNA COME OVER FOR DINNER?
SURE.
WHY AREN'T I INVITED?
SORRY! I THOUGHT YOU'D HAVE TO GO HOME!
YOU'RE TOTALLY INVITED!

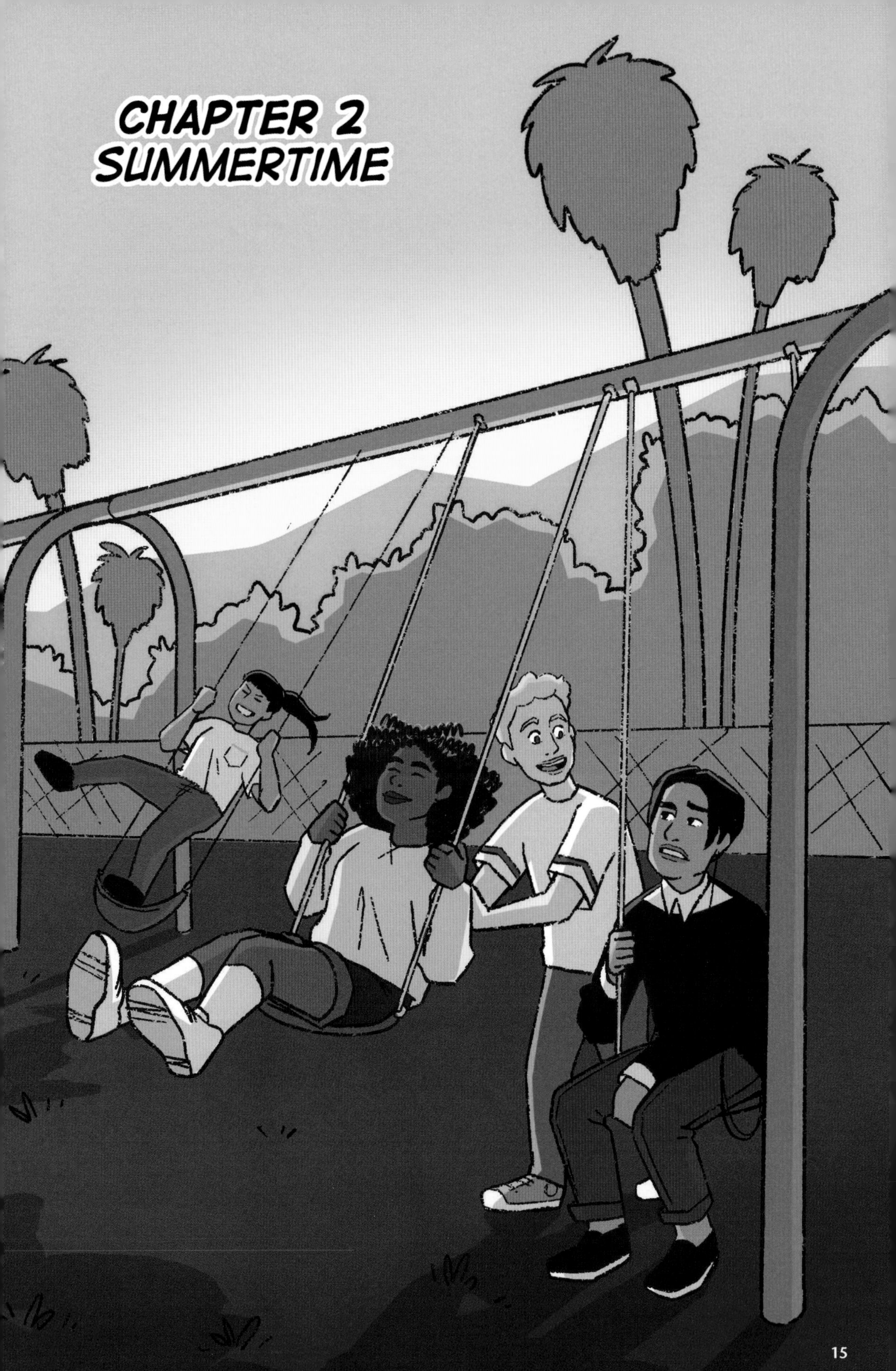
CHAPTER 2
SUMMERTIME

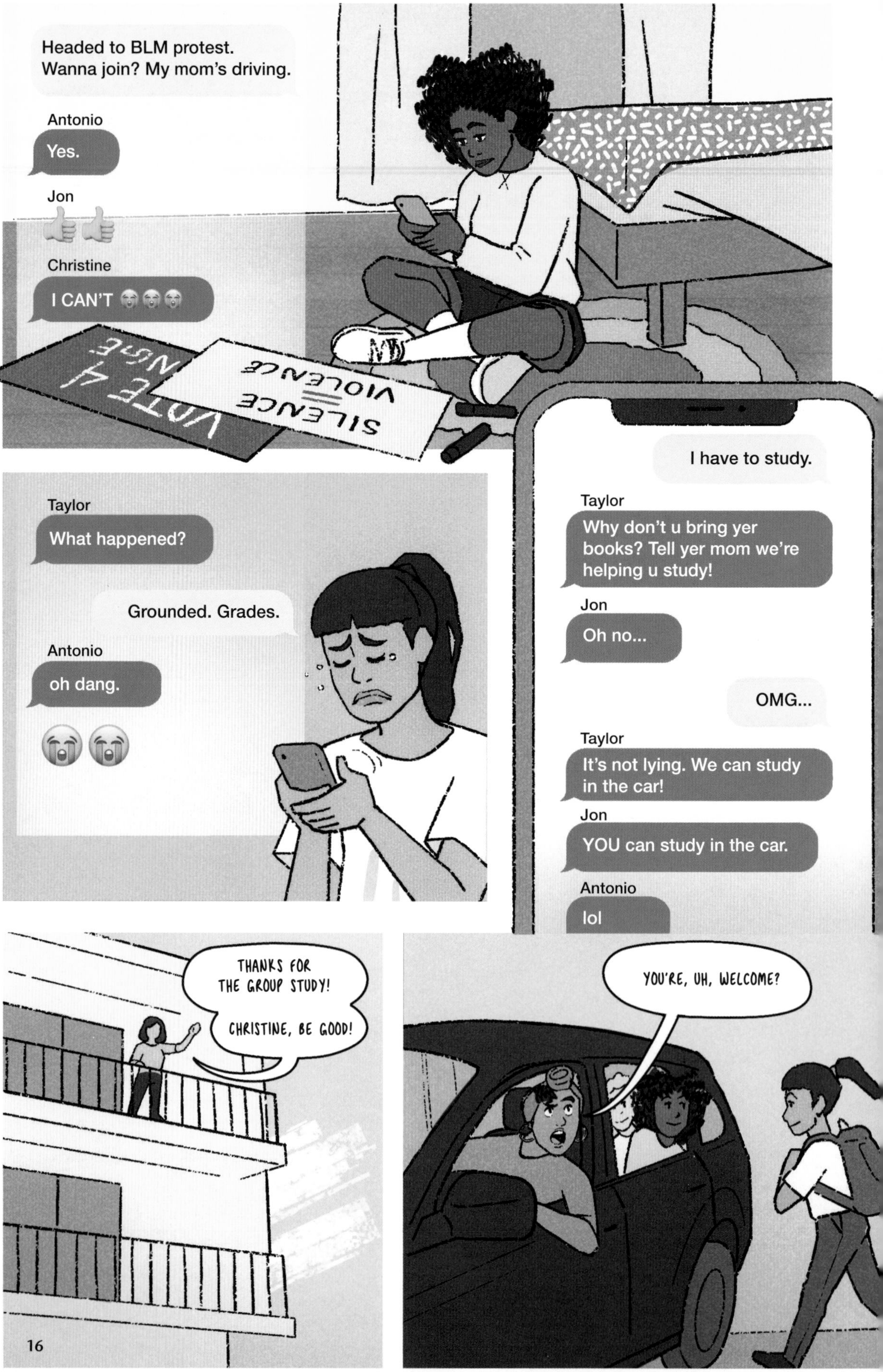
Headed to BLM protest. Wanna join? My mom's driving.
Antonio
Yes.
Jon
👍👍
Christine
I CAN'T 😱😱😱
SILENCE = VIOLENCE
I have to study.
Taylor
Why don't u bring yer books? Tell yer mom we're helping u study!
Jon
Oh no...
OMG...
Taylor
It's not lying. We can study in the car!
Jon
YOU can study in the car.
Antonio
lol
Taylor
What happened?
Grounded. Grades.
Antonio
oh dang.
😭😭
THANKS FOR THE GROUP STUDY!
CHRISTINE, BE GOOD!
YOU'RE, UH, WELCOME?

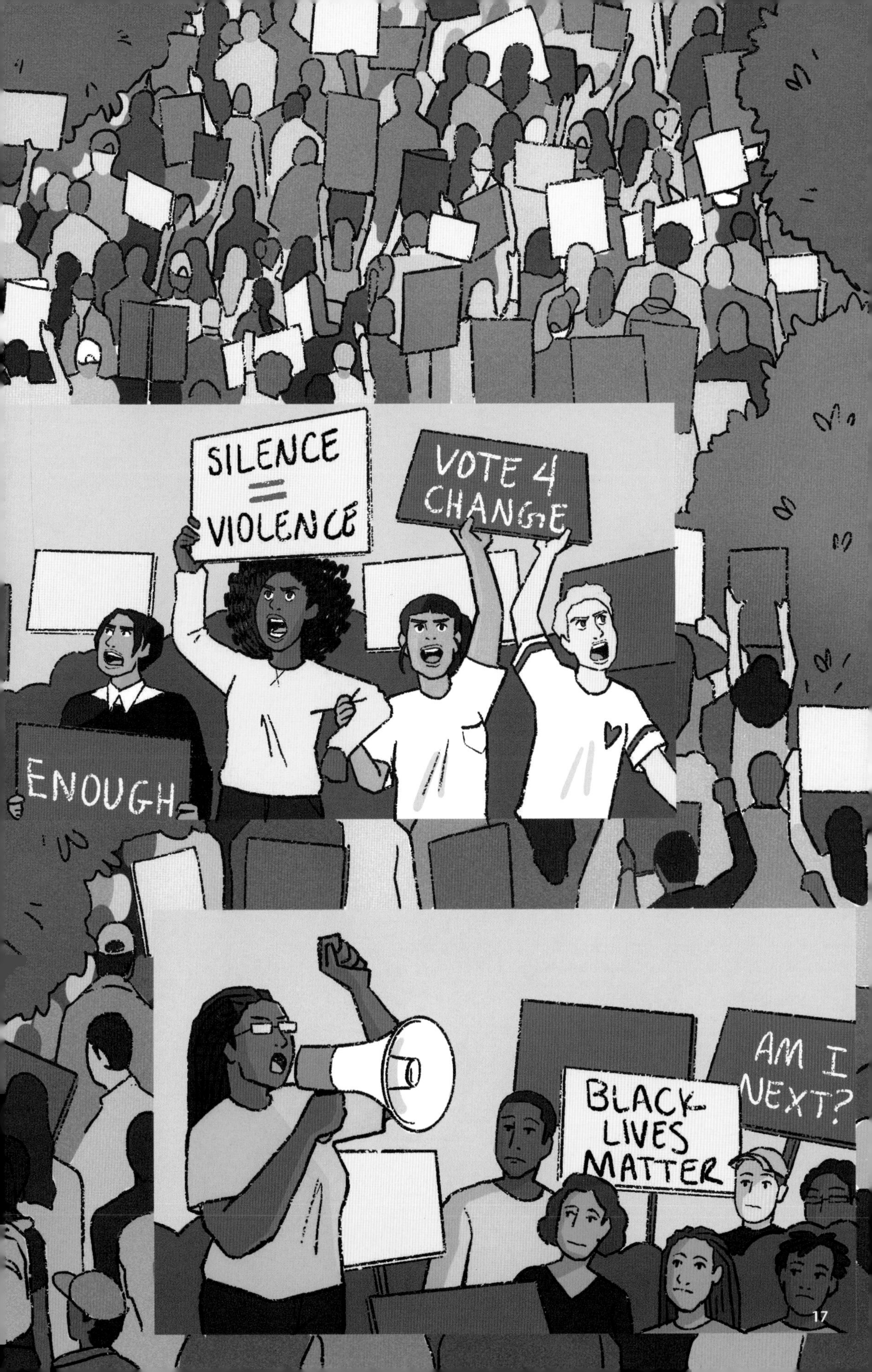
SILENCE
=
VIOLENCE
VOTE 4
CHANGE
ENOUGH
BLACK
LIVES
MATTER
AM I
NEXT?

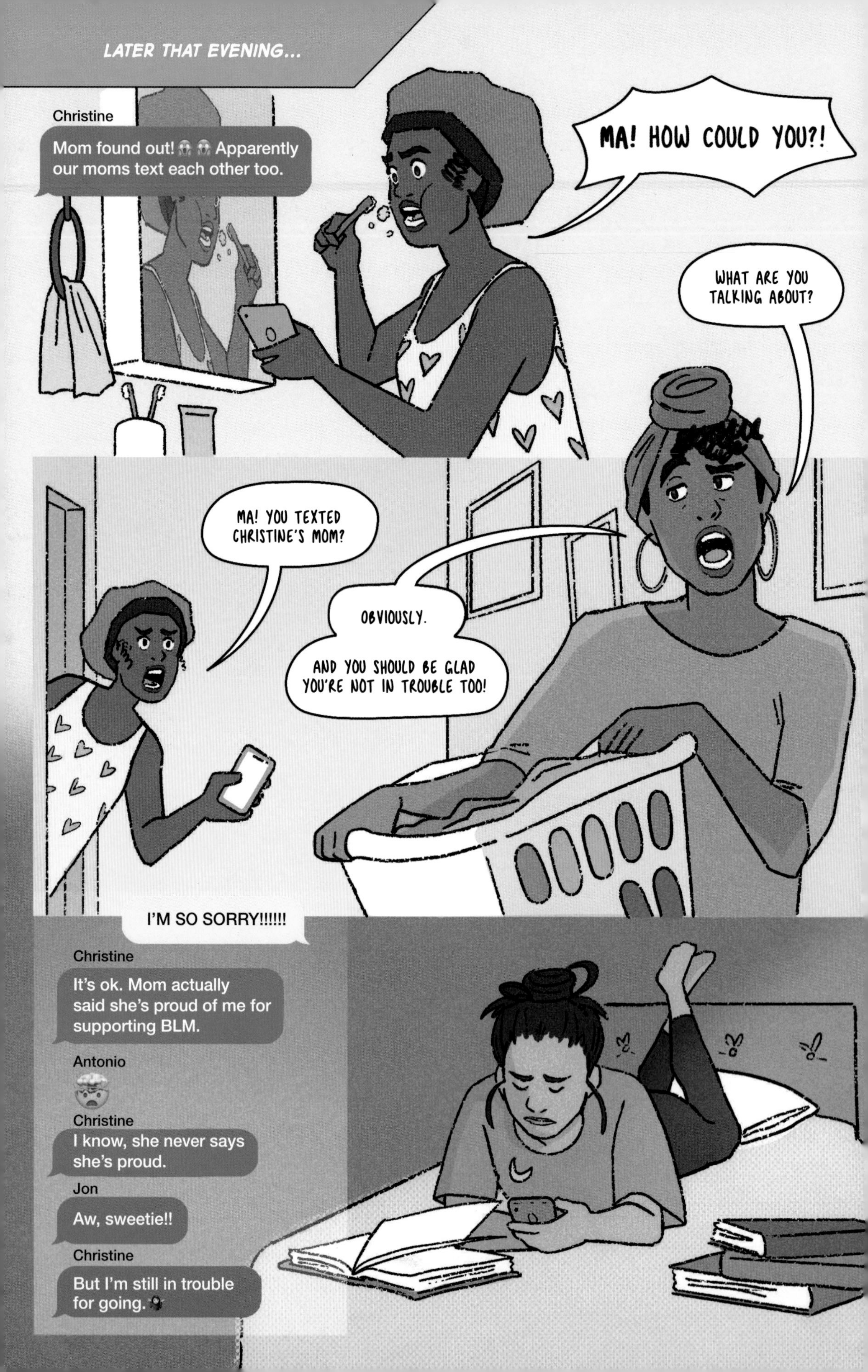
LATER THAT EVENING...
Christine
Mom found out! 😱😱 Apparently our moms text each other too.
MA! HOW COULD YOU?!
WHAT ARE YOU TALKING ABOUT?
MA! YOU TEXTED CHRISTINE'S MOM?
OBVIOUSLY.
AND YOU SHOULD BE GLAD YOU'RE NOT IN TROUBLE TOO!
I'M SO SORRY!!!!!!
Christine
It's ok. Mom actually said she's proud of me for supporting BLM.
Antonio
🤯
Christine
I know, she never says she's proud.
Jon
Aw, sweetie!!
Christine
But I'm still in trouble for going.

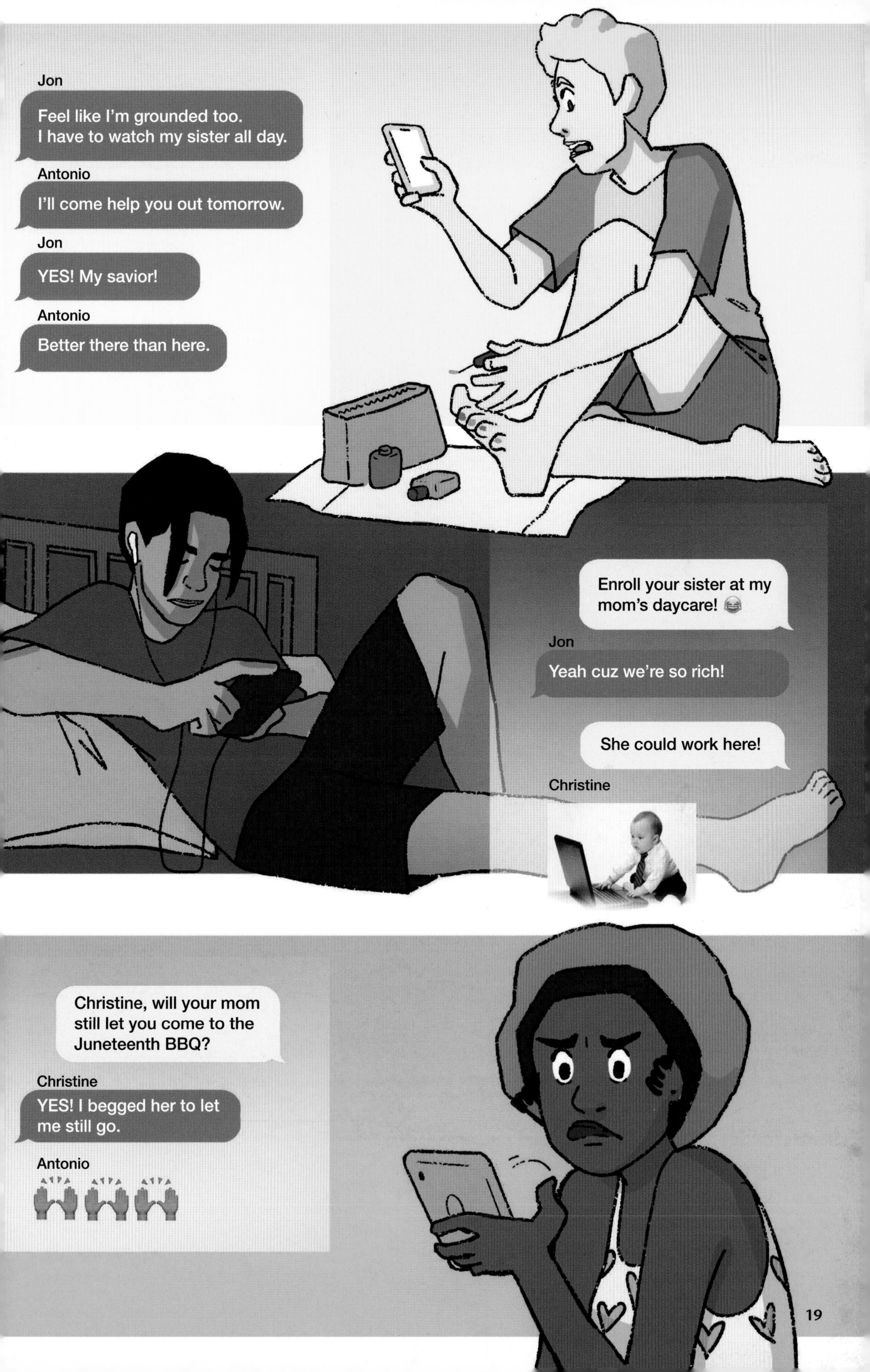

Jon
Feel like I'm grounded too. I have to watch my sister all day.
Antonio
I'll come help you out tomorrow.
Jon
YES! My savior!
Antonio
Better there than here.
Enroll your sister at my mom's daycare! 😂
Jon
Yeah cuz we're so rich!
She could work here!
Christine
Christine, will your mom still let you come to the Juneteenth BBQ?
Christine
YES! I begged her to let me still go.
Antonio
🙌🙌🙌

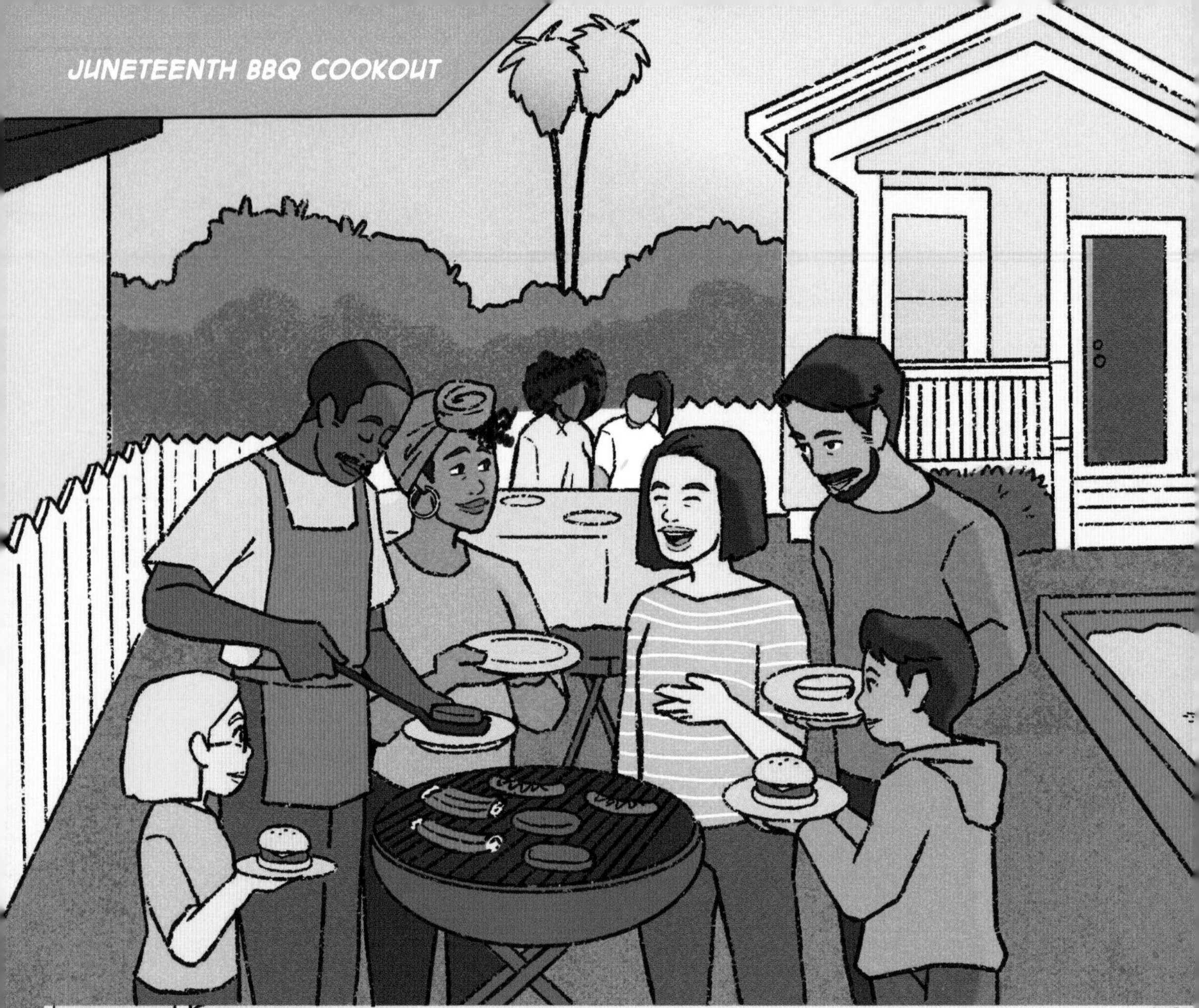
JUNETEENTH BBQ COOKOUT

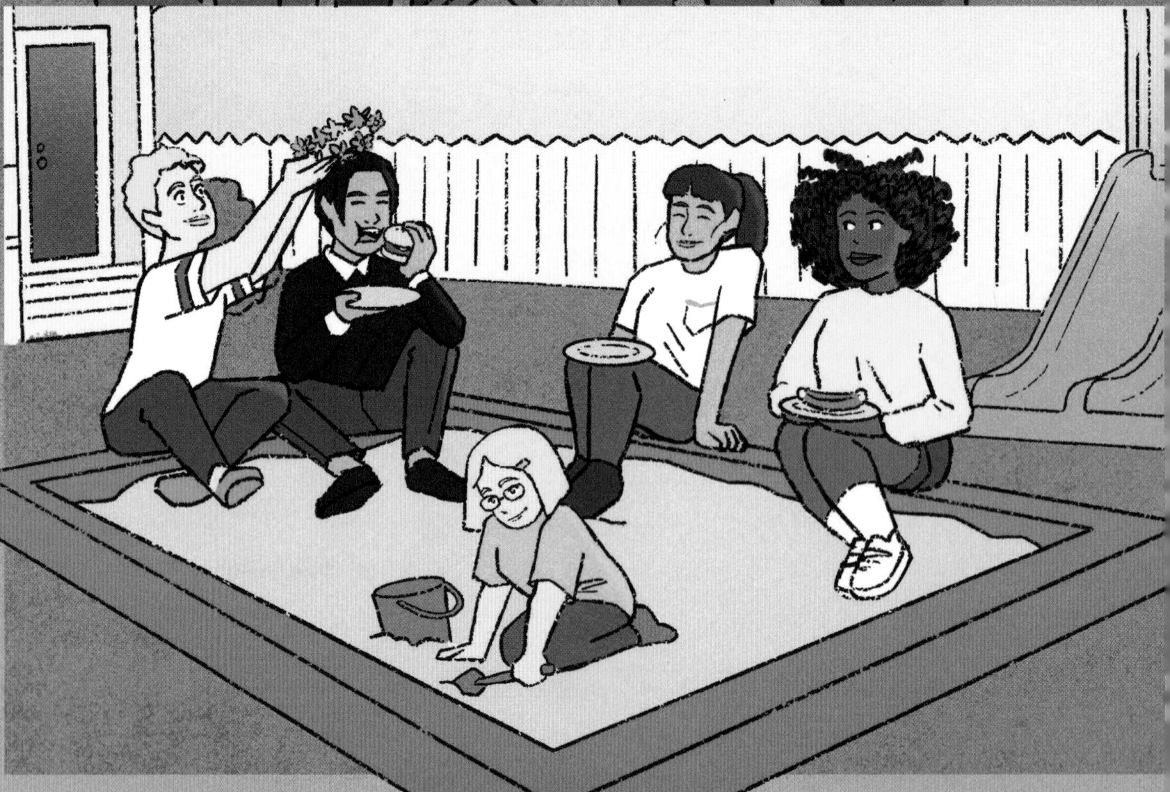

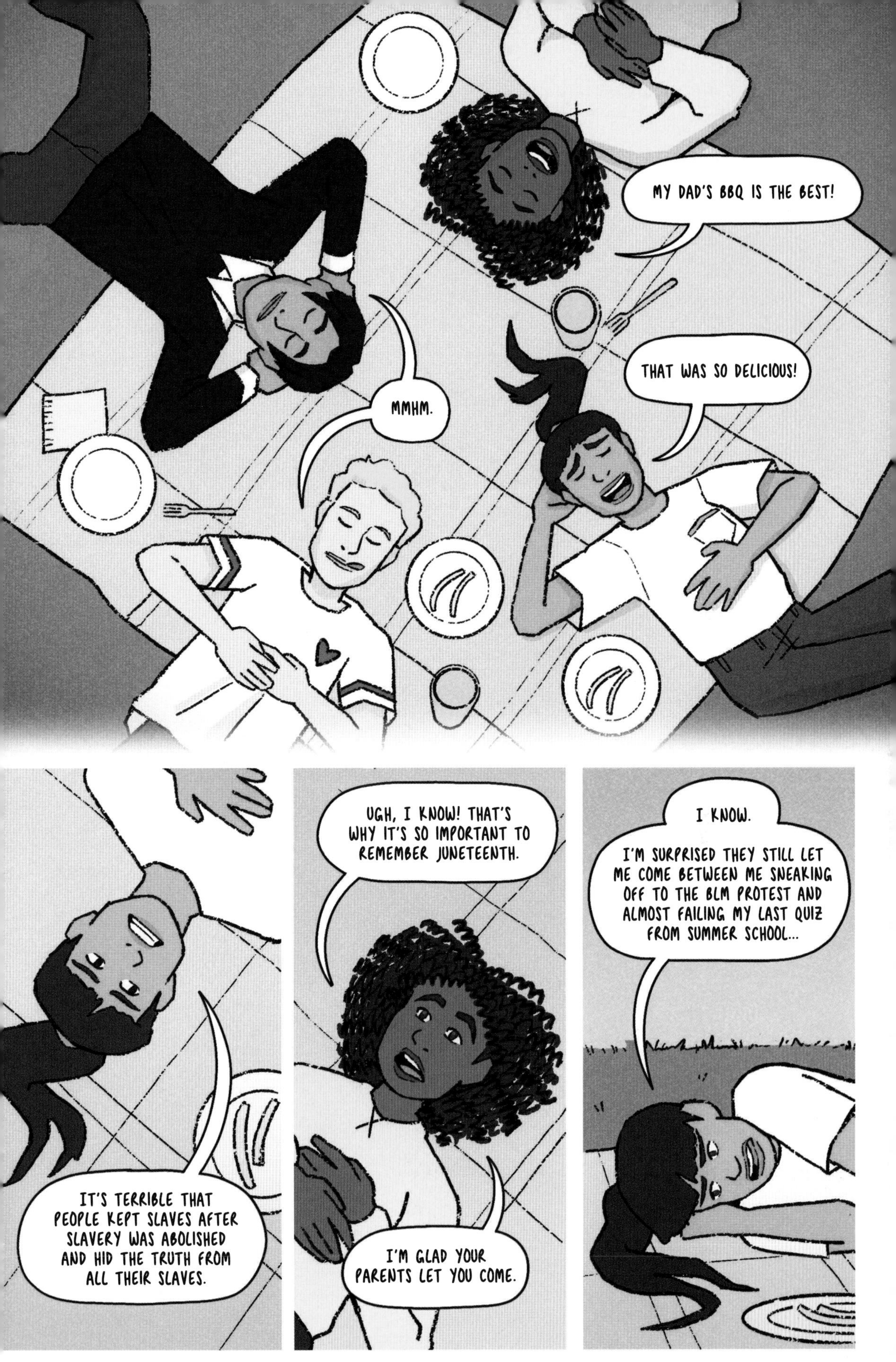
MY DAD'S BBQ IS THE BEST!
MMHM.
THAT WAS SO DELICIOUS!
IT'S TERRIBLE THAT PEOPLE KEPT SLAVES AFTER SLAVERY WAS ABOLISHED AND HID THE TRUTH FROM ALL THEIR SLAVES.
UGH, I KNOW! THAT'S WHY IT'S SO IMPORTANT TO REMEMBER JUNETEENTH.
I'M GLAD YOUR PARENTS LET YOU COME.
I KNOW.
I'M SURPRISED THEY STILL LET ME COME BETWEEN ME SNEAKING OFF TO THE BLM PROTEST AND ALMOST FAILING MY LAST QUIZ FROM SUMMER SCHOOL...

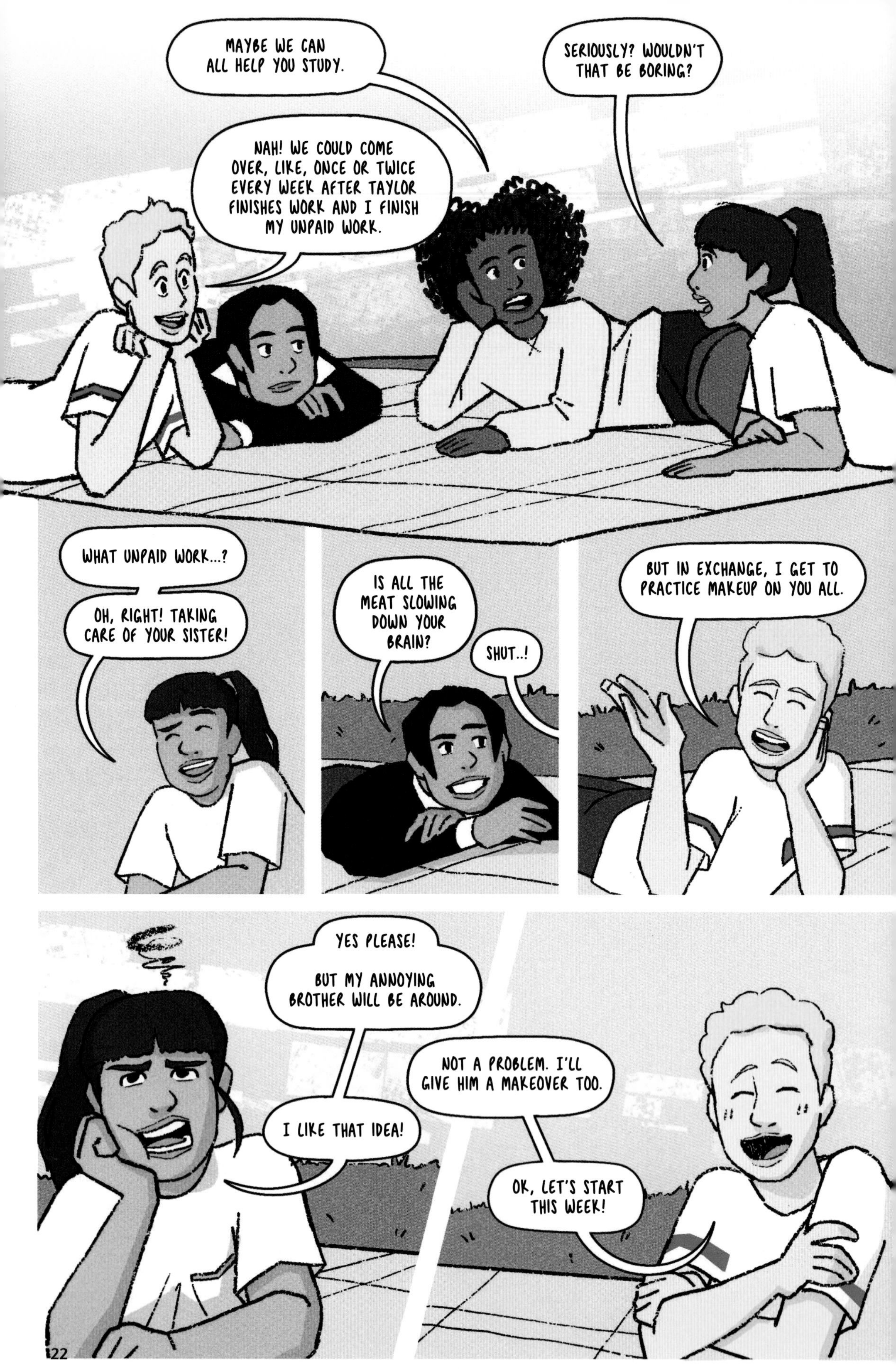
MAYBE WE CAN ALL HELP YOU STUDY.
SERIOUSLY? WOULDN'T THAT BE BORING?
NAH! WE COULD COME OVER, LIKE, ONCE OR TWICE EVERY WEEK AFTER TAYLOR FINISHES WORK AND I FINISH MY UNPAID WORK.
WHAT UNPAID WORK...?
OH, RIGHT! TAKING CARE OF YOUR SISTER!
IS ALL THE MEAT SLOWING DOWN YOUR BRAIN?
SHUT..!
BUT IN EXCHANGE, I GET TO PRACTICE MAKEUP ON YOU ALL.
YES PLEASE!
BUT MY ANNOYING BROTHER WILL BE AROUND.
I LIKE THAT IDEA!
NOT A PROBLEM. I'LL GIVE HIM A MAKEOVER TOO.
OK, LET'S START THIS WEEK!

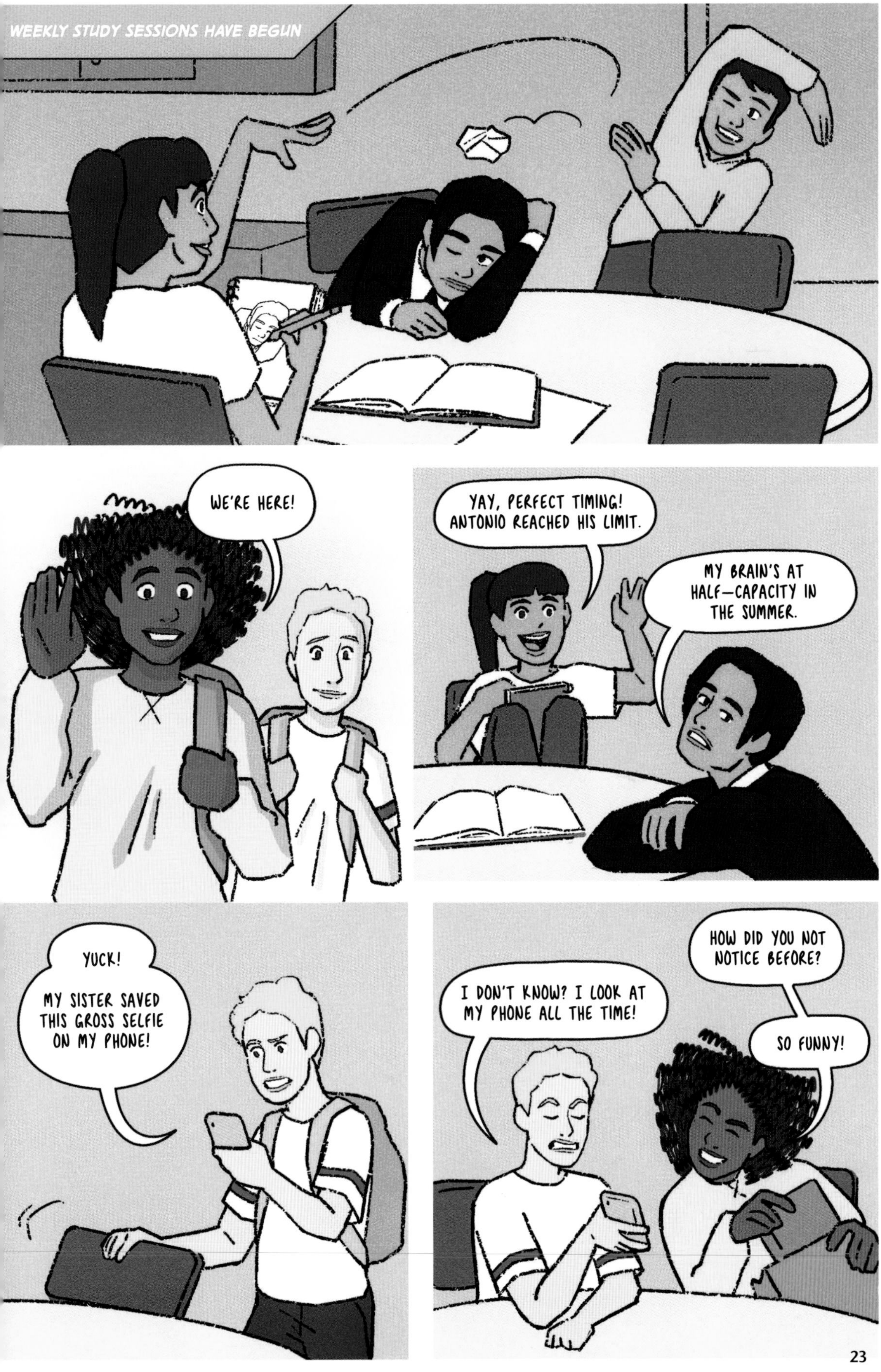
WEEKLY STUDY SESSIONS HAVE BEGUN
WE'RE HERE!
YAY, PERFECT TIMING! ANTONIO REACHED HIS LIMIT.
MY BRAIN'S AT HALF–CAPACITY IN THE SUMMER.
YUCK!
MY SISTER SAVED THIS GROSS SELFIE ON MY PHONE!
HOW DID YOU NOT NOTICE BEFORE?
I DON'T KNOW? I LOOK AT MY PHONE ALL THE TIME!
SO FUNNY!

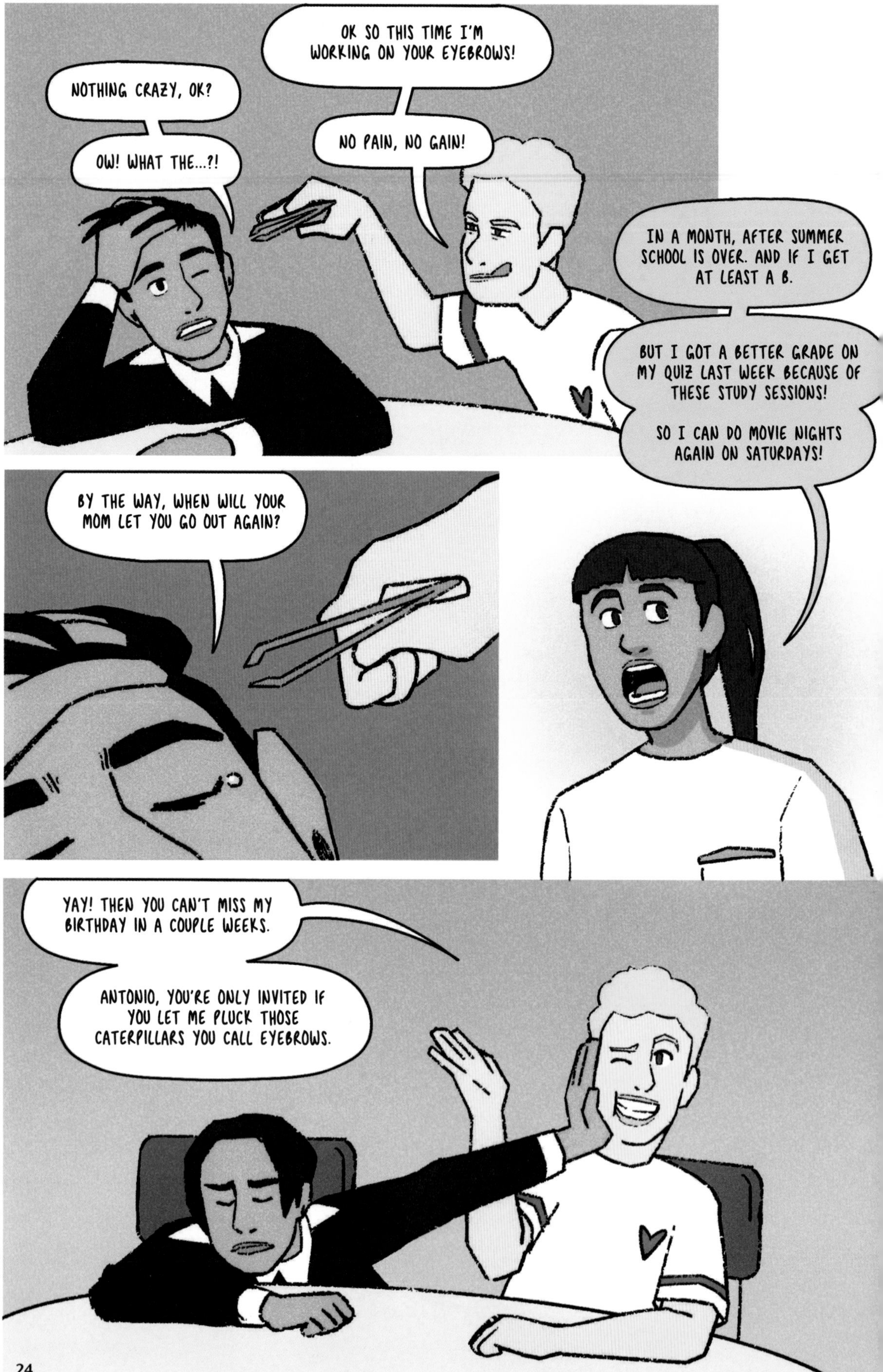

OK SO THIS TIME I'M WORKING ON YOUR EYEBROWS!
NOTHING CRAZY, OK?
NO PAIN, NO GAIN!
OW! WHAT THE...?!
IN A MONTH, AFTER SUMMER SCHOOL IS OVER. AND IF I GET AT LEAST A B.
BUT I GOT A BETTER GRADE ON MY QUIZ LAST WEEK BECAUSE OF THESE STUDY SESSIONS!
SO I CAN DO MOVIE NIGHTS AGAIN ON SATURDAYS!
BY THE WAY, WHEN WILL YOUR MOM LET YOU GO OUT AGAIN?
YAY! THEN YOU CAN'T MISS MY BIRTHDAY IN A COUPLE WEEKS.
ANTONIO, YOU'RE ONLY INVITED IF YOU LET ME PLUCK THOSE CATERPILLARS YOU CALL EYEBROWS.

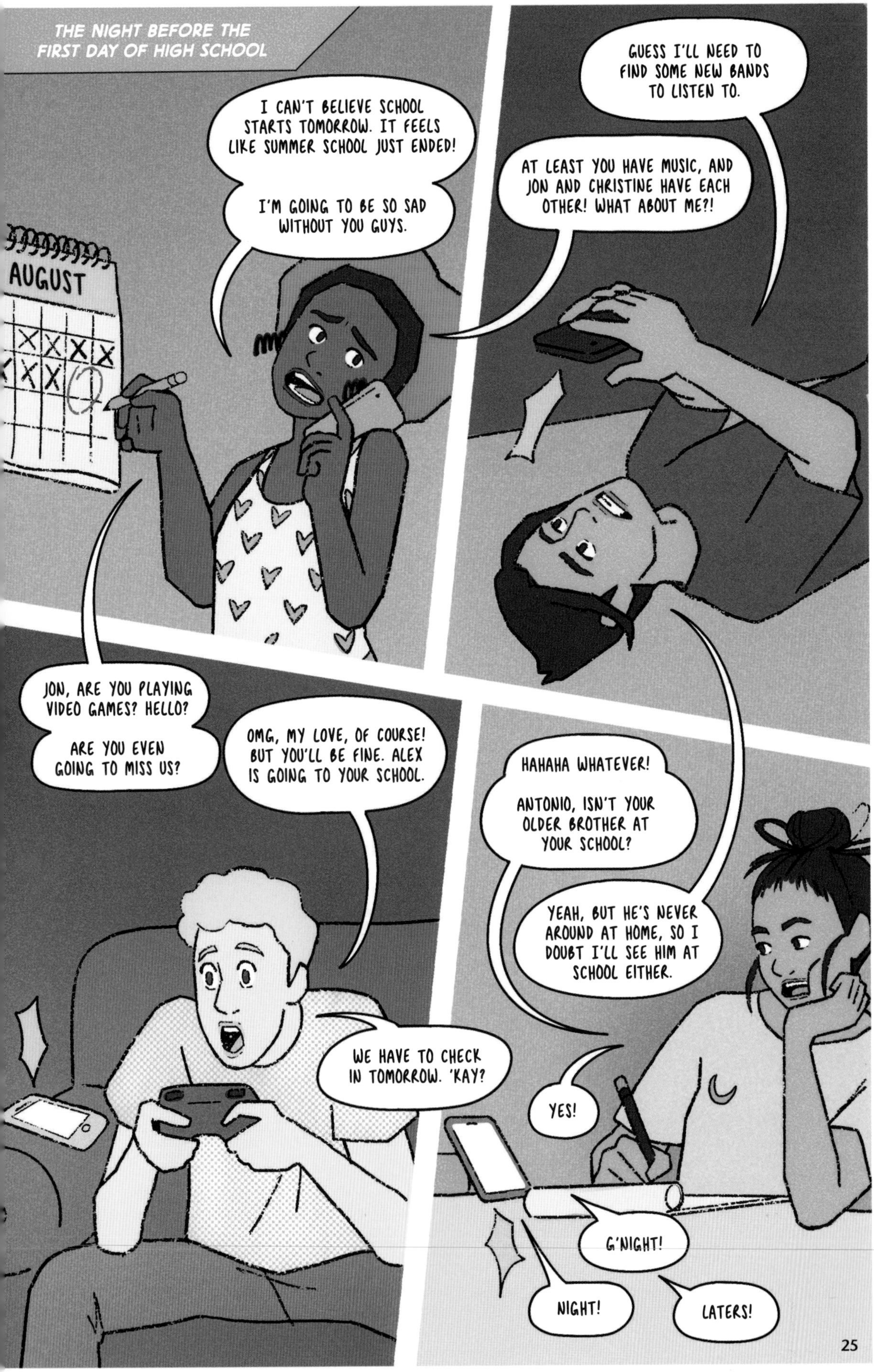
THE NIGHT BEFORE THE FIRST DAY OF HIGH SCHOOL
AUGUST
I CAN'T BELIEVE SCHOOL STARTS TOMORROW. IT FEELS LIKE SUMMER SCHOOL JUST ENDED!
I'M GOING TO BE SO SAD WITHOUT YOU GUYS.
GUESS I'LL NEED TO FIND SOME NEW BANDS TO LISTEN TO.
AT LEAST YOU HAVE MUSIC, AND JON AND CHRISTINE HAVE EACH OTHER! WHAT ABOUT ME?!
JON, ARE YOU PLAYING VIDEO GAMES? HELLO?
ARE YOU EVEN GOING TO MISS US?
OMG, MY LOVE, OF COURSE! BUT YOU'LL BE FINE. ALEX IS GOING TO YOUR SCHOOL.
HAHAHA WHATEVER!
ANTONIO, ISN'T YOUR OLDER BROTHER AT YOUR SCHOOL?
YEAH, BUT HE'S NEVER AROUND AT HOME, SO I DOUBT I'LL SEE HIM AT SCHOOL EITHER.
WE HAVE TO CHECK IN TOMORROW. 'KAY?
YES!
G'NIGHT!
NIGHT!
LATERS!

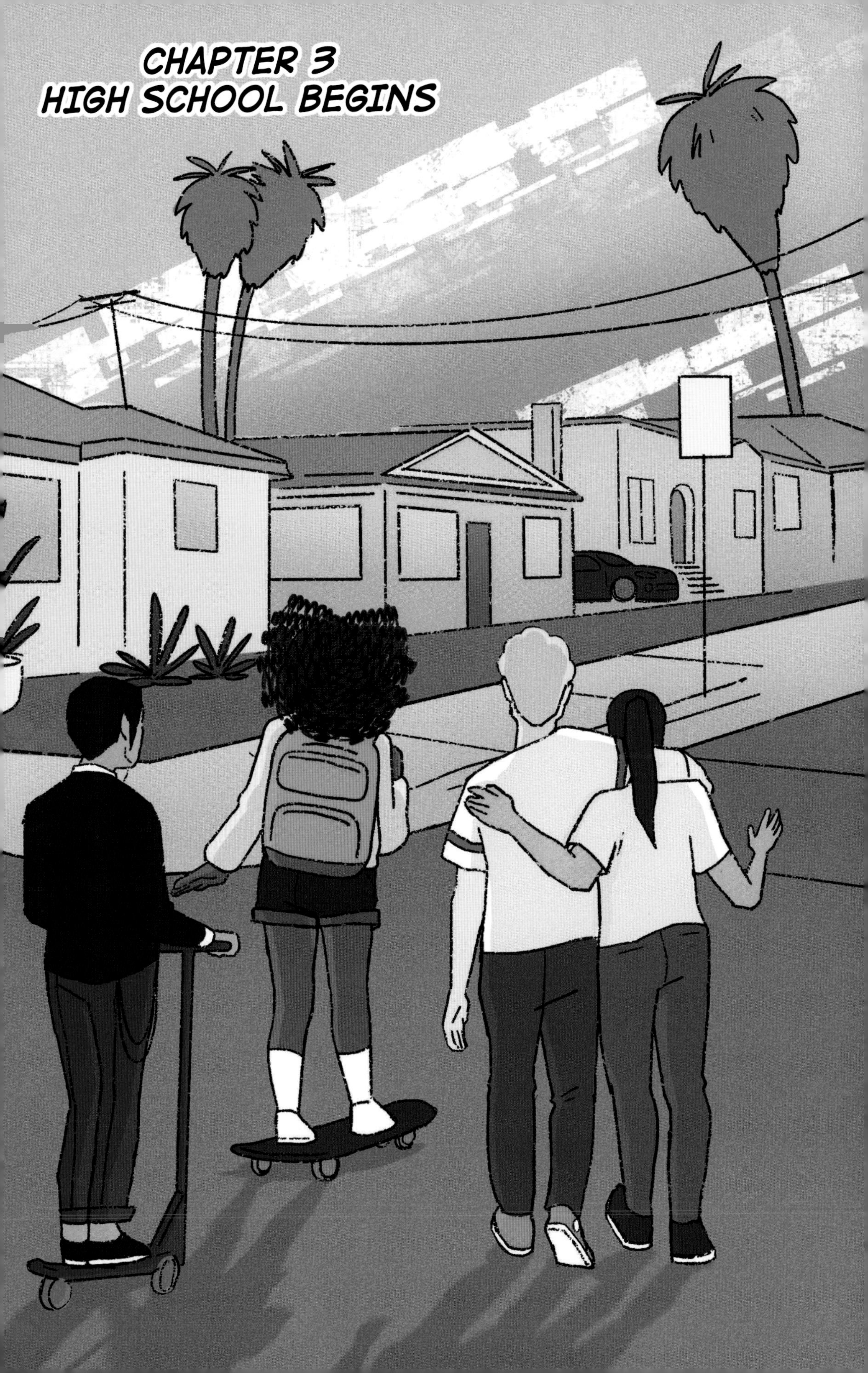
CHAPTER 3
HIGH SCHOOL BEGINS

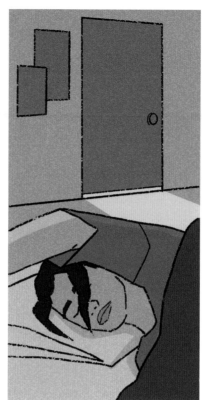

5:30 A.M.

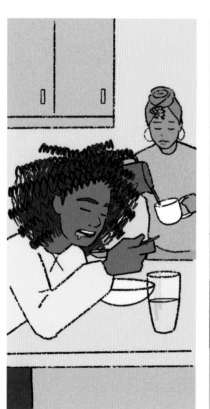

¡ESPERA, DESPIERTA
A TU HERMANO!

*"WAIT, WAKE UP YOUR BROTHER!"

6:30 A.M.

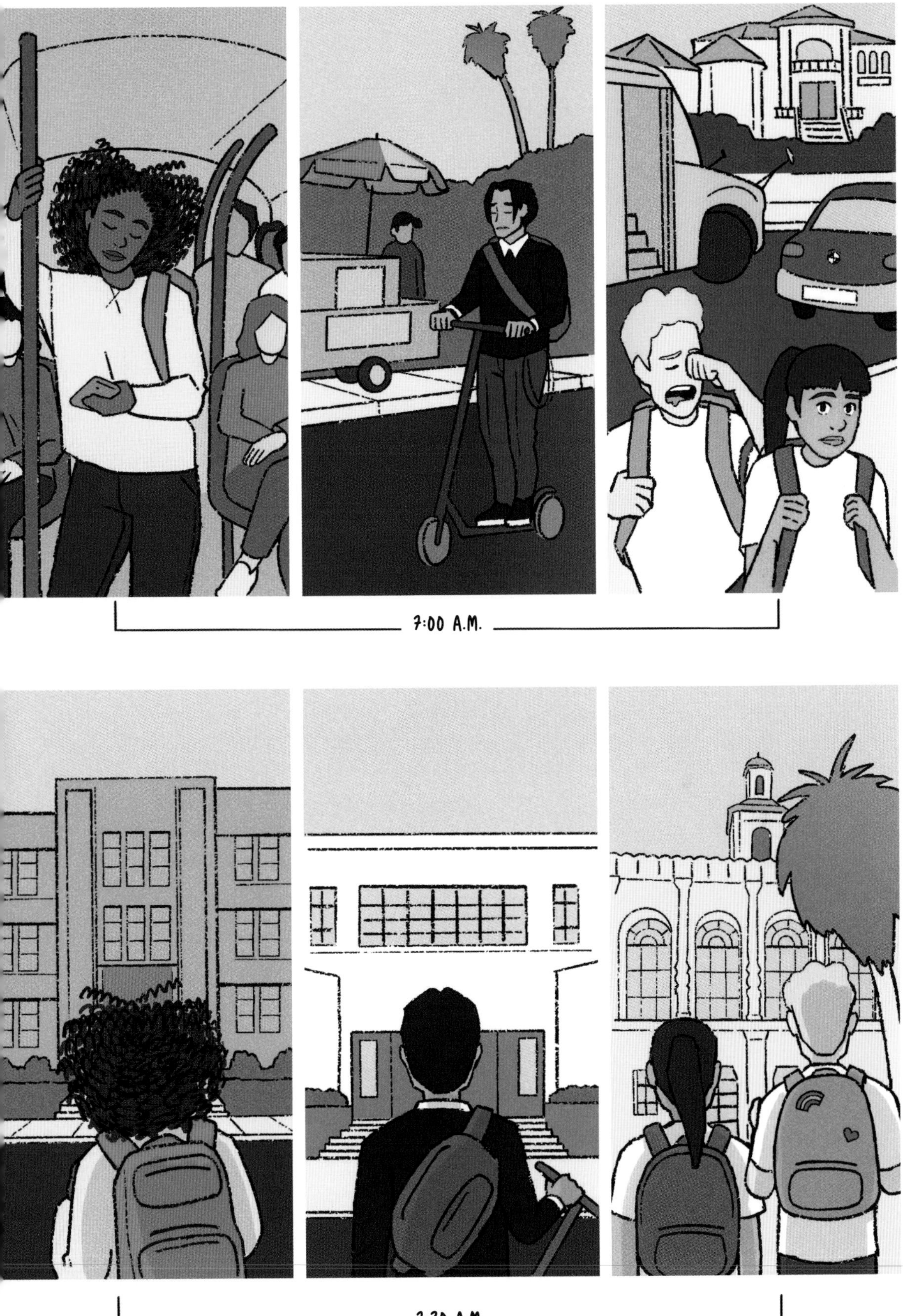
7:00 A.M.
7:30 A.M.

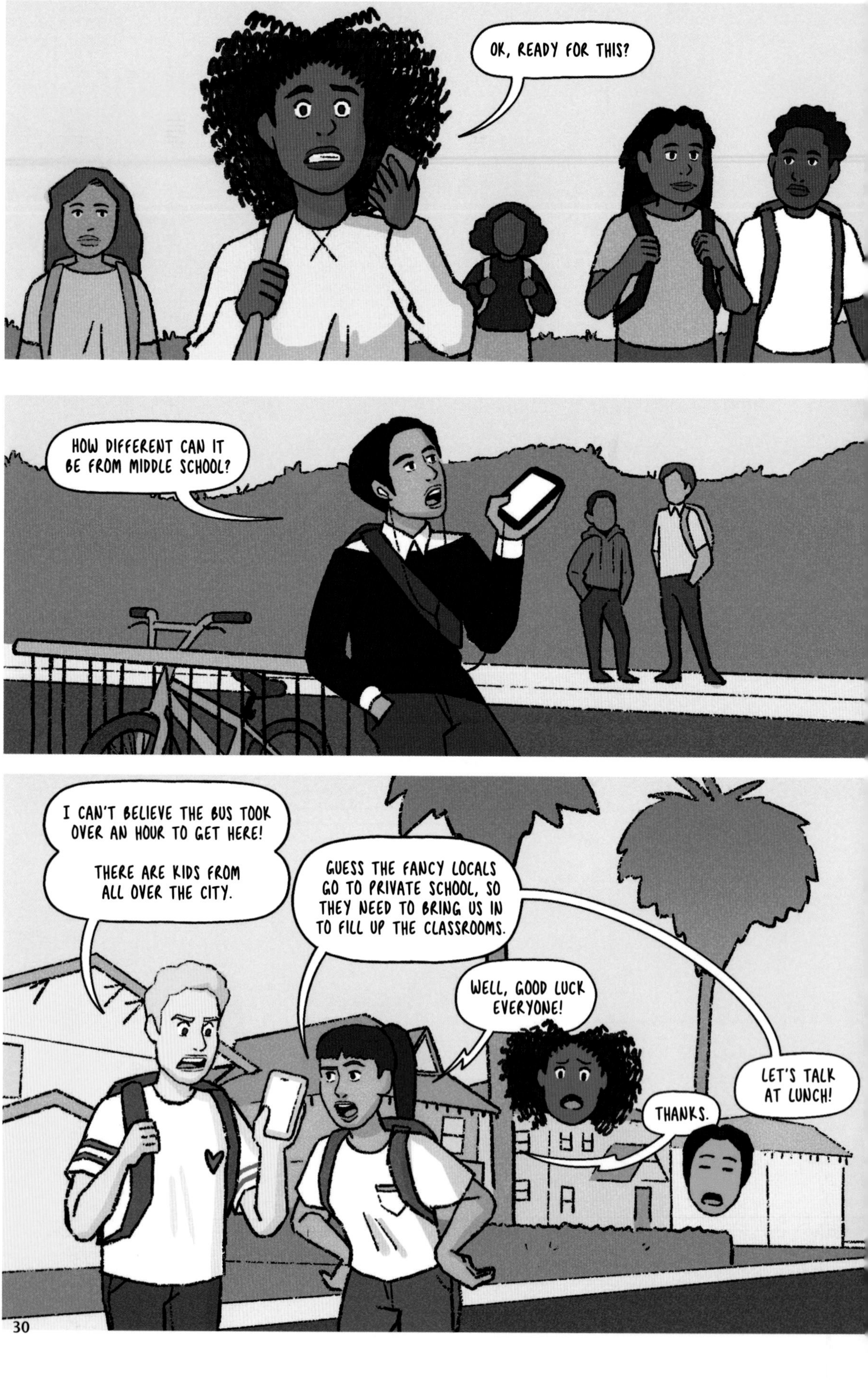
OK, READY FOR THIS?
HOW DIFFERENT CAN IT BE FROM MIDDLE SCHOOL?
I CAN'T BELIEVE THE BUS TOOK OVER AN HOUR TO GET HERE!
THERE ARE KIDS FROM ALL OVER THE CITY.
GUESS THE FANCY LOCALS GO TO PRIVATE SCHOOL, SO THEY NEED TO BRING US IN TO FILL UP THE CLASSROOMS.
WELL, GOOD LUCK EVERYONE!
THANKS.
LET'S TALK AT LUNCH!

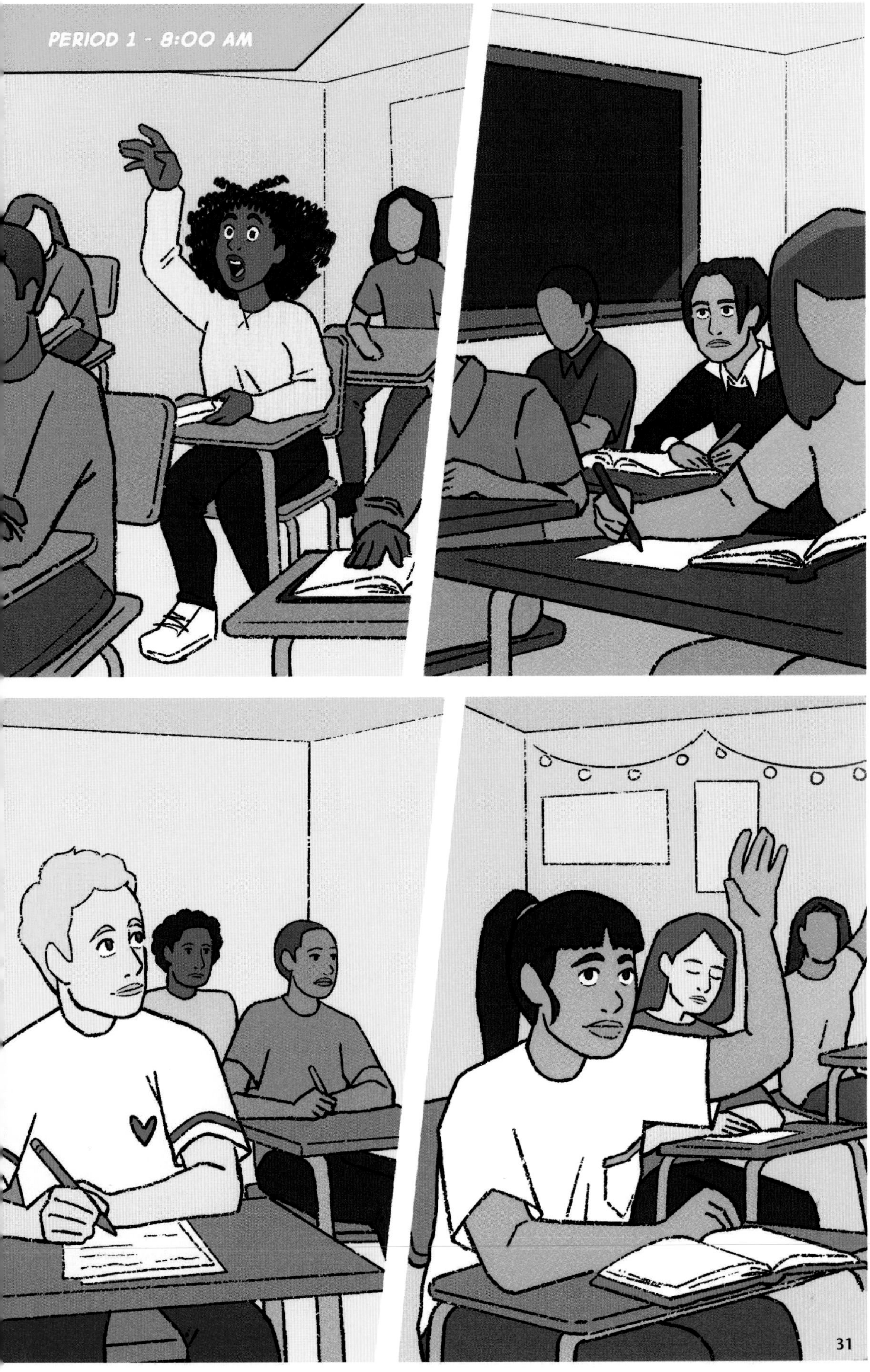
PERIOD 1 - 8:00 AM

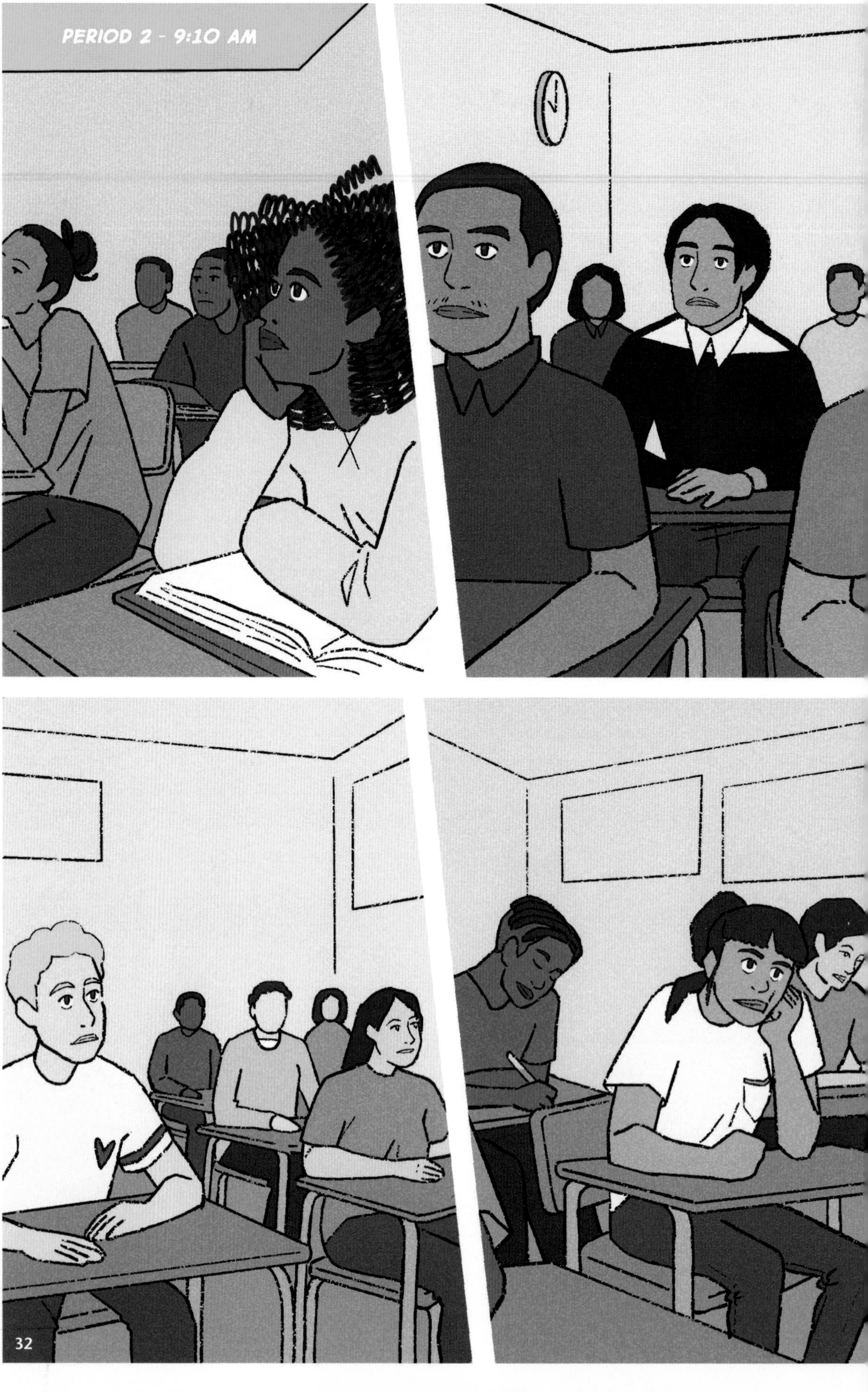
PERIOD 2 - 9:10 AM

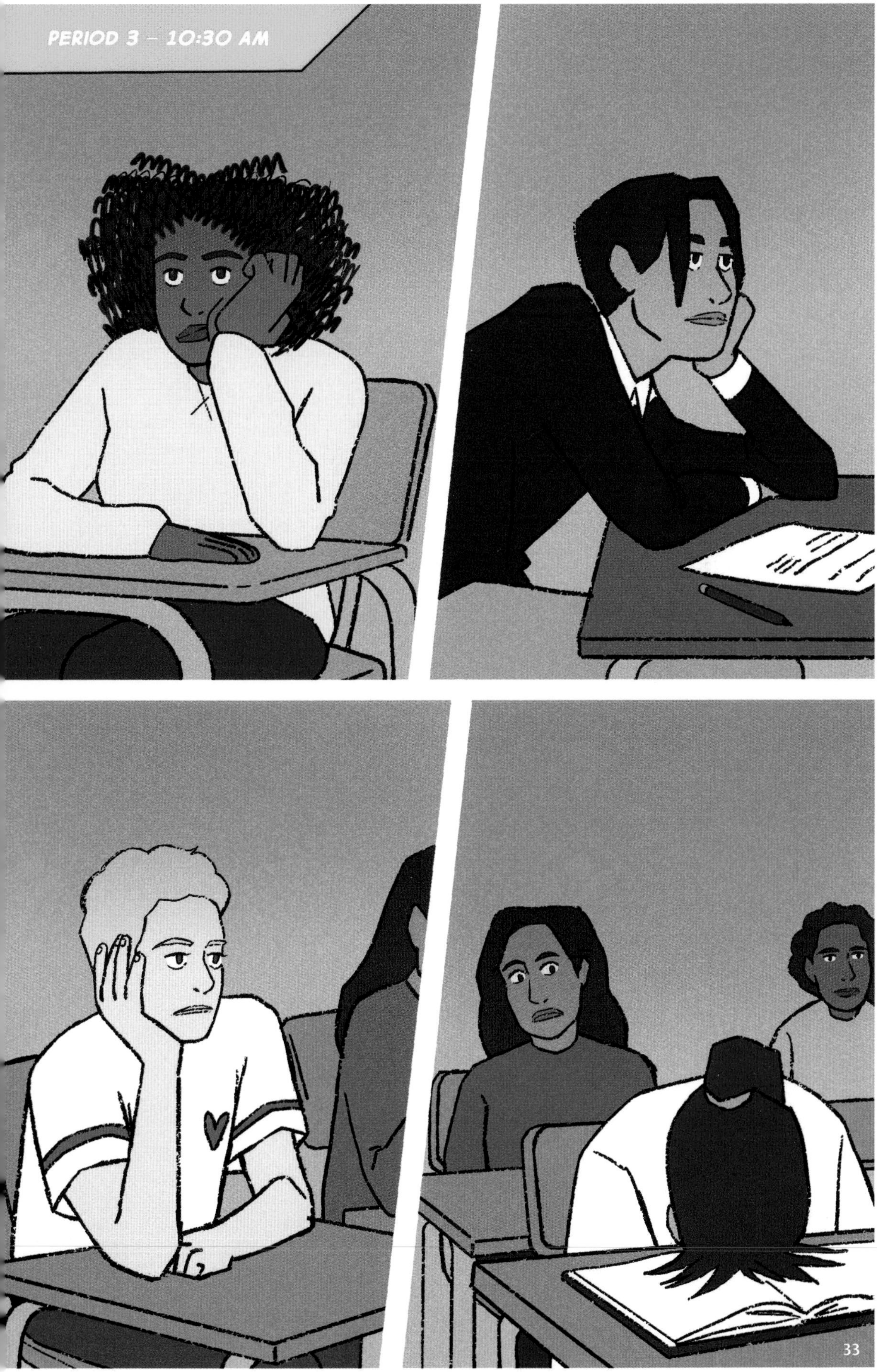
PERIOD 3 – 10:30 AM

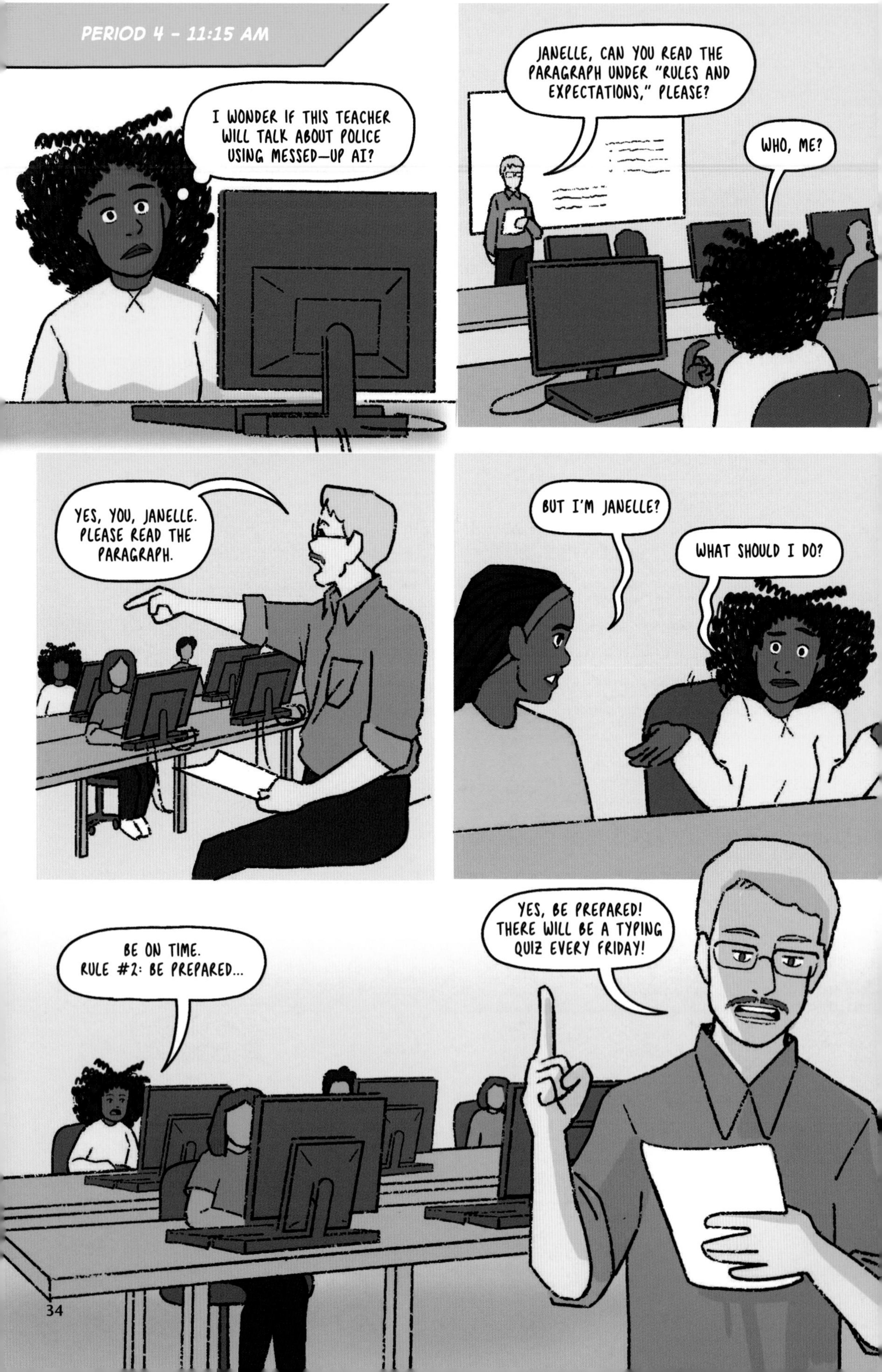
PERIOD 4 - 11:15 AM
I WONDER IF THIS TEACHER WILL TALK ABOUT POLICE USING MESSED-UP AI?
JANELLE, CAN YOU READ THE PARAGRAPH UNDER "RULES AND EXPECTATIONS," PLEASE?
WHO, ME?
YES, YOU, JANELLE. PLEASE READ THE PARAGRAPH.
BUT I'M JANELLE?
WHAT SHOULD I DO?
BE ON TIME. RULE #2: BE PREPARED...
YES, BE PREPARED! THERE WILL BE A TYPING QUIZ EVERY FRIDAY!

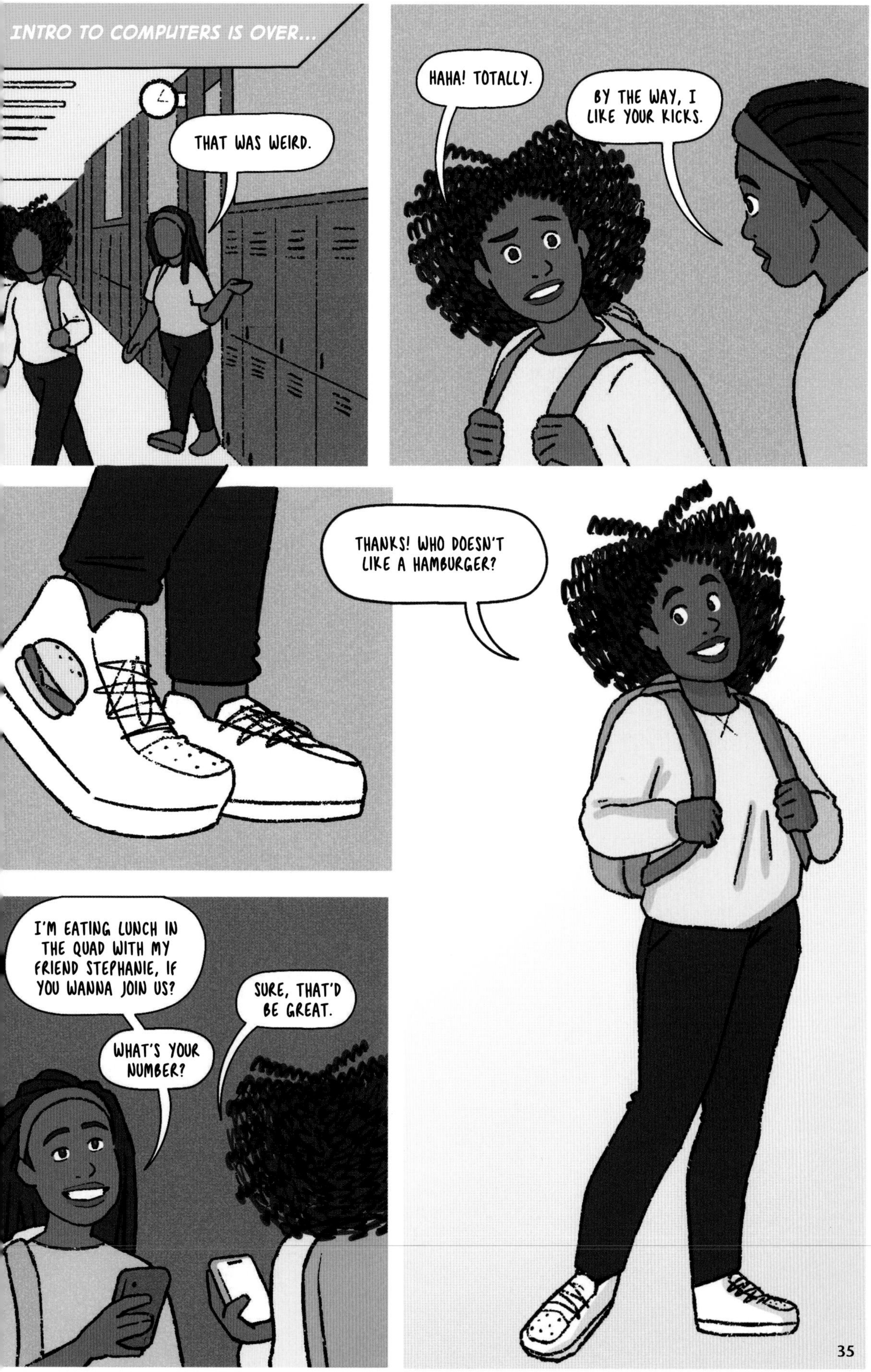
INTRO TO COMPUTERS IS OVER...
THAT WAS WEIRD.
HAHA! TOTALLY.
BY THE WAY, I LIKE YOUR KICKS.
THANKS! WHO DOESN'T LIKE A HAMBURGER?
I'M EATING LUNCH IN THE QUAD WITH MY FRIEND STEPHANIE, IF YOU WANNA JOIN US?
WHAT'S YOUR NUMBER?
SURE, THAT'D BE GREAT.

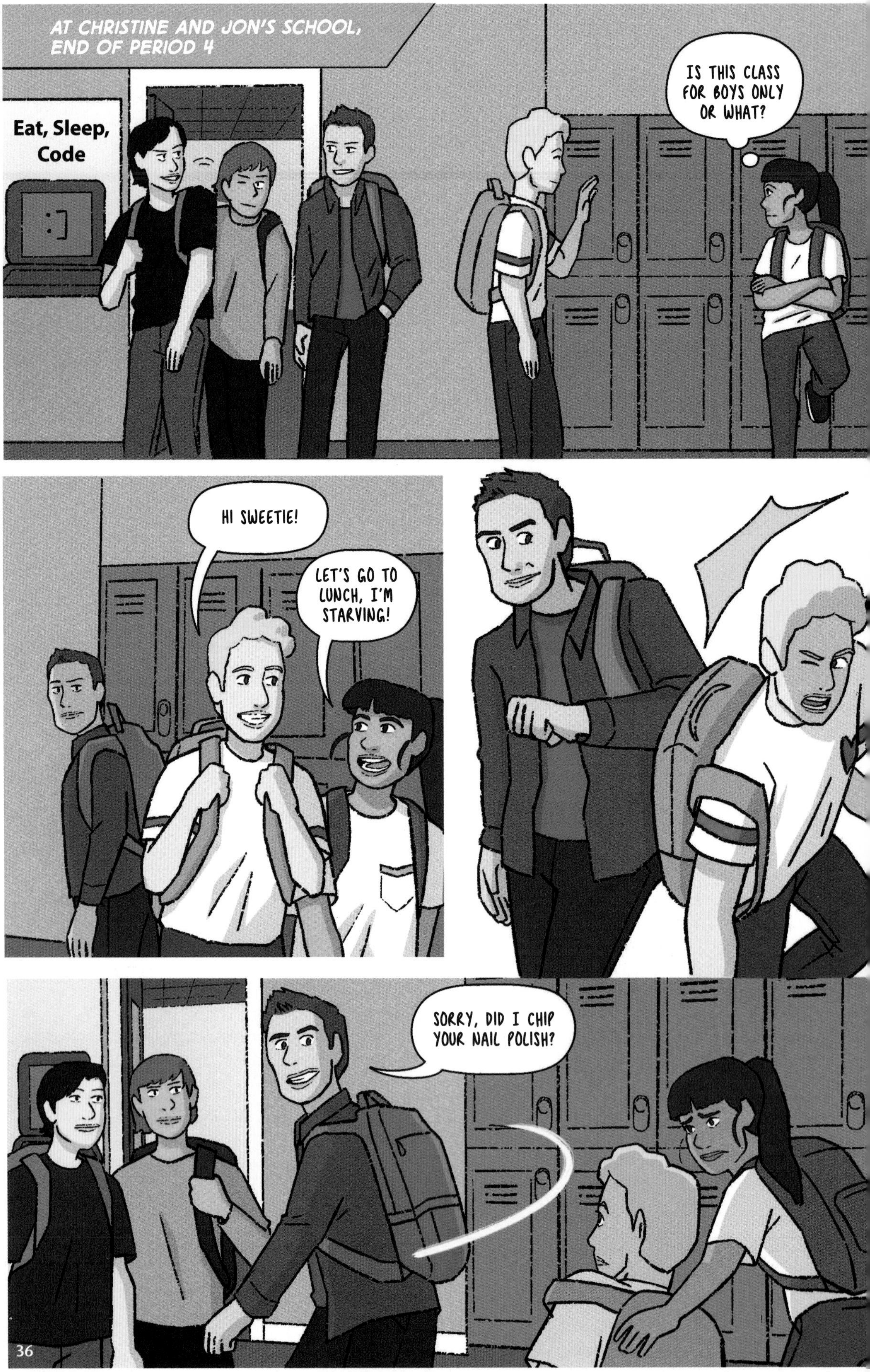
AT CHRISTINE AND JON'S SCHOOL, END OF PERIOD 4
Eat, Sleep, Code
IS THIS CLASS FOR BOYS ONLY OR WHAT?
HI SWEETIE!
LET'S GO TO LUNCH, I'M STARVING!
SORRY, DID I CHIP YOUR NAIL POLISH?

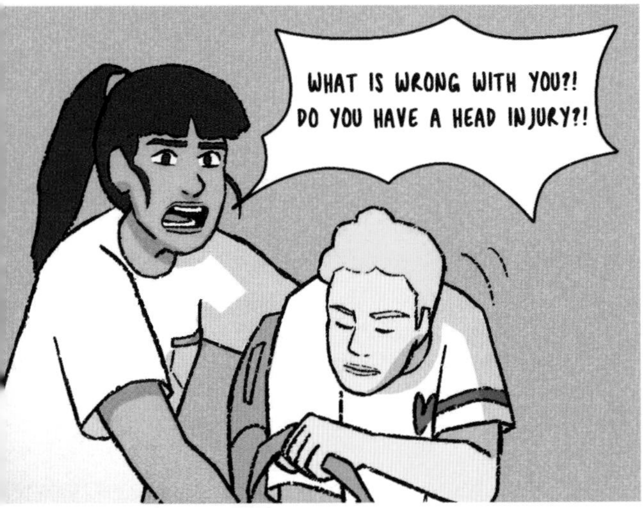
WHAT IS WRONG WITH YOU?! DO YOU HAVE A HEAD INJURY?!

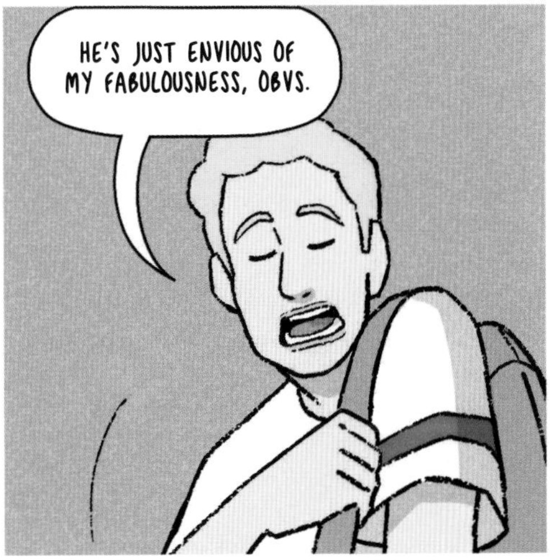
HE'S JUST ENVIOUS OF MY FABULOUSNESS, OBVS.

WE MUST WORK TOGETHER TO STOP BULLYING. IN US HIGH SCHOOLS, **59.1%** OF STUDENTS WHO SELF-IDENTIFY AS LESBIAN, GAY, BISEXUAL, TRANSGENDER, OR QUEER (LGBTQ) FEEL UNSAFE AT SCHOOL, WITH **MOST AVOIDING SCHOOL FUNCTIONS (77.6%) AND EXTRACURRICULAR ACTIVITIES (71.8%)** BECAUSE THEY FEEL UNSAFE OR UNCOMFORTABLE.

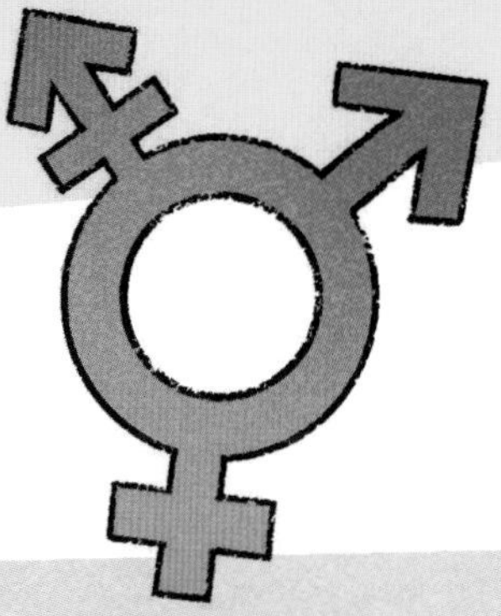

LGBTQ STUDENTS EXPERIENCE **BEING BULLIED ON SCHOOL PROPERTY (33%) AND CYBERBULLIED (27.1%)**, MORE THAN THEIR HETEROSEXUAL PEERS (17.1% AND 13.3%, RESPECTIVELY).

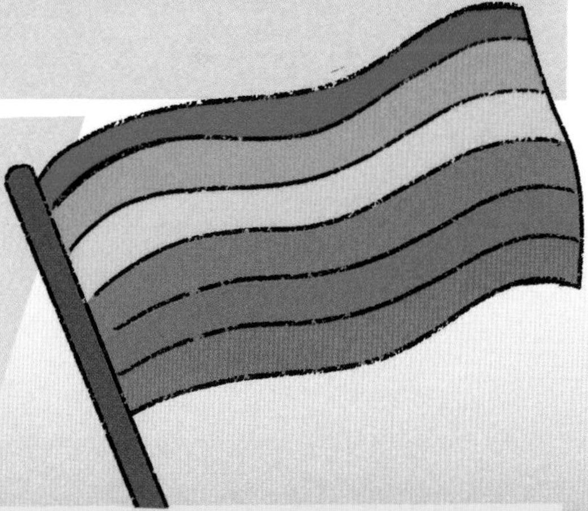

NON-WHITE LGBTQ STUDENTS EXPERIENCE EVEN WORSE TREATMENT: **67% OF BLACK AND AFRICAN AMERICAN LGBTQ YOUTH—AND 82% OF TRANSGENDER AND GENDER-EXPANSIVE YOUTH**—RESPONDING TO A HUMAN RIGHTS CAMPAIGN SURVEY HAVE BEEN VERBALLY INSULTED BECAUSE OF THEIR LGBTQ IDENTITY.[1]

IF YOU ARE LGBTQ AND WANT RESOURCES/SUPPORT, OR IF YOU ARE AN ALLY WHO WANTS TO SUPPORT YOUR LGBTQ FRIENDS AND FAMILY, CHECK OUT THESE RESOURCES:

- THE TREVOR PROJECT: WWW.THETREVORPROJECT.ORG
- HUMAN RIGHTS CAMPAIGN: WWW.HRC.ORG
- THE US GOVERNMENT STOP BULLYING WEBSITE: WWW.STOPBULLYING.GOV/BULLYING/LGBTQ
- GLSEN: WWW.GLSEN.ORG/

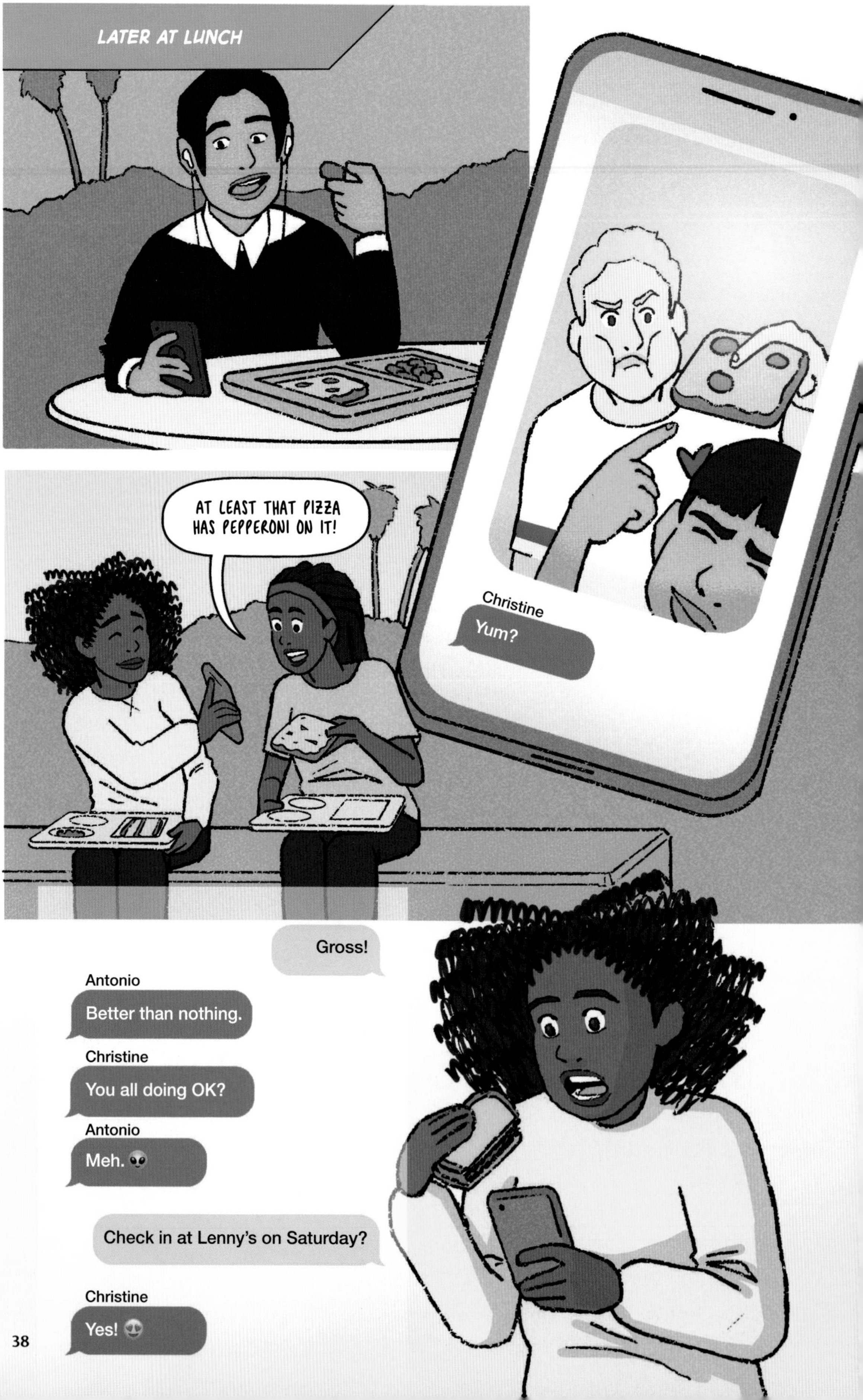
LATER AT LUNCH
Christine
Yum?
AT LEAST THAT PIZZA HAS PEPPERONI ON IT!
Gross!
Antonio
Better than nothing.
Christine
You all doing OK?
Antonio
Meh.
Check in at Lenny's on Saturday?
Christine
Yes!

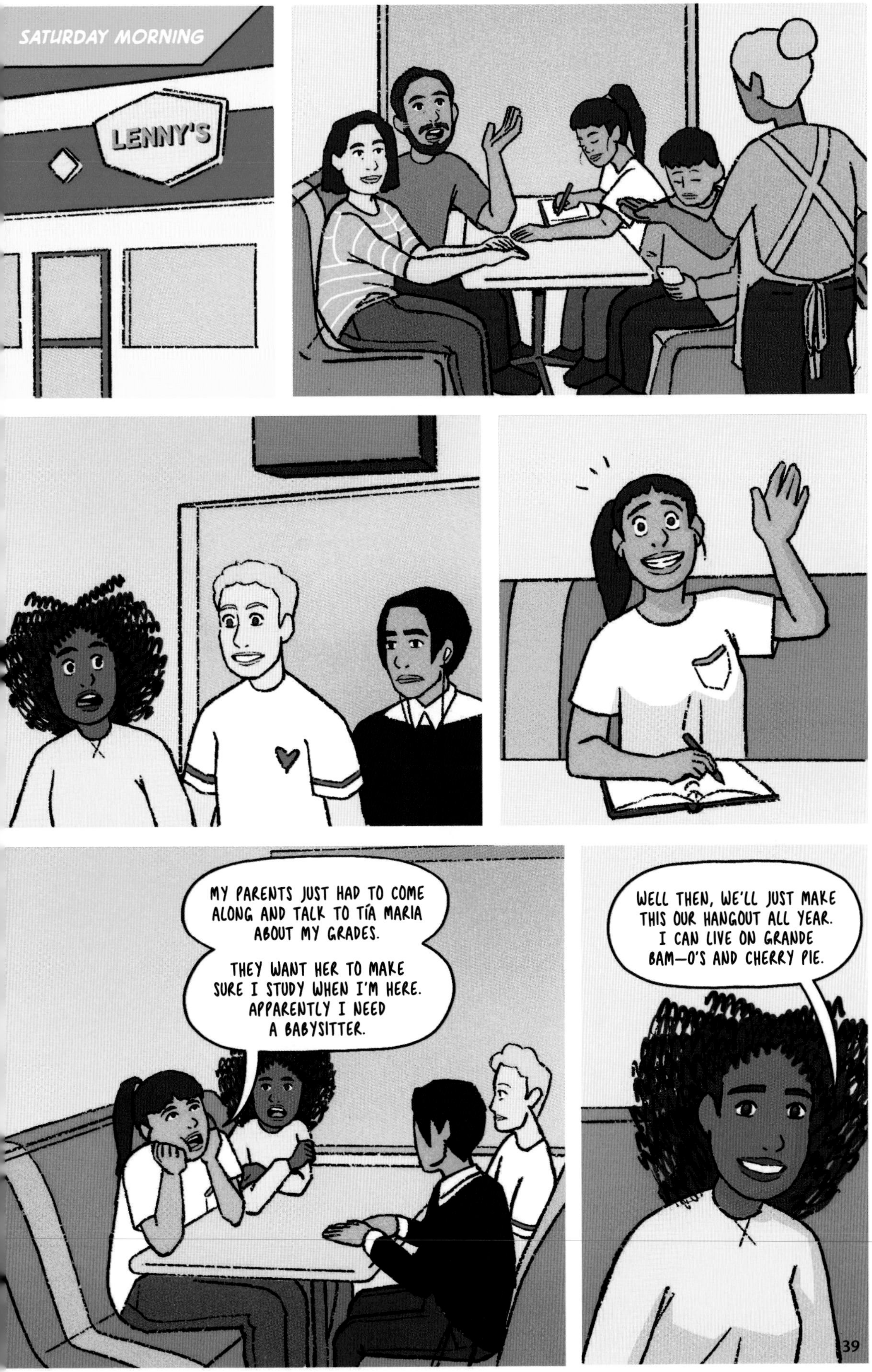
SATURDAY MORNING
LENNY'S
MY PARENTS JUST HAD TO COME ALONG AND TALK TO TÍA MARIA ABOUT MY GRADES.
THEY WANT HER TO MAKE SURE I STUDY WHEN I'M HERE. APPARENTLY I NEED A BABYSITTER.
WELL THEN, WE'LL JUST MAKE THIS OUR HANGOUT ALL YEAR. I CAN LIVE ON GRANDE BAM—O'S AND CHERRY PIE.

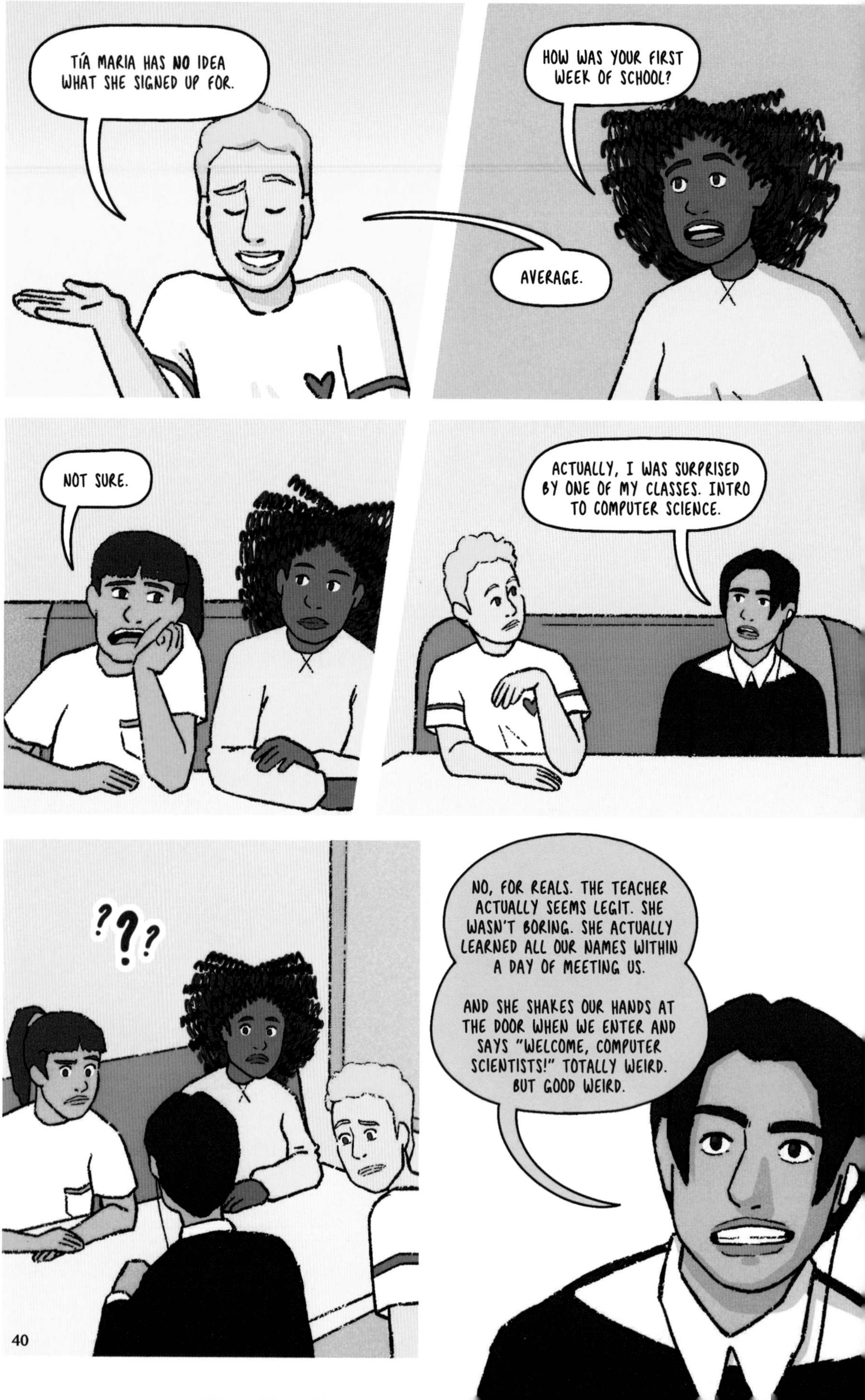
TÍA MARIA HAS NO IDEA WHAT SHE SIGNED UP FOR.
HOW WAS YOUR FIRST WEEK OF SCHOOL?
AVERAGE.
NOT SURE.
ACTUALLY, I WAS SURPRISED BY ONE OF MY CLASSES. INTRO TO COMPUTER SCIENCE.
???
NO, FOR REALS. THE TEACHER ACTUALLY SEEMS LEGIT. SHE WASN'T BORING. SHE ACTUALLY LEARNED ALL OUR NAMES WITHIN A DAY OF MEETING US.
AND SHE SHAKES OUR HANDS AT THE DOOR WHEN WE ENTER AND SAYS "WELCOME, COMPUTER SCIENTISTS!" TOTALLY WEIRD. BUT GOOD WEIRD.

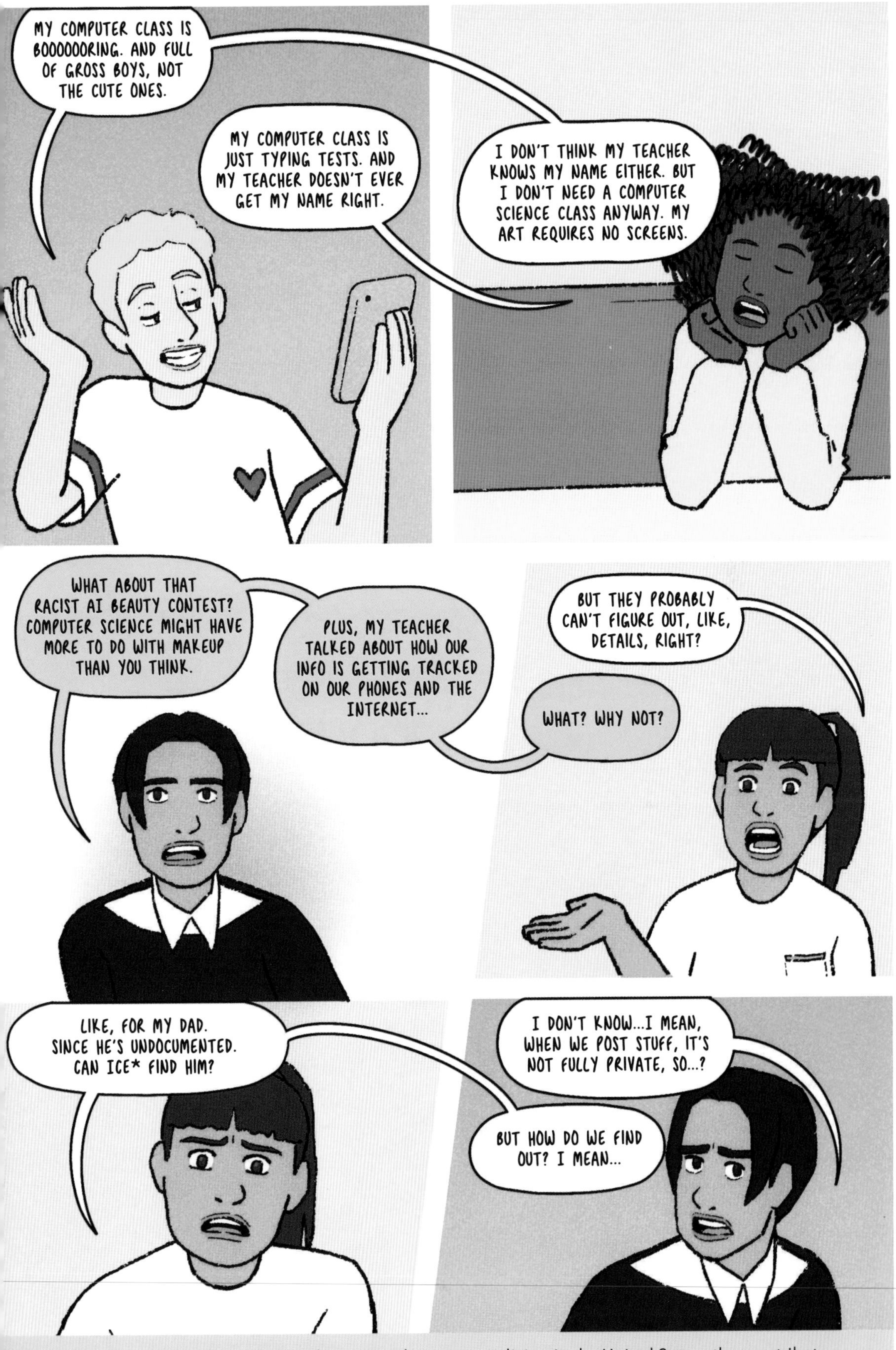
MY COMPUTER CLASS IS BOOOOOORING. AND FULL OF GROSS BOYS, NOT THE CUTE ONES.
MY COMPUTER CLASS IS JUST TYPING TESTS. AND MY TEACHER DOESN'T EVER GET MY NAME RIGHT.
I DON'T THINK MY TEACHER KNOWS MY NAME EITHER. BUT I DON'T NEED A COMPUTER SCIENCE CLASS ANYWAY. MY ART REQUIRES NO SCREENS.
WHAT ABOUT THAT RACIST AI BEAUTY CONTEST? COMPUTER SCIENCE MIGHT HAVE MORE TO DO WITH MAKEUP THAN YOU THINK.
PLUS, MY TEACHER TALKED ABOUT HOW OUR INFO IS GETTING TRACKED ON OUR PHONES AND THE INTERNET...
WHAT? WHY NOT?
BUT THEY PROBABLY CAN'T FIGURE OUT, LIKE, DETAILS, RIGHT?
LIKE, FOR MY DAD. SINCE HE'S UNDOCUMENTED. CAN ICE* FIND HIM?
I DON'T KNOW...I MEAN, WHEN WE POST STUFF, IT'S NOT FULLY PRIVATE, SO...?
BUT HOW DO WE FIND OUT? I MEAN...

*There are an estimated 11 million undocumented immigrants living in the United States; they contribute to our economy, pay taxes, enrich our culture, and are vital members of our communities.[2]

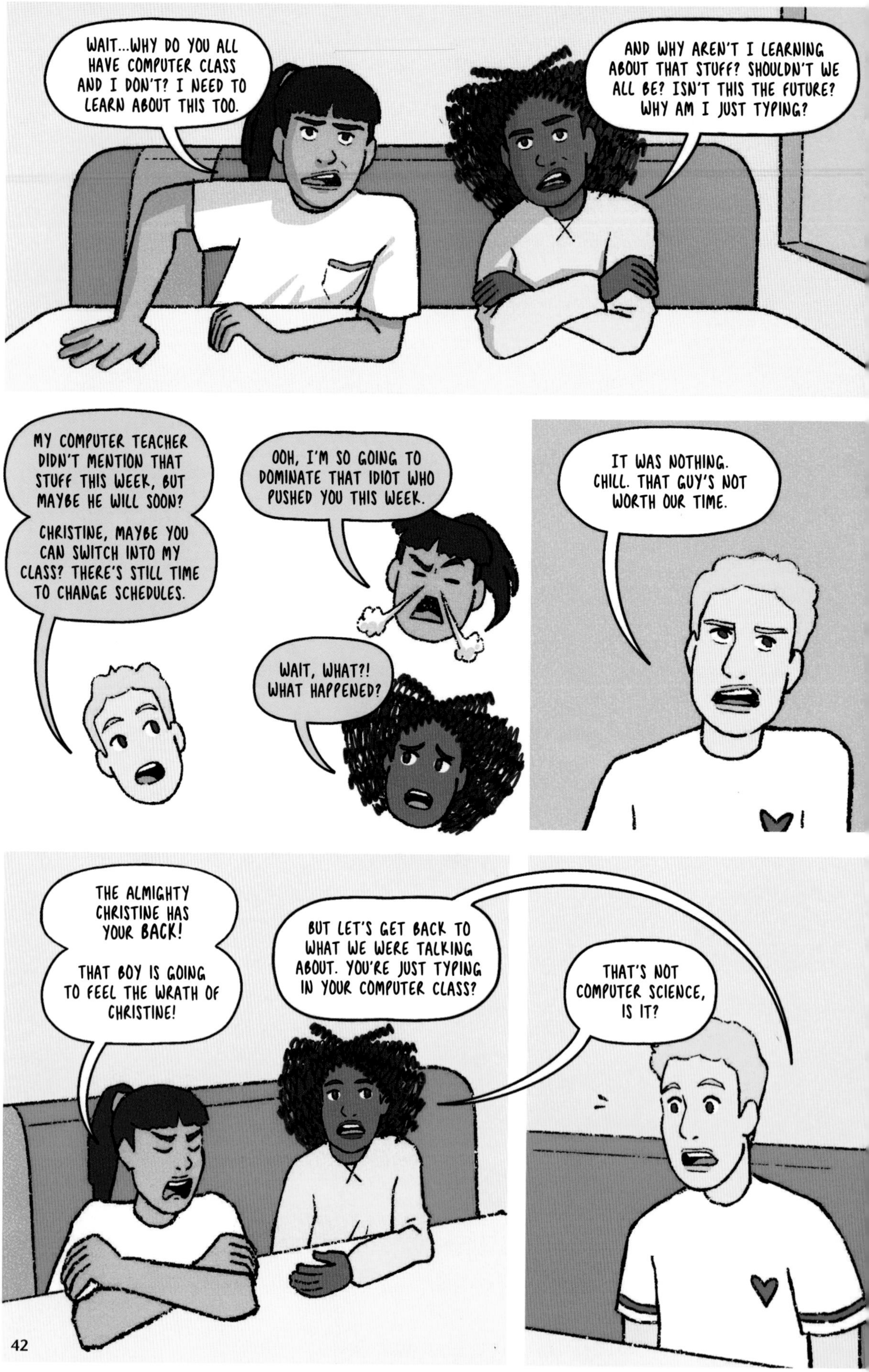
WAIT...WHY DO YOU ALL HAVE COMPUTER CLASS AND I DON'T? I NEED TO LEARN ABOUT THIS TOO.
AND WHY AREN'T I LEARNING ABOUT THAT STUFF? SHOULDN'T WE ALL BE? ISN'T THIS THE FUTURE? WHY AM I JUST TYPING?
MY COMPUTER TEACHER DIDN'T MENTION THAT STUFF THIS WEEK, BUT MAYBE HE WILL SOON?
CHRISTINE, MAYBE YOU CAN SWITCH INTO MY CLASS? THERE'S STILL TIME TO CHANGE SCHEDULES.
OOH, I'M SO GOING TO DOMINATE THAT IDIOT WHO PUSHED YOU THIS WEEK.
WAIT, WHAT?! WHAT HAPPENED?
IT WAS NOTHING. CHILL. THAT GUY'S NOT WORTH OUR TIME.
THE ALMIGHTY CHRISTINE HAS YOUR BACK!
THAT BOY IS GOING TO FEEL THE WRATH OF CHRISTINE!
BUT LET'S GET BACK TO WHAT WE WERE TALKING ABOUT. YOU'RE JUST TYPING IN YOUR COMPUTER CLASS?
THAT'S NOT COMPUTER SCIENCE, IS IT?

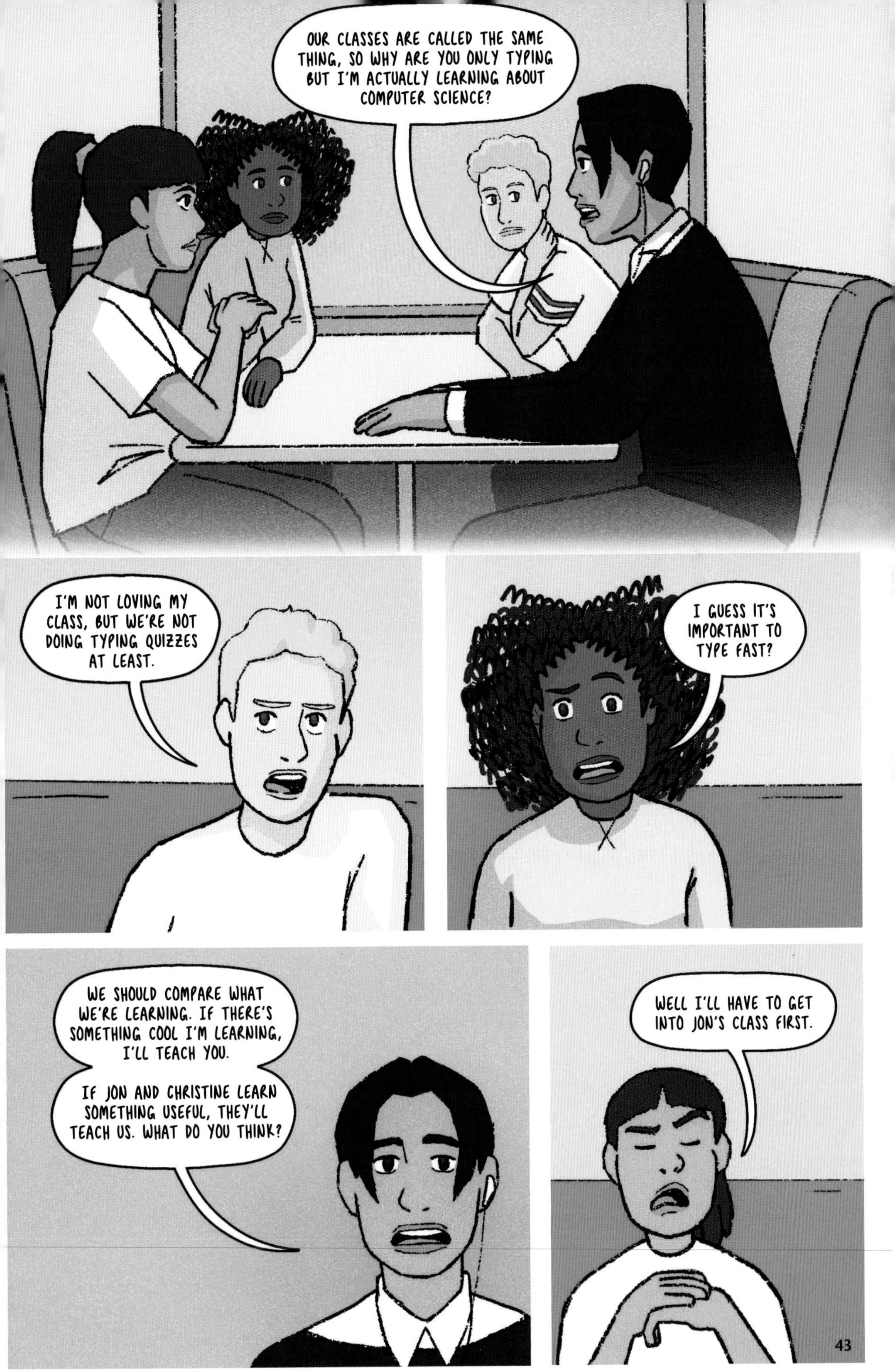
OUR CLASSES ARE CALLED THE SAME THING, SO WHY ARE YOU ONLY TYPING BUT I'M ACTUALLY LEARNING ABOUT COMPUTER SCIENCE?
I'M NOT LOVING MY CLASS, BUT WE'RE NOT DOING TYPING QUIZZES AT LEAST.
I GUESS IT'S IMPORTANT TO TYPE FAST?
WE SHOULD COMPARE WHAT WE'RE LEARNING. IF THERE'S SOMETHING COOL I'M LEARNING, I'LL TEACH YOU.
IF JON AND CHRISTINE LEARN SOMETHING USEFUL, THEY'LL TEACH US. WHAT DO YOU THINK?
WELL I'LL HAVE TO GET INTO JON'S CLASS FIRST.

What is computer science, anyway?

Computer science isn't just typing or learning how to make spreadsheets. **Computer science is about the study of computers, including both hardware and software, and how they can be applied to solving real-world problems.** Computer scientists use creativity and critical thinking to design innovations.

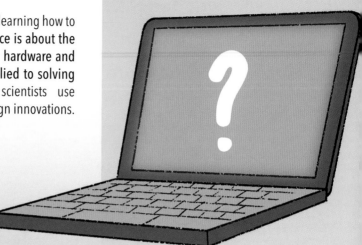

Computer science is changing every field: it is used to mix beats and make all genres of music, create special effects and animation in films/TV, create medicine and vaccines or help doctors and nurses decide on treatments for patients, help athletes monitor their health and skills during training on and off the field, collect data and information for scientists working anywhere from forests to labs, improve how people learn in school, and more. Everyone needs to learn computer science because it affects everything we touch and do. Computing determines how we understand what is going on in the world.

Using computers to develop vaccines: In computational immunology, scientists use mathematical models that can predict which part of a new virus will be recognized by the immune system. This helps speed up the development and testing of vaccines.

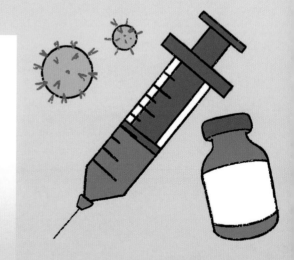

Using computer science to revolutionize fashion: Designers can incorporate and sew microcomputers, sensors, LEDs, and more into fabric so that clothing can make sounds, light up, and sense and react to the environment.

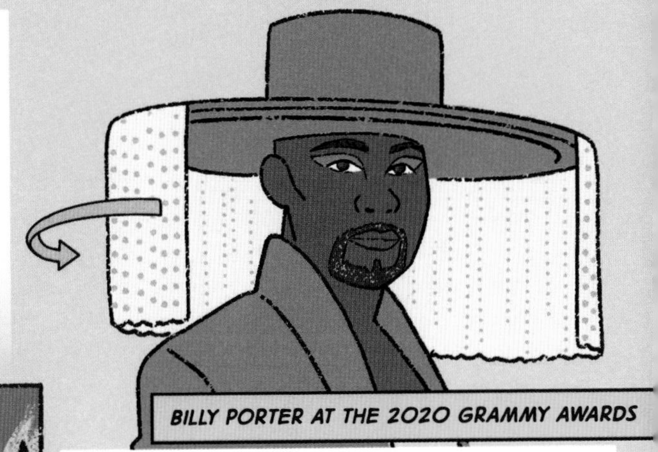

BILLY PORTER AT THE 2020 GRAMMY AWARDS

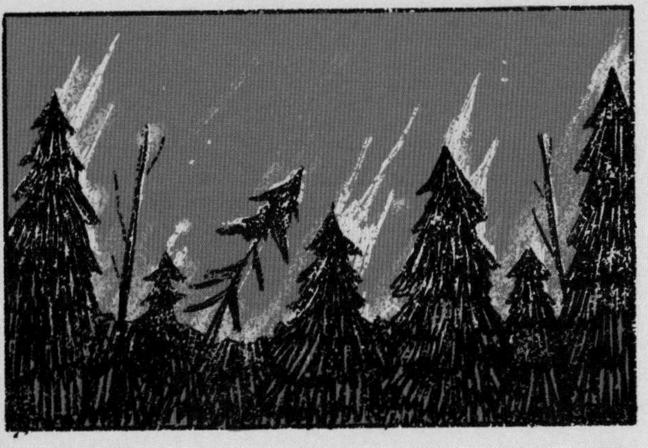

Addressing climate change: Computer scientists analyze data to address how trapped greenhouse gases are affecting sea levels, droughts, hurricanes, fires, and heat waves.

Finding life on other planets: Scientists program a computer that serves as the Mars Rover's brain—controlling its motors, science instruments, and communication functions—as it sends data back and forth between Mars and Earth.

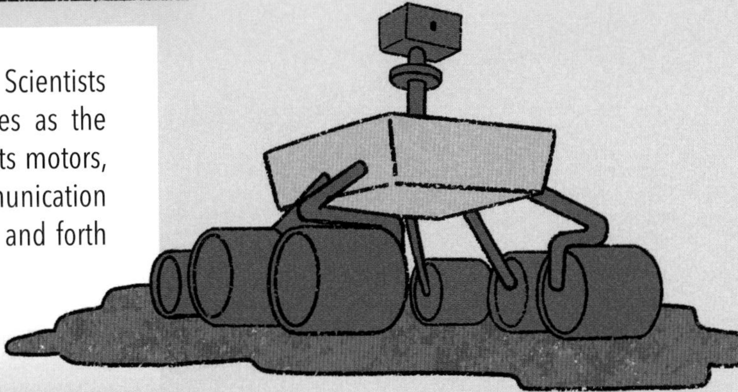

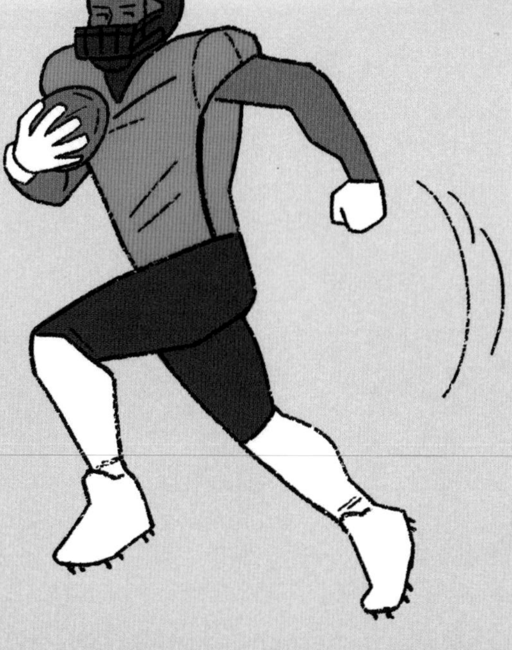

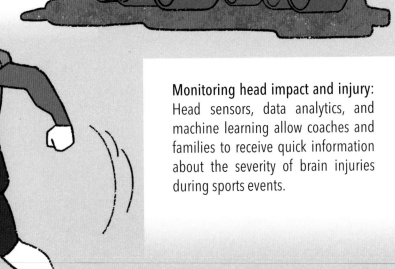

Monitoring head impact and injury: Head sensors, data analytics, and machine learning allow coaches and families to receive quick information about the severity of brain injuries during sports events.

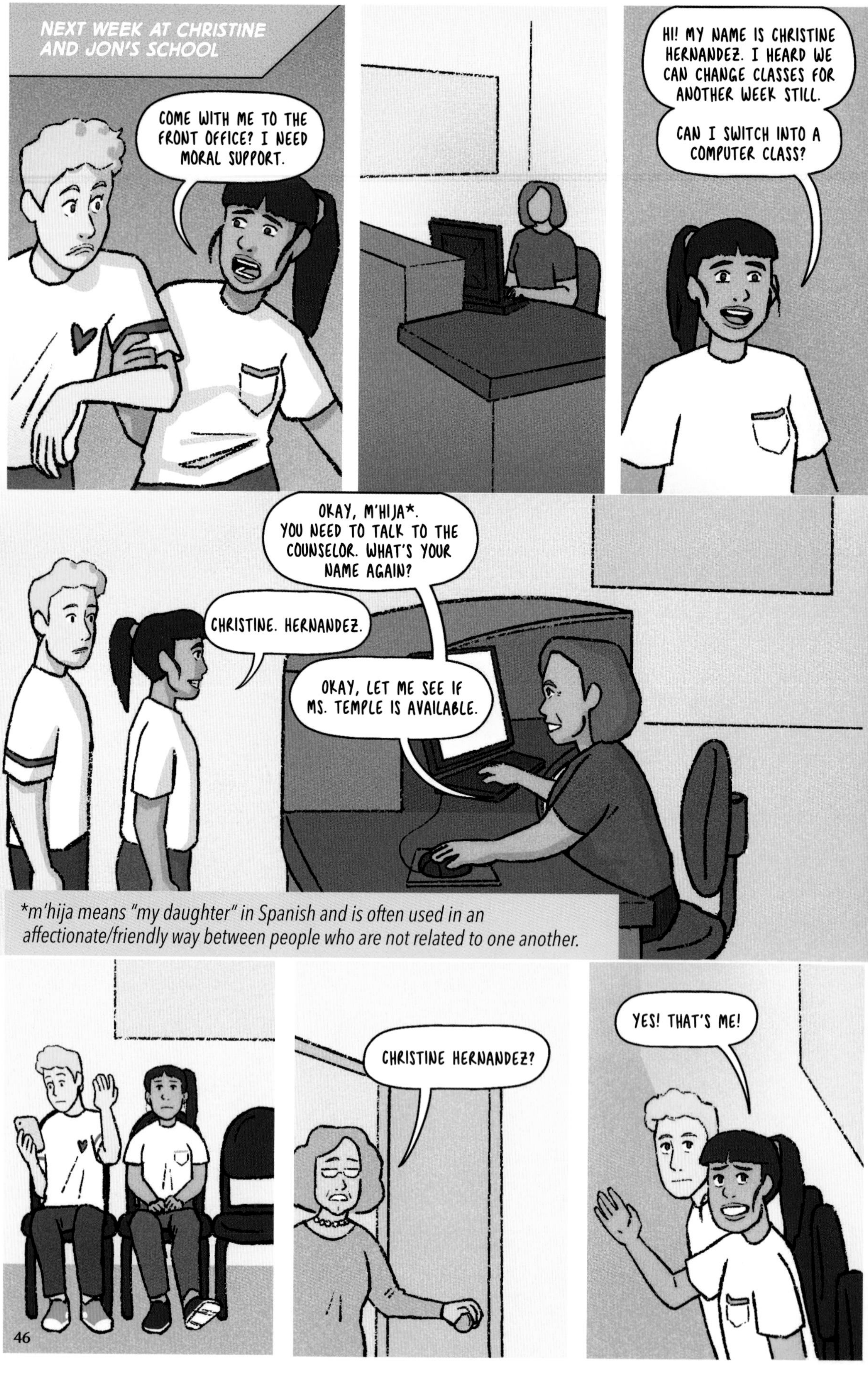
NEXT WEEK AT CHRISTINE AND JON'S SCHOOL
COME WITH ME TO THE FRONT OFFICE? I NEED MORAL SUPPORT.
HI! MY NAME IS CHRISTINE HERNANDEZ. I HEARD WE CAN CHANGE CLASSES FOR ANOTHER WEEK STILL.
CAN I SWITCH INTO A COMPUTER CLASS?
OKAY, M'HIJA*. YOU NEED TO TALK TO THE COUNSELOR. WHAT'S YOUR NAME AGAIN?
CHRISTINE. HERNANDEZ.
OKAY, LET ME SEE IF MS. TEMPLE IS AVAILABLE.
*m'hija means "my daughter" in Spanish and is often used in an affectionate/friendly way between people who are not related to one another.
CHRISTINE HERNANDEZ?
YES! THAT'S ME!

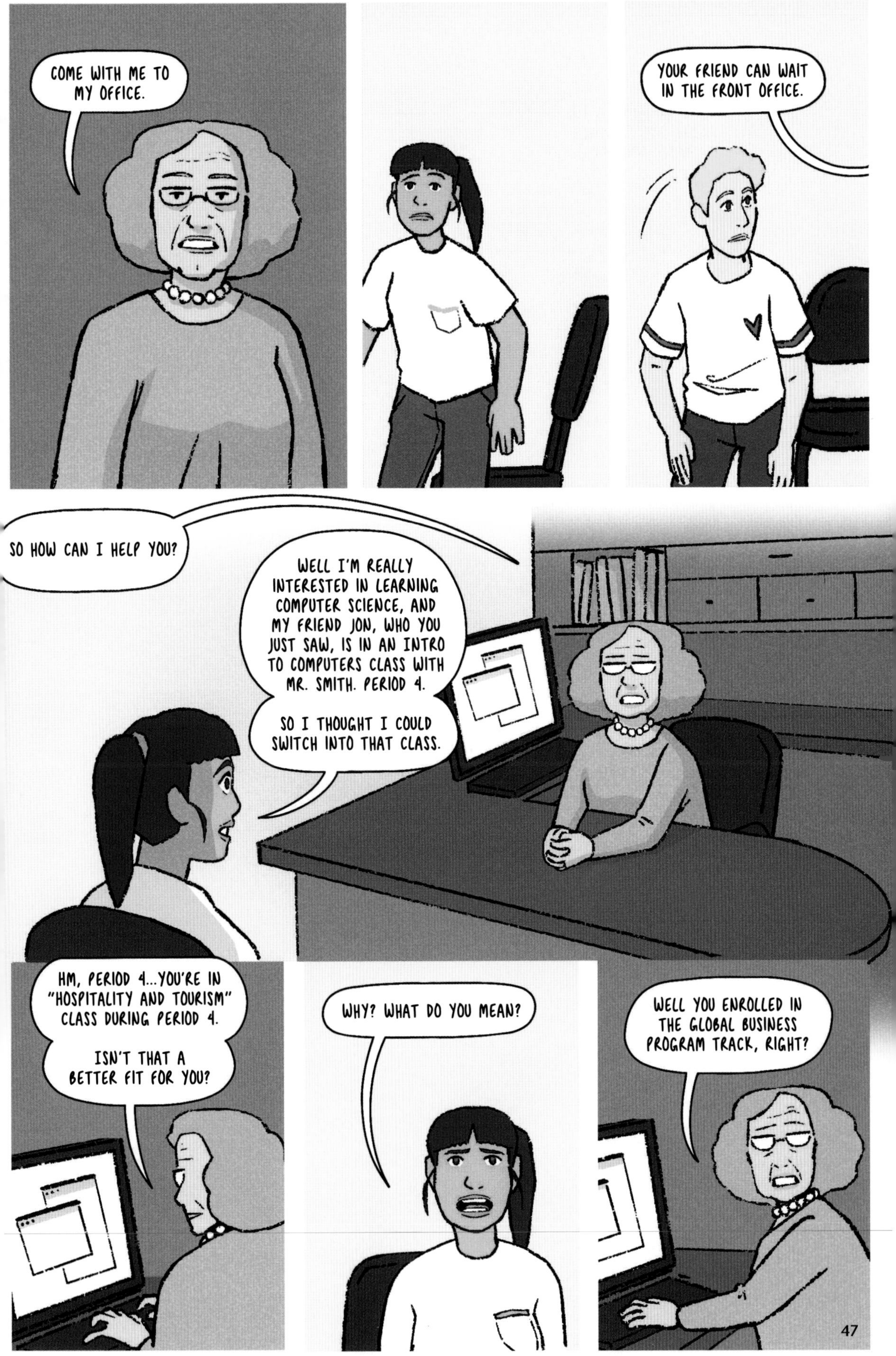
COME WITH ME TO MY OFFICE.
YOUR FRIEND CAN WAIT IN THE FRONT OFFICE.
SO HOW CAN I HELP YOU?
WELL I'M REALLY INTERESTED IN LEARNING COMPUTER SCIENCE, AND MY FRIEND JON, WHO YOU JUST SAW, IS IN AN INTRO TO COMPUTERS CLASS WITH MR. SMITH. PERIOD 4.
SO I THOUGHT I COULD SWITCH INTO THAT CLASS.
HM, PERIOD 4...YOU'RE IN "HOSPITALITY AND TOURISM" CLASS DURING PERIOD 4.
ISN'T THAT A BETTER FIT FOR YOU?
WHY? WHAT DO YOU MEAN?
WELL YOU ENROLLED IN THE GLOBAL BUSINESS PROGRAM TRACK, RIGHT?

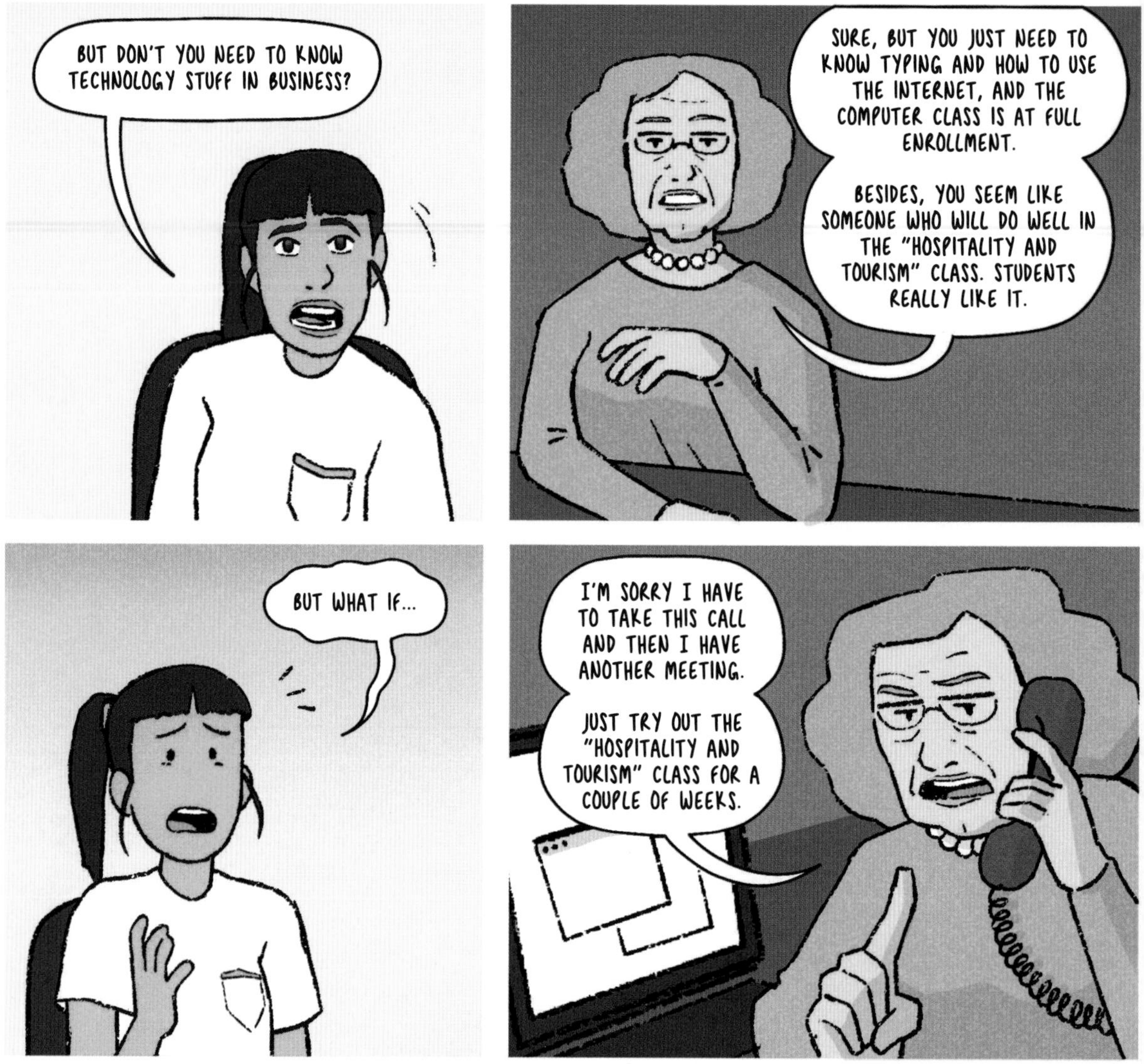
BUT DON'T YOU NEED TO KNOW TECHNOLOGY STUFF IN BUSINESS?
SURE, BUT YOU JUST NEED TO KNOW TYPING AND HOW TO USE THE INTERNET, AND THE COMPUTER CLASS IS AT FULL ENROLLMENT.
BESIDES, YOU SEEM LIKE SOMEONE WHO WILL DO WELL IN THE "HOSPITALITY AND TOURISM" CLASS. STUDENTS REALLY LIKE IT.
BUT WHAT IF...
I'M SORRY I HAVE TO TAKE THIS CALL AND THEN I HAVE ANOTHER MEETING.
JUST TRY OUT THE "HOSPITALITY AND TOURISM" CLASS FOR A COUPLE OF WEEKS.

Christine's experience with her counselor is based on the real experiences of a female high school student in a very overcrowded school who wanted to learn computer programming but was told by her counselor that the Programming class was filled and that she should take Floristry instead. She did not want to take Floristry, but was told that it filled the Technical Arts requirement (the same requirement filled by Computer Science at the school). This is described in *Stuck in the Shallow End: Education, Race, and Computing.*[3]

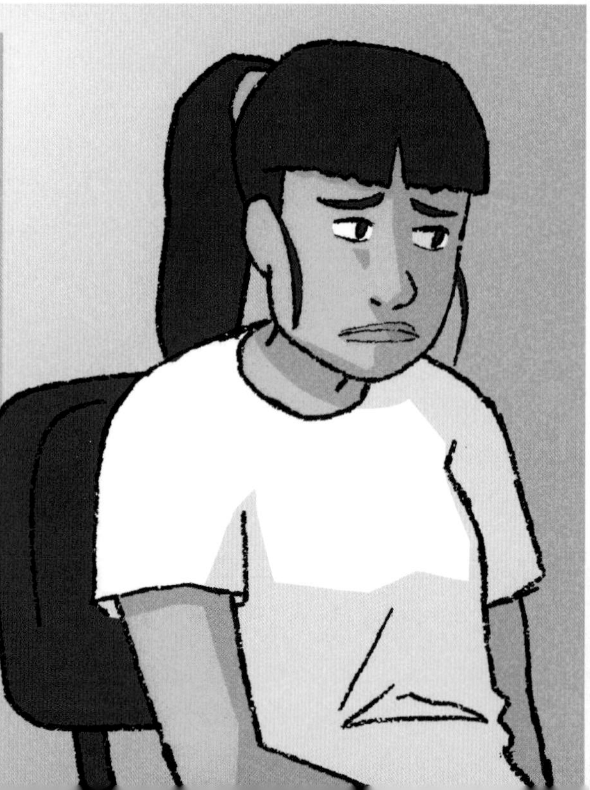

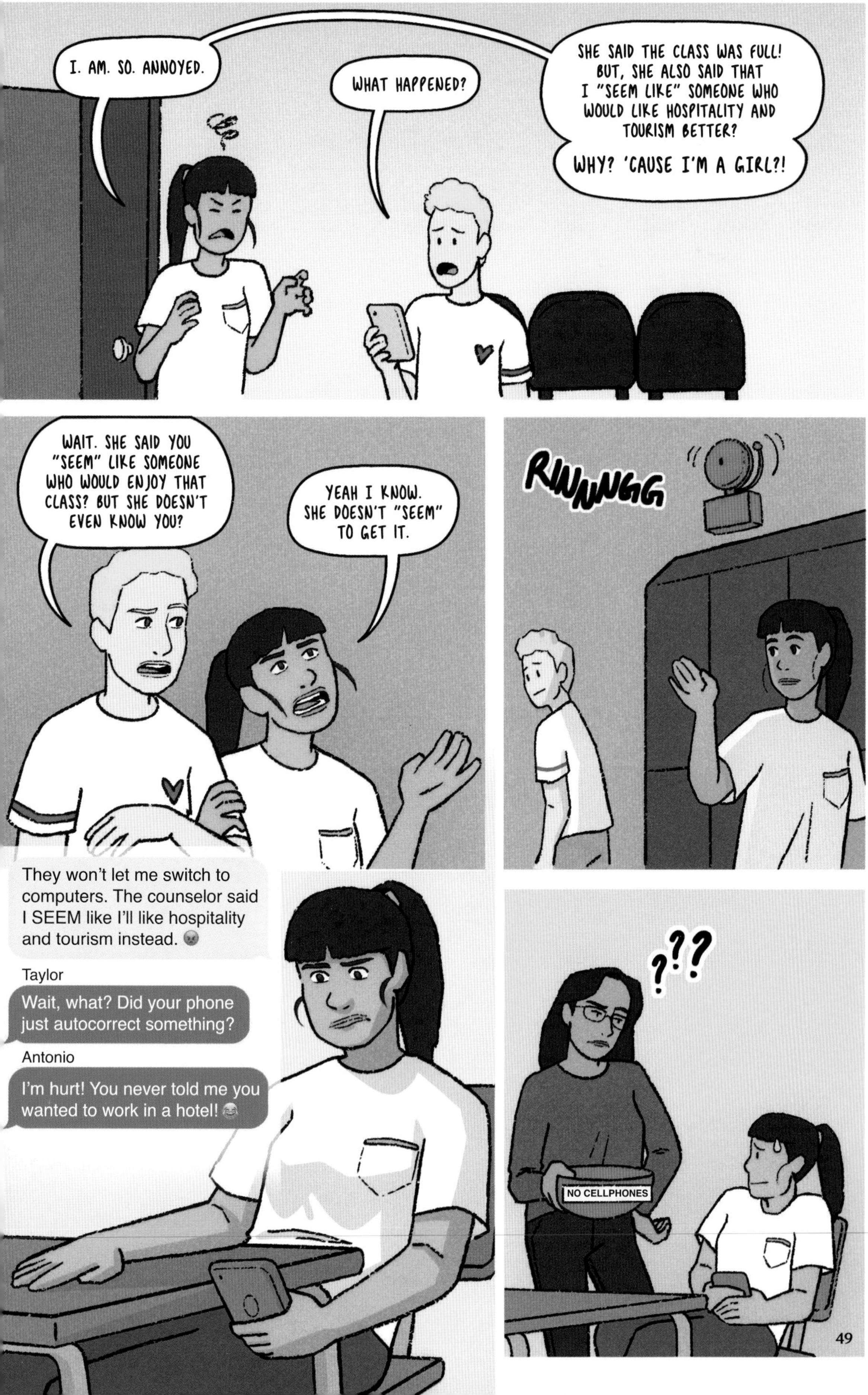
I. AM. SO. ANNOYED.
WHAT HAPPENED?
SHE SAID THE CLASS WAS FULL! BUT, SHE ALSO SAID THAT I "SEEM LIKE" SOMEONE WHO WOULD LIKE HOSPITALITY AND TOURISM BETTER?
WHY? 'CAUSE I'M A GIRL?!
WAIT. SHE SAID YOU "SEEM" LIKE SOMEONE WHO WOULD ENJOY THAT CLASS? BUT SHE DOESN'T EVEN KNOW YOU?
YEAH I KNOW. SHE DOESN'T "SEEM" TO GET IT.
RIINNNGG
They won't let me switch to computers. The counselor said I SEEM like I'll like hospitality and tourism instead.
Taylor
Wait, what? Did your phone just autocorrect something?
Antonio
I'm hurt! You never told me you wanted to work in a hotel!
???
NO CELLPHONES

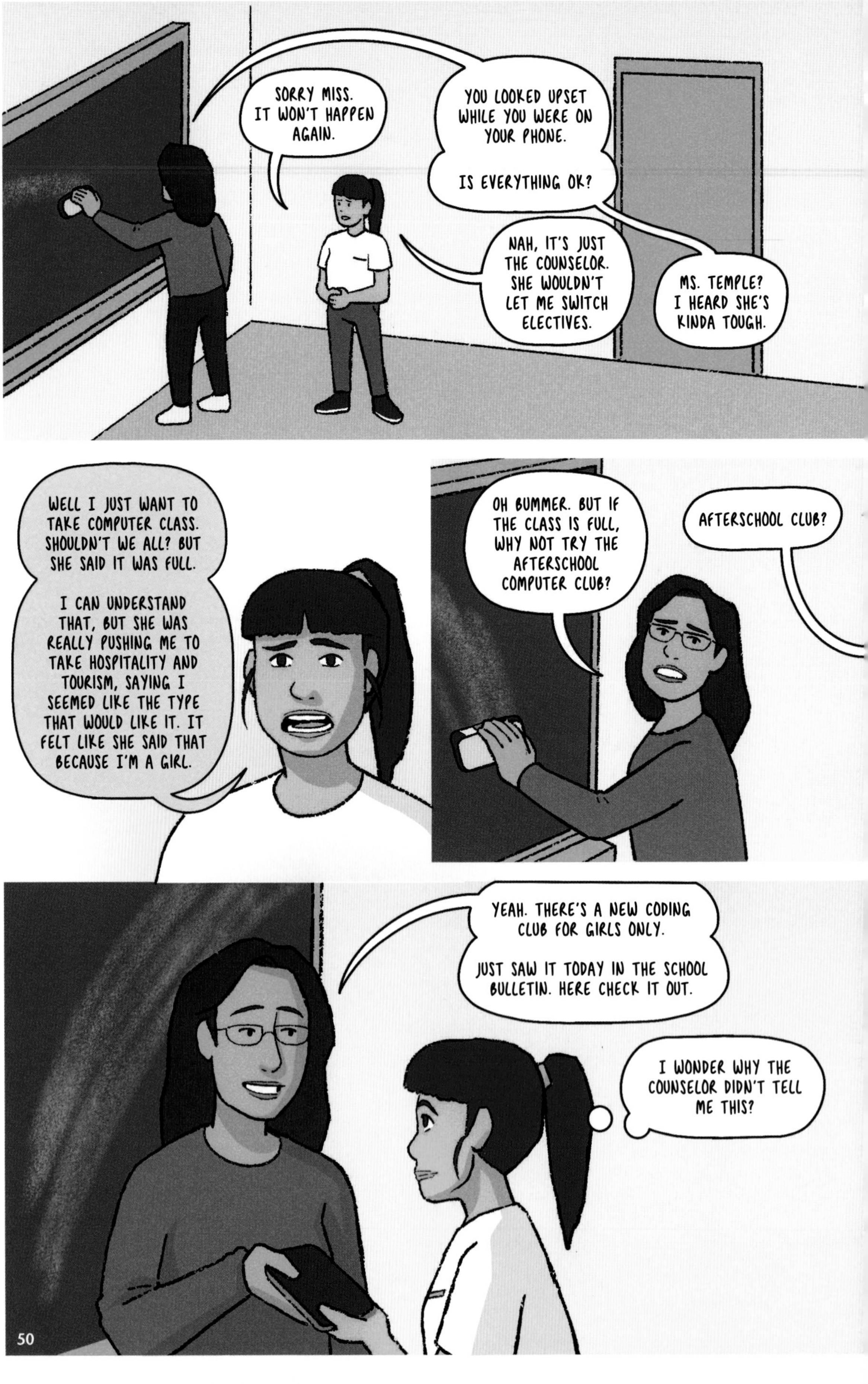
SORRY MISS. IT WON'T HAPPEN AGAIN.
YOU LOOKED UPSET WHILE YOU WERE ON YOUR PHONE.
IS EVERYTHING OK?
NAH, IT'S JUST THE COUNSELOR. SHE WOULDN'T LET ME SWITCH ELECTIVES.
MS. TEMPLE? I HEARD SHE'S KINDA TOUGH.
WELL I JUST WANT TO TAKE COMPUTER CLASS. SHOULDN'T WE ALL? BUT SHE SAID IT WAS FULL.
I CAN UNDERSTAND THAT, BUT SHE WAS REALLY PUSHING ME TO TAKE HOSPITALITY AND TOURISM, SAYING I SEEMED LIKE THE TYPE THAT WOULD LIKE IT. IT FELT LIKE SHE SAID THAT BECAUSE I'M A GIRL.
OH BUMMER. BUT IF THE CLASS IS FULL, WHY NOT TRY THE AFTERSCHOOL COMPUTER CLUB?
AFTERSCHOOL CLUB?
YEAH. THERE'S A NEW CODING CLUB FOR GIRLS ONLY.
JUST SAW IT TODAY IN THE SCHOOL BULLETIN. HERE CHECK IT OUT.
I WONDER WHY THE COUNSELOR DIDN'T TELL ME THIS?

CHAPTER 4

WHY DO WE NEED TO LEARN COMPUTER SCIENCE?

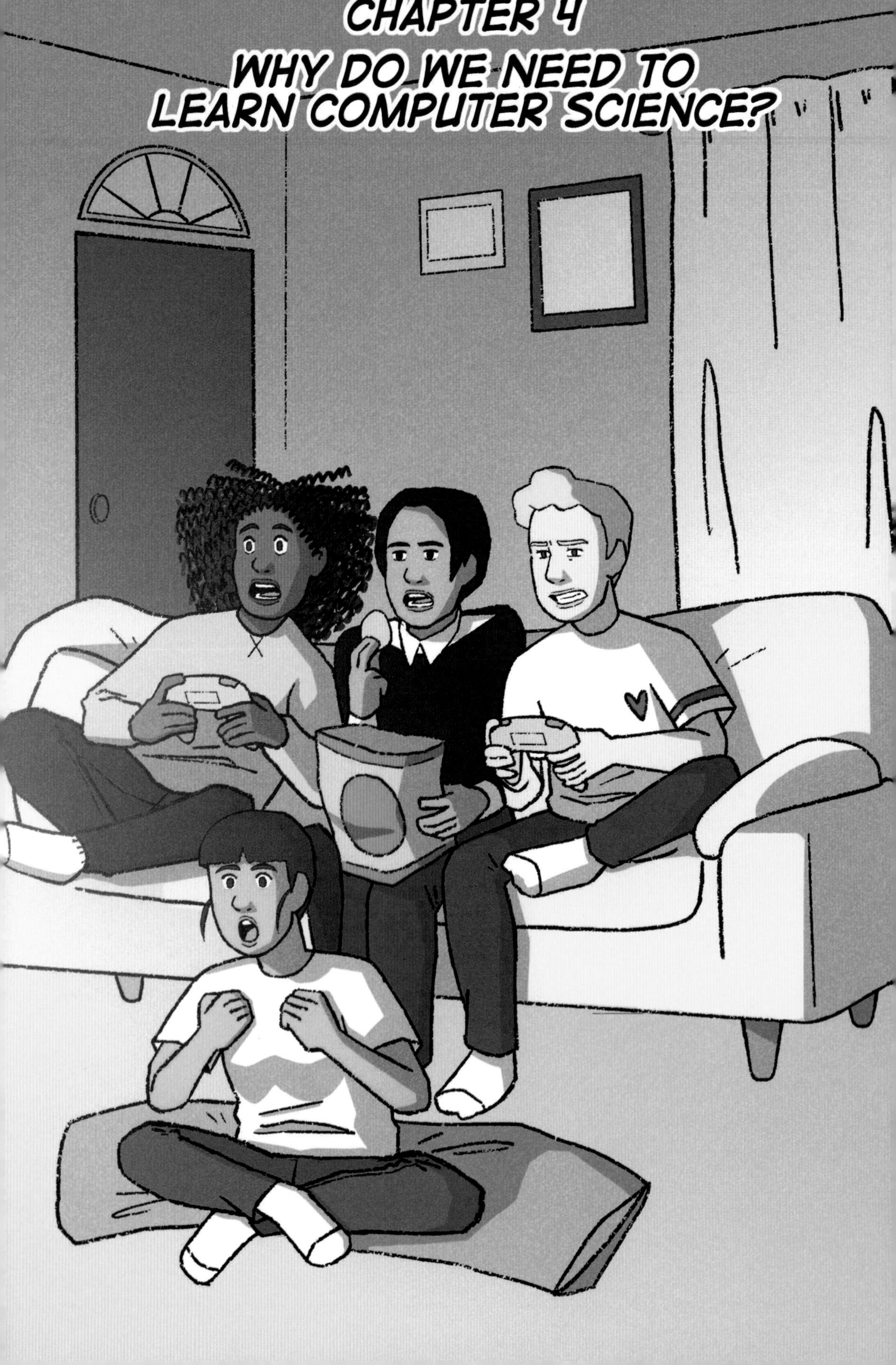

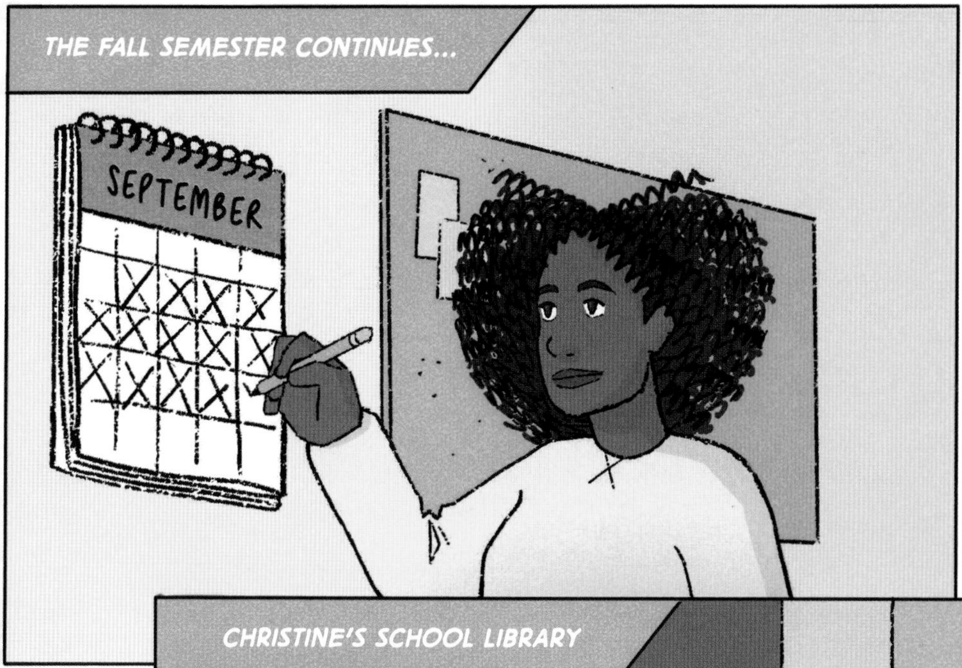

THE FALL SEMESTER CONTINUES...
SEPTEMBER

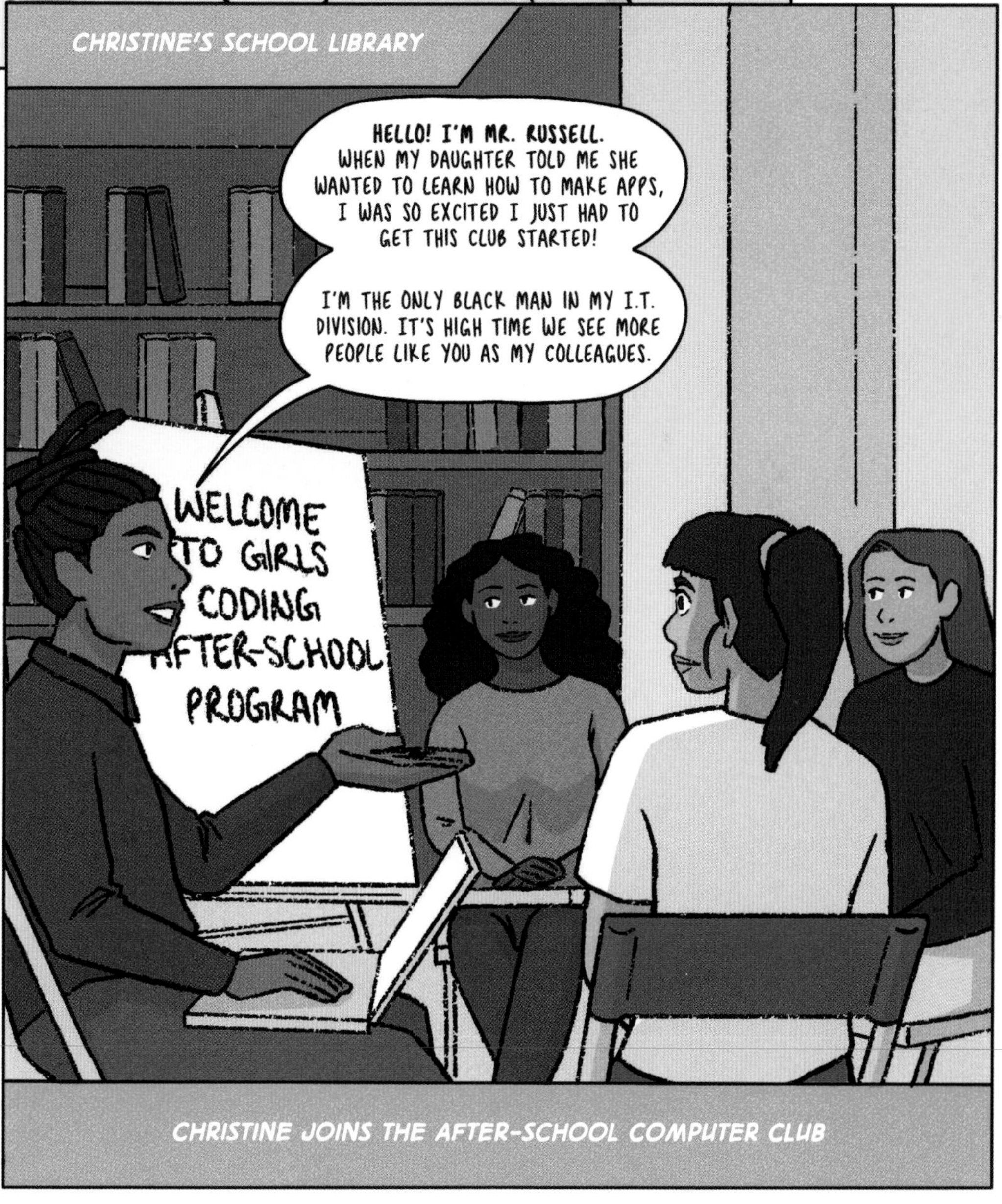

CHRISTINE'S SCHOOL LIBRARY
HELLO! I'M MR. RUSSELL. WHEN MY DAUGHTER TOLD ME SHE WANTED TO LEARN HOW TO MAKE APPS, I WAS SO EXCITED I JUST HAD TO GET THIS CLUB STARTED!
I'M THE ONLY BLACK MAN IN MY I.T. DIVISION. IT'S HIGH TIME WE SEE MORE PEOPLE LIKE YOU AS MY COLLEAGUES.
WELCOME TO GIRLS CODING AFTER-SCHOOL PROGRAM
CHRISTINE JOINS THE AFTER-SCHOOL COMPUTER CLUB

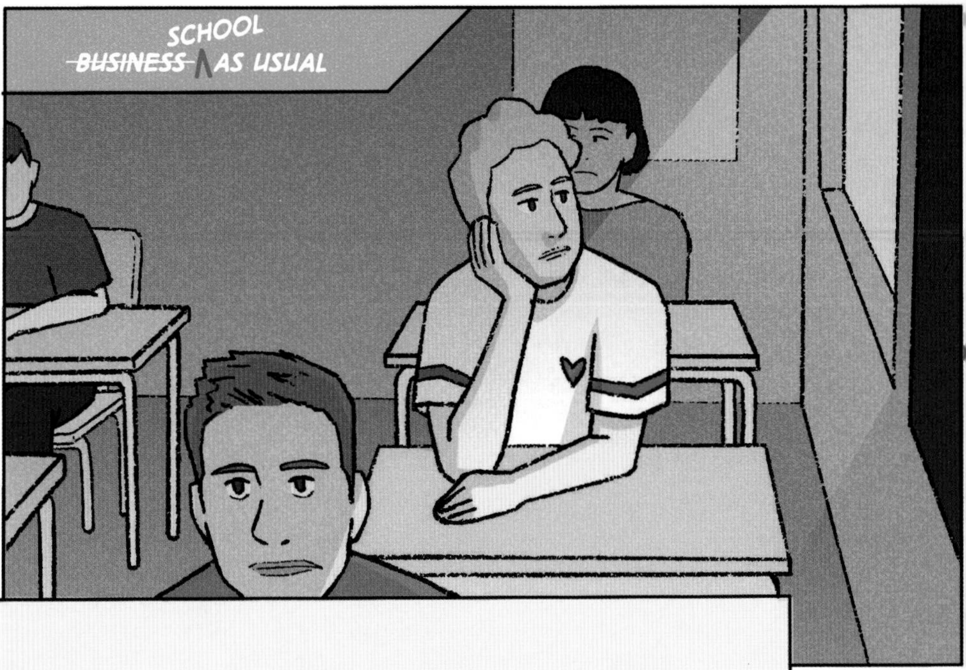
~~BUSINESS~~ SCHOOL AS USUAL

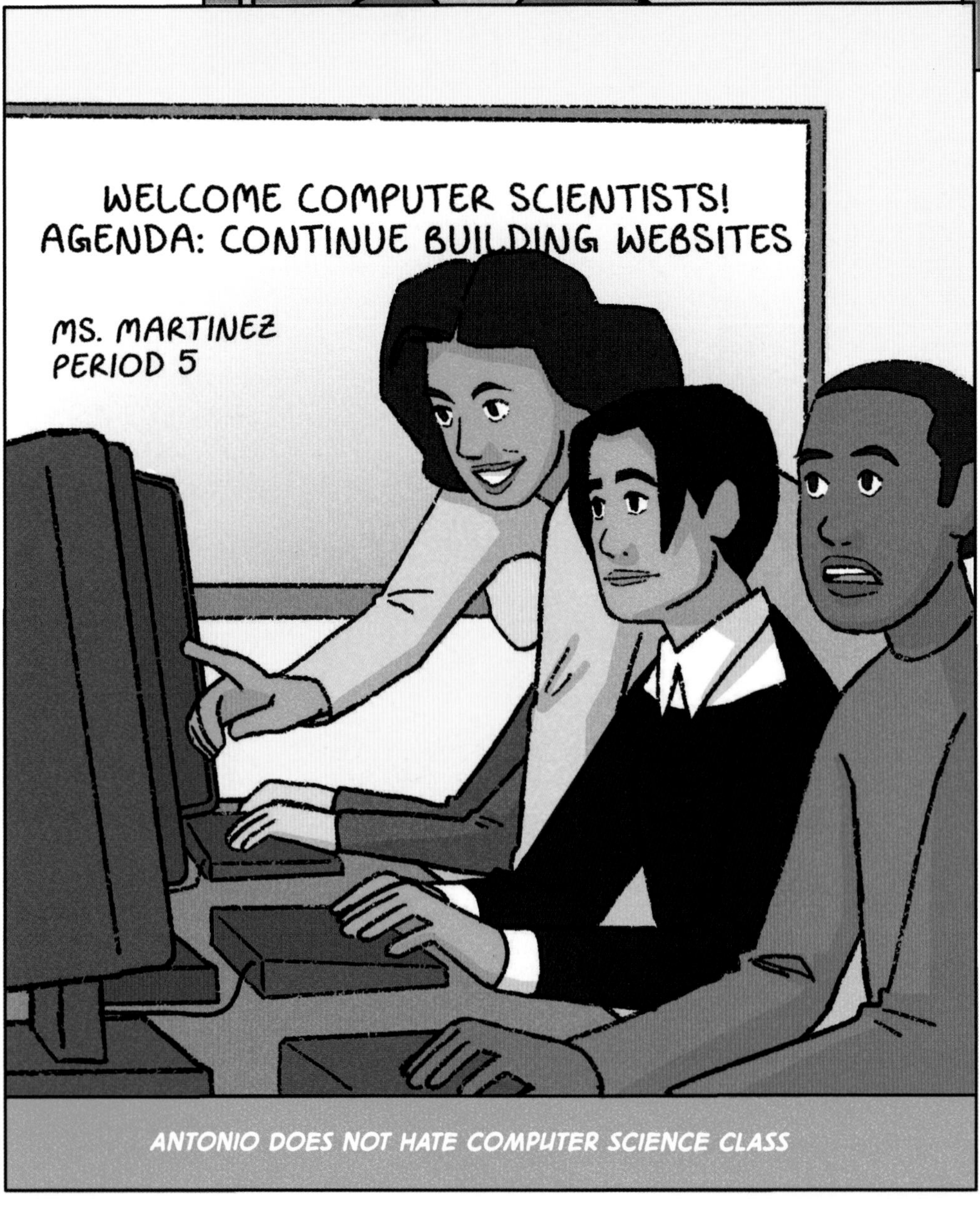
WELCOME COMPUTER SCIENTISTS!
AGENDA: CONTINUE BUILDING WEBSITES
MS. MARTINEZ
PERIOD 5
ANTONIO DOES NOT HATE COMPUTER SCIENCE CLASS

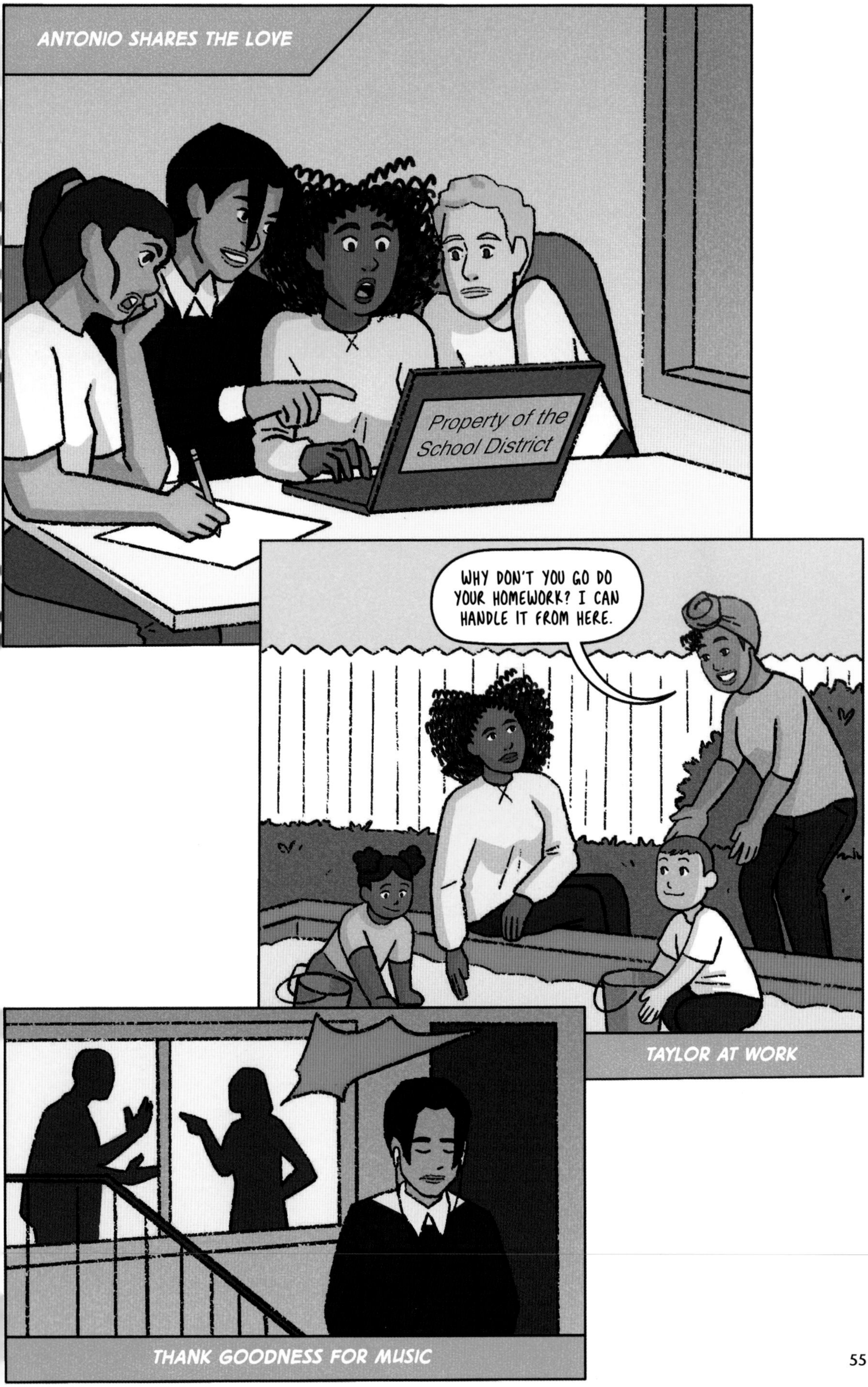
ANTONIO SHARES THE LOVE
Property of the School District
WHY DON'T YOU GO DO YOUR HOMEWORK? I CAN HANDLE IT FROM HERE.
TAYLOR AT WORK
THANK GOODNESS FOR MUSIC

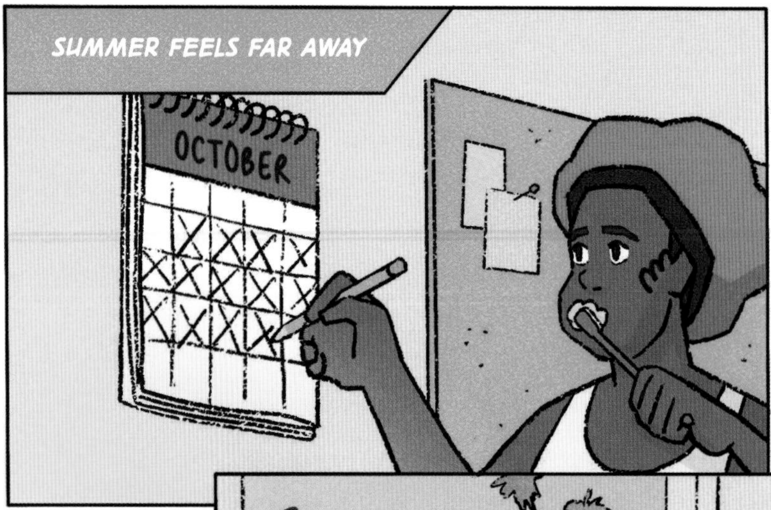
SUMMER FEELS FAR AWAY
OCTOBER

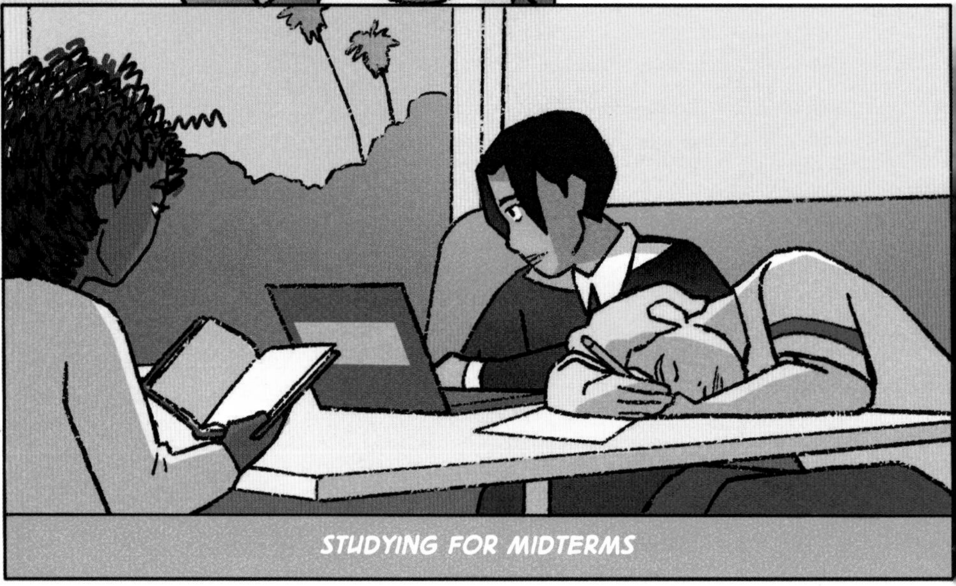
STUDYING FOR MIDTERMS

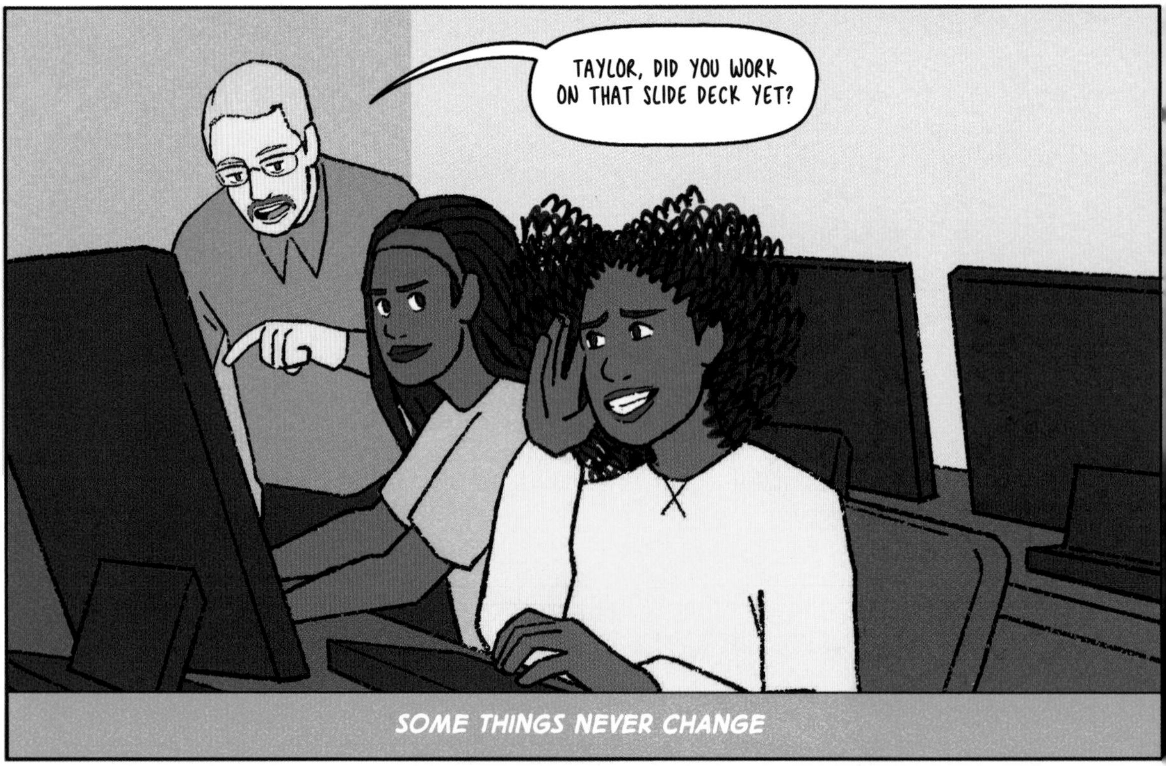
TAYLOR, DID YOU WORK ON THAT SLIDE DECK YET?
SOME THINGS NEVER CHANGE

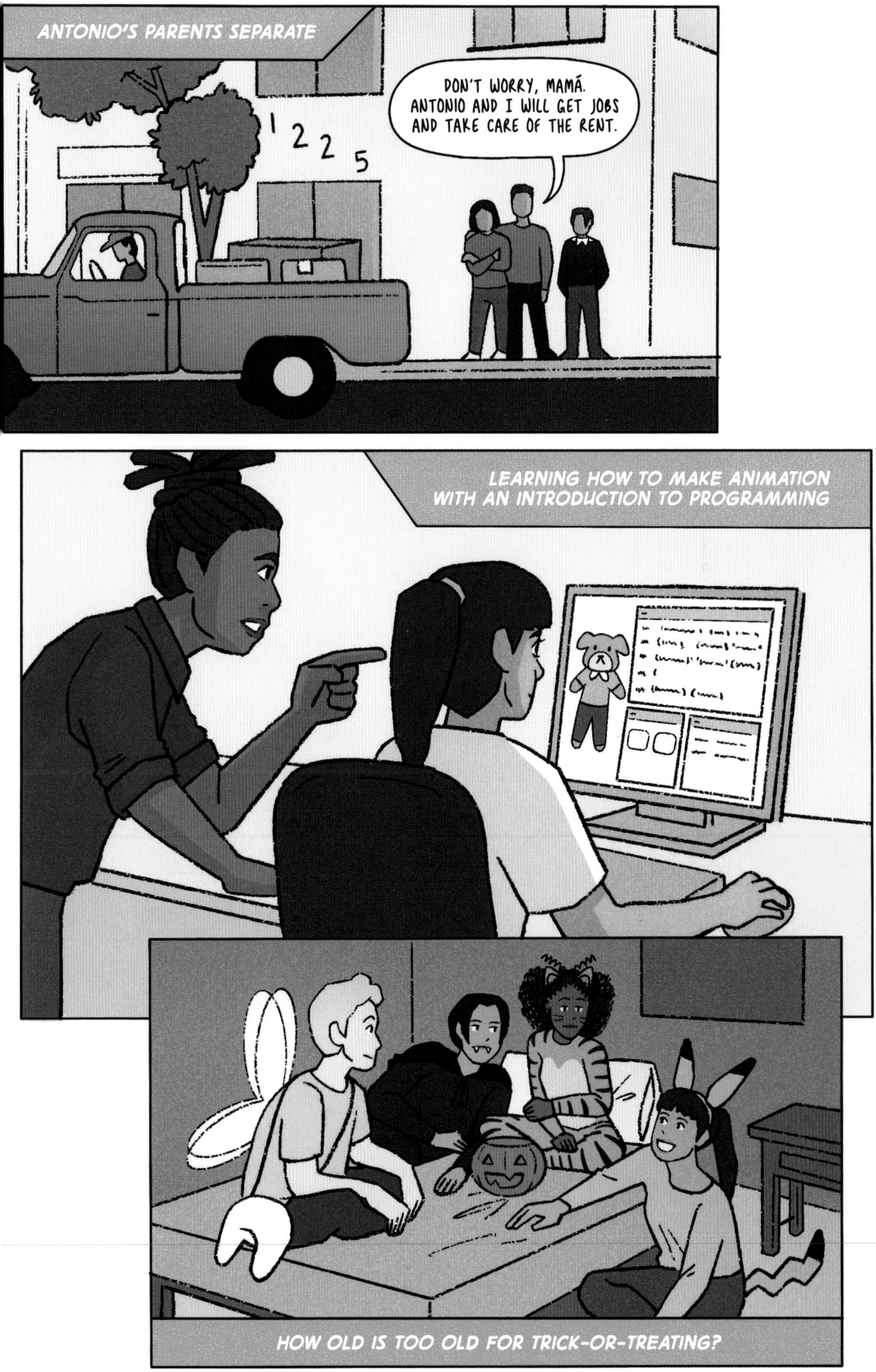
ANTONIO'S PARENTS SEPARATE
1225
DON'T WORRY, MAMÁ. ANTONIO AND I WILL GET JOBS AND TAKE CARE OF THE RENT.
LEARNING HOW TO MAKE ANIMATION WITH AN INTRODUCTION TO PROGRAMMING
HOW OLD IS TOO OLD FOR TRICK-OR-TREATING?

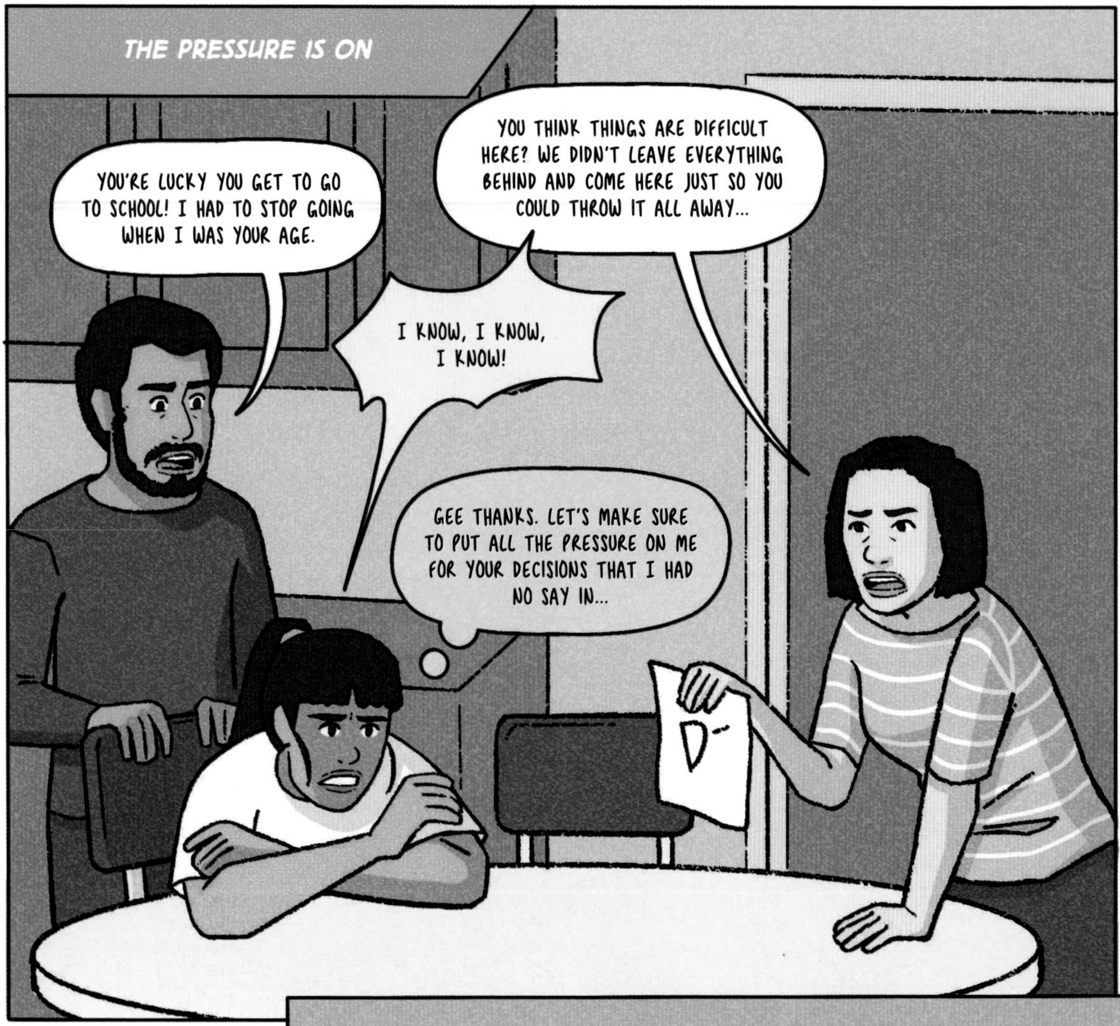
THE PRESSURE IS ON
YOU'RE LUCKY YOU GET TO GO TO SCHOOL! I HAD TO STOP GOING WHEN I WAS YOUR AGE.
YOU THINK THINGS ARE DIFFICULT HERE? WE DIDN'T LEAVE EVERYTHING BEHIND AND COME HERE JUST SO YOU COULD THROW IT ALL AWAY...
I KNOW, I KNOW, I KNOW!
GEE THANKS. LET'S MAKE SURE TO PUT ALL THE PRESSURE ON ME FOR YOUR DECISIONS THAT I HAD NO SAY IN...
D-

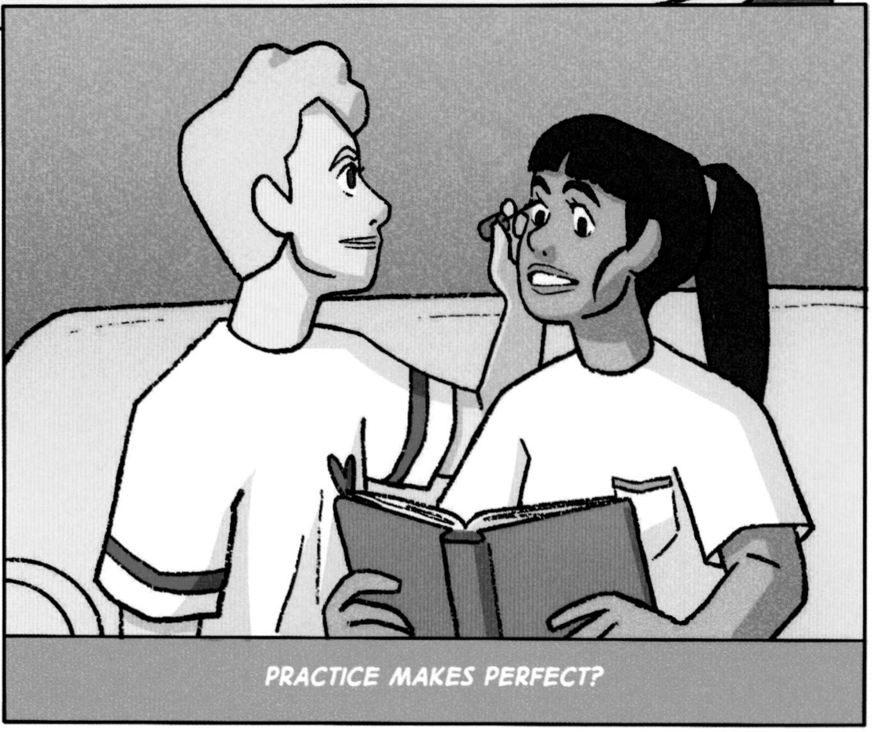
PRACTICE MAKES PERFECT?

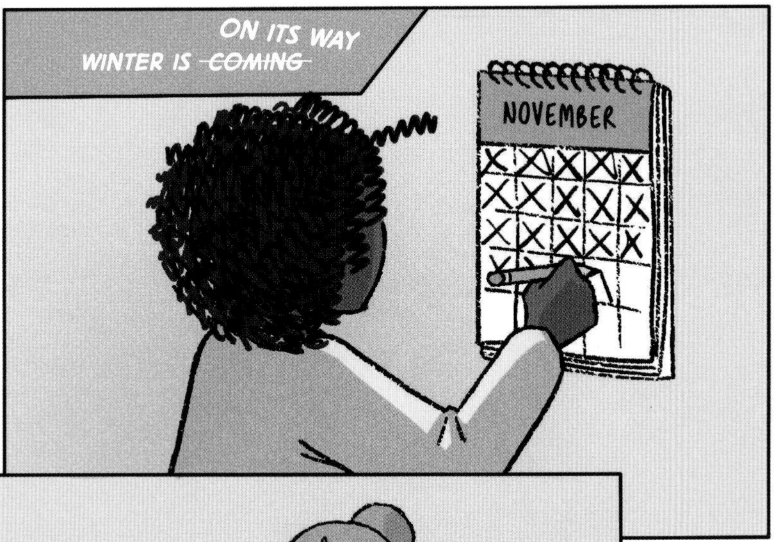
WINTER IS ~~COMING~~ ON ITS WAY
NOVEMBER

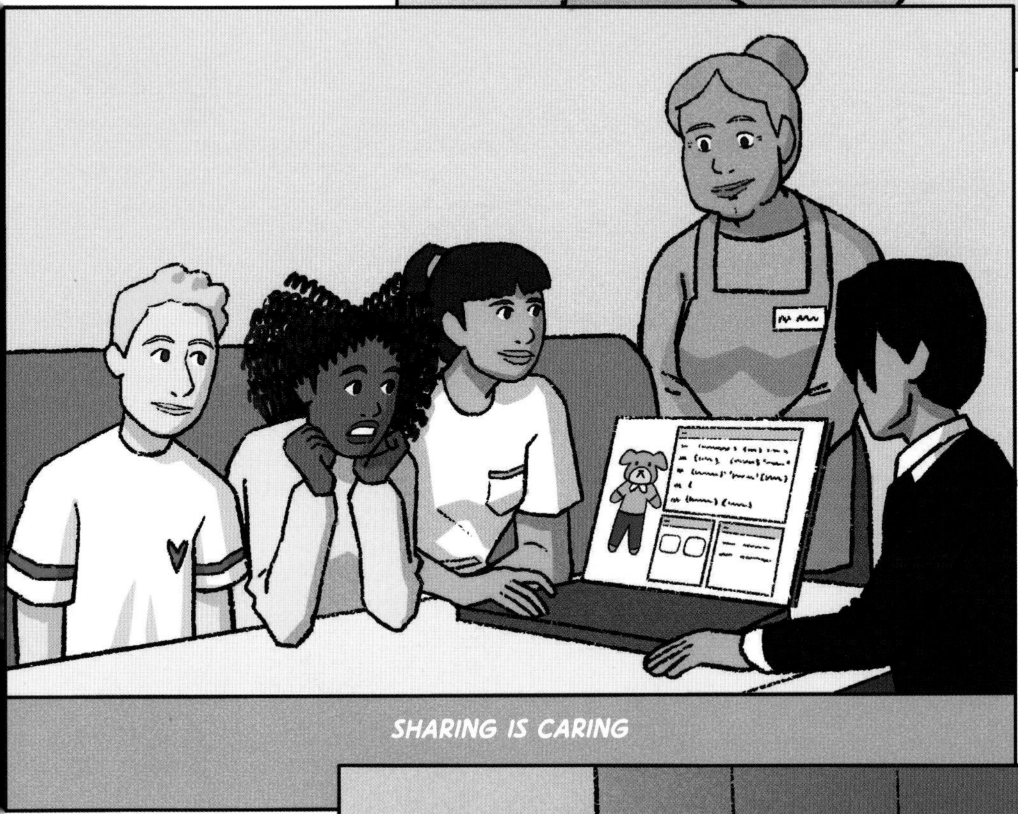
SHARING IS CARING

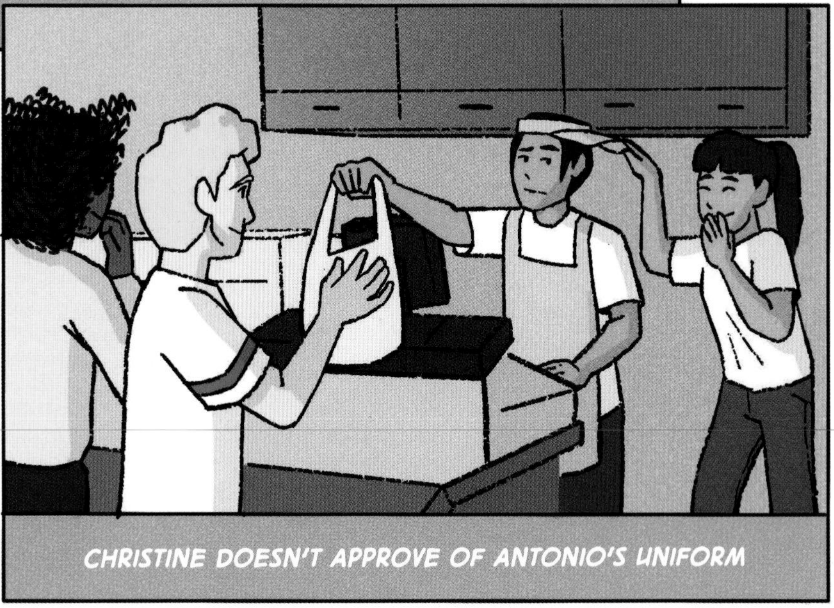
CHRISTINE DOESN'T APPROVE OF ANTONIO'S UNIFORM

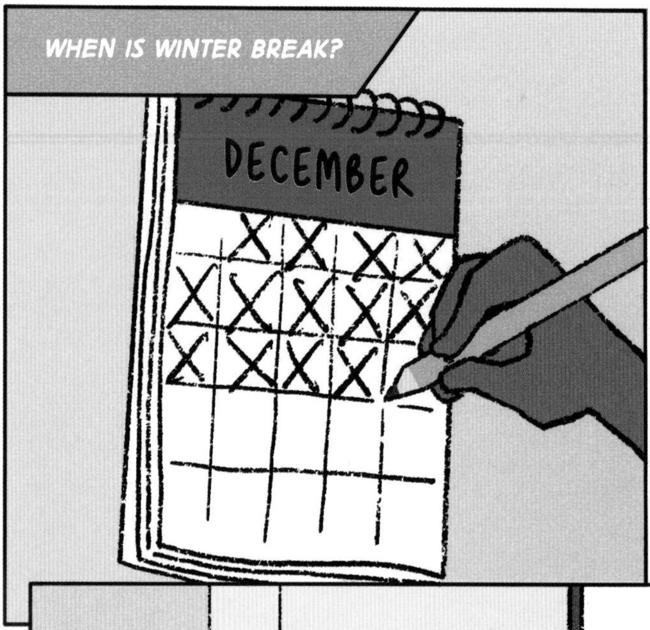
WHEN IS WINTER BREAK?
DECEMBER

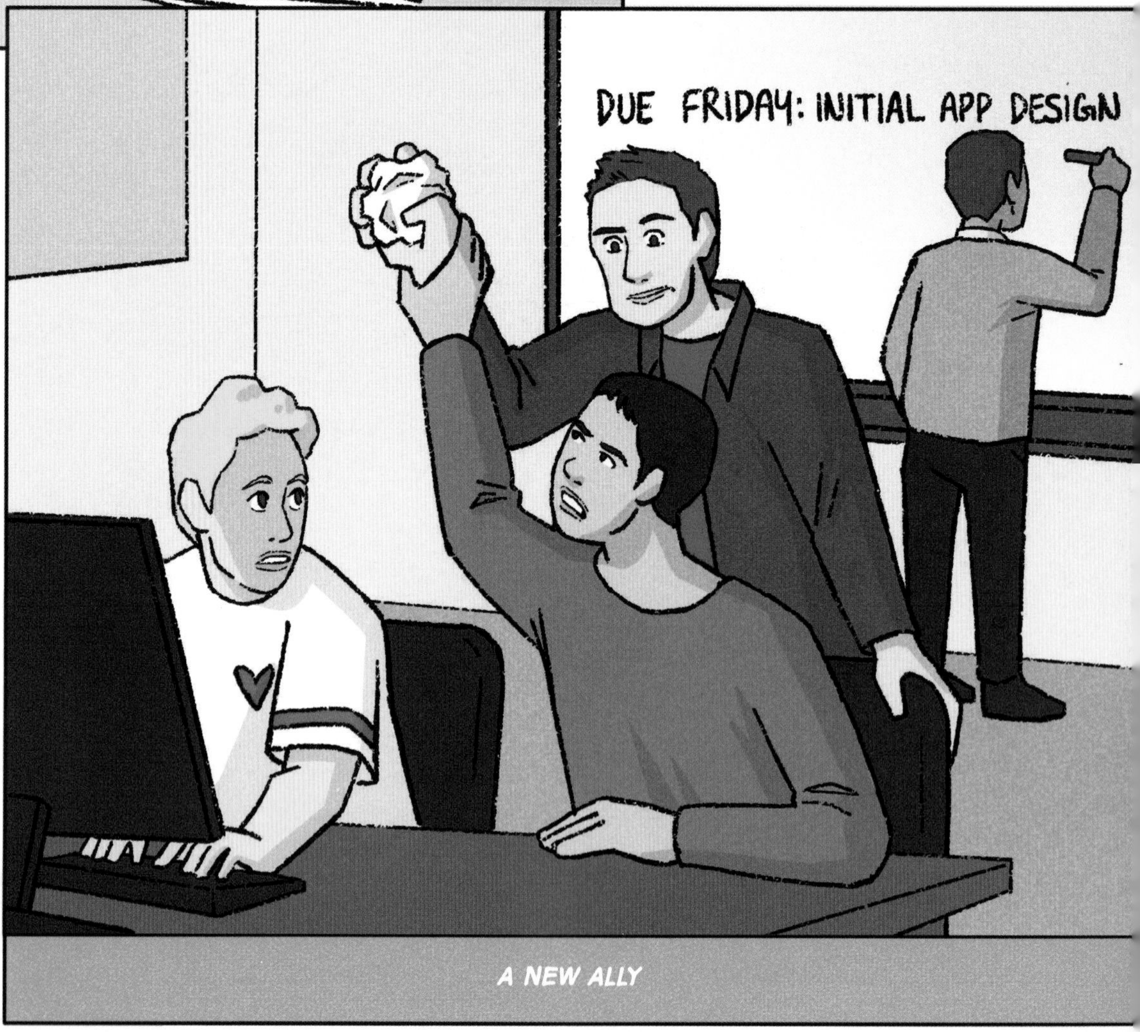
DUE FRIDAY: INITIAL APP DESIGN
A NEW ALLY

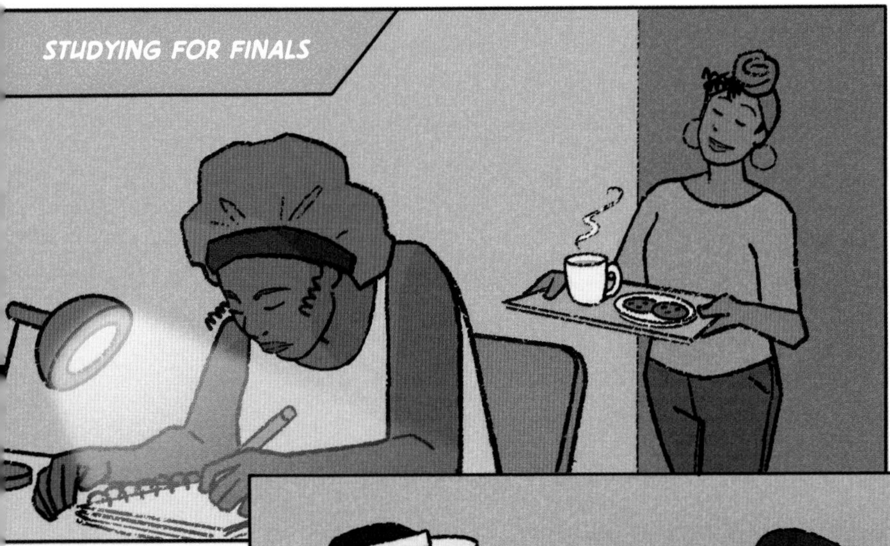
STUDYING FOR FINALS

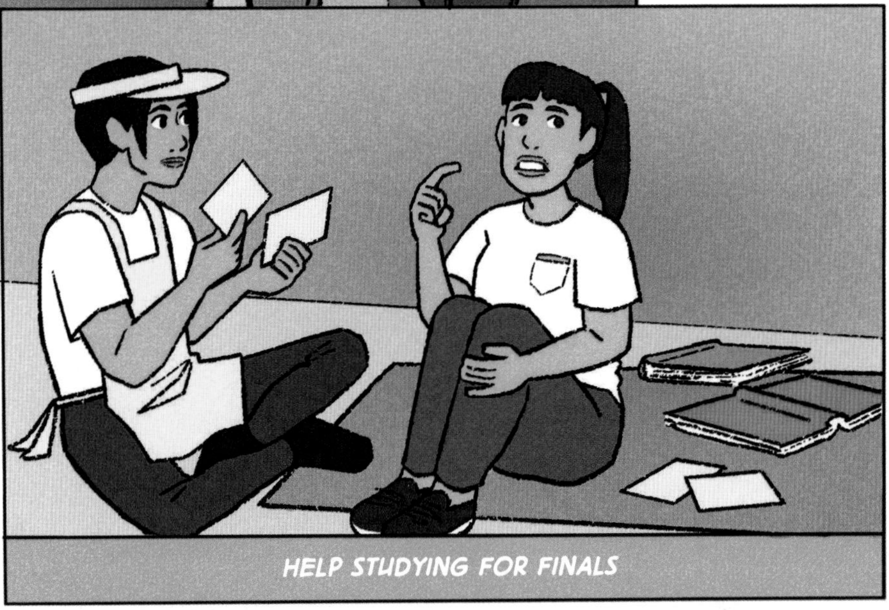
HELP STUDYING FOR FINALS

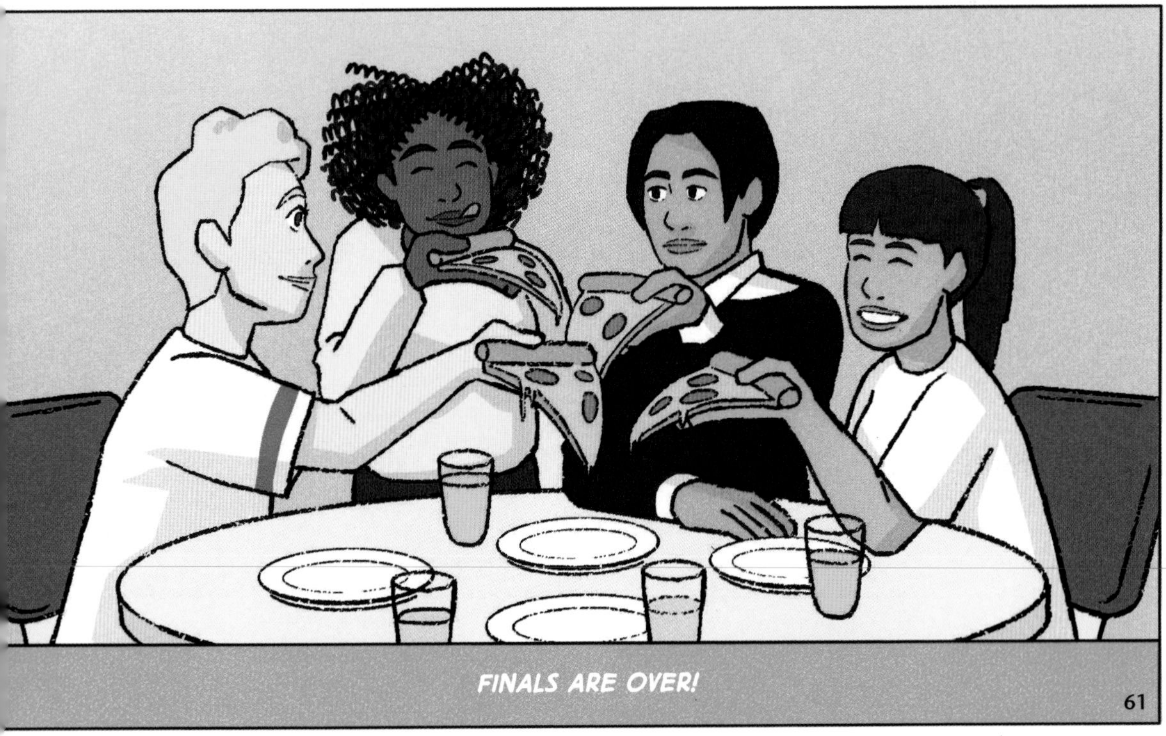
FINALS ARE OVER!

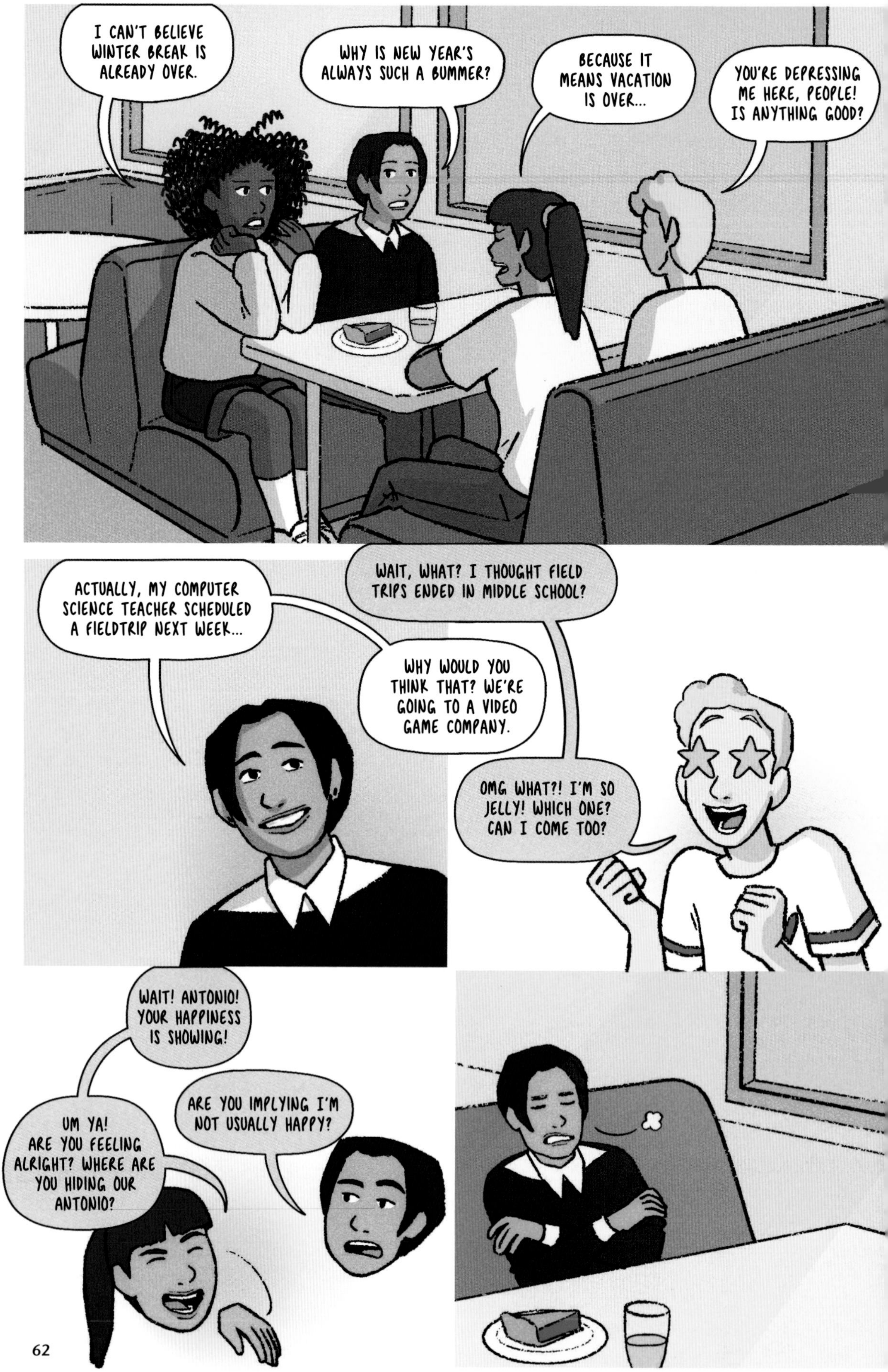
I CAN'T BELIEVE WINTER BREAK IS ALREADY OVER.
WHY IS NEW YEAR'S ALWAYS SUCH A BUMMER?
BECAUSE IT MEANS VACATION IS OVER...
YOU'RE DEPRESSING ME HERE, PEOPLE! IS ANYTHING GOOD?
ACTUALLY, MY COMPUTER SCIENCE TEACHER SCHEDULED A FIELDTRIP NEXT WEEK...
WAIT, WHAT? I THOUGHT FIELD TRIPS ENDED IN MIDDLE SCHOOL?
WHY WOULD YOU THINK THAT? WE'RE GOING TO A VIDEO GAME COMPANY.
OMG WHAT?! I'M SO JELLY! WHICH ONE? CAN I COME TOO?
WAIT! ANTONIO! YOUR HAPPINESS IS SHOWING!
UM YA! ARE YOU FEELING ALRIGHT? WHERE ARE YOU HIDING OUR ANTONIO?
ARE YOU IMPLYING I'M NOT USUALLY HAPPY?

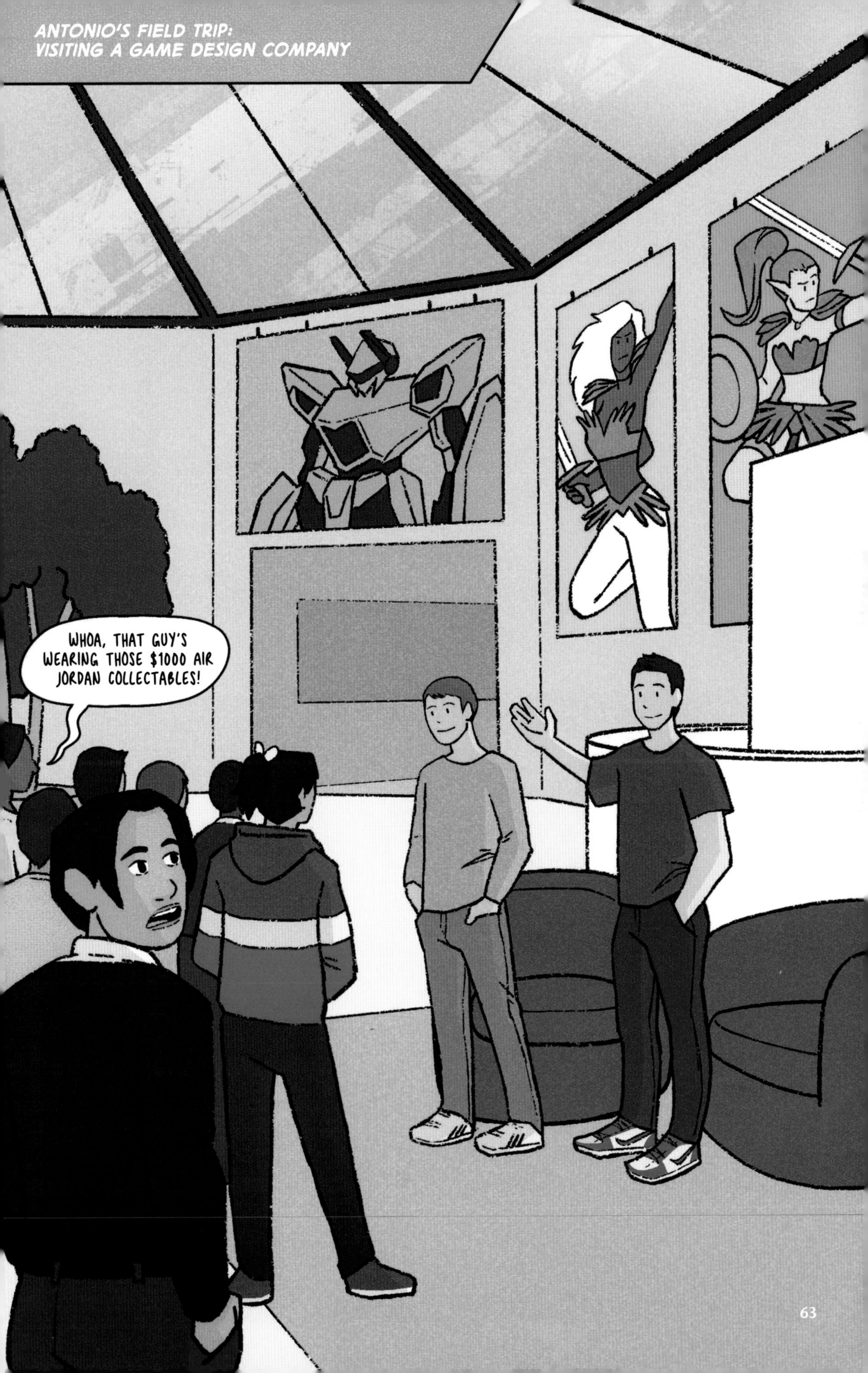
ANTONIO'S FIELD TRIP:
VISITING A GAME DESIGN COMPANY
WHOA, THAT GUY'S WEARING THOSE $1000 AIR JORDAN COLLECTABLES!

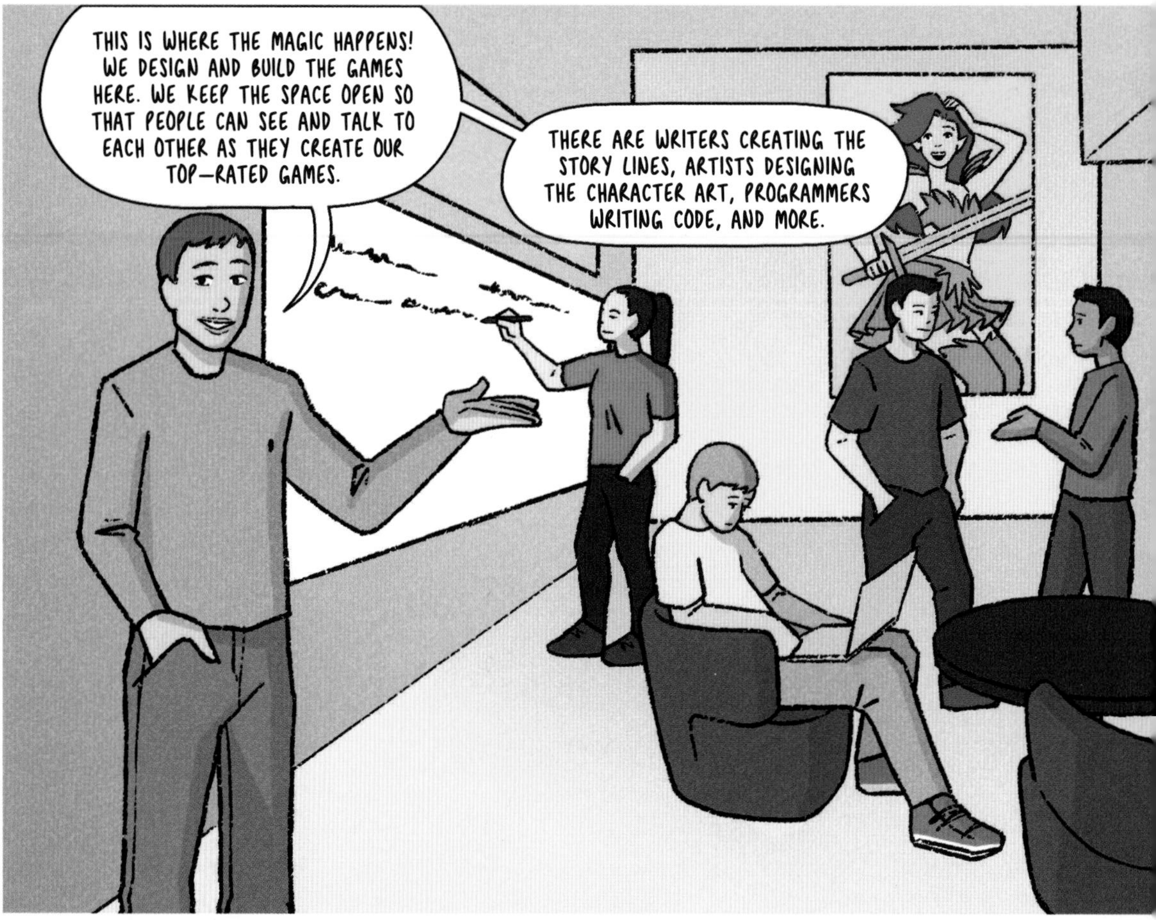
THIS IS WHERE THE MAGIC HAPPENS! WE DESIGN AND BUILD THE GAMES HERE. WE KEEP THE SPACE OPEN SO THAT PEOPLE CAN SEE AND TALK TO EACH OTHER AS THEY CREATE OUR TOP-RATED GAMES.
THERE ARE WRITERS CREATING THE STORY LINES, ARTISTS DESIGNING THE CHARACTER ART, PROGRAMMERS WRITING CODE, AND MORE.

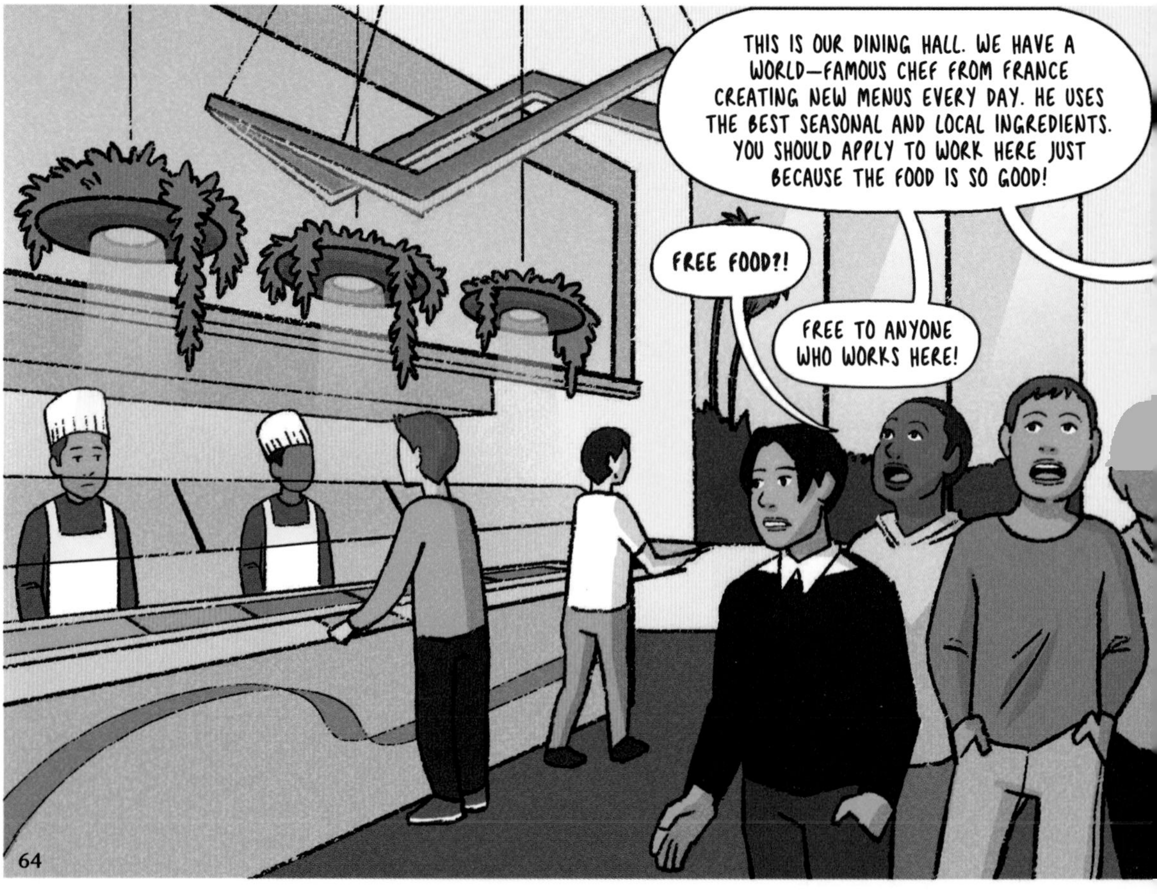
THIS IS OUR DINING HALL. WE HAVE A WORLD-FAMOUS CHEF FROM FRANCE CREATING NEW MENUS EVERY DAY. HE USES THE BEST SEASONAL AND LOCAL INGREDIENTS. YOU SHOULD APPLY TO WORK HERE JUST BECAUSE THE FOOD IS SO GOOD!
FREE FOOD?!
FREE TO ANYONE WHO WORKS HERE!

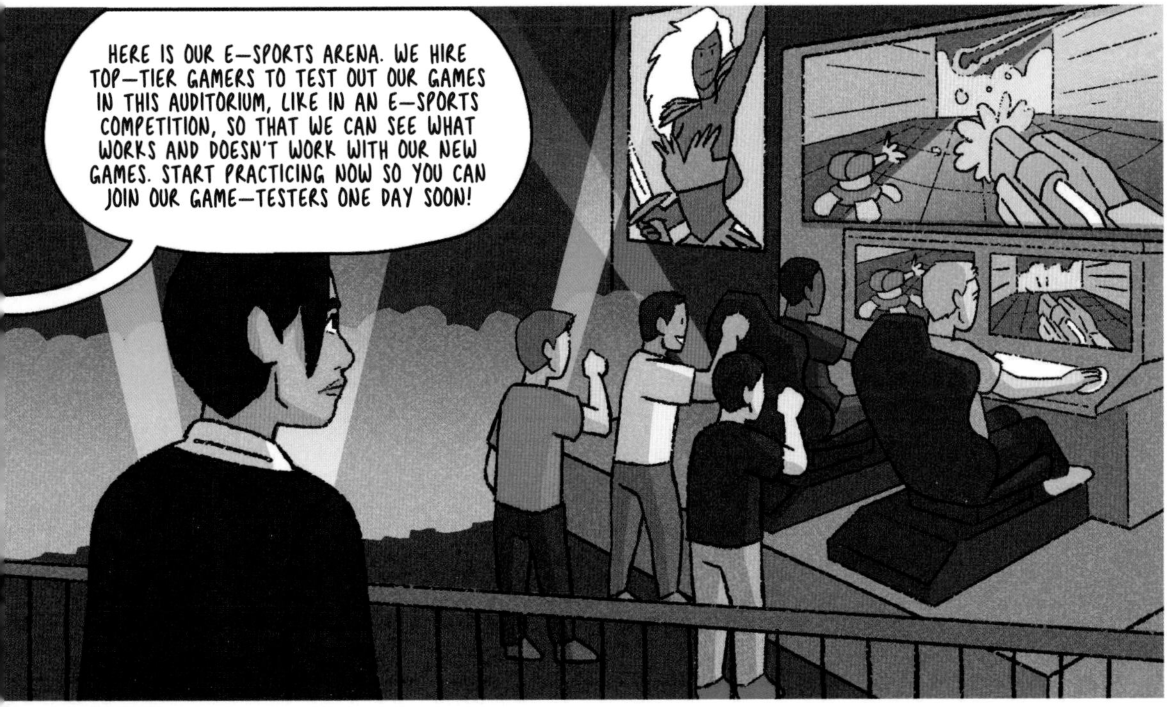
HERE IS OUR E-SPORTS ARENA. WE HIRE TOP-TIER GAMERS TO TEST OUT OUR GAMES IN THIS AUDITORIUM, LIKE IN AN E-SPORTS COMPETITION, SO THAT WE CAN SEE WHAT WORKS AND DOESN'T WORK WITH OUR NEW GAMES. START PRACTICING NOW SO YOU CAN JOIN OUR GAME-TESTERS ONE DAY SOON!

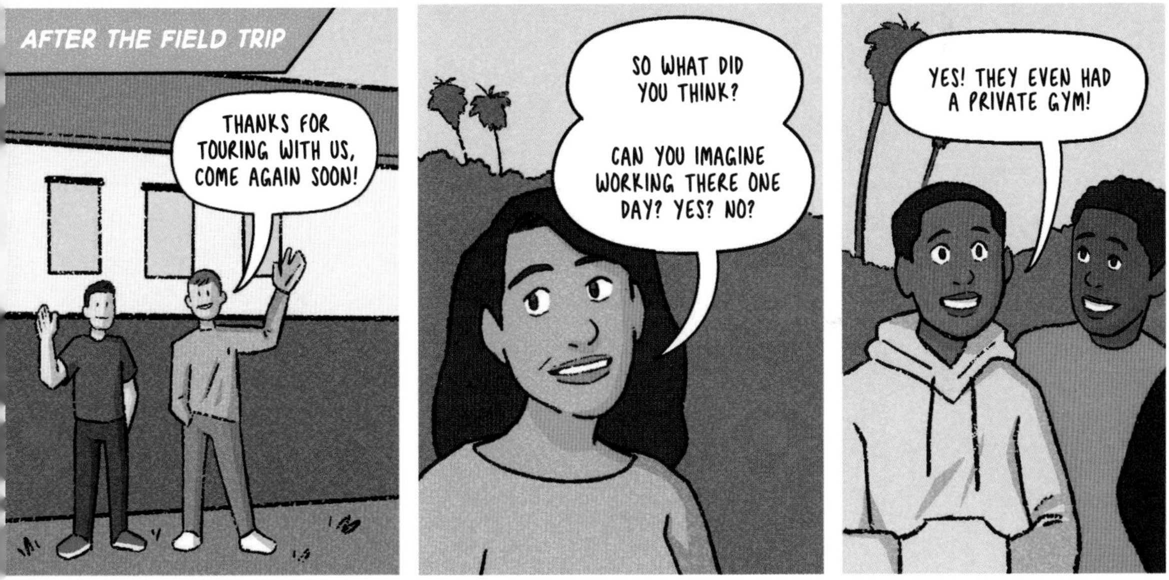
AFTER THE FIELD TRIP
THANKS FOR TOURING WITH US, COME AGAIN SOON!
SO WHAT DID YOU THINK?
CAN YOU IMAGINE WORKING THERE ONE DAY? YES? NO?
YES! THEY EVEN HAD A PRIVATE GYM!

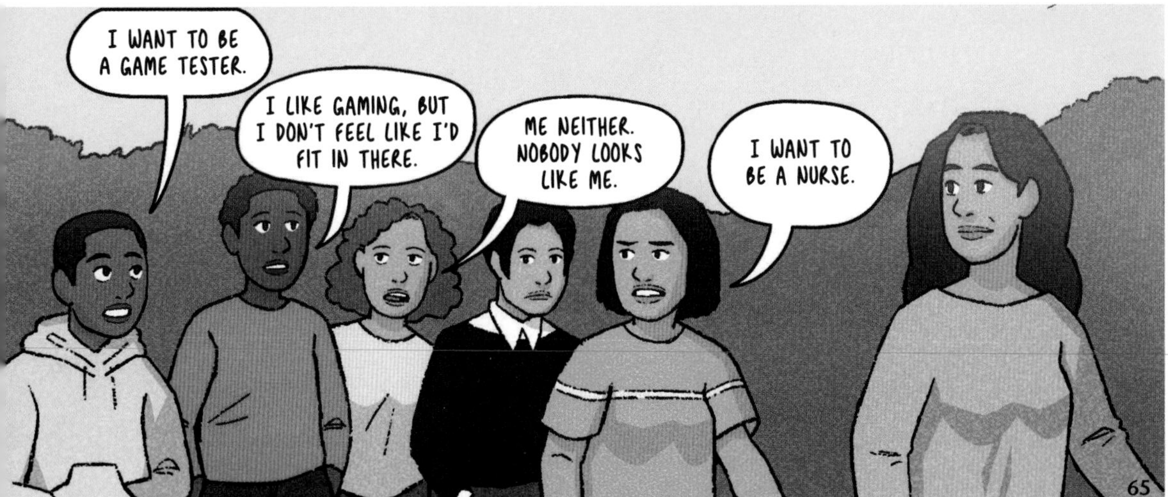
I WANT TO BE A GAME TESTER.
I LIKE GAMING, BUT I DON'T FEEL LIKE I'D FIT IN THERE.
ME NEITHER. NOBODY LOOKS LIKE ME.
I WANT TO BE A NURSE.

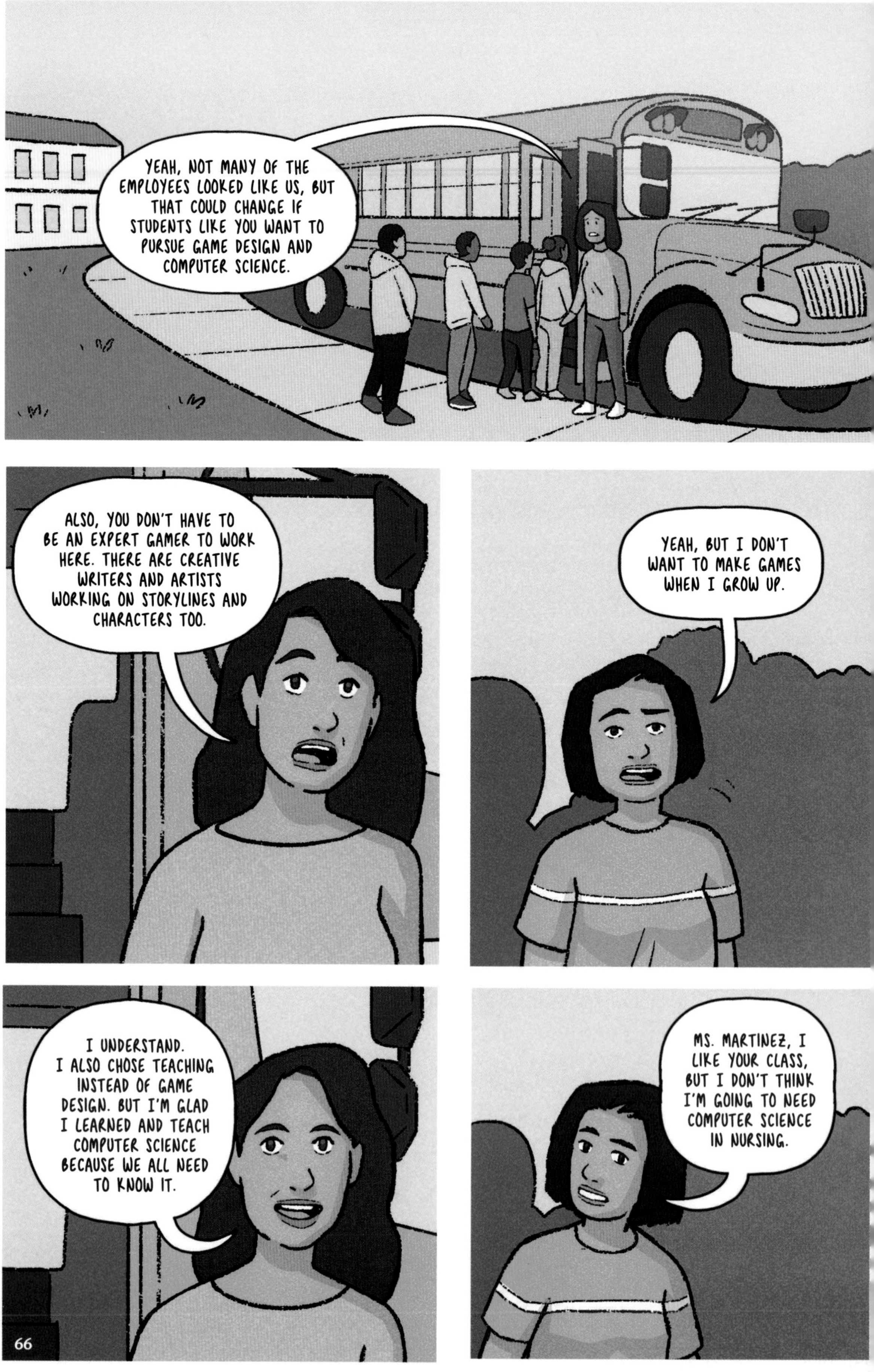
YEAH, NOT MANY OF THE EMPLOYEES LOOKED LIKE US, BUT THAT COULD CHANGE IF STUDENTS LIKE YOU WANT TO PURSUE GAME DESIGN AND COMPUTER SCIENCE.
ALSO, YOU DON'T HAVE TO BE AN EXPERT GAMER TO WORK HERE. THERE ARE CREATIVE WRITERS AND ARTISTS WORKING ON STORYLINES AND CHARACTERS TOO.
YEAH, BUT I DON'T WANT TO MAKE GAMES WHEN I GROW UP.
I UNDERSTAND. I ALSO CHOSE TEACHING INSTEAD OF GAME DESIGN. BUT I'M GLAD I LEARNED AND TEACH COMPUTER SCIENCE BECAUSE WE ALL NEED TO KNOW IT.
MS. MARTINEZ, I LIKE YOUR CLASS, BUT I DON'T THINK I'M GOING TO NEED COMPUTER SCIENCE IN NURSING.

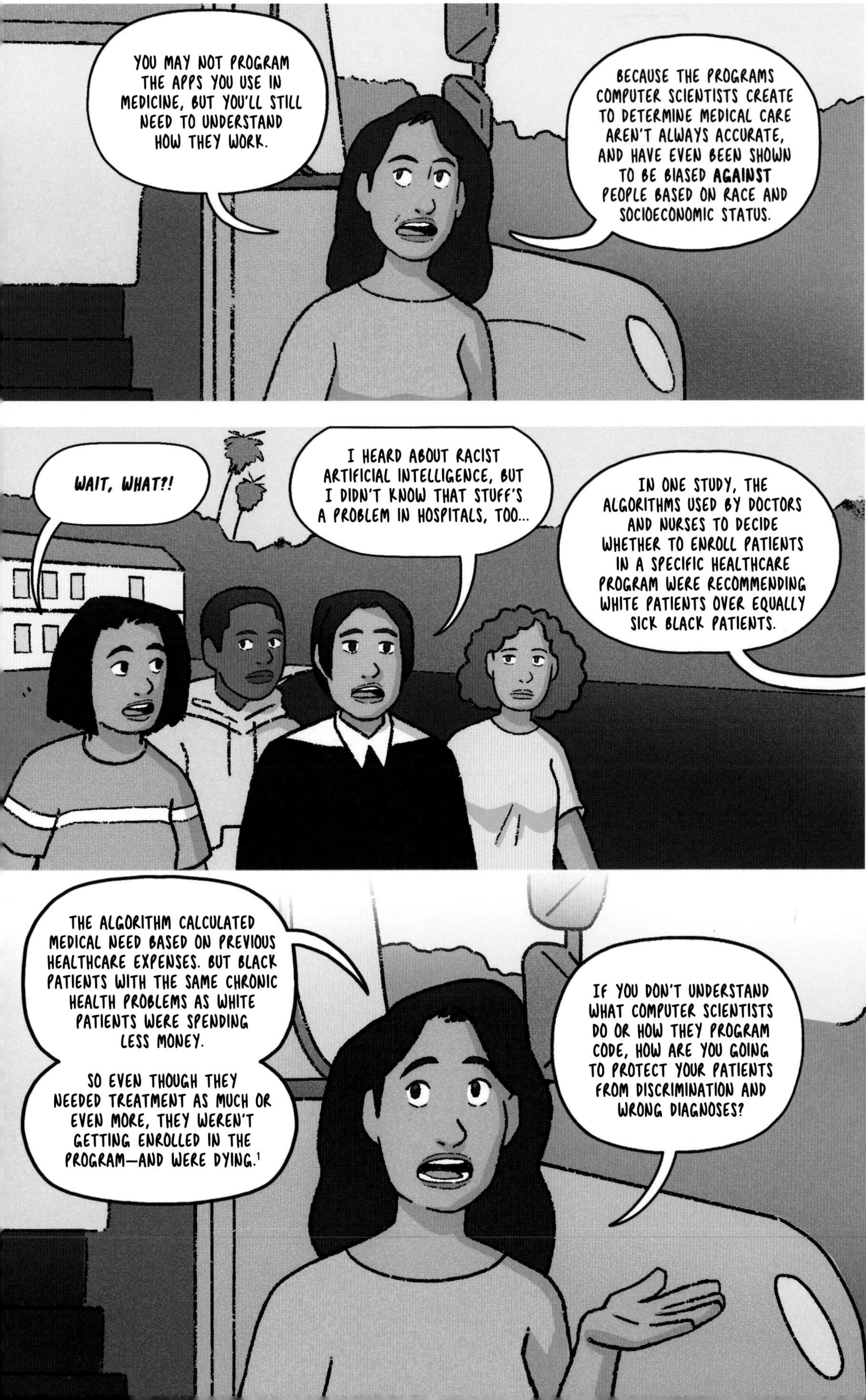
YOU MAY NOT PROGRAM THE APPS YOU USE IN MEDICINE, BUT YOU'LL STILL NEED TO UNDERSTAND HOW THEY WORK.
BECAUSE THE PROGRAMS COMPUTER SCIENTISTS CREATE TO DETERMINE MEDICAL CARE AREN'T ALWAYS ACCURATE, AND HAVE EVEN BEEN SHOWN TO BE BIASED **AGAINST** PEOPLE BASED ON RACE AND SOCIOECONOMIC STATUS.
WAIT, WHAT?!
I HEARD ABOUT RACIST ARTIFICIAL INTELLIGENCE, BUT I DIDN'T KNOW THAT STUFF'S A PROBLEM IN HOSPITALS, TOO...
IN ONE STUDY, THE ALGORITHMS USED BY DOCTORS AND NURSES TO DECIDE WHETHER TO ENROLL PATIENTS IN A SPECIFIC HEALTHCARE PROGRAM WERE RECOMMENDING WHITE PATIENTS OVER EQUALLY SICK BLACK PATIENTS.
THE ALGORITHM CALCULATED MEDICAL NEED BASED ON PREVIOUS HEALTHCARE EXPENSES. BUT BLACK PATIENTS WITH THE SAME CHRONIC HEALTH PROBLEMS AS WHITE PATIENTS WERE SPENDING LESS MONEY.
SO EVEN THOUGH THEY NEEDED TREATMENT AS MUCH OR EVEN MORE, THEY WEREN'T GETTING ENROLLED IN THE PROGRAM—AND WERE DYING.[1]
IF YOU DON'T UNDERSTAND WHAT COMPUTER SCIENTISTS DO OR HOW THEY PROGRAM CODE, HOW ARE YOU GOING TO PROTECT YOUR PATIENTS FROM DISCRIMINATION AND WRONG DIAGNOSES?

In *Weapons of Math Destruction,* **Cathy O'Neil** researches the ways medical and auto insurance companies track people and behavior (with cell phone data, online shopping habits, etc.), using computers to calculate whether someone is "high risk" and should pay more for insurance than other people. She calls these algorithms "weapons of math destruction" because they inevitably treat certain people—usually low-income families, people of color, etc.—unfairly based on assumptions around people's personal data.[2]

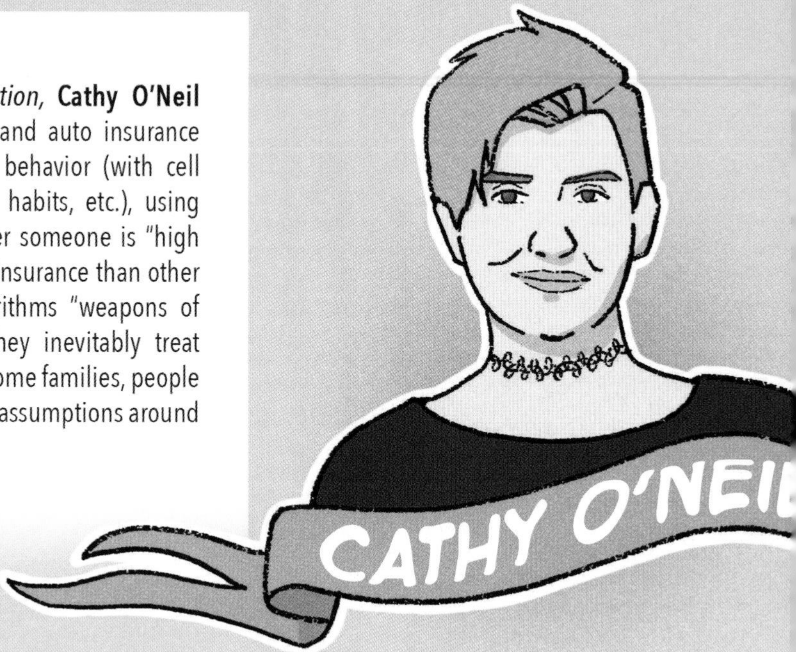
CATHY O'NEIL

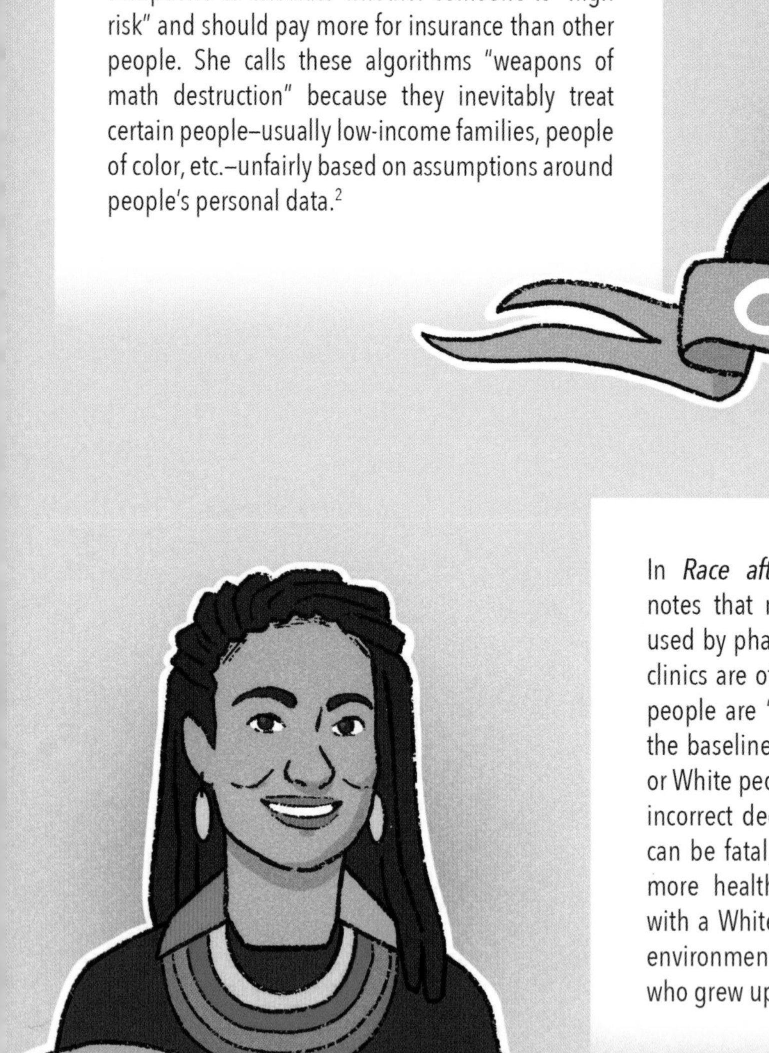
RUHA BENJAMIN

In *Race after Technology,* **Ruha Benjamin** notes that machines and computing systems used by pharmaceutical companies and certain clinics are often designed in ways that assume people are "healthy" based on their race, with the baseline "normal" being different for Black or White people, for example. But this results in incorrect decisions made about treatment that can be fatal, because a Black person can have more health-related and physical similarities with a White person who grew up in a similar environment than with another Black person who grew up in a completely different context.[3]

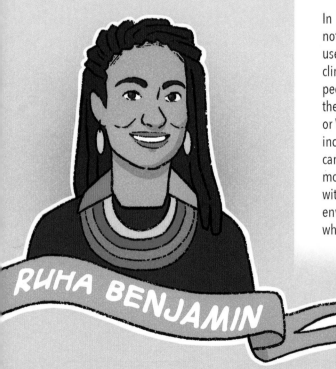

In *Algorithms of Oppression: How Search Engines Reinforce Racism,* **Safiya Umoja Noble** reveals how search algorithms and search engines like Google reflect and reinforce prejudices and biases in our society, especially against people of color, specifically women of color. In this pathbreaking book, Noble discusses how computer scientists, who are mostly White and Asian males, too often design these systems without any consideration of the built-in biases or their societal impact, especially on communities of color and women.[4]

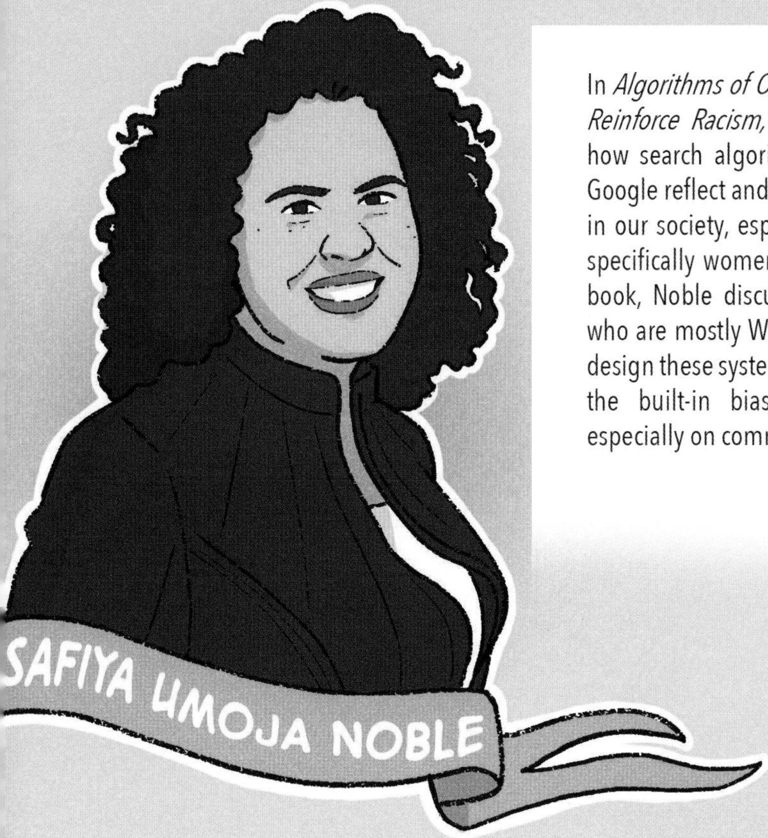
SAFIYA UMOJA NOBLE

In *Automating Inequality,* **Virginia Eubanks** reports on extensive research showing that these computing tools end up profiling, tracking, and punishing people of low socioeconomic status the most, across urban, suburban, and rural landscapes. Eubanks calls this new world the "digital poorhouse" that prevents people from accessing the resources they need, punishing them if they do not act in very specific ways and inevitably allowing a computer to decide whether they "deserve" to live well or not. She has studied algorithms discriminating against poorer families in Indiana, families who are homeless in Los Angeles, and children in Allegheny County, Pennsylvania.[5]

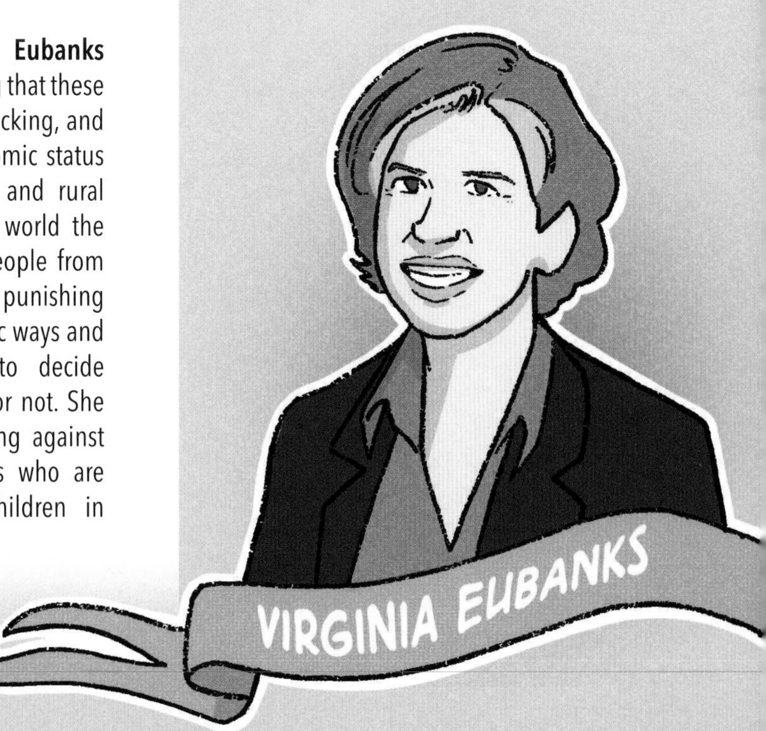
VIRGINIA EUBANKS

CHAPTER 5
SOMEONE LIKE ME

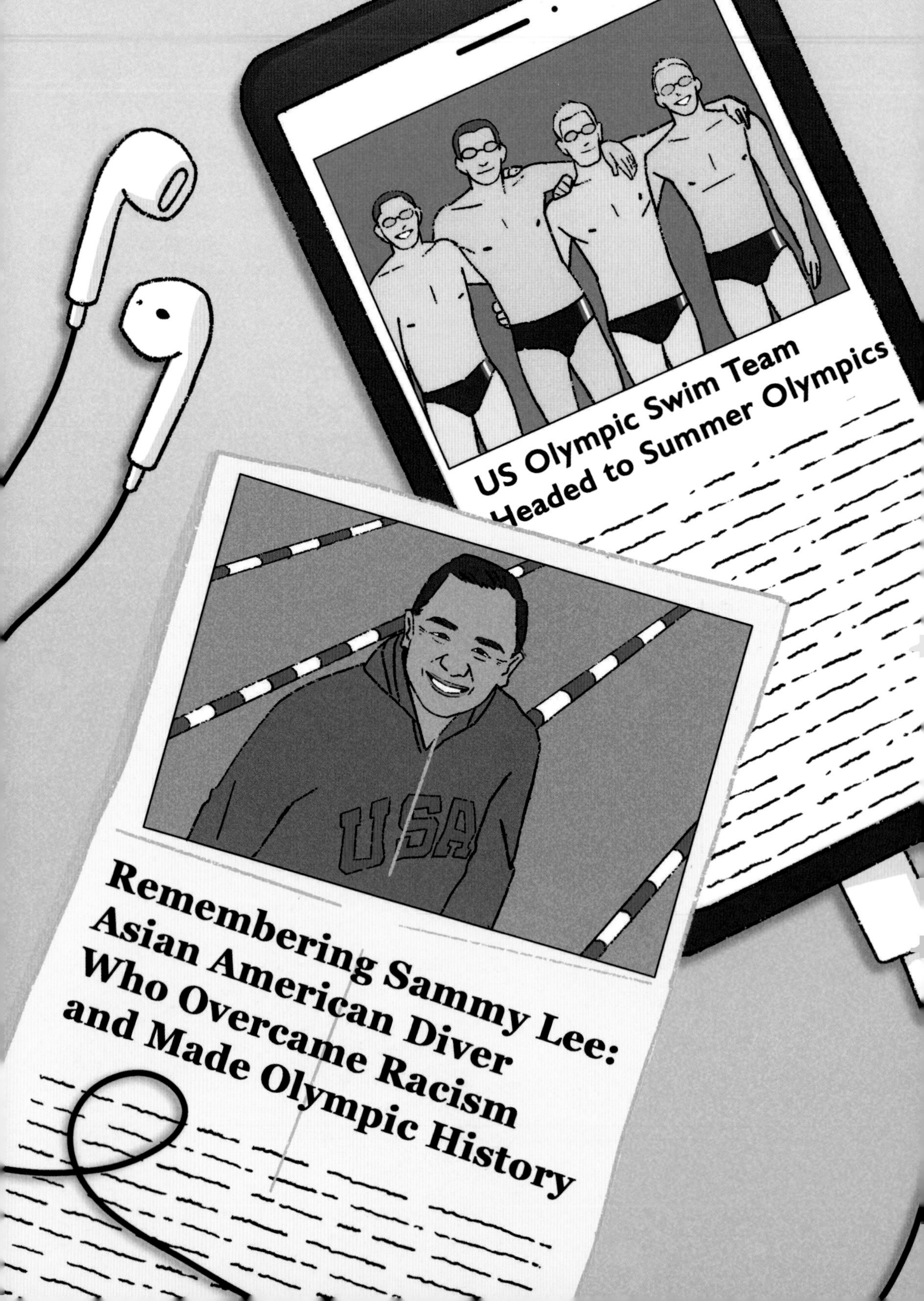
US Olympic Swim Team
Headed to Summer Olympics
USA
Remembering Sammy Lee:
Asian American Diver
Who Overcame Racism
and Made Olympic History

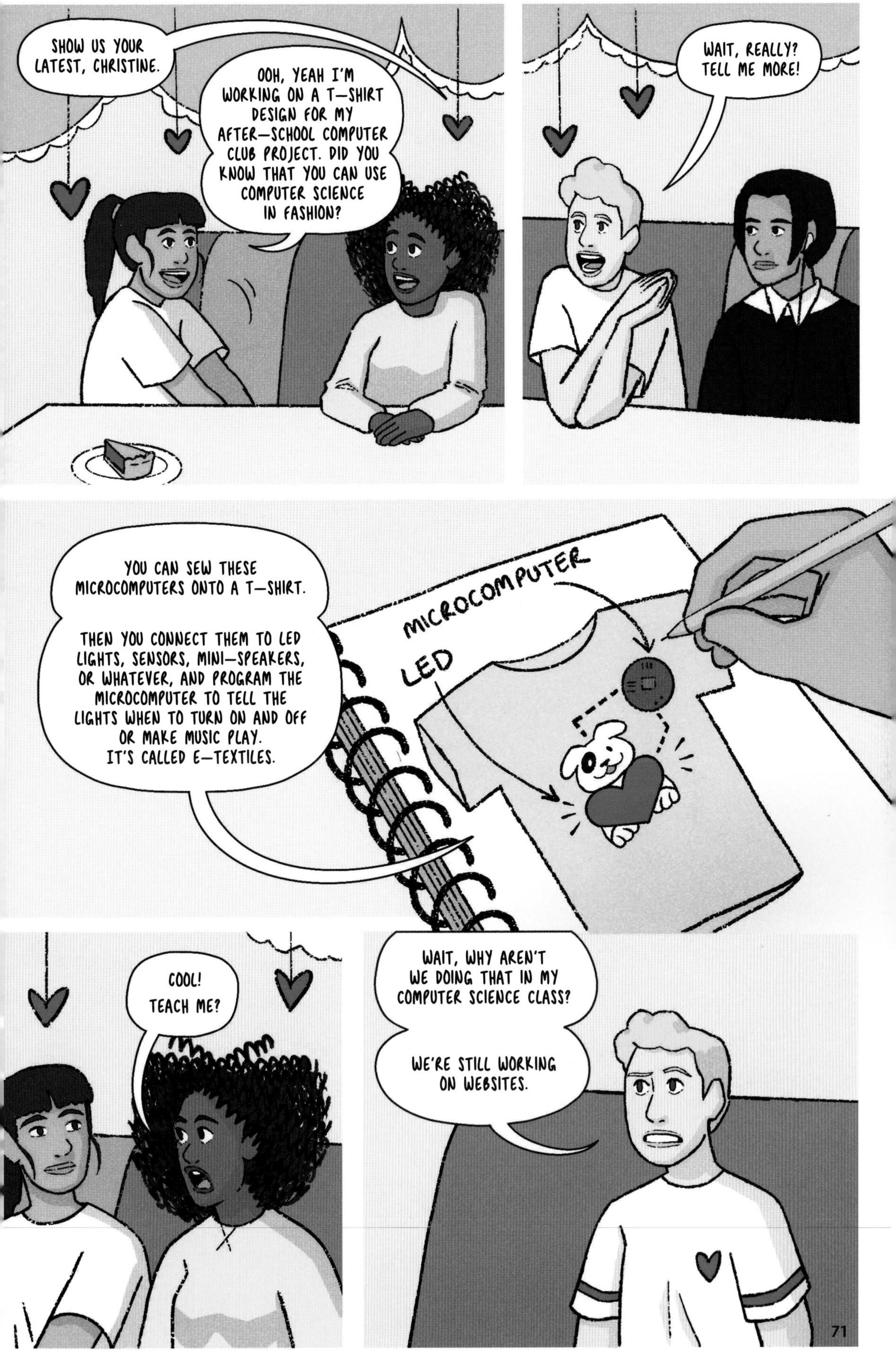
SHOW US YOUR LATEST, CHRISTINE.
OOH, YEAH I'M WORKING ON A T-SHIRT DESIGN FOR MY AFTER-SCHOOL COMPUTER CLUB PROJECT. DID YOU KNOW THAT YOU CAN USE COMPUTER SCIENCE IN FASHION?
WAIT, REALLY? TELL ME MORE!
YOU CAN SEW THESE MICROCOMPUTERS ONTO A T-SHIRT.
THEN YOU CONNECT THEM TO LED LIGHTS, SENSORS, MINI-SPEAKERS, OR WHATEVER, AND PROGRAM THE MICROCOMPUTER TO TELL THE LIGHTS WHEN TO TURN ON AND OFF OR MAKE MUSIC PLAY. IT'S CALLED E-TEXTILES.
MICROCOMPUTER
LED
COOL! TEACH ME?
WAIT, WHY AREN'T WE DOING THAT IN MY COMPUTER SCIENCE CLASS?
WE'RE STILL WORKING ON WEBSITES.

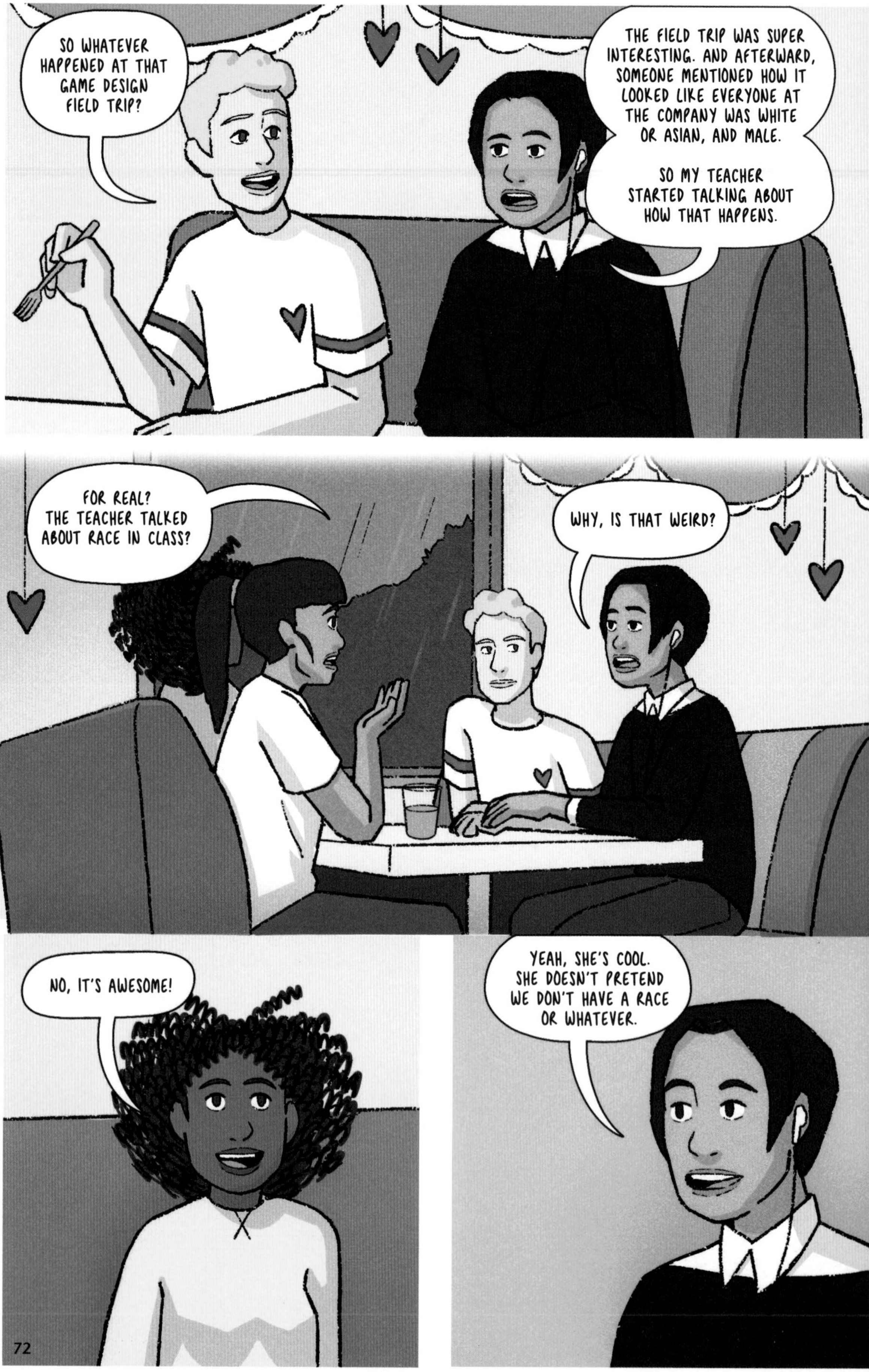
SO WHATEVER HAPPENED AT THAT GAME DESIGN FIELD TRIP?
THE FIELD TRIP WAS SUPER INTERESTING. AND AFTERWARD, SOMEONE MENTIONED HOW IT LOOKED LIKE EVERYONE AT THE COMPANY WAS WHITE OR ASIAN, AND MALE.
SO MY TEACHER STARTED TALKING ABOUT HOW THAT HAPPENS.
FOR REAL? THE TEACHER TALKED ABOUT RACE IN CLASS?
WHY, IS THAT WEIRD?
NO, IT'S AWESOME!
YEAH, SHE'S COOL. SHE DOESN'T PRETEND WE DON'T HAVE A RACE OR WHATEVER.

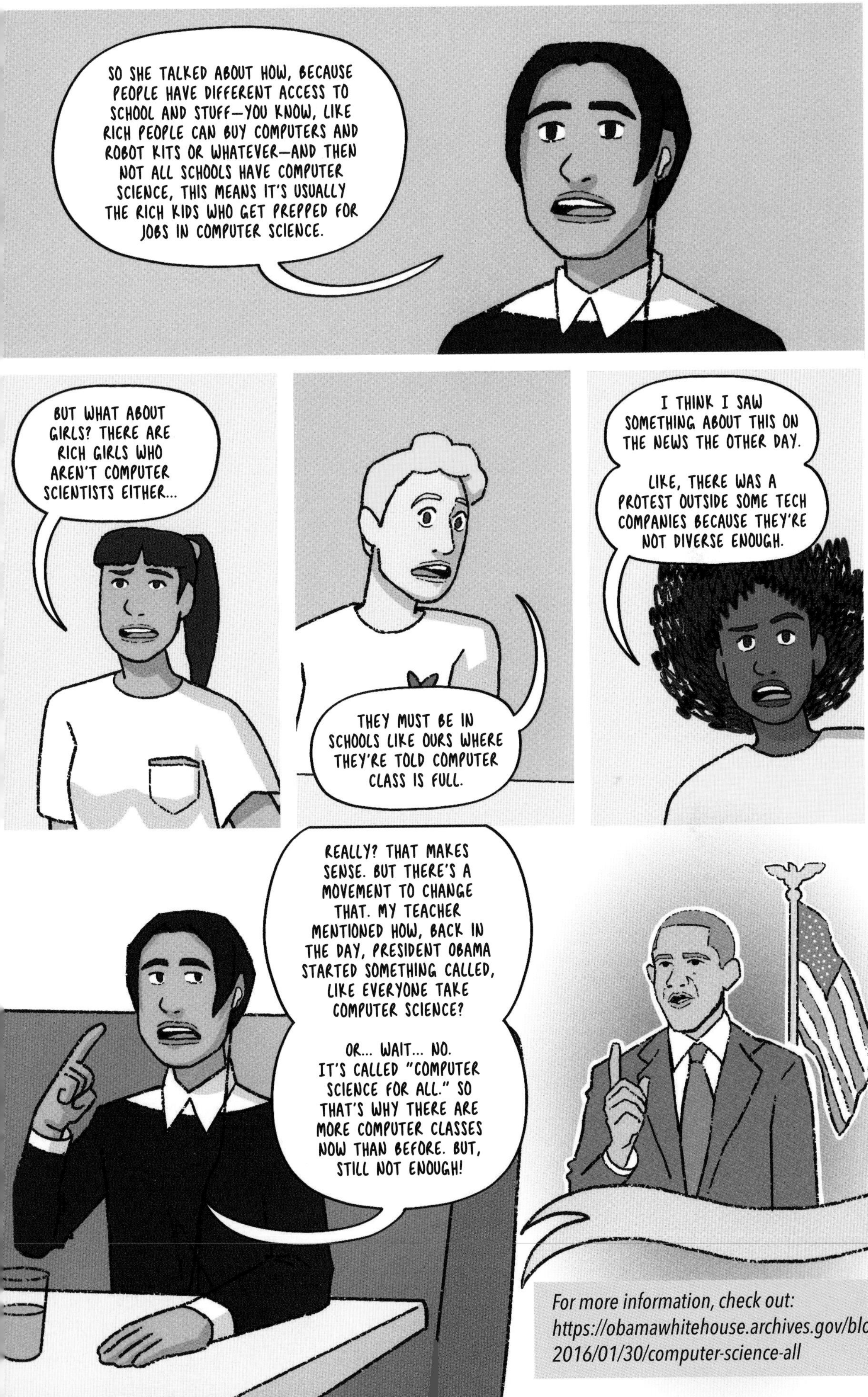
SO SHE TALKED ABOUT HOW, BECAUSE PEOPLE HAVE DIFFERENT ACCESS TO SCHOOL AND STUFF—YOU KNOW, LIKE RICH PEOPLE CAN BUY COMPUTERS AND ROBOT KITS OR WHATEVER—AND THEN NOT ALL SCHOOLS HAVE COMPUTER SCIENCE, THIS MEANS IT'S USUALLY THE RICH KIDS WHO GET PREPPED FOR JOBS IN COMPUTER SCIENCE.
BUT WHAT ABOUT GIRLS? THERE ARE RICH GIRLS WHO AREN'T COMPUTER SCIENTISTS EITHER...
THEY MUST BE IN SCHOOLS LIKE OURS WHERE THEY'RE TOLD COMPUTER CLASS IS FULL.
I THINK I SAW SOMETHING ABOUT THIS ON THE NEWS THE OTHER DAY.
LIKE, THERE WAS A PROTEST OUTSIDE SOME TECH COMPANIES BECAUSE THEY'RE NOT DIVERSE ENOUGH.
REALLY? THAT MAKES SENSE. BUT THERE'S A MOVEMENT TO CHANGE THAT. MY TEACHER MENTIONED HOW, BACK IN THE DAY, PRESIDENT OBAMA STARTED SOMETHING CALLED, LIKE EVERYONE TAKE COMPUTER SCIENCE?
OR... WAIT... NO. IT'S CALLED "COMPUTER SCIENCE FOR ALL." SO THAT'S WHY THERE ARE MORE COMPUTER CLASSES NOW THAN BEFORE. BUT, STILL NOT ENOUGH!
For more information, check out: https://obamawhitehouse.archives.gov/blog/2016/01/30/computer-science-all

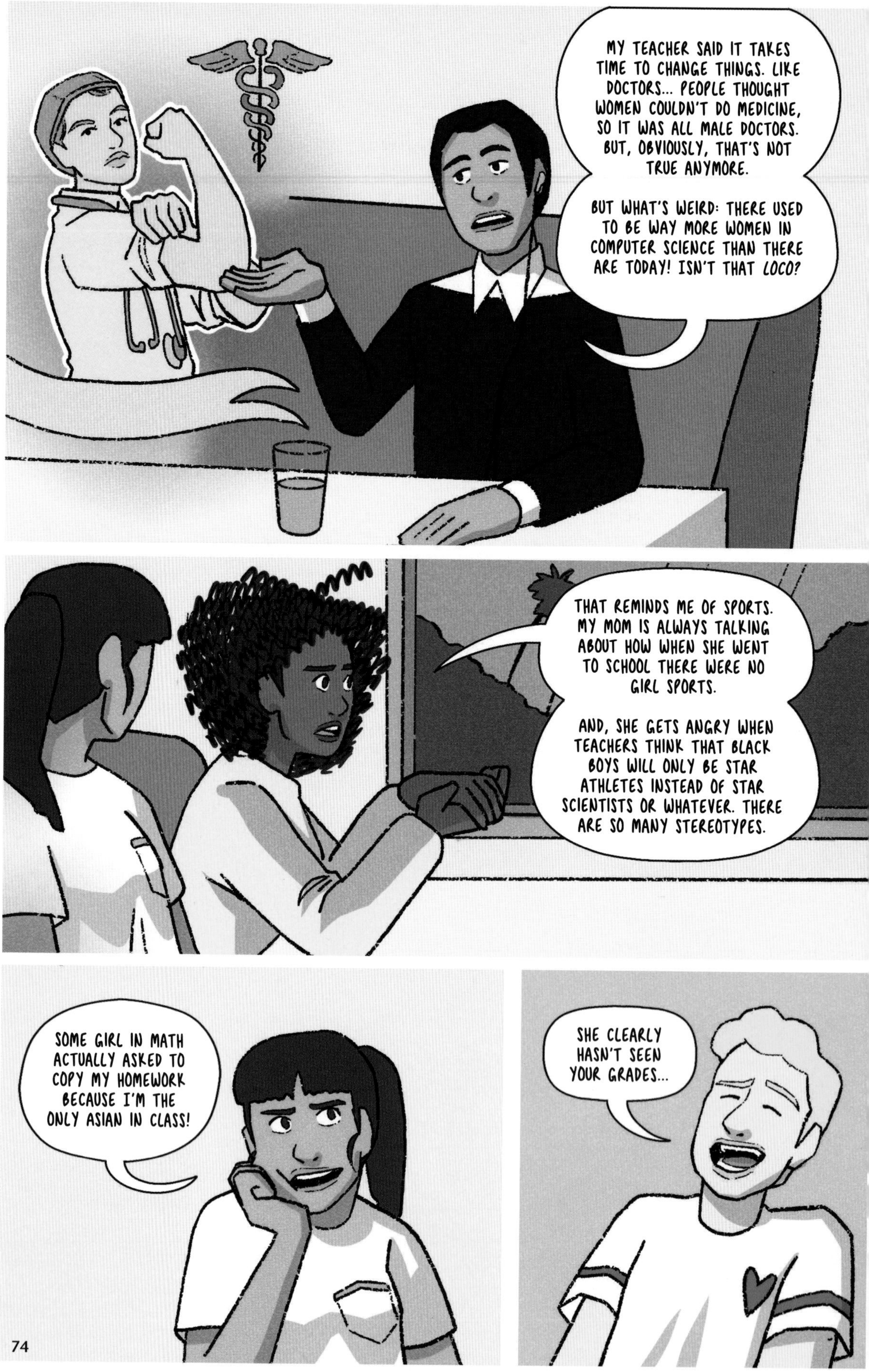
MY TEACHER SAID IT TAKES TIME TO CHANGE THINGS. LIKE DOCTORS... PEOPLE THOUGHT WOMEN COULDN'T DO MEDICINE, SO IT WAS ALL MALE DOCTORS. BUT, OBVIOUSLY, THAT'S NOT TRUE ANYMORE.
BUT WHAT'S WEIRD: THERE USED TO BE WAY MORE WOMEN IN COMPUTER SCIENCE THAN THERE ARE TODAY! ISN'T THAT *LOCO?*
THAT REMINDS ME OF SPORTS. MY MOM IS ALWAYS TALKING ABOUT HOW WHEN SHE WENT TO SCHOOL THERE WERE NO GIRL SPORTS.
AND, SHE GETS ANGRY WHEN TEACHERS THINK THAT BLACK BOYS WILL ONLY BE STAR ATHLETES INSTEAD OF STAR SCIENTISTS OR WHATEVER. THERE ARE SO MANY STEREOTYPES.
SOME GIRL IN MATH ACTUALLY ASKED TO COPY MY HOMEWORK BECAUSE I'M THE ONLY ASIAN IN CLASS!
SHE CLEARLY HASN'T SEEN YOUR GRADES...

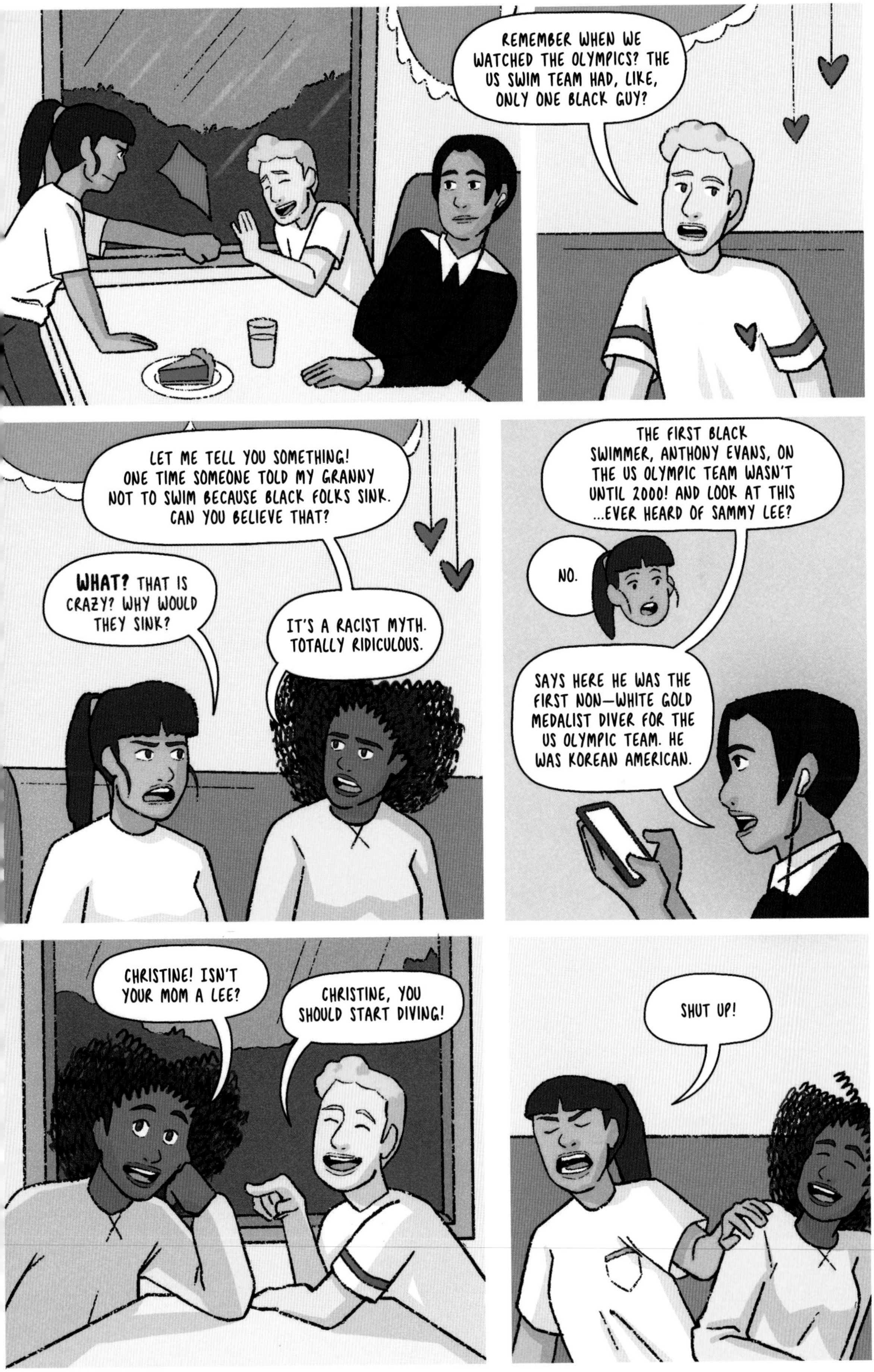
REMEMBER WHEN WE WATCHED THE OLYMPICS? THE US SWIM TEAM HAD, LIKE, ONLY ONE BLACK GUY?
LET ME TELL YOU SOMETHING! ONE TIME SOMEONE TOLD MY GRANNY NOT TO SWIM BECAUSE BLACK FOLKS SINK. CAN YOU BELIEVE THAT?
WHAT? THAT IS CRAZY? WHY WOULD THEY SINK?
IT'S A RACIST MYTH. TOTALLY RIDICULOUS.
THE FIRST BLACK SWIMMER, ANTHONY EVANS, ON THE US OLYMPIC TEAM WASN'T UNTIL 2000! AND LOOK AT THIS ...EVER HEARD OF SAMMY LEE?
NO.
SAYS HERE HE WAS THE FIRST NON–WHITE GOLD MEDALIST DIVER FOR THE US OLYMPIC TEAM. HE WAS KOREAN AMERICAN.
CHRISTINE! ISN'T YOUR MOM A LEE?
CHRISTINE, YOU SHOULD START DIVING!
SHUT UP!

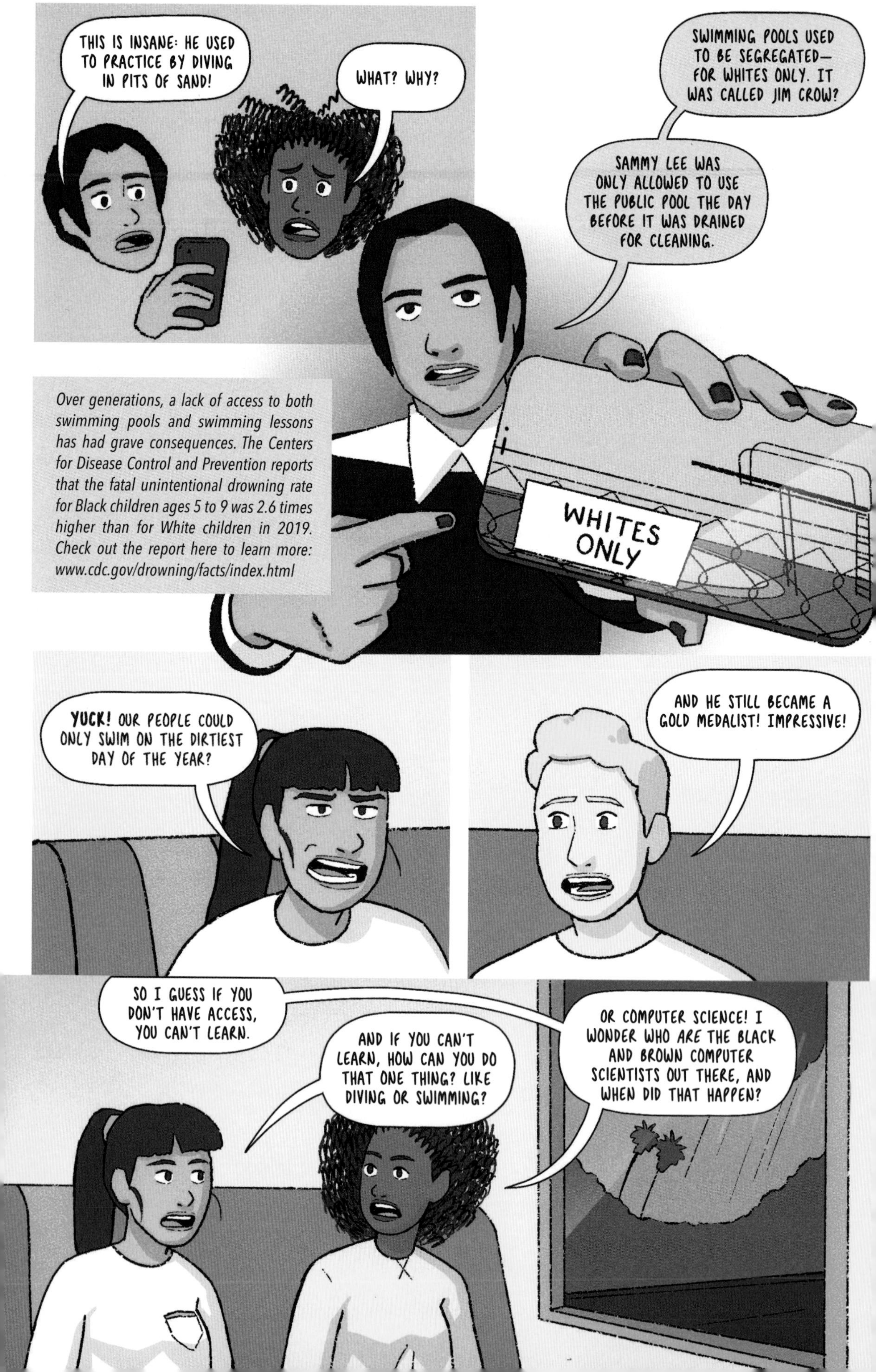
THIS IS INSANE: HE USED TO PRACTICE BY DIVING IN PITS OF SAND!
WHAT? WHY?
SWIMMING POOLS USED TO BE SEGREGATED—FOR WHITES ONLY. IT WAS CALLED JIM CROW?
SAMMY LEE WAS ONLY ALLOWED TO USE THE PUBLIC POOL THE DAY BEFORE IT WAS DRAINED FOR CLEANING.
Over generations, a lack of access to both swimming pools and swimming lessons has had grave consequences. The Centers for Disease Control and Prevention reports that the fatal unintentional drowning rate for Black children ages 5 to 9 was 2.6 times higher than for White children in 2019. Check out the report here to learn more: www.cdc.gov/drowning/facts/index.html
WHITES ONLY
YUCK! OUR PEOPLE COULD ONLY SWIM ON THE DIRTIEST DAY OF THE YEAR?
AND HE STILL BECAME A GOLD MEDALIST! IMPRESSIVE!
SO I GUESS IF YOU DON'T HAVE ACCESS, YOU CAN'T LEARN.
AND IF YOU CAN'T LEARN, HOW CAN YOU DO THAT ONE THING? LIKE DIVING OR SWIMMING?
OR COMPUTER SCIENCE! I WONDER WHO ARE THE BLACK AND BROWN COMPUTER SCIENTISTS OUT THERE, AND WHEN DID THAT HAPPEN?

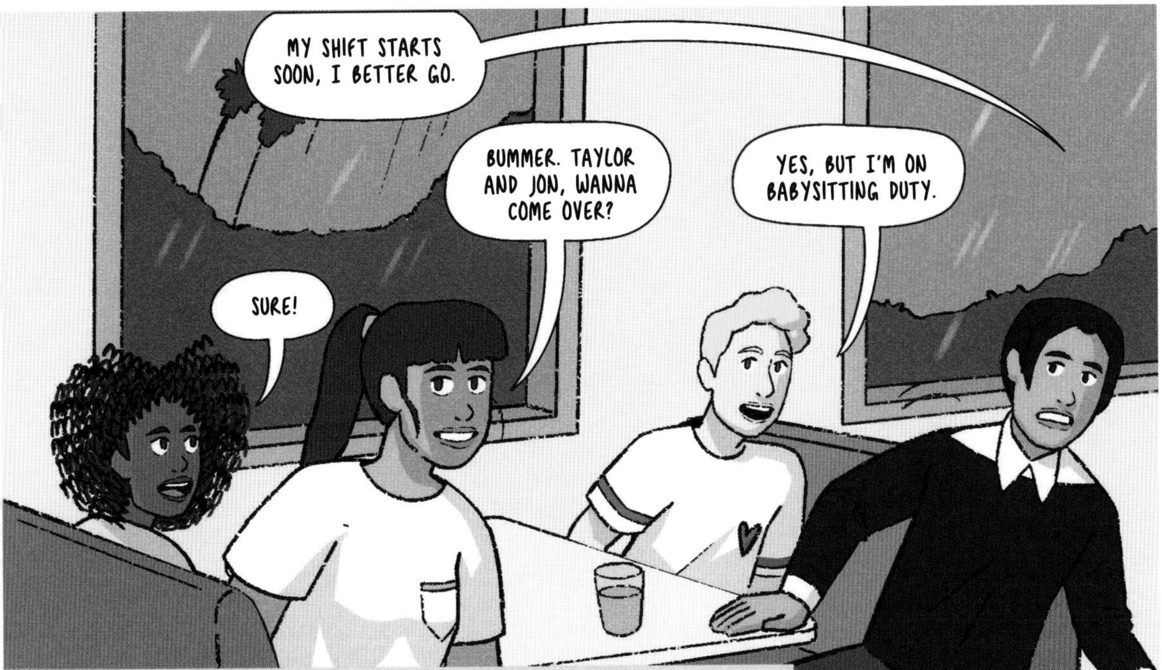
MY SHIFT STARTS SOON, I BETTER GO.
SURE!
BUMMER. TAYLOR AND JON, WANNA COME OVER?
YES, BUT I'M ON BABYSITTING DUTY.

To learn more about the history of this kind of segregation, check out *Stuck in the Shallow End: Education, Race, and Computing*.

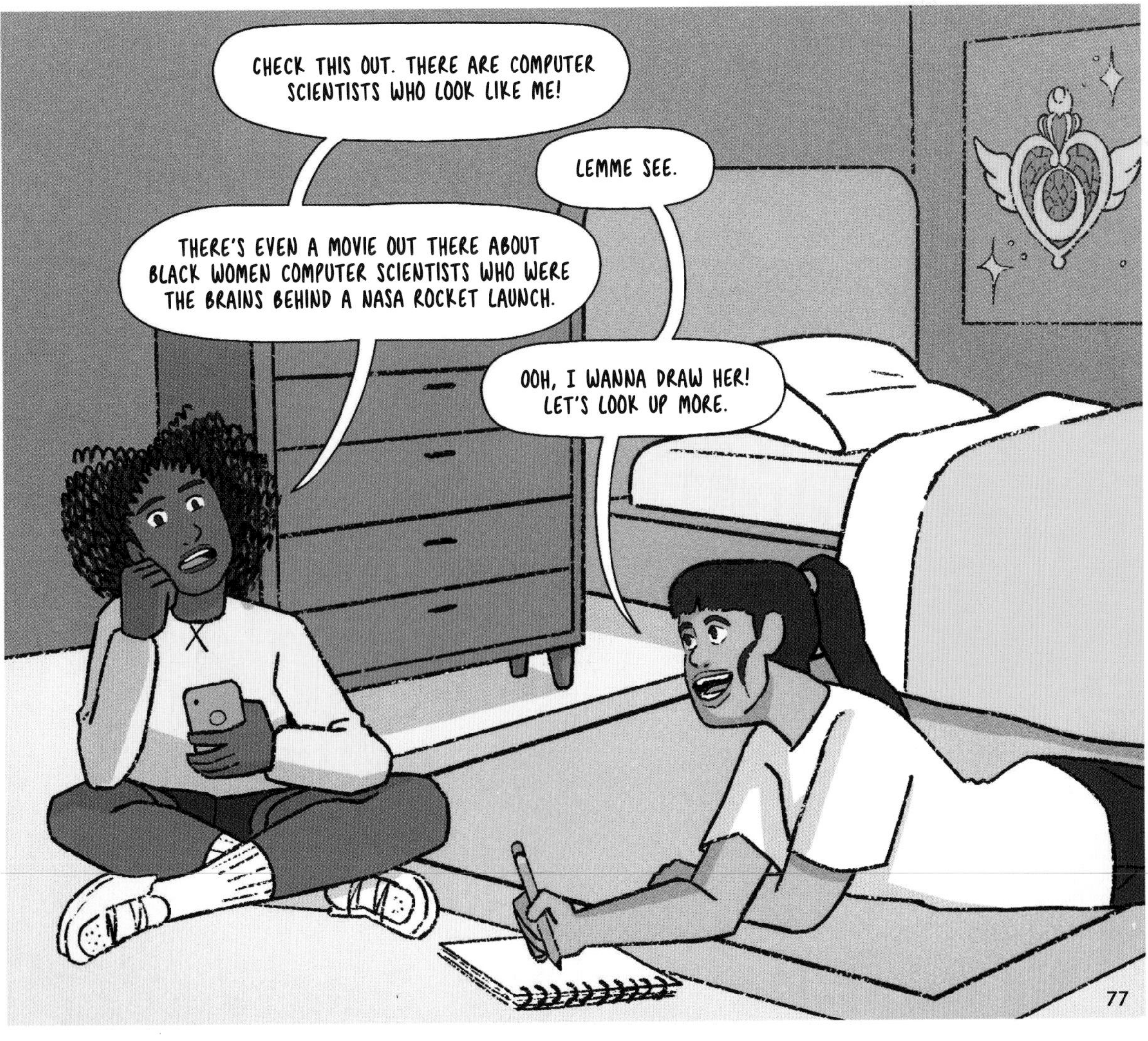
CHECK THIS OUT. THERE ARE COMPUTER SCIENTISTS WHO LOOK LIKE ME!
THERE'S EVEN A MOVIE OUT THERE ABOUT BLACK WOMEN COMPUTER SCIENTISTS WHO WERE THE BRAINS BEHIND A NASA ROCKET LAUNCH.
LEMME SEE.
OOH, I WANNA DRAW HER! LET'S LOOK UP MORE.

Katherine Johnson was an African American physicist and mathematician whose story is described in the book and film *Hidden Figures*.[1] She started working at NASA as a "human computer" in 1953. Due to her incredible skills in math calculations, NASA turned to her to confirm the accuracy of early computer calculations. Her work was key to the success of missions such as Project Mercury and Apollo 11. President Obama awarded her the Presidential Medal of Freedom in 2015.

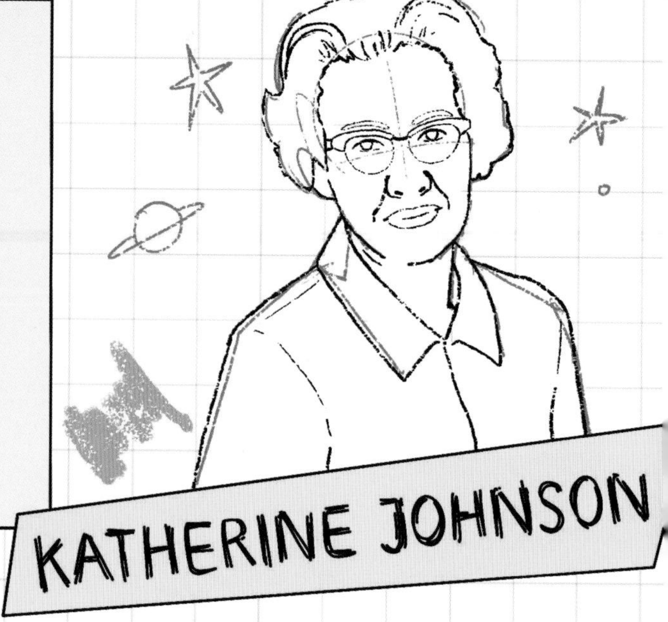
KATHERINE JOHNSON

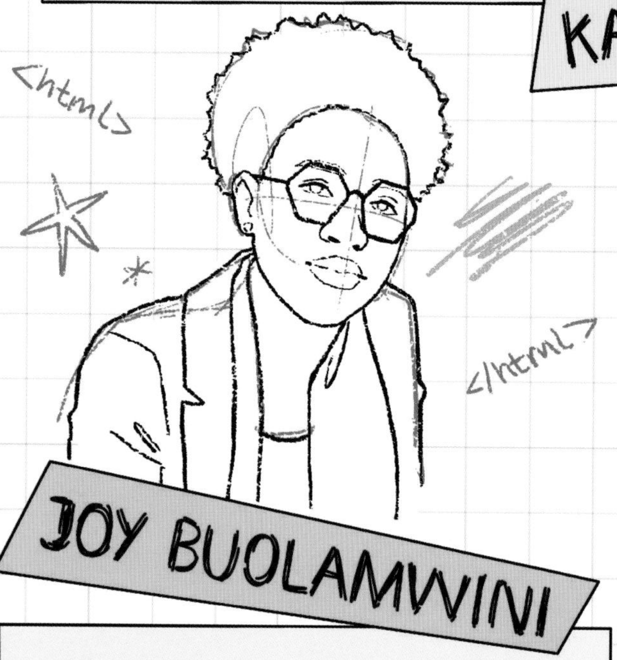
<html>
</html>
JOY BUOLAMWINI

Joy Buolamwini is a Ghanaian American who was born in Canada, raised in Mississippi, and taught herself XHTML, JavaScript, and PHP after getting inspired by Kismet, a robot created at MIT. She studied computer science at Georgia Institute of Technology. She later joined the MIT Media Lab and founded the Algorithmic Justice League. Her research focuses on human bias and how it shapes computer science. She conducts research about racist and sexist artificial intelligence systems, and had to wear a white mask in order for the system to even recognize her face. Look for her TEDx talk at Beacon Street entitled "How I'm Fighting Bias in Algorithms."

Tristan Walker was born and raised in a low-income community of New York City. He eventually became an intern for Twitter, worked for Foursquare Labs, and then started his own African American health and beauty products company called Walker and Company Brands, Inc. He created this company after increasing frustration that companies lack focus on people of color and what they want and need. He couldn't find the right products for himself, and so wanted to create products for other people like him. Walker also cofounded Code2040, a nonprofit working to build a bridge between Black and Latinx students and career opportunities in computer science and tech. Their mission is to ensure the full representation of Black and Latinx people in tech by 2040.

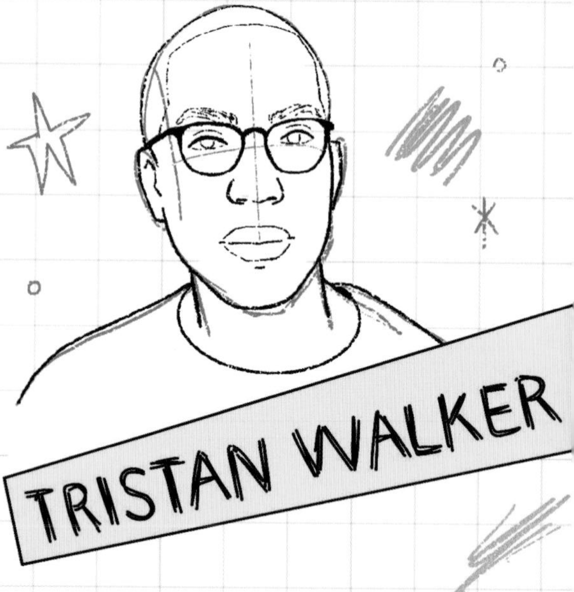
TRISTAN WALKER

Laura Gomez is a Mexican American computer scientist who was born in Central Mexico. Her mother–a migrant farmer–moved to the United States to seek medical treatment when diagnosed with cancer when Laura was only eight years old. A couple of years later, Laura and her siblings joined their mother as undocumented immigrants. Over time, they became legal residents and lived in a low-income neighborhood in Silicon Valley, where Laura's mother raised the four children as a single mom. Laura was introduced to computer science in high school and liked it, so she began studying engineering in college. But she was discouraged by the lack of diversity in the department and switched majors. Her counselor didn't push her to stick with engineering, but eventually Laura returned to tech after college. She has since worked at Twitter, Jawbone, YouTube, Google Brasil, AKQA London, and founded the company Atipica, focused on building diversity and inclusion in the field of artificial intelligence. She is dedicated to mentoring other women of color in the field and helping them deal with the racism, sexism, and heterosexism that is so prevalent in computer science.

LAURA GOMEZ

Rediet Abebe is an Ethiopian computer scientist who went to Harvard University where she studied math. She was the first woman computer scientist to be inducted into the Harvard Society of Fellows. She is now a professor at the University of California, Berkeley. She cofounded Mechanism Design for Social Good (MD4SG), a multi-institutional and interdisciplinary group working to improve the lives of minoritized communities. She is also the cofounder of Black in AI and is dedicated to developing algorithmic and computational techniques that address issues of socioeconomic inequality.

REDIET ABEBE

Chanpory Rith was born in Thailand in a refugee camp near the border of Thailand and Cambodia. Chanpory came to the United States as a Cambodian War refugee during the aftermath of the Killing Fields. He grew up Mormon and was raised with nine people in a one-bedroom Oakland apartment, surviving on $24,000 a year of government assistance. He was always the poorest person in class at his all-African-American school, an outsider racially and ethnically with parents who didn't speak English, and often unwelcome as a gay man. But he forged his own path, beginning with design at Move Design (started by former IDEO designers), which led to learning programming, working for Youth Radio, MetaDesign, Dubberly Design Office, and eventually with Google, where he joined the Gmail team as one of its first full-time designers.

CHANPORY RITH

Timnit Gebru is an Eritrean American computer scientist and an expert in artificial intelligence. Her work focuses on algorithmic bias and data mining. She is also cofounder of Black in AI, a community of Black researchers working in artificial intelligence. Gebru was born in Eritrea and lived in Ethiopia. During forced deportation by the Ethiopian government to Eritrea, she traveled to Ireland, and then moved to the United States to join her mother and two older sisters. She has worked with Joy Buolamwini to examine racial and gender bias in facial recognition software. She is dedicated to addressing issues of ethics and bias in computing. Dr. Gebru became a leader of the Ethics@AI team at Google and was a vocal critic of Google's hiring practices that have resulted in the underrepresentation of people of color and women. In 2020, Gebru was fired from Google. Her firing outraged many and she received large support from Google employees, academic researchers, and computer science educators around the country. Gebru's case became a symbol of the struggle against underrepresentation and racial bias in tech.

TIMNIT GEBRU

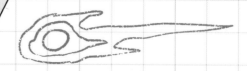

Lynn Conway is a computer scientist, electrical engineer, inventor, and transgender activist. She went to MIT in 1955 but left after a failed gender transition attempt in 1957–58, impacted by the medical context of that time. She eventually completed her education at Columbia University and worked at IBM in the 1960s. However, she was fired by IBM in 1968 after sharing her intention to transition from male to female, and following her transition she lost legal access to her children. Since the 1990s, Conway has been working in transgender activism and working toward protecting the rights of transgender people.

LYNN CONWAY

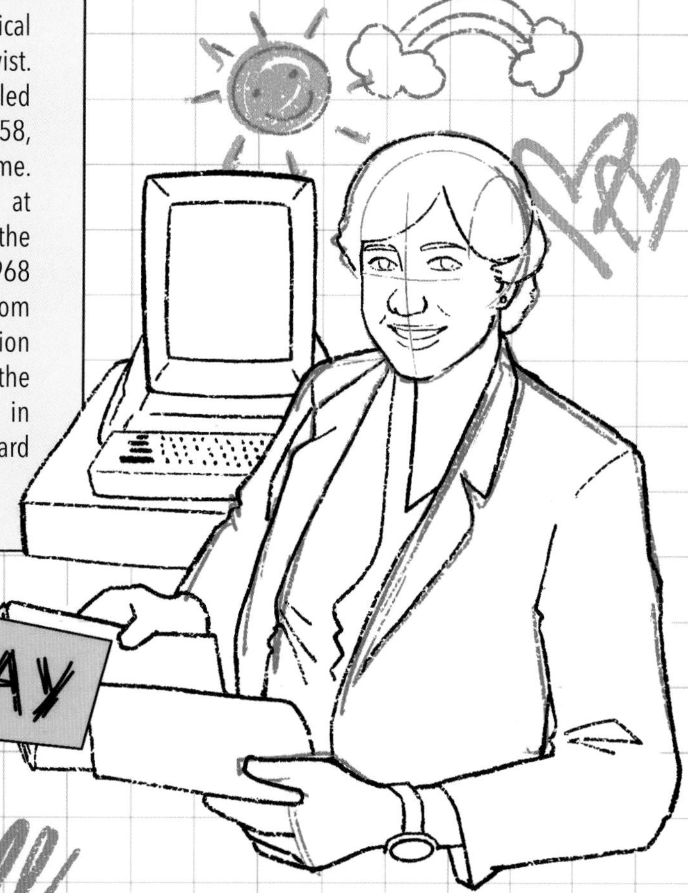

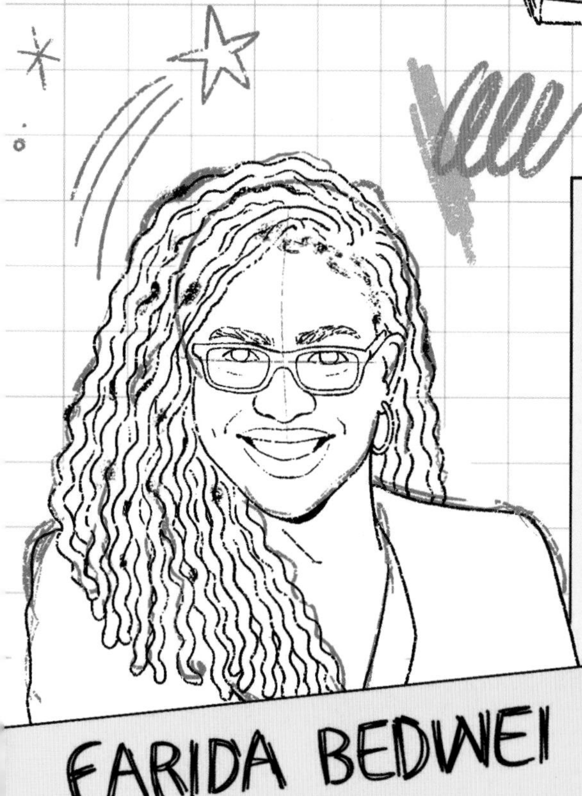

FARIDA BEDWEI

Farida Bedwei is the cofounder and Chief Technology Officer of a microfinance software company in Ghana called Logiciel. Diagnosed with cerebral palsy at the age of one (cerebral palsy is an incurable neurological disorder that affects one's ability to speak and move), Farida often had to use technology to verbally communicate. However, when she started using a computer for written communication, she realized it could be a tool for much more than typing, which was when she decided to learn computer science. Farida is not only a successful software developer who was named one of the most successful women in finance technology in Africa in 2013, she is also an advocate for women and people with disabilities in science, technology, engineering, and math, as well as the author of the comic book Karmzah about an archaeologist superhero with cerebral palsy.

Erin Spiceland is Choctaw and Chickasaw, and grew up in rural south Georgia. Today she is a software engineer for the SpaceX Flight Test Team, testing rocket parts and software, as well as writing flight control software with the goal of sending people to Mars and revolutionizing travel. Erin's life has not been easy, but she is proud to be a Native computer scientist and mother of two, while having overcome the challenges of growing up in poverty, losing her mother to leukemia at a young age, surviving domestic abuse, and not finishing college. Erin is a primarily self-taught software engineer who has, thus far, learned Java/JSP, Python, JavaScript/CSS, and Node.js, as well as MySQL, PostgreSQL, and distributed systems architecture. She also is active in running online Choctaw communities, digitizes Mississippian and Southeastern Native imagery to be freely available online for Natives, makes handmade Native American beadwork, studies her tribe's language, and supports Native people in researching their genealogy and tribal history.

ERIN SPICELAND

Joshua Miele is a blind computer scientist whose work focuses on adaptive technology design to enable blind and visually impaired people to use technology. He received his bachelor's degree in physics and University of California, Berkeley, where he also received a PhD in psychoacoustics to understand the science of sound perception, which has informed his work in designing nonvisual interfaces for information systems. He created Tactile Maps Automated Production, which is web-based software that creates tactile street maps that can be printed using home-based Braille embossers. These maps have been incorporated into the Bay Area Rapid Transit system, supporting blind travelers to help them explore their route through the metro system. He has also developed features for smartphones and portable devices to make them more accessible for the blind, as well as the YouDescribe platform that supports descriptive audio and video to synchronize in ways that blind people can understand. He is the recipient of a MacArthur Foundation fellowship.

JOSHUA MIELE

CHAPTER 6

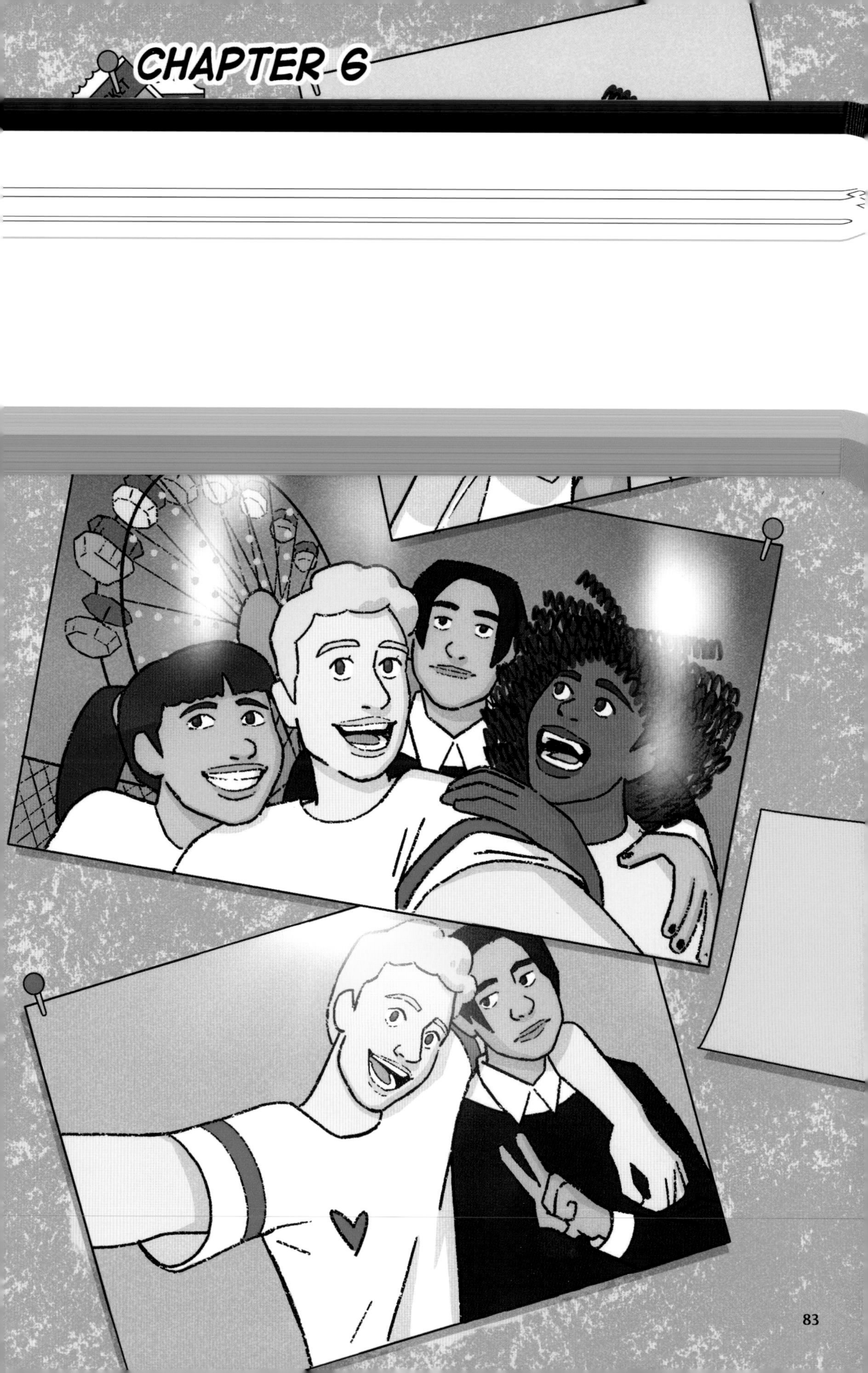

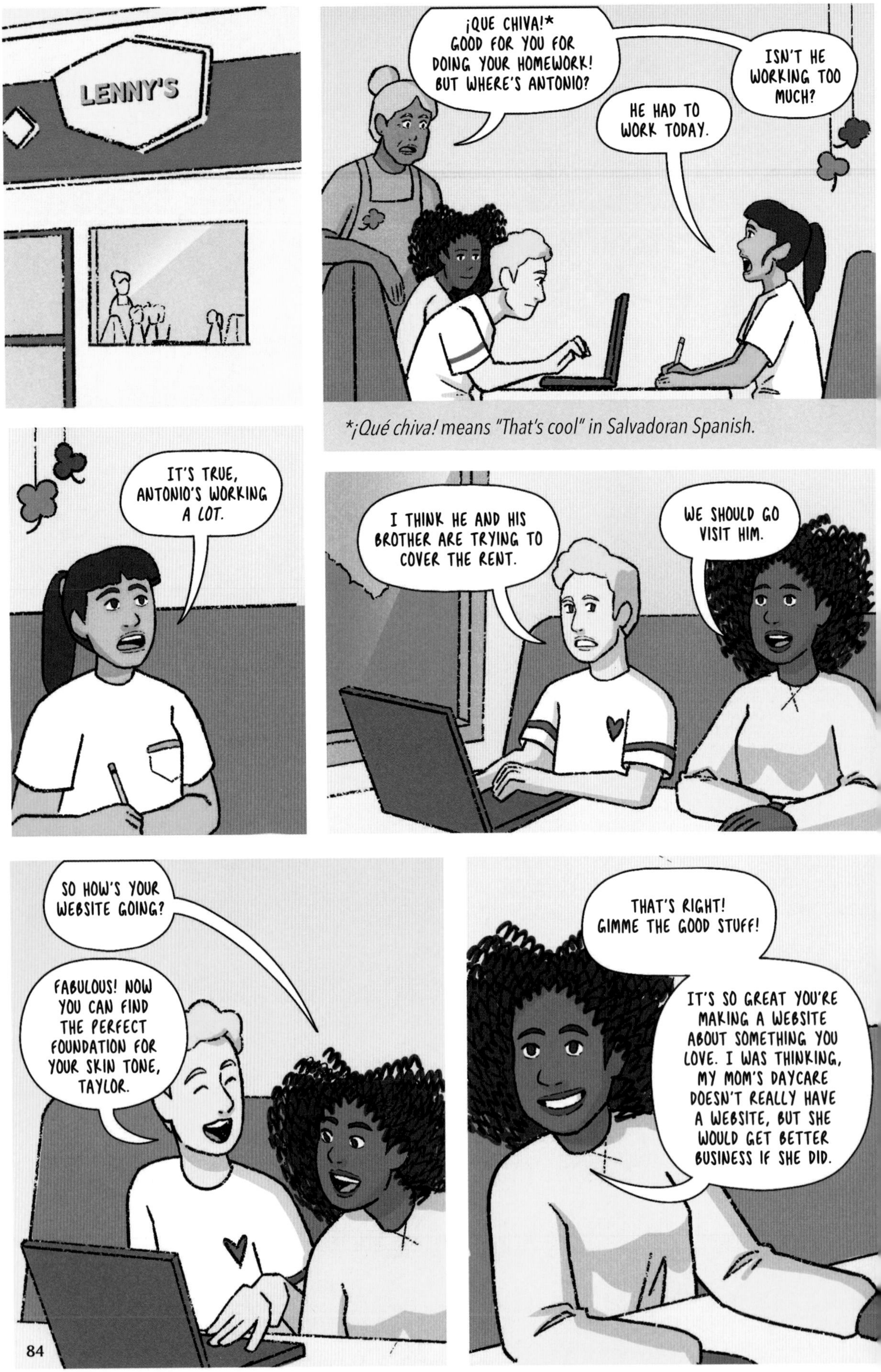
LENNY'S
¡QUE CHIVA!*
GOOD FOR YOU FOR DOING YOUR HOMEWORK! BUT WHERE'S ANTONIO?
HE HAD TO WORK TODAY.
ISN'T HE WORKING TOO MUCH?
IT'S TRUE, ANTONIO'S WORKING A LOT.
I THINK HE AND HIS BROTHER ARE TRYING TO COVER THE RENT.
WE SHOULD GO VISIT HIM.
SO HOW'S YOUR WEBSITE GOING?
FABULOUS! NOW YOU CAN FIND THE PERFECT FOUNDATION FOR YOUR SKIN TONE, TAYLOR.
THAT'S RIGHT! GIMME THE GOOD STUFF!
IT'S SO GREAT YOU'RE MAKING A WEBSITE ABOUT SOMETHING YOU LOVE. I WAS THINKING, MY MOM'S DAYCARE DOESN'T REALLY HAVE A WEBSITE, BUT SHE WOULD GET BETTER BUSINESS IF SHE DID.

¡Qué chiva! means "That's cool" in Salvadoran Spanish.

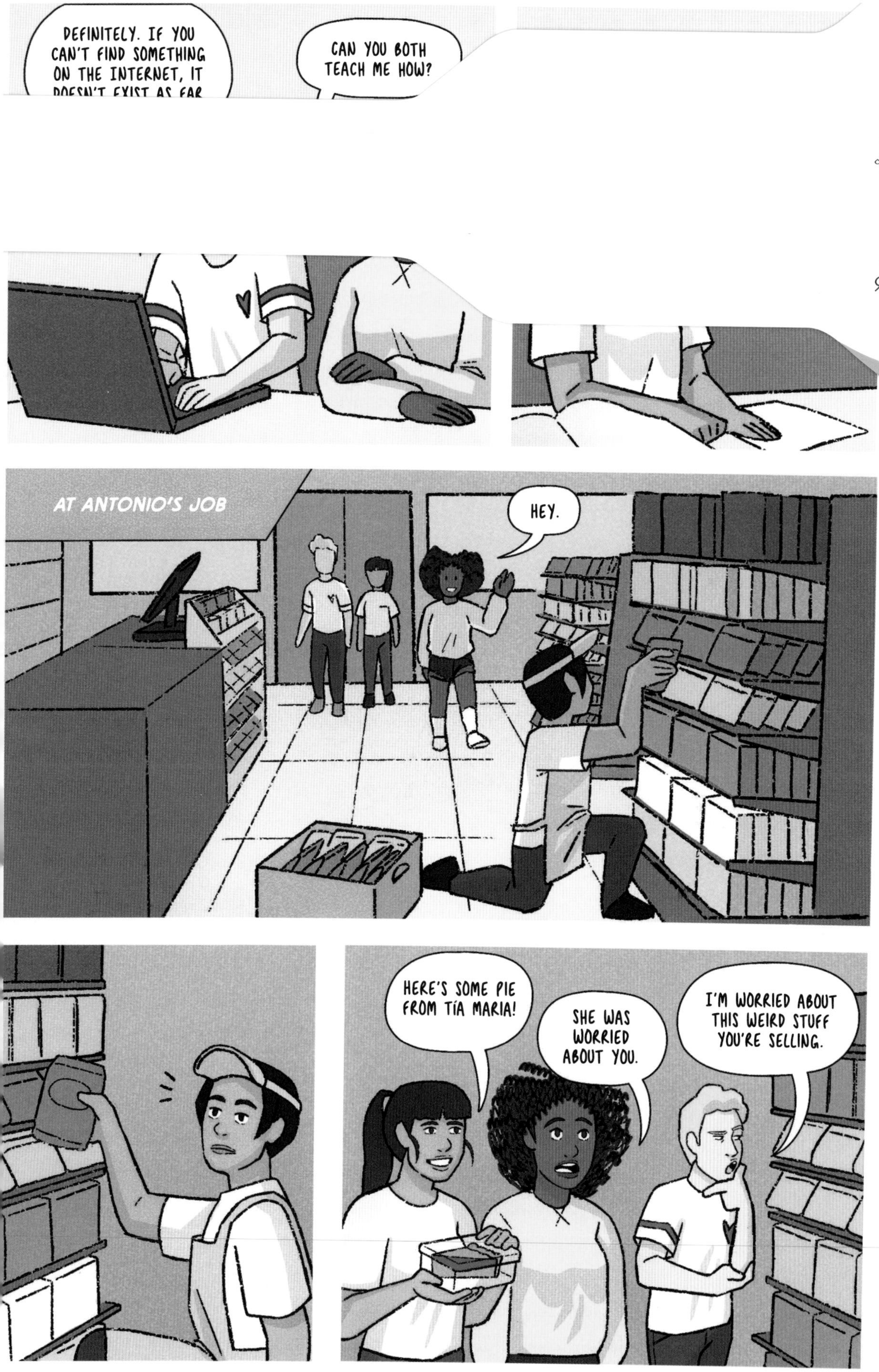

DEFINITELY. IF YOU CAN'T FIND SOMETHING ON THE INTERNET, IT
CAN YOU BOTH TEACH ME HOW?
AT ANTONIO'S JOB
HEY.
HERE'S SOME PIE FROM TÍA MARIA!
SHE WAS WORRIED ABOUT YOU.
I'M WORRIED ABOUT THIS WEIRD STUFF YOU'RE SELLING.

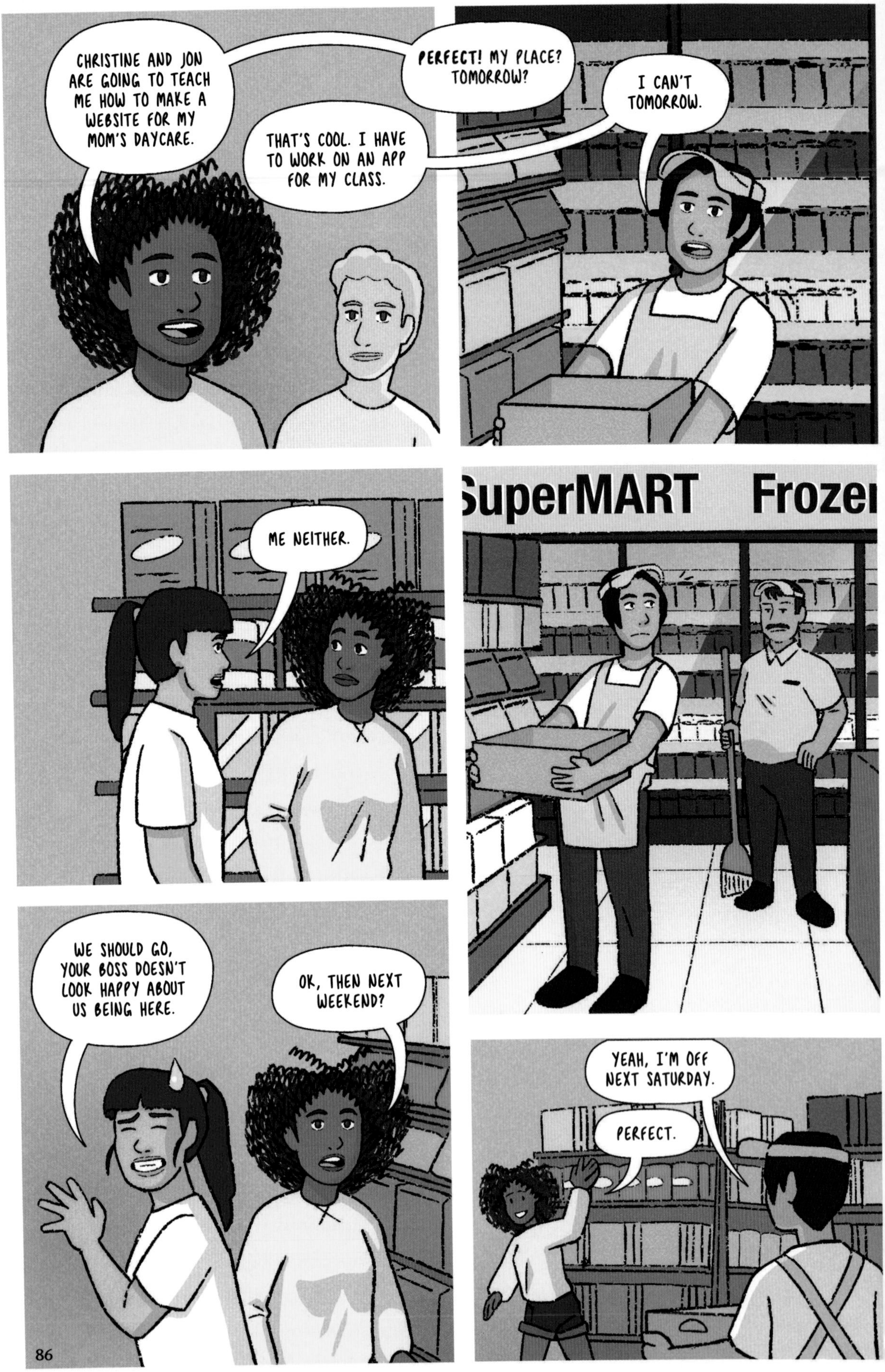
CHRISTINE AND JON ARE GOING TO TEACH ME HOW TO MAKE A WEBSITE FOR MY MOM'S DAYCARE.
THAT'S COOL. I HAVE TO WORK ON AN APP FOR MY CLASS.
PERFECT! MY PLACE? TOMORROW?
I CAN'T TOMORROW.
ME NEITHER.
SuperMART Frozen
WE SHOULD GO, YOUR BOSS DOESN'T LOOK HAPPY ABOUT US BEING HERE.
OK, THEN NEXT WEEKEND?
YEAH, I'M OFF NEXT SATURDAY.
PERFECT.

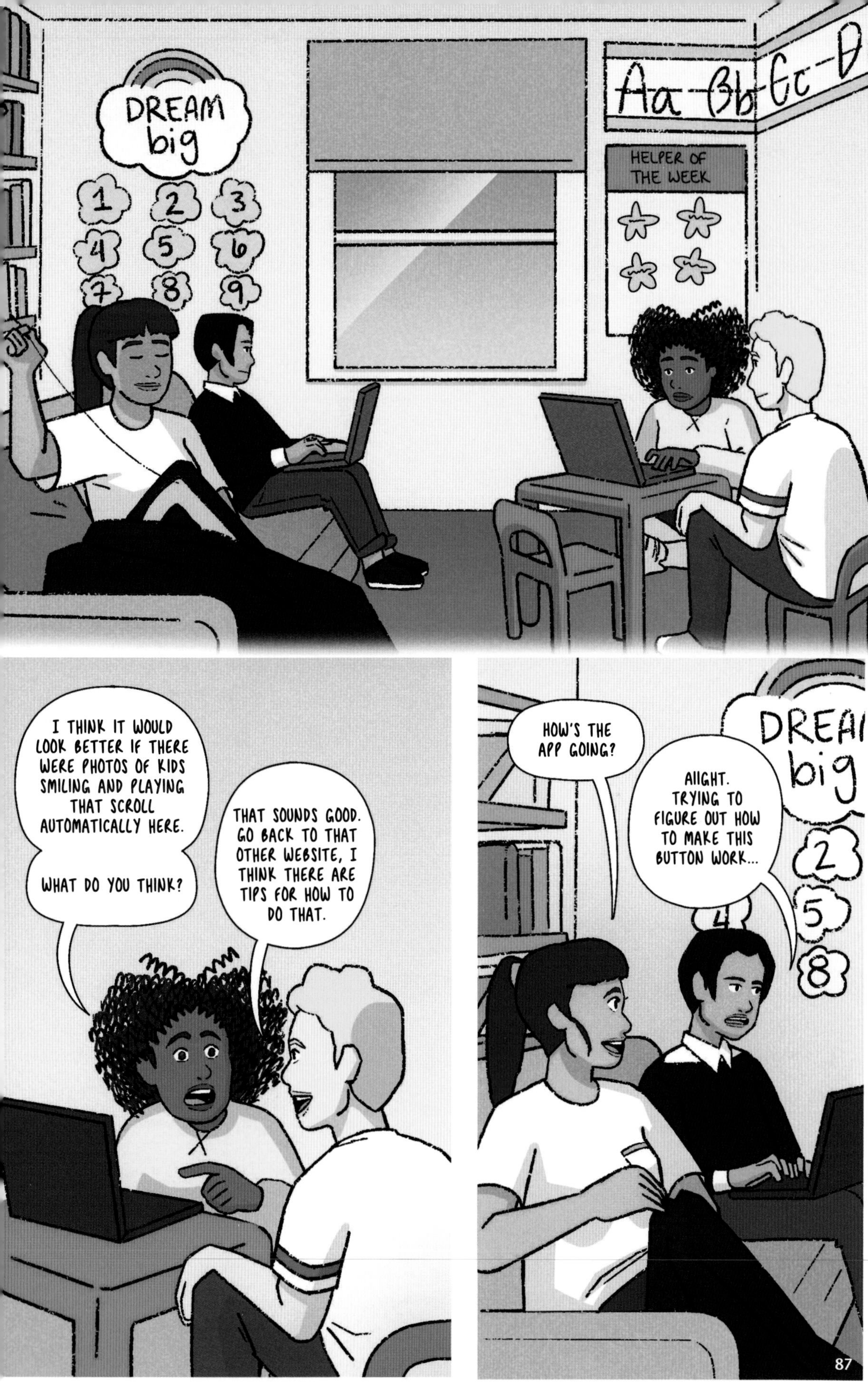
DREAM big
1 2 3 4 5 6 7 8 9
Aa Bb Cc Dd
HELPER OF THE WEEK
I THINK IT WOULD LOOK BETTER IF THERE WERE PHOTOS OF KIDS SMILING AND PLAYING THAT SCROLL AUTOMATICALLY HERE.
WHAT DO YOU THINK?
THAT SOUNDS GOOD. GO BACK TO THAT OTHER WEBSITE, I THINK THERE ARE TIPS FOR HOW TO DO THAT.
HOW'S THE APP GOING?
AIIGHT. TRYING TO FIGURE OUT HOW TO MAKE THIS BUTTON WORK...

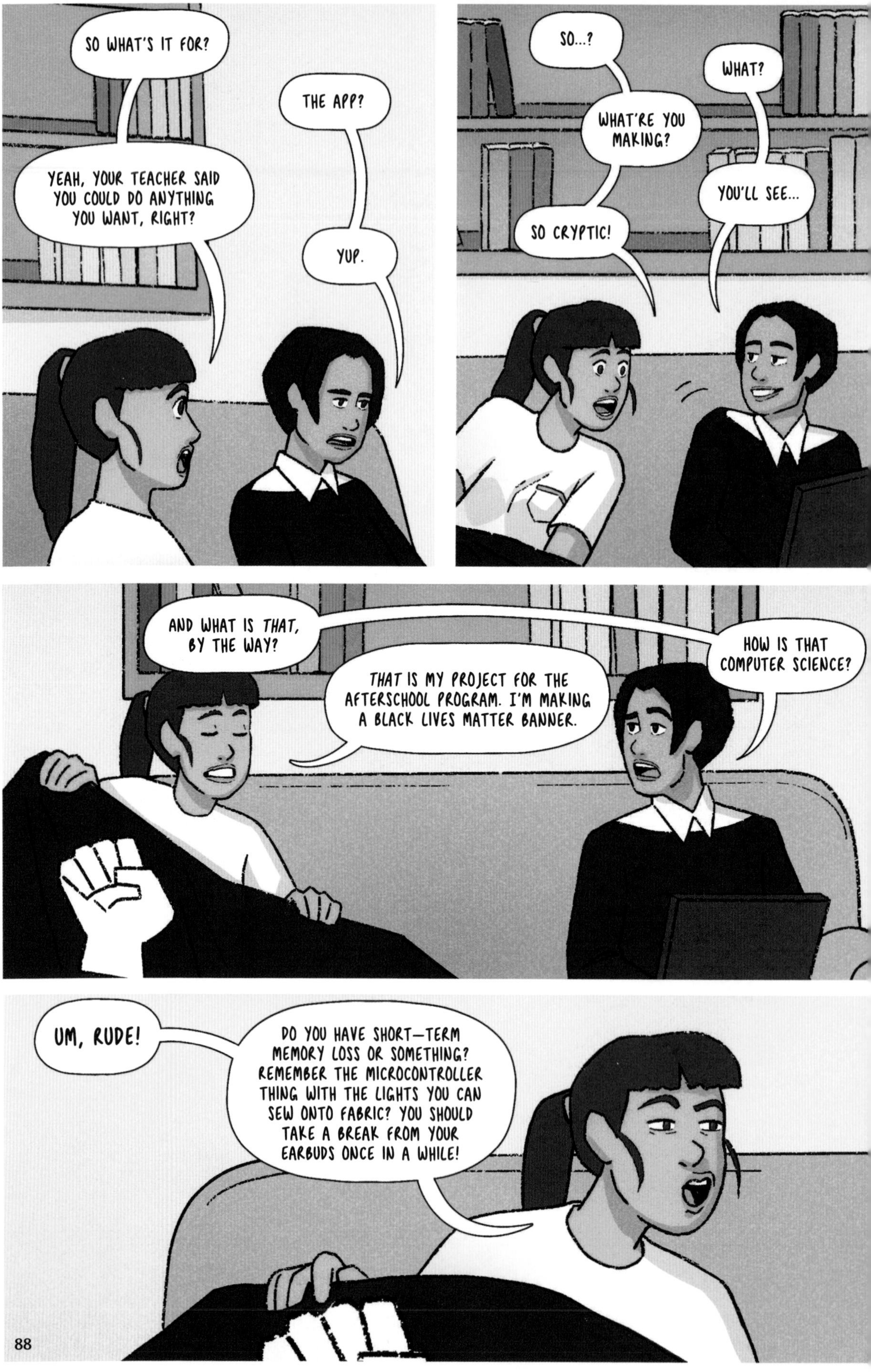

SO WHAT'S IT FOR?
THE APP?
YEAH, YOUR TEACHER SAID YOU COULD DO ANYTHING YOU WANT, RIGHT?
YUP.
SO...?
WHAT?
WHAT'RE YOU MAKING?
YOU'LL SEE...
SO CRYPTIC!
AND WHAT IS *THAT*, BY THE WAY?
THAT IS MY PROJECT FOR THE AFTERSCHOOL PROGRAM. I'M MAKING A BLACK LIVES MATTER BANNER.
HOW IS THAT COMPUTER SCIENCE?
UM, RUDE!
DO YOU HAVE SHORT-TERM MEMORY LOSS OR SOMETHING? REMEMBER THE MICROCONTROLLER THING WITH THE LIGHTS YOU CAN SEW ONTO FABRIC? YOU SHOULD TAKE A BREAK FROM YOUR EARBUDS ONCE IN A WHILE!

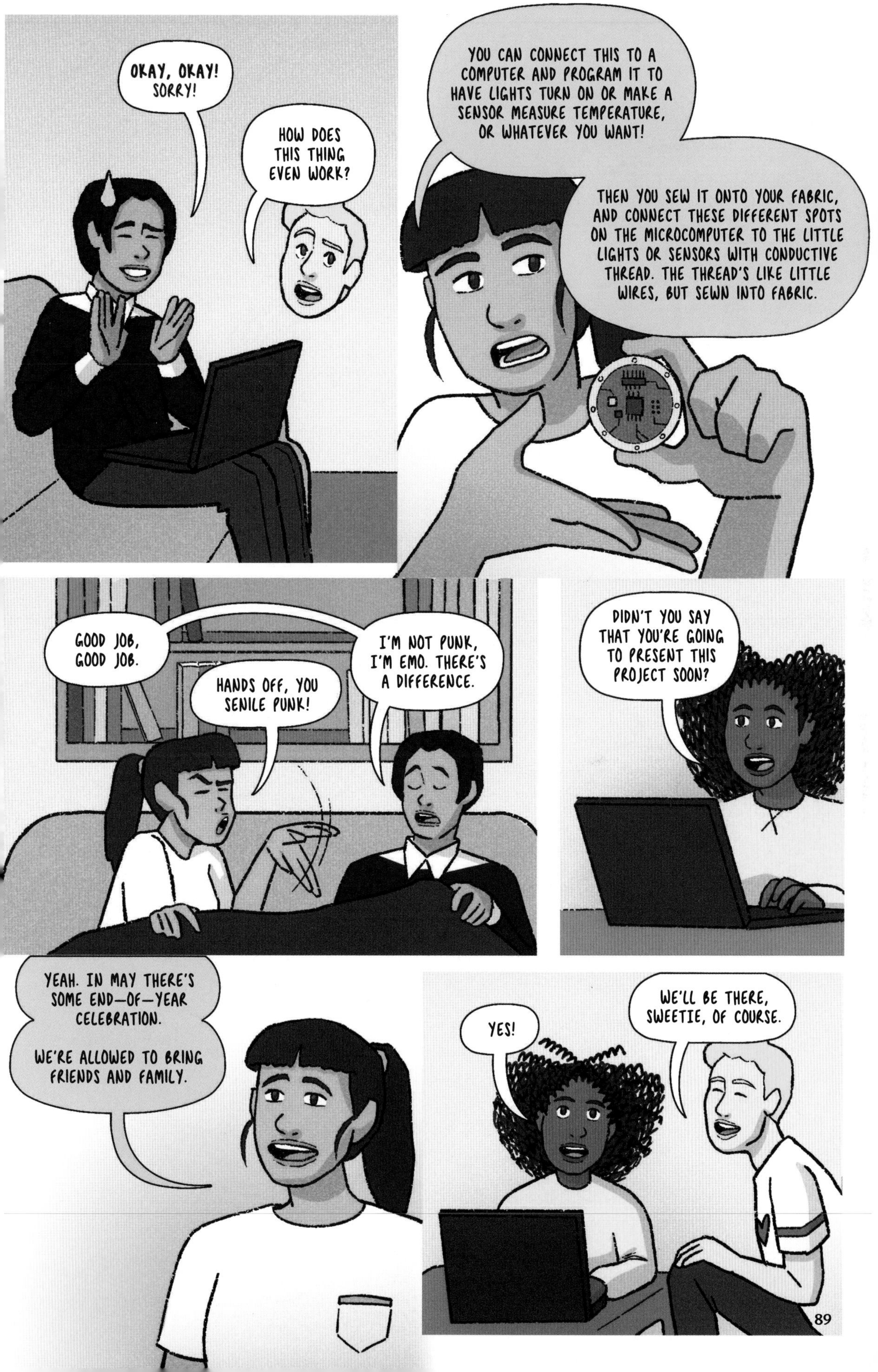
OKAY, OKAY! SORRY!
HOW DOES THIS THING EVEN WORK?
YOU CAN CONNECT THIS TO A COMPUTER AND PROGRAM IT TO HAVE LIGHTS TURN ON OR MAKE A SENSOR MEASURE TEMPERATURE, OR WHATEVER YOU WANT!
THEN YOU SEW IT ONTO YOUR FABRIC, AND CONNECT THESE DIFFERENT SPOTS ON THE MICROCOMPUTER TO THE LITTLE LIGHTS OR SENSORS WITH CONDUCTIVE THREAD. THE THREAD'S LIKE LITTLE WIRES, BUT SEWN INTO FABRIC.
GOOD JOB, GOOD JOB.
HANDS OFF, YOU SENILE PUNK!
I'M NOT PUNK, I'M EMO. THERE'S A DIFFERENCE.
DIDN'T YOU SAY THAT YOU'RE GOING TO PRESENT THIS PROJECT SOON?
YEAH. IN MAY THERE'S SOME END-OF-YEAR CELEBRATION.
WE'RE ALLOWED TO BRING FRIENDS AND FAMILY.
YES!
WE'LL BE THERE, SWEETIE, OF COURSE.

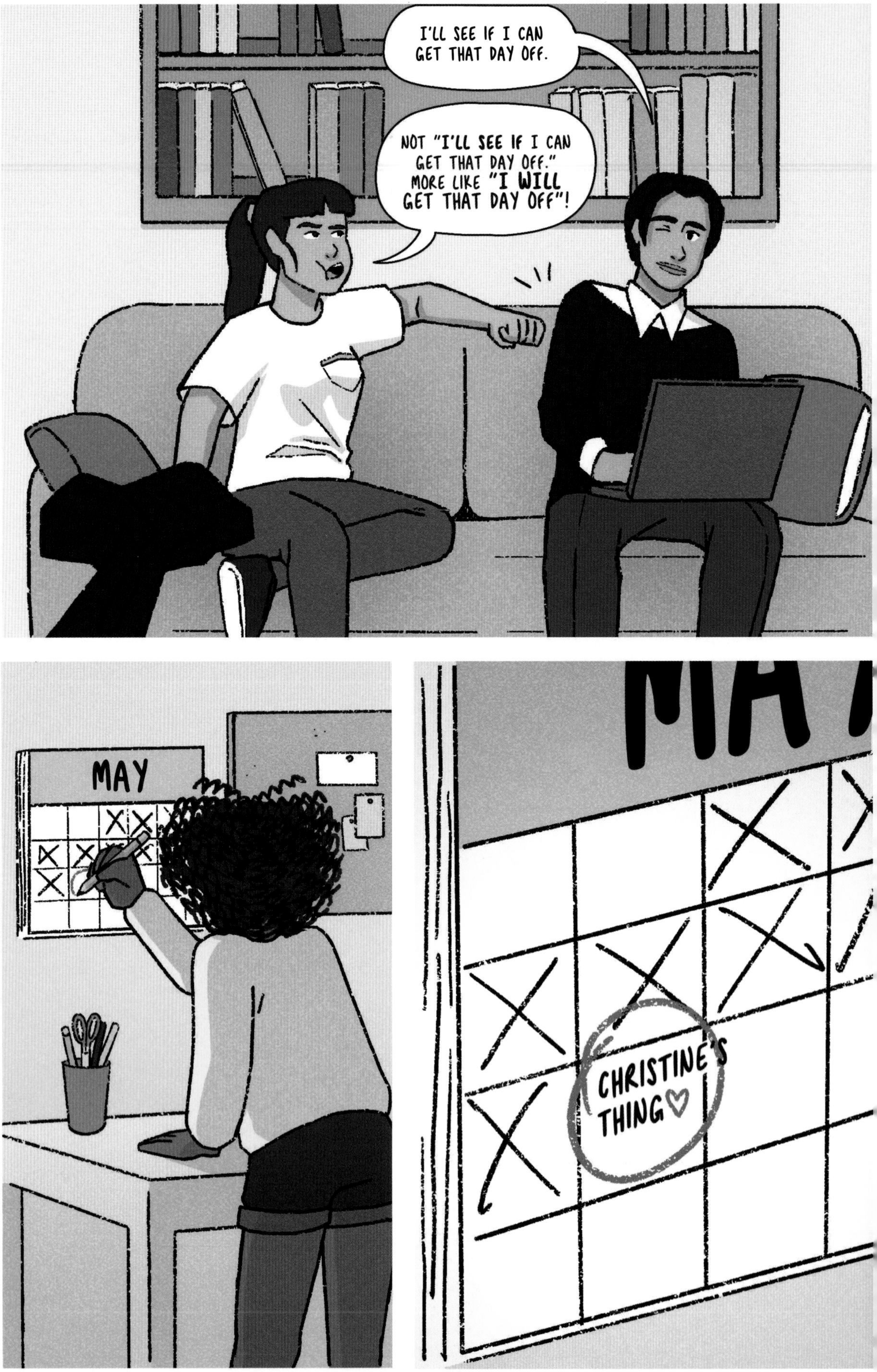
I'LL SEE IF I CAN GET THAT DAY OFF.
NOT "I'LL SEE IF I CAN GET THAT DAY OFF." MORE LIKE "I WILL GET THAT DAY OFF"!
MAY
CHRISTINE'S THING

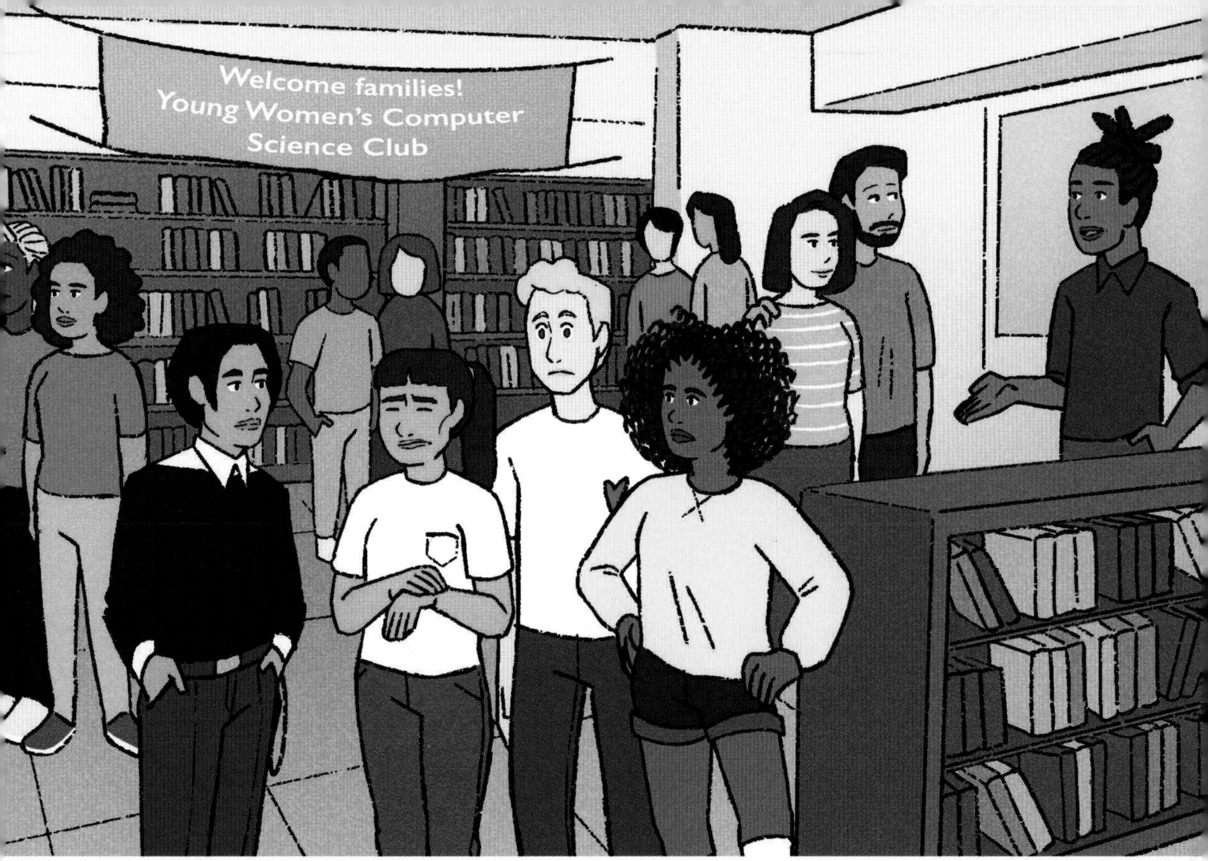
Welcome families!
Young Women's Computer
Science Club

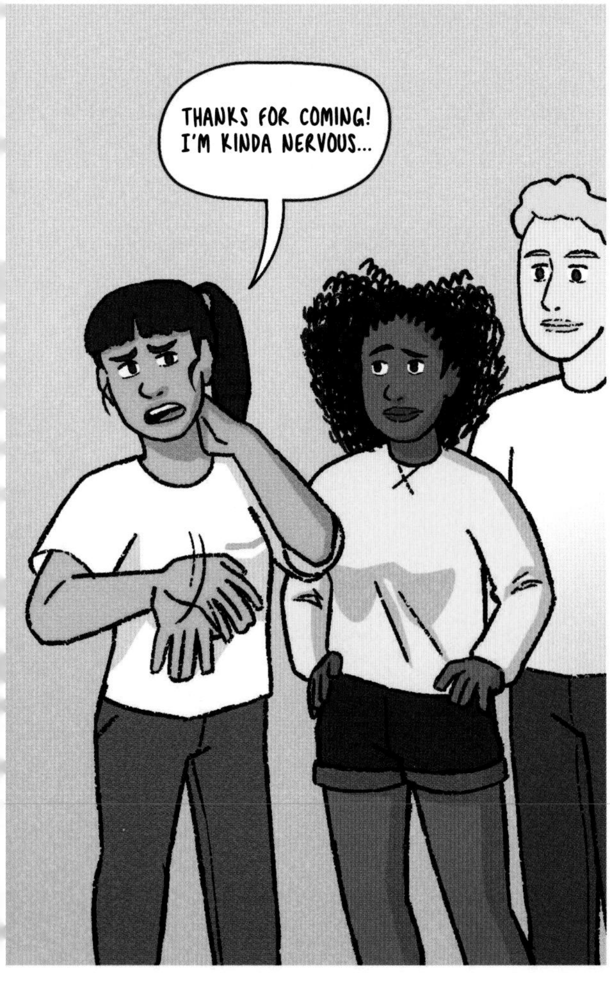
THANKS FOR COMING!
I'M KINDA NERVOUS...

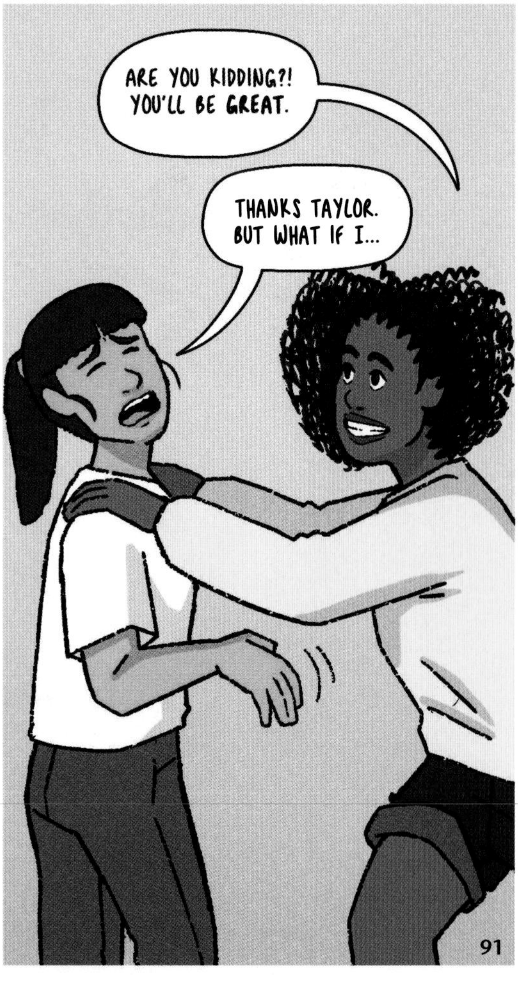
ARE YOU KIDDING?!
YOU'LL BE GREAT.
THANKS TAYLOR.
BUT WHAT IF I...

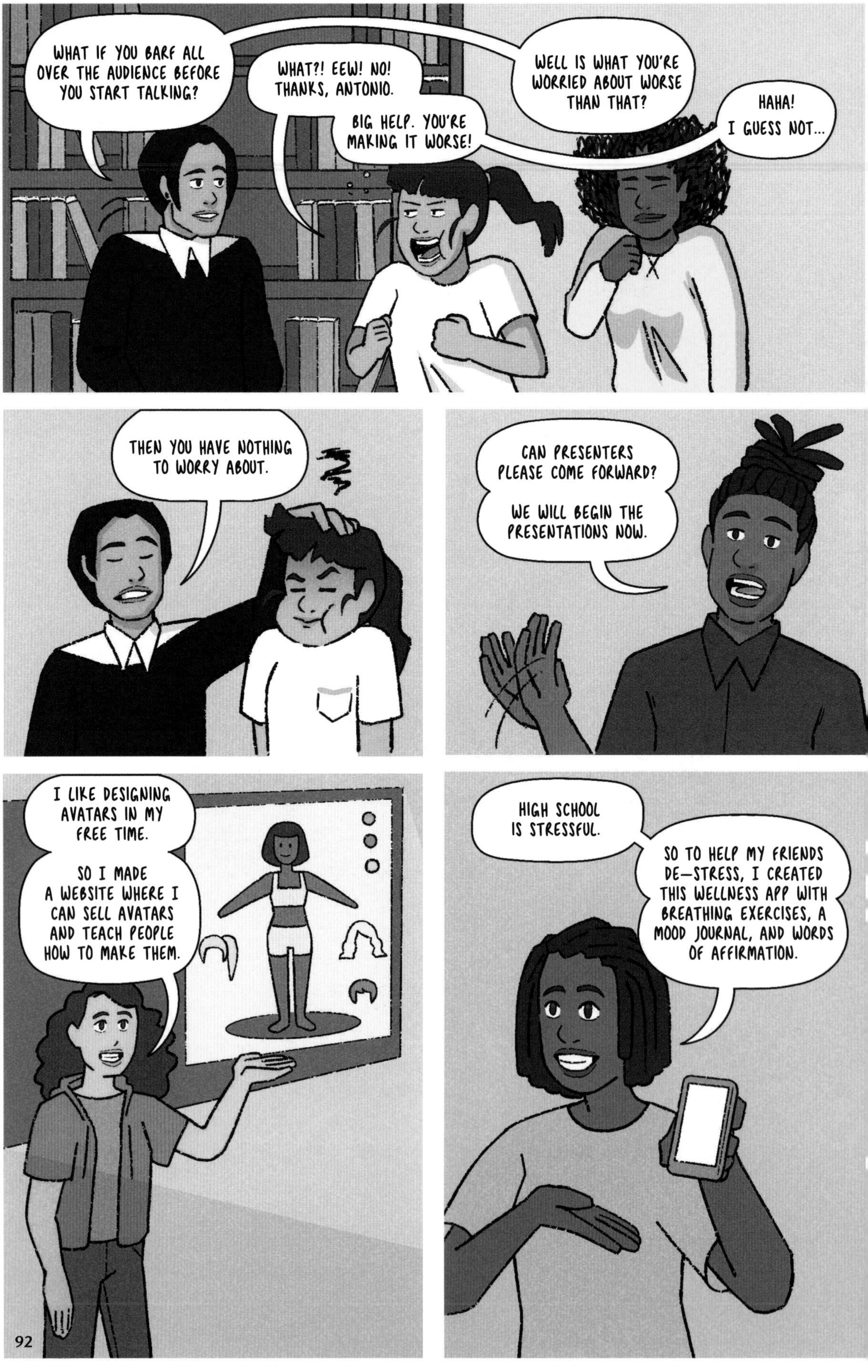
WHAT IF YOU BARF ALL OVER THE AUDIENCE BEFORE YOU START TALKING?
WHAT?! EEW! NO! THANKS, ANTONIO.
BIG HELP. YOU'RE MAKING IT WORSE!
WELL IS WHAT YOU'RE WORRIED ABOUT WORSE THAN THAT?
HAHA! I GUESS NOT...
THEN YOU HAVE NOTHING TO WORRY ABOUT.
CAN PRESENTERS PLEASE COME FORWARD?
WE WILL BEGIN THE PRESENTATIONS NOW.
I LIKE DESIGNING AVATARS IN MY FREE TIME.
SO I MADE A WEBSITE WHERE I CAN SELL AVATARS AND TEACH PEOPLE HOW TO MAKE THEM.
HIGH SCHOOL IS STRESSFUL.
SO TO HELP MY FRIENDS DE-STRESS, I CREATED THIS WELLNESS APP WITH BREATHING EXERCISES, A MOOD JOURNAL, AND WORDS OF AFFIRMATION.

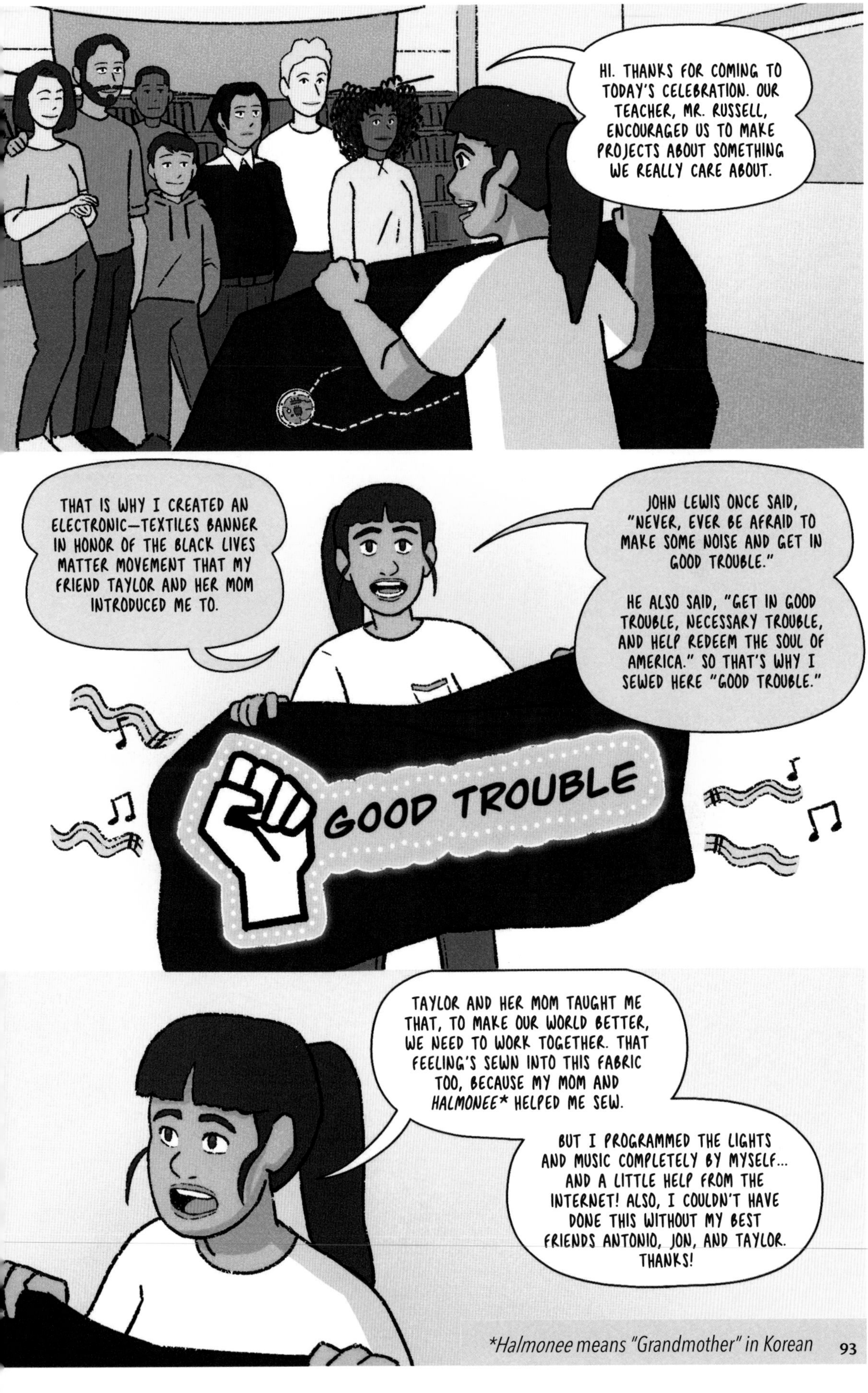
HI. THANKS FOR COMING TO TODAY'S CELEBRATION. OUR TEACHER, MR. RUSSELL, ENCOURAGED US TO MAKE PROJECTS ABOUT SOMETHING WE REALLY CARE ABOUT.
THAT IS WHY I CREATED AN ELECTRONIC—TEXTILES BANNER IN HONOR OF THE BLACK LIVES MATTER MOVEMENT THAT MY FRIEND TAYLOR AND HER MOM INTRODUCED ME TO.
JOHN LEWIS ONCE SAID, "NEVER, EVER BE AFRAID TO MAKE SOME NOISE AND GET IN GOOD TROUBLE."
HE ALSO SAID, "GET IN GOOD TROUBLE, NECESSARY TROUBLE, AND HELP REDEEM THE SOUL OF AMERICA." SO THAT'S WHY I SEWED HERE "GOOD TROUBLE."
GOOD TROUBLE
TAYLOR AND HER MOM TAUGHT ME THAT, TO MAKE OUR WORLD BETTER, WE NEED TO WORK TOGETHER. THAT FEELING'S SEWN INTO THIS FABRIC TOO, BECAUSE MY MOM AND *HALMONEE** HELPED ME SEW.
BUT I PROGRAMMED THE LIGHTS AND MUSIC COMPLETELY BY MYSELF... AND A LITTLE HELP FROM THE INTERNET! ALSO, I COULDN'T HAVE DONE THIS WITHOUT MY BEST FRIENDS ANTONIO, JON, AND TAYLOR. THANKS!

**Halmonee* means "Grandmother" in Korean

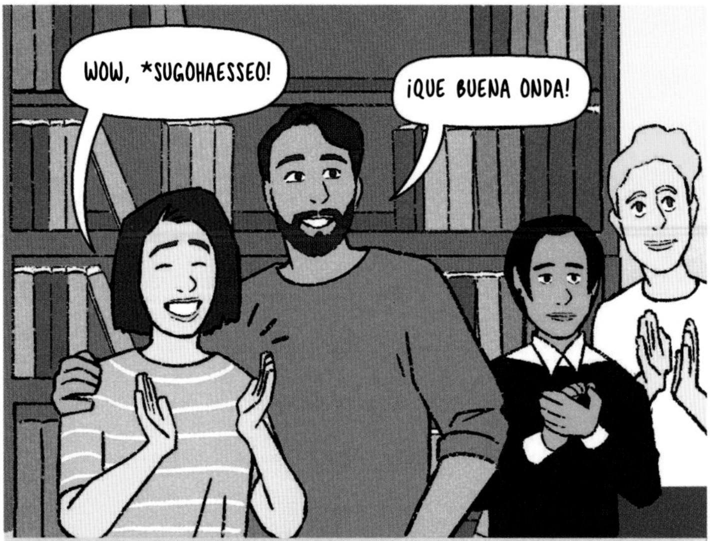
WOW, *SUGOHAESSEO!
¡QUE BUENA ONDA!
*Sugohaesseo means "Good job, you worked hard!" in Korean; ¡Que buena onda! means "Beautiful work!" in Salvadoran Spanish

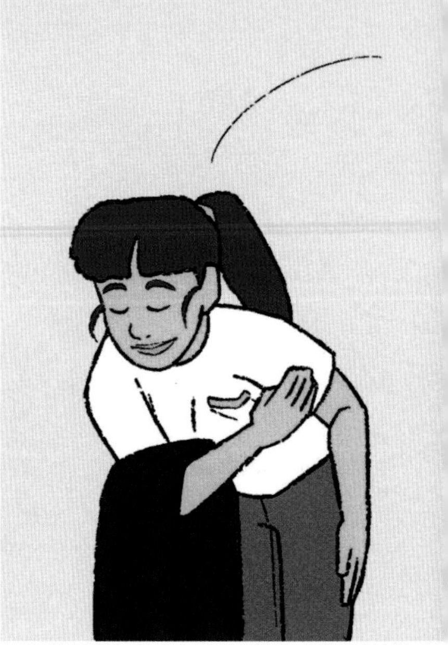

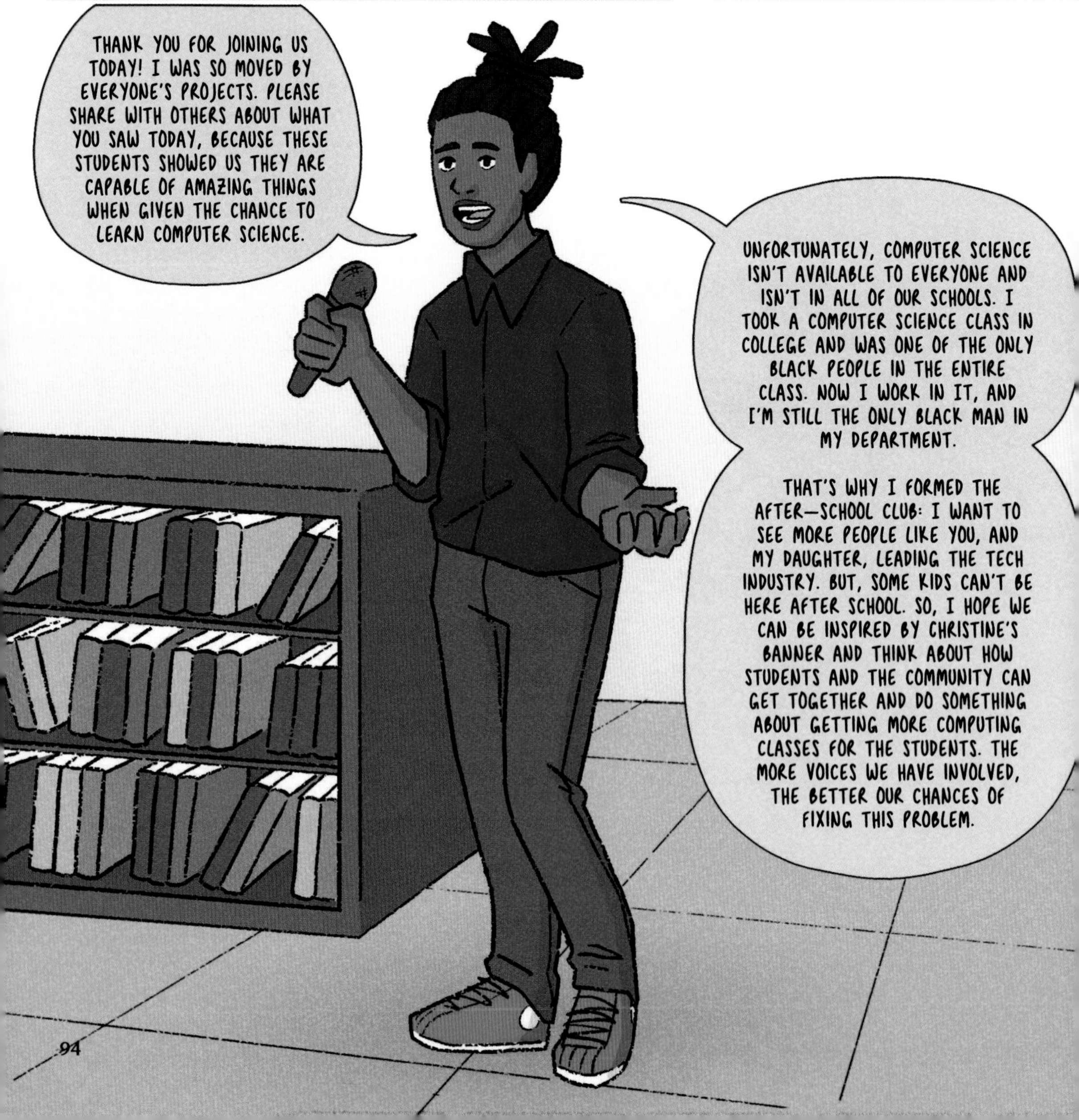
THANK YOU FOR JOINING US TODAY! I WAS SO MOVED BY EVERYONE'S PROJECTS. PLEASE SHARE WITH OTHERS ABOUT WHAT YOU SAW TODAY, BECAUSE THESE STUDENTS SHOWED US THEY ARE CAPABLE OF AMAZING THINGS WHEN GIVEN THE CHANCE TO LEARN COMPUTER SCIENCE.
UNFORTUNATELY, COMPUTER SCIENCE ISN'T AVAILABLE TO EVERYONE AND ISN'T IN ALL OF OUR SCHOOLS. I TOOK A COMPUTER SCIENCE CLASS IN COLLEGE AND WAS ONE OF THE ONLY BLACK PEOPLE IN THE ENTIRE CLASS. NOW I WORK IN IT, AND I'M STILL THE ONLY BLACK MAN IN MY DEPARTMENT.
THAT'S WHY I FORMED THE AFTER-SCHOOL CLUB: I WANT TO SEE MORE PEOPLE LIKE YOU, AND MY DAUGHTER, LEADING THE TECH INDUSTRY. BUT, SOME KIDS CAN'T BE HERE AFTER SCHOOL. SO, I HOPE WE CAN BE INSPIRED BY CHRISTINE'S BANNER AND THINK ABOUT HOW STUDENTS AND THE COMMUNITY CAN GET TOGETHER AND DO SOMETHING ABOUT GETTING MORE COMPUTING CLASSES FOR THE STUDENTS. THE MORE VOICES WE HAVE INVOLVED, THE BETTER OUR CHANCES OF FIXING THIS PROBLEM.

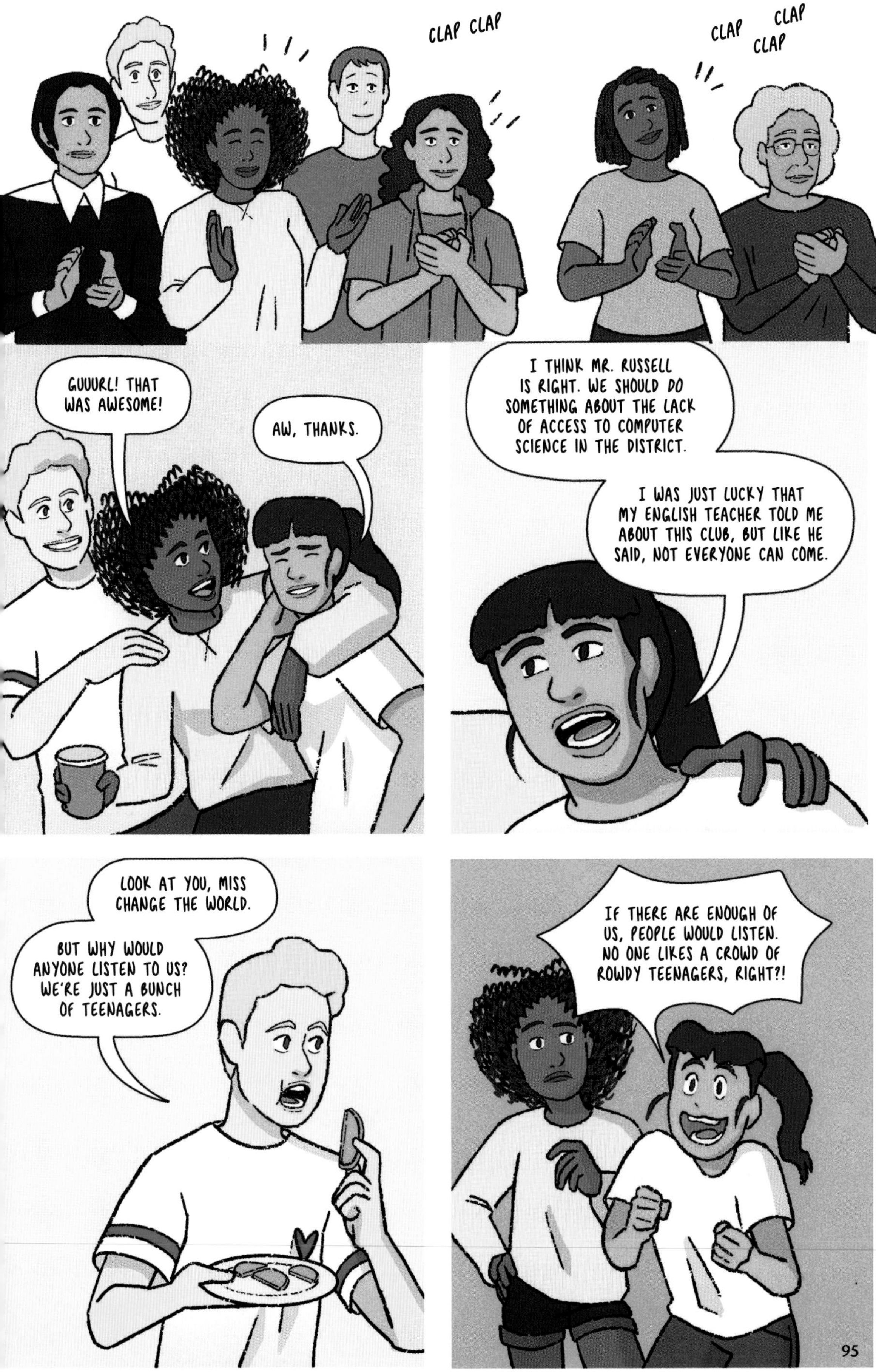
CLAP CLAP
CLAP CLAP
CLAP
GUUURL! THAT WAS AWESOME!
AW, THANKS.
I THINK MR. RUSSELL IS RIGHT. WE SHOULD DO SOMETHING ABOUT THE LACK OF ACCESS TO COMPUTER SCIENCE IN THE DISTRICT.
I WAS JUST LUCKY THAT MY ENGLISH TEACHER TOLD ME ABOUT THIS CLUB, BUT LIKE HE SAID, NOT EVERYONE CAN COME.
LOOK AT YOU, MISS CHANGE THE WORLD.
BUT WHY WOULD ANYONE LISTEN TO US? WE'RE JUST A BUNCH OF TEENAGERS.
IF THERE ARE ENOUGH OF US, PEOPLE WOULD LISTEN. NO ONE LIKES A CROWD OF ROWDY TEENAGERS, RIGHT?!

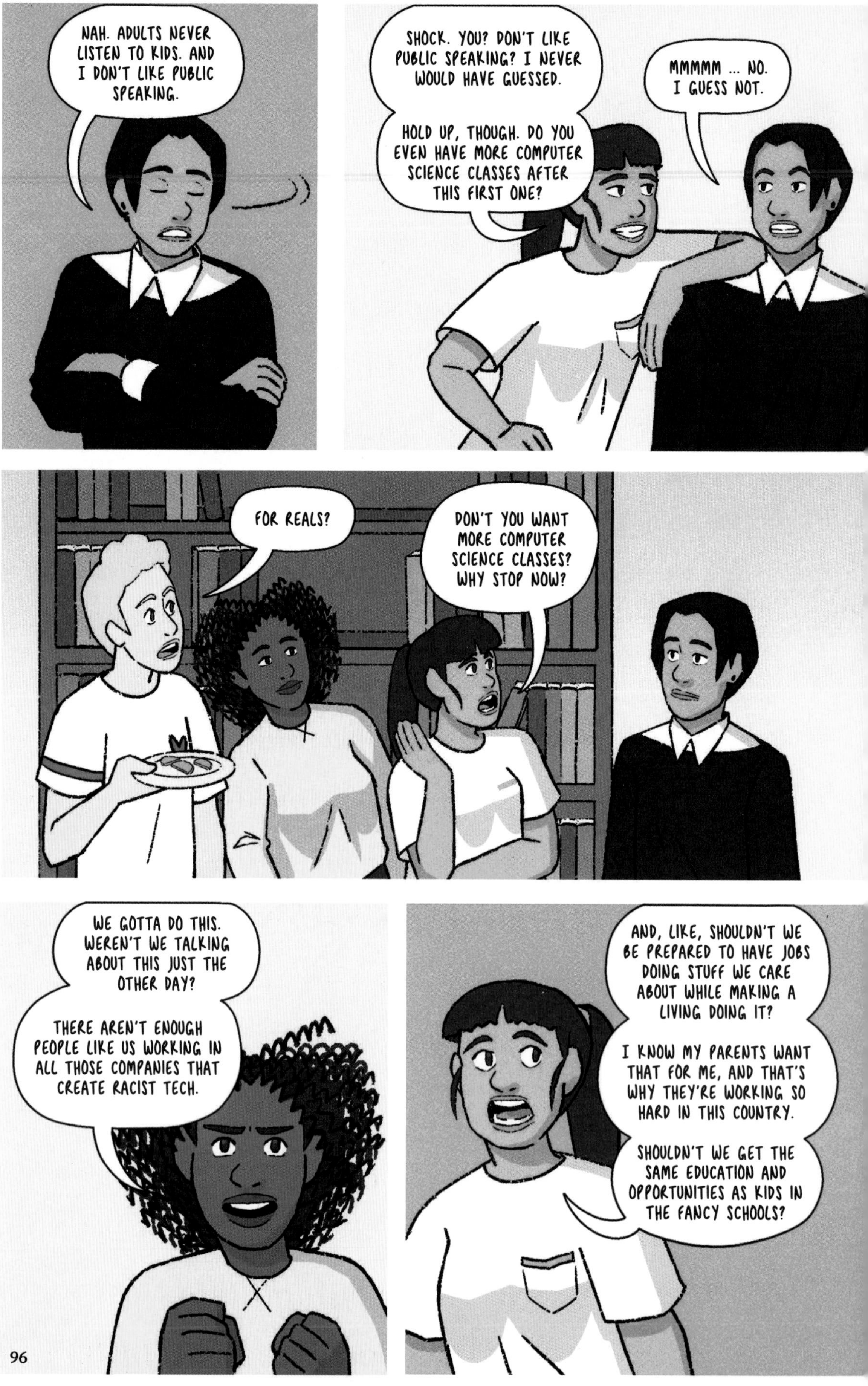
NAH. ADULTS NEVER LISTEN TO KIDS. AND I DON'T LIKE PUBLIC SPEAKING.
SHOCK. YOU? DON'T LIKE PUBLIC SPEAKING? I NEVER WOULD HAVE GUESSED.
HOLD UP, THOUGH. DO YOU EVEN HAVE MORE COMPUTER SCIENCE CLASSES AFTER THIS FIRST ONE?
MMMMM ... NO. I GUESS NOT.
FOR REALS?
DON'T YOU WANT MORE COMPUTER SCIENCE CLASSES? WHY STOP NOW?
WE GOTTA DO THIS. WEREN'T WE TALKING ABOUT THIS JUST THE OTHER DAY?
THERE AREN'T ENOUGH PEOPLE LIKE US WORKING IN ALL THOSE COMPANIES THAT CREATE RACIST TECH.
AND, LIKE, SHOULDN'T WE BE PREPARED TO HAVE JOBS DOING STUFF WE CARE ABOUT WHILE MAKING A LIVING DOING IT?
I KNOW MY PARENTS WANT THAT FOR ME, AND THAT'S WHY THEY'RE WORKING SO HARD IN THIS COUNTRY.
SHOULDN'T WE GET THE SAME EDUCATION AND OPPORTUNITIES AS KIDS IN THE FANCY SCHOOLS?

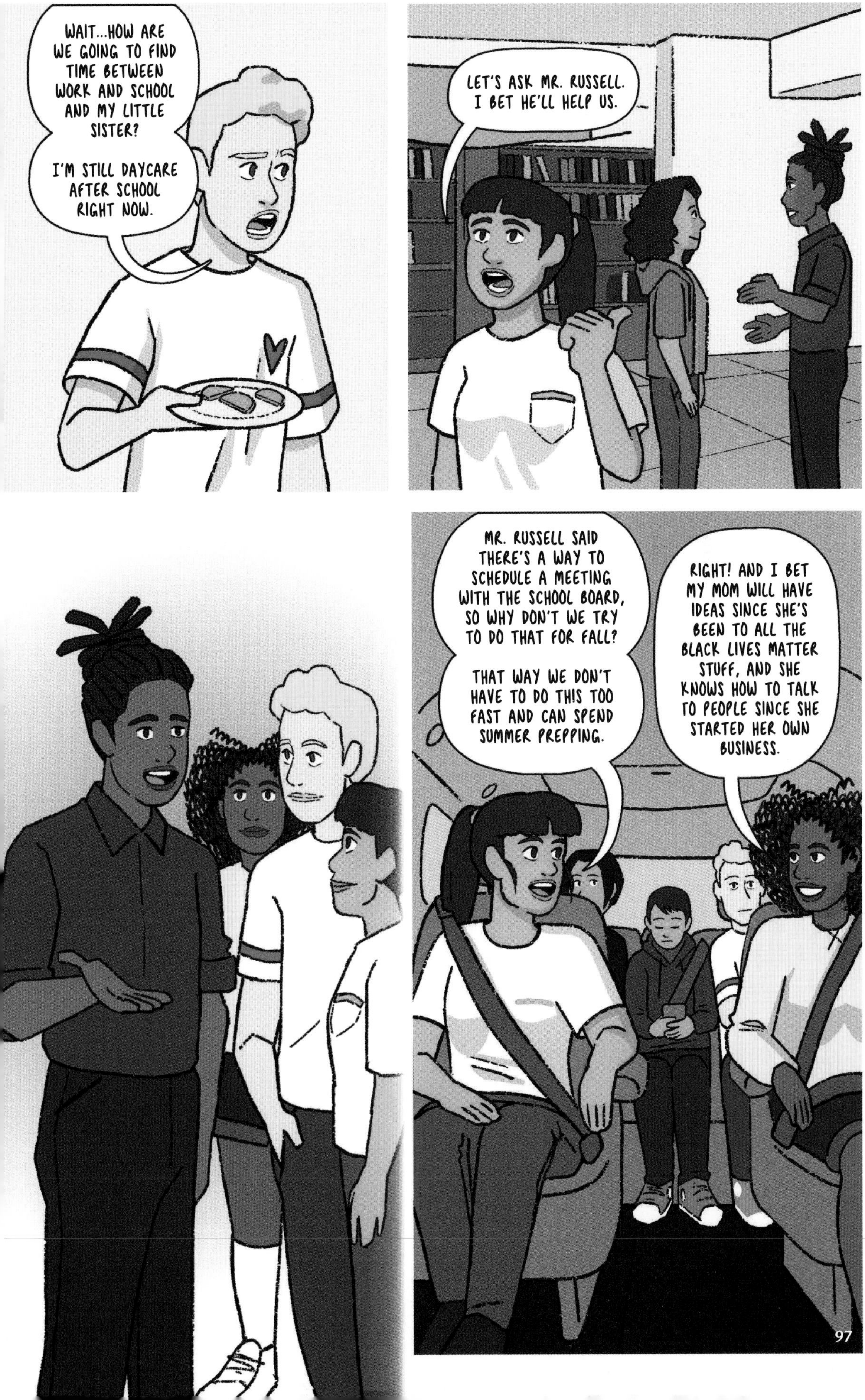
WAIT...HOW ARE WE GOING TO FIND TIME BETWEEN WORK AND SCHOOL AND MY LITTLE SISTER?
I'M STILL DAYCARE AFTER SCHOOL RIGHT NOW.
LET'S ASK MR. RUSSELL. I BET HE'LL HELP US.
MR. RUSSELL SAID THERE'S A WAY TO SCHEDULE A MEETING WITH THE SCHOOL BOARD, SO WHY DON'T WE TRY TO DO THAT FOR FALL?
THAT WAY WE DON'T HAVE TO DO THIS TOO FAST AND CAN SPEND SUMMER PREPPING.
RIGHT! AND I BET MY MOM WILL HAVE IDEAS SINCE SHE'S BEEN TO ALL THE BLACK LIVES MATTER STUFF, AND SHE KNOWS HOW TO TALK TO PEOPLE SINCE SHE STARTED HER OWN BUSINESS.

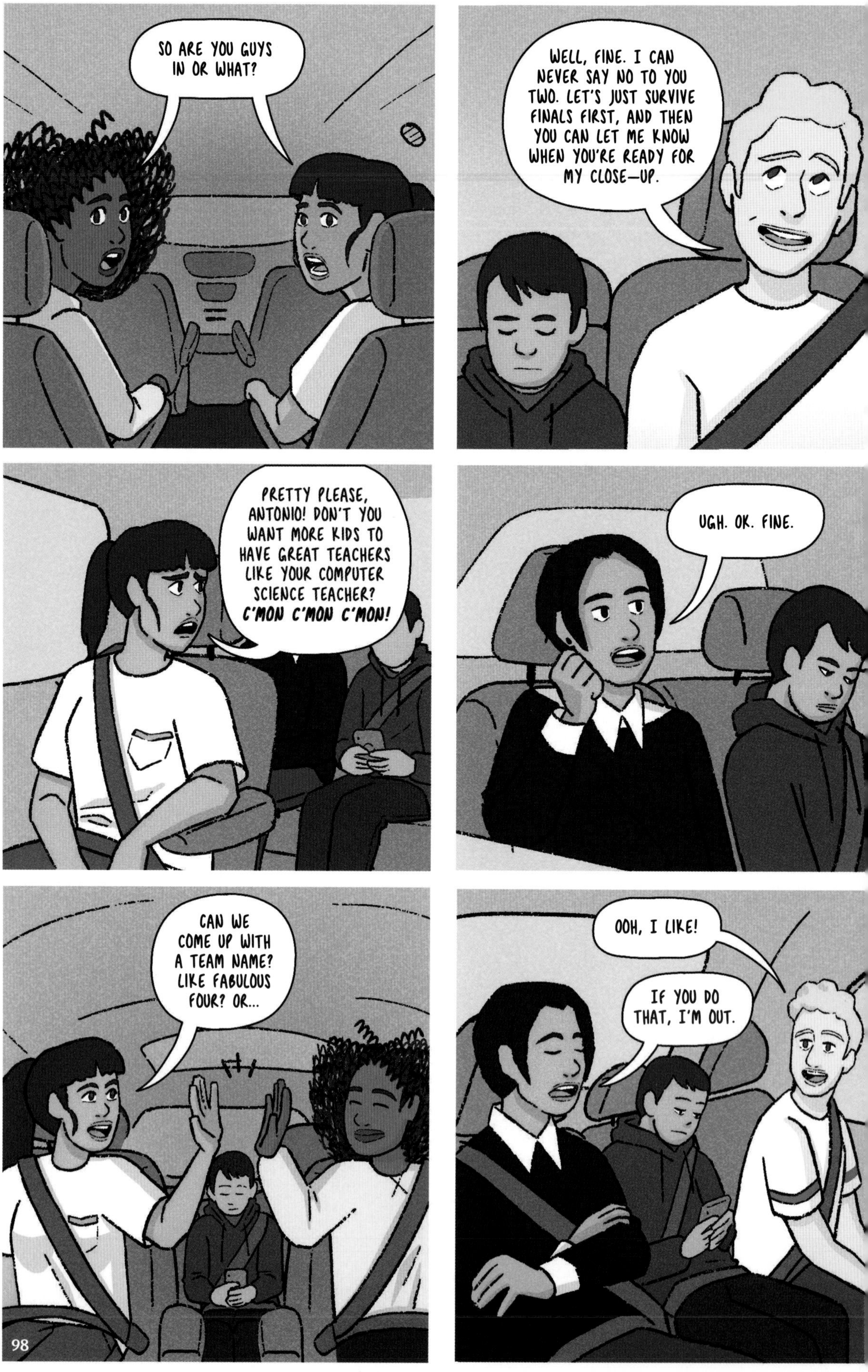
SO ARE YOU GUYS IN OR WHAT?
WELL, FINE. I CAN NEVER SAY NO TO YOU TWO. LET'S JUST SURVIVE FINALS FIRST, AND THEN YOU CAN LET ME KNOW WHEN YOU'RE READY FOR MY CLOSE-UP.
PRETTY PLEASE, ANTONIO! DON'T YOU WANT MORE KIDS TO HAVE GREAT TEACHERS LIKE YOUR COMPUTER SCIENCE TEACHER? C'MON C'MON C'MON!
UGH. OK. FINE.
CAN WE COME UP WITH A TEAM NAME? LIKE FABULOUS FOUR? OR...
OOH, I LIKE!
IF YOU DO THAT, I'M OUT.

CHAPTER 7

STUDENTS TAKE LEAD: COMPUTER SCIENCE FOR ALL

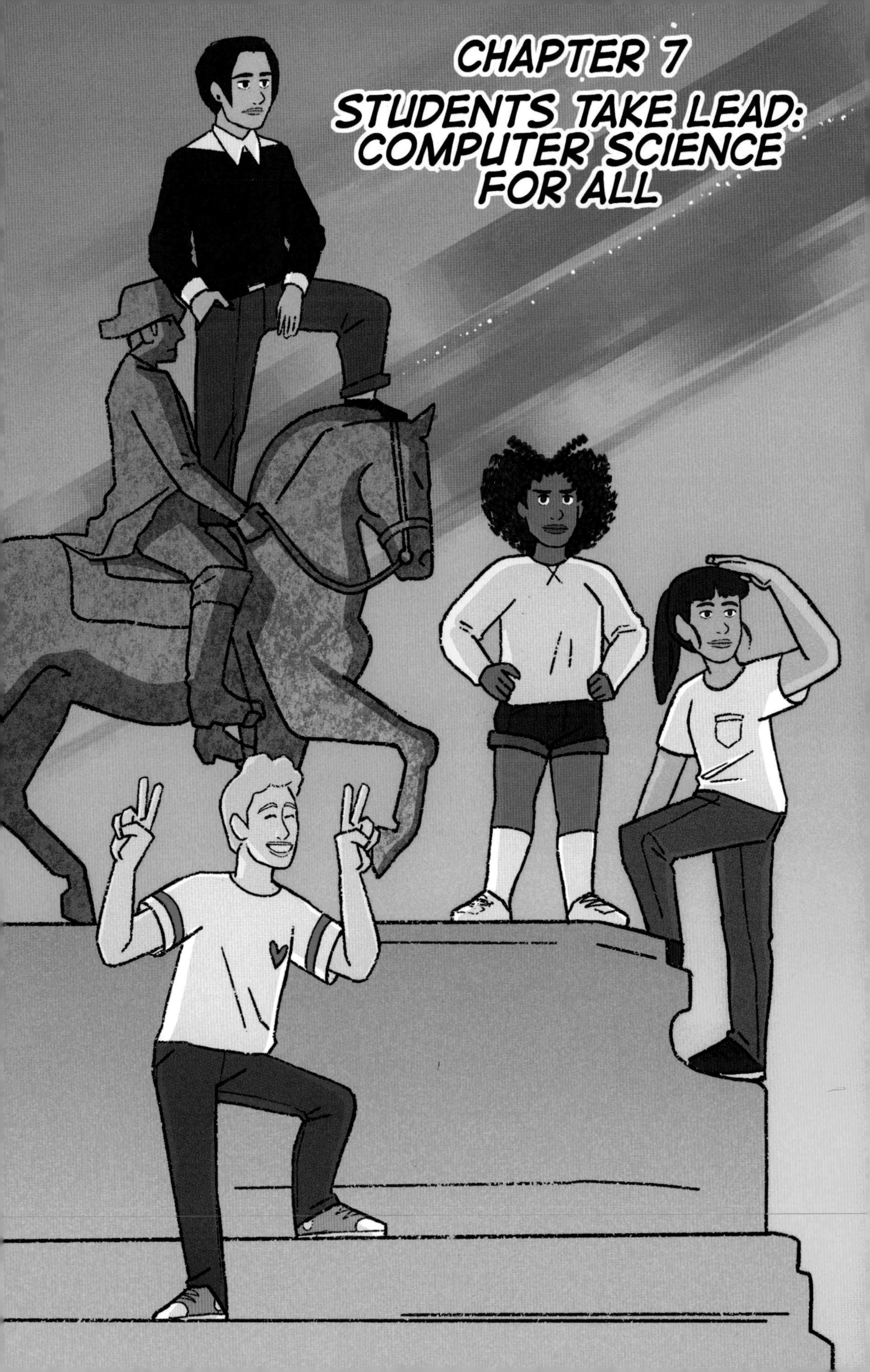

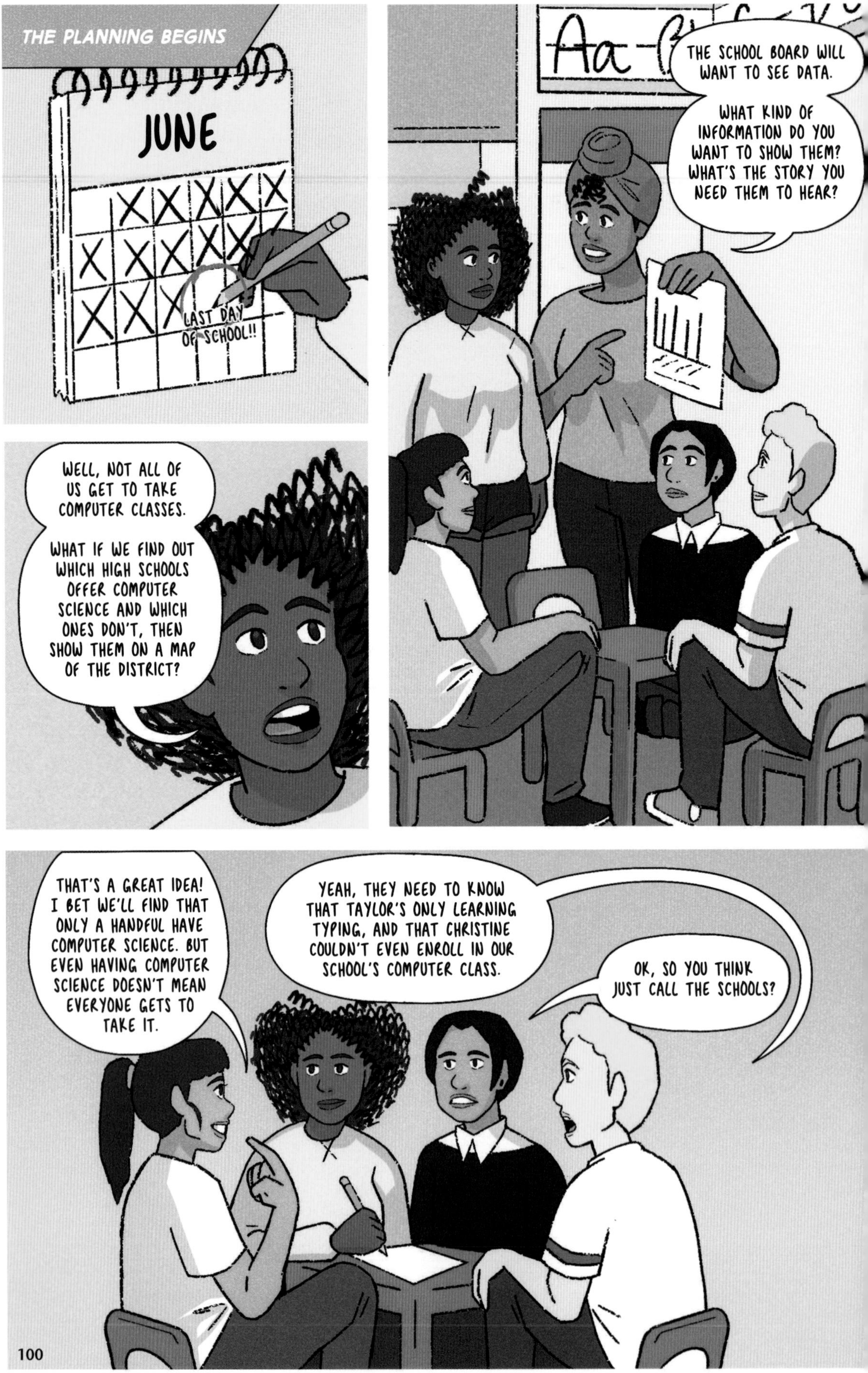
THE PLANNING BEGINS
JUNE
LAST DAY OF SCHOOL!!
THE SCHOOL BOARD WILL WANT TO SEE DATA.
WHAT KIND OF INFORMATION DO YOU WANT TO SHOW THEM? WHAT'S THE STORY YOU NEED THEM TO HEAR?
WELL, NOT ALL OF US GET TO TAKE COMPUTER CLASSES.
WHAT IF WE FIND OUT WHICH HIGH SCHOOLS OFFER COMPUTER SCIENCE AND WHICH ONES DON'T, THEN SHOW THEM ON A MAP OF THE DISTRICT?
THAT'S A GREAT IDEA! I BET WE'LL FIND THAT ONLY A HANDFUL HAVE COMPUTER SCIENCE. BUT EVEN HAVING COMPUTER SCIENCE DOESN'T MEAN EVERYONE GETS TO TAKE IT.
YEAH, THEY NEED TO KNOW THAT TAYLOR'S ONLY LEARNING TYPING, AND THAT CHRISTINE COULDN'T EVEN ENROLL IN OUR SCHOOL'S COMPUTER CLASS.
OK, SO YOU THINK JUST CALL THE SCHOOLS?

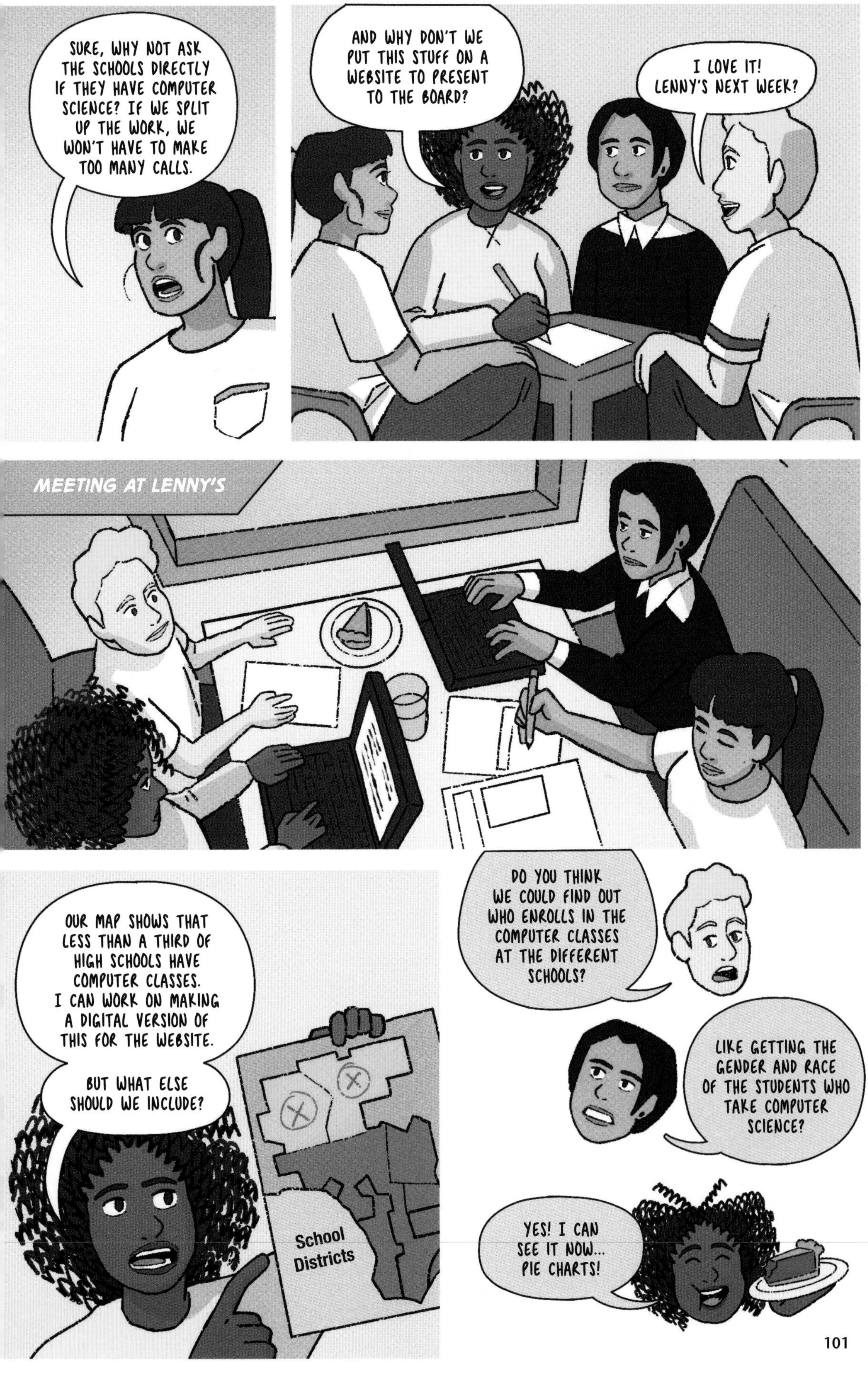

SURE, WHY NOT ASK THE SCHOOLS DIRECTLY IF THEY HAVE COMPUTER SCIENCE? IF WE SPLIT UP THE WORK, WE WON'T HAVE TO MAKE TOO MANY CALLS.
AND WHY DON'T WE PUT THIS STUFF ON A WEBSITE TO PRESENT TO THE BOARD?
I LOVE IT! LENNY'S NEXT WEEK?
MEETING AT LENNY'S
OUR MAP SHOWS THAT LESS THAN A THIRD OF HIGH SCHOOLS HAVE COMPUTER CLASSES. I CAN WORK ON MAKING A DIGITAL VERSION OF THIS FOR THE WEBSITE.
BUT WHAT ELSE SHOULD WE INCLUDE?
School Districts
DO YOU THINK WE COULD FIND OUT WHO ENROLLS IN THE COMPUTER CLASSES AT THE DIFFERENT SCHOOLS?
LIKE GETTING THE GENDER AND RACE OF THE STUDENTS WHO TAKE COMPUTER SCIENCE?
YES! I CAN SEE IT NOW... PIE CHARTS!

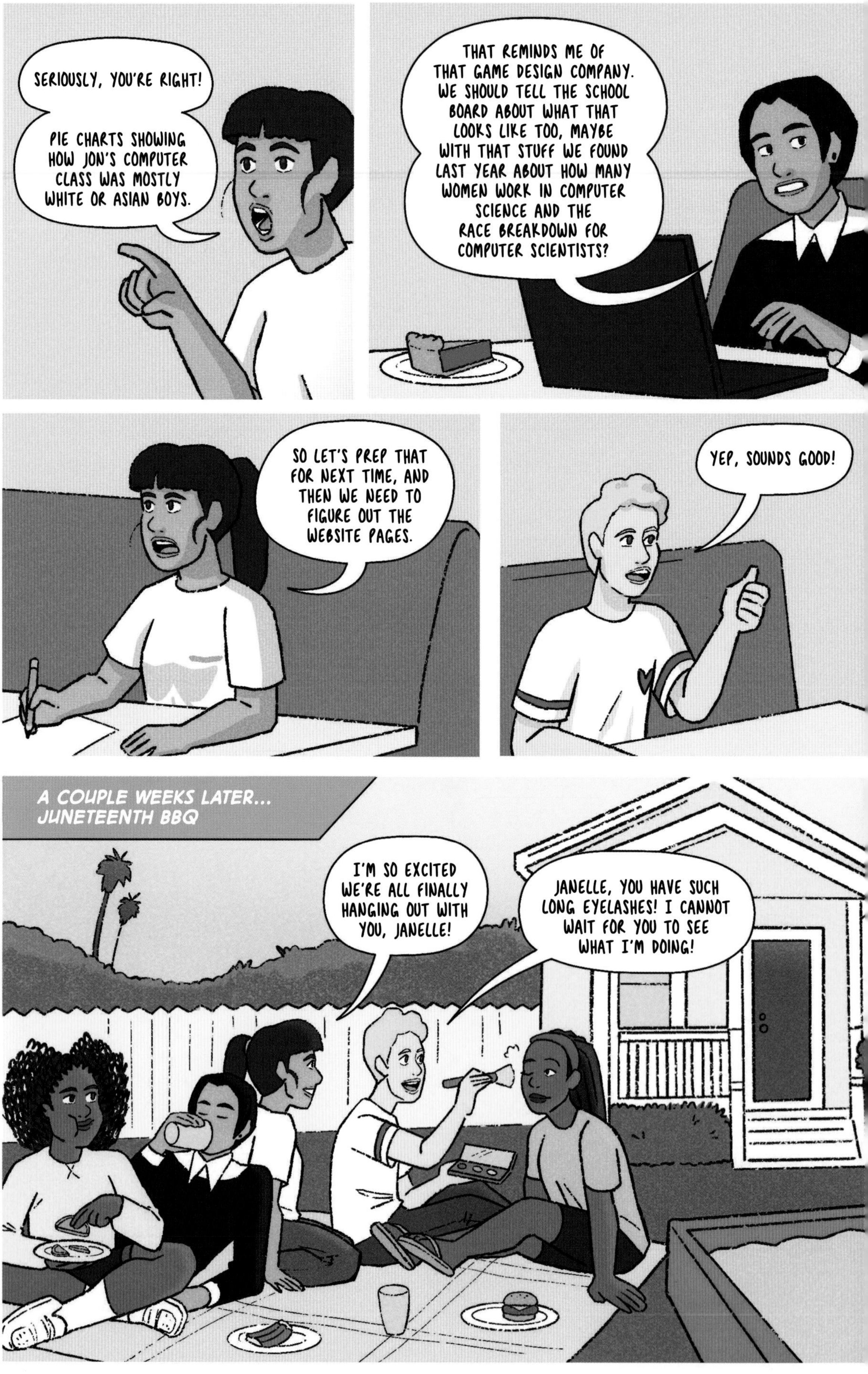
SERIOUSLY, YOU'RE RIGHT!
PIE CHARTS SHOWING HOW JON'S COMPUTER CLASS WAS MOSTLY WHITE OR ASIAN BOYS.
THAT REMINDS ME OF THAT GAME DESIGN COMPANY. WE SHOULD TELL THE SCHOOL BOARD ABOUT WHAT THAT LOOKS LIKE TOO, MAYBE WITH THAT STUFF WE FOUND LAST YEAR ABOUT HOW MANY WOMEN WORK IN COMPUTER SCIENCE AND THE RACE BREAKDOWN FOR COMPUTER SCIENTISTS?
SO LET'S PREP THAT FOR NEXT TIME, AND THEN WE NEED TO FIGURE OUT THE WEBSITE PAGES.
YEP, SOUNDS GOOD!
A COUPLE WEEKS LATER...
JUNETEENTH BBQ
I'M SO EXCITED WE'RE ALL FINALLY HANGING OUT WITH YOU, JANELLE!
JANELLE, YOU HAVE SUCH LONG EYELASHES! I CANNOT WAIT FOR YOU TO SEE WHAT I'M DOING!

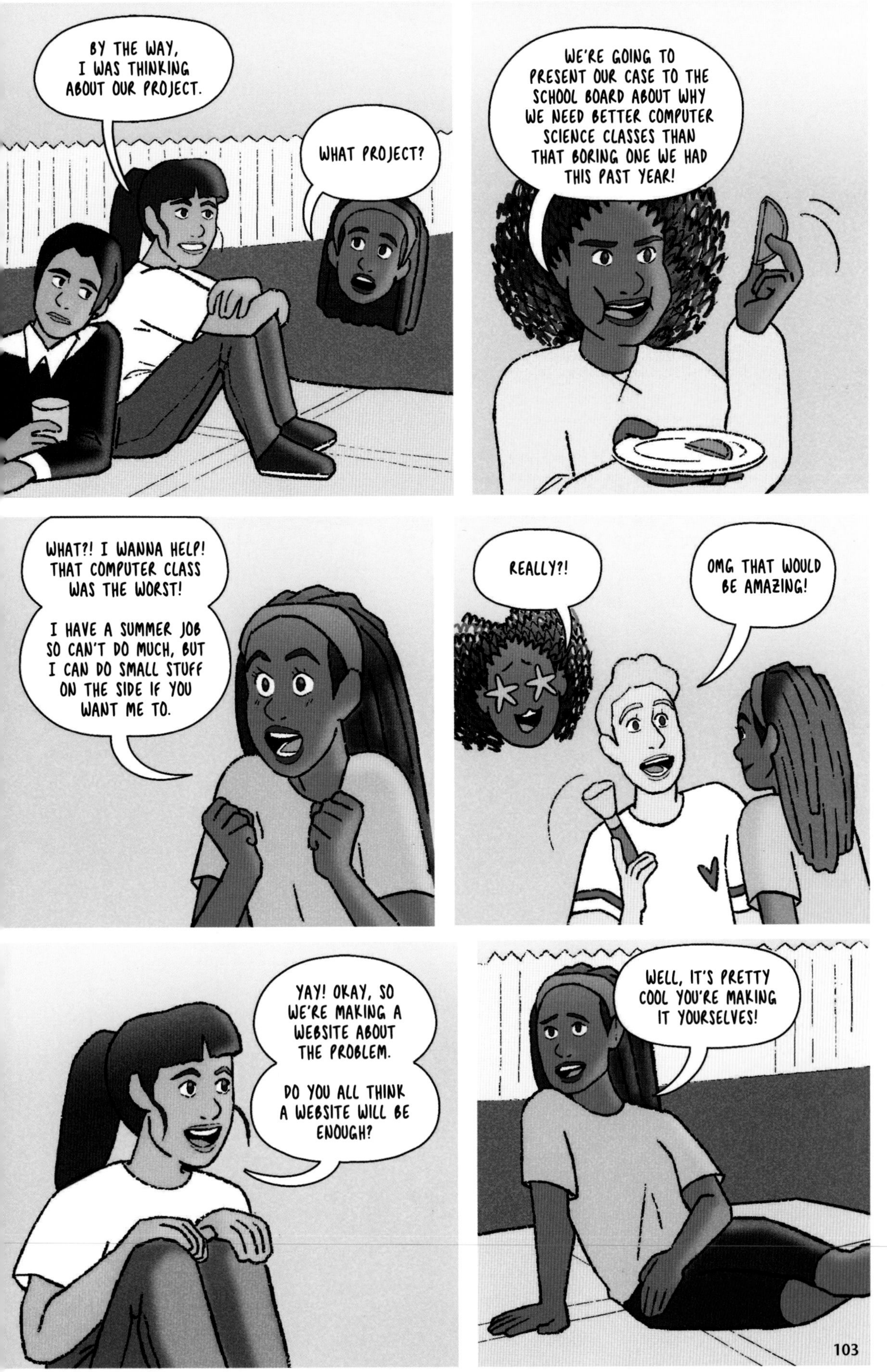
BY THE WAY, I WAS THINKING ABOUT OUR PROJECT.
WHAT PROJECT?
WE'RE GOING TO PRESENT OUR CASE TO THE SCHOOL BOARD ABOUT WHY WE NEED BETTER COMPUTER SCIENCE CLASSES THAN THAT BORING ONE WE HAD THIS PAST YEAR!
WHAT?! I WANNA HELP! THAT COMPUTER CLASS WAS THE WORST!
I HAVE A SUMMER JOB SO CAN'T DO MUCH, BUT I CAN DO SMALL STUFF ON THE SIDE IF YOU WANT ME TO.
REALLY?!
OMG THAT WOULD BE AMAZING!
YAY! OKAY, SO WE'RE MAKING A WEBSITE ABOUT THE PROBLEM.
DO YOU ALL THINK A WEBSITE WILL BE ENOUGH?
WELL, IT'S PRETTY COOL YOU'RE MAKING IT YOURSELVES!

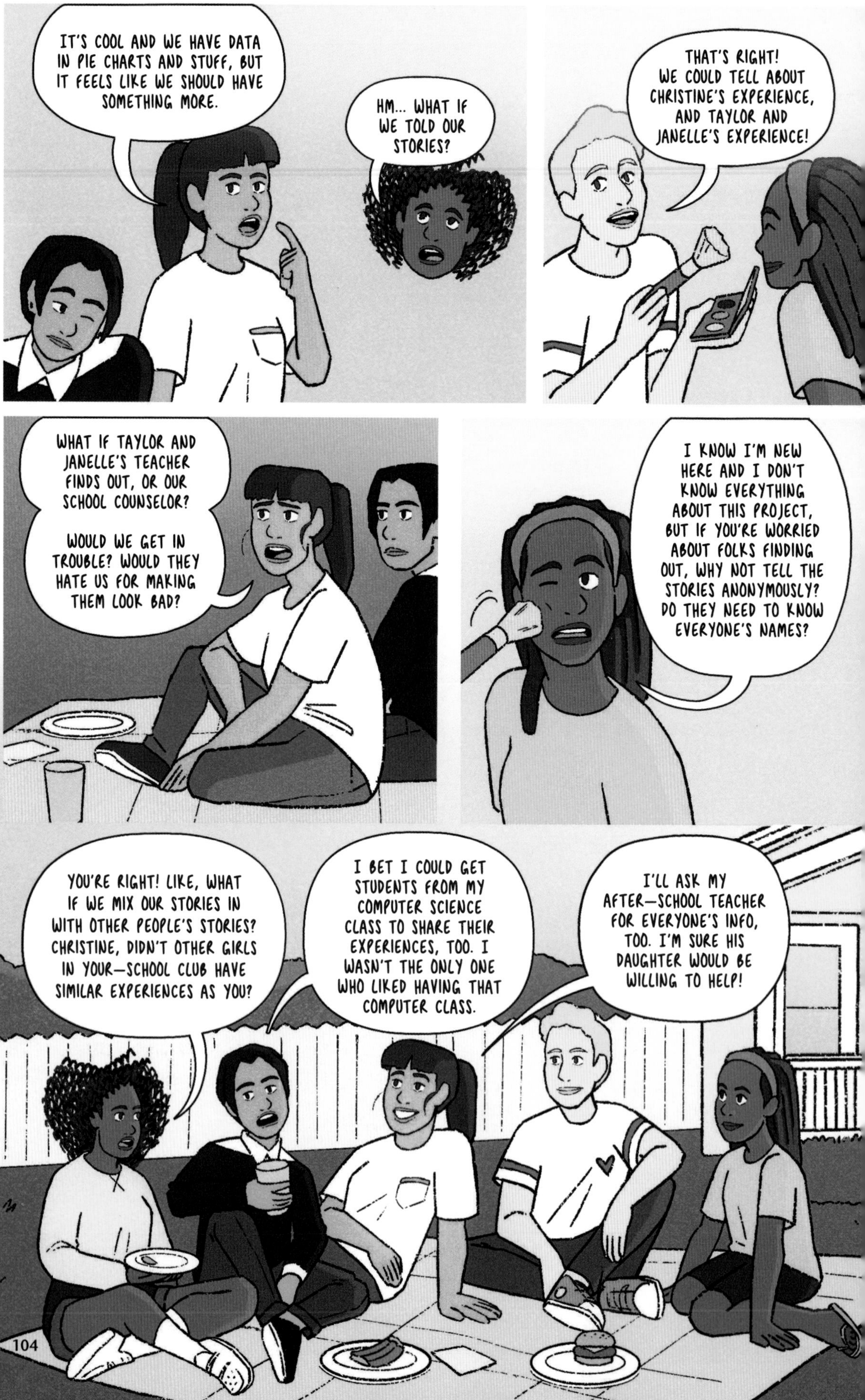
IT'S COOL AND WE HAVE DATA IN PIE CHARTS AND STUFF, BUT IT FEELS LIKE WE SHOULD HAVE SOMETHING MORE.
HM... WHAT IF WE TOLD OUR STORIES?
THAT'S RIGHT! WE COULD TELL ABOUT CHRISTINE'S EXPERIENCE, AND TAYLOR AND JANELLE'S EXPERIENCE!
WHAT IF TAYLOR AND JANELLE'S TEACHER FINDS OUT, OR OUR SCHOOL COUNSELOR?
WOULD WE GET IN TROUBLE? WOULD THEY HATE US FOR MAKING THEM LOOK BAD?
I KNOW I'M NEW HERE AND I DON'T KNOW EVERYTHING ABOUT THIS PROJECT, BUT IF YOU'RE WORRIED ABOUT FOLKS FINDING OUT, WHY NOT TELL THE STORIES ANONYMOUSLY? DO THEY NEED TO KNOW EVERYONE'S NAMES?
YOU'RE RIGHT! LIKE, WHAT IF WE MIX OUR STORIES IN WITH OTHER PEOPLE'S STORIES? CHRISTINE, DIDN'T OTHER GIRLS IN YOUR—SCHOOL CLUB HAVE SIMILAR EXPERIENCES AS YOU?
I BET I COULD GET STUDENTS FROM MY COMPUTER SCIENCE CLASS TO SHARE THEIR EXPERIENCES, TOO. I WASN'T THE ONLY ONE WHO LIKED HAVING THAT COMPUTER CLASS.
I'LL ASK MY AFTER—SCHOOL TEACHER FOR EVERYONE'S INFO, TOO. I'M SURE HIS DAUGHTER WOULD BE WILLING TO HELP!

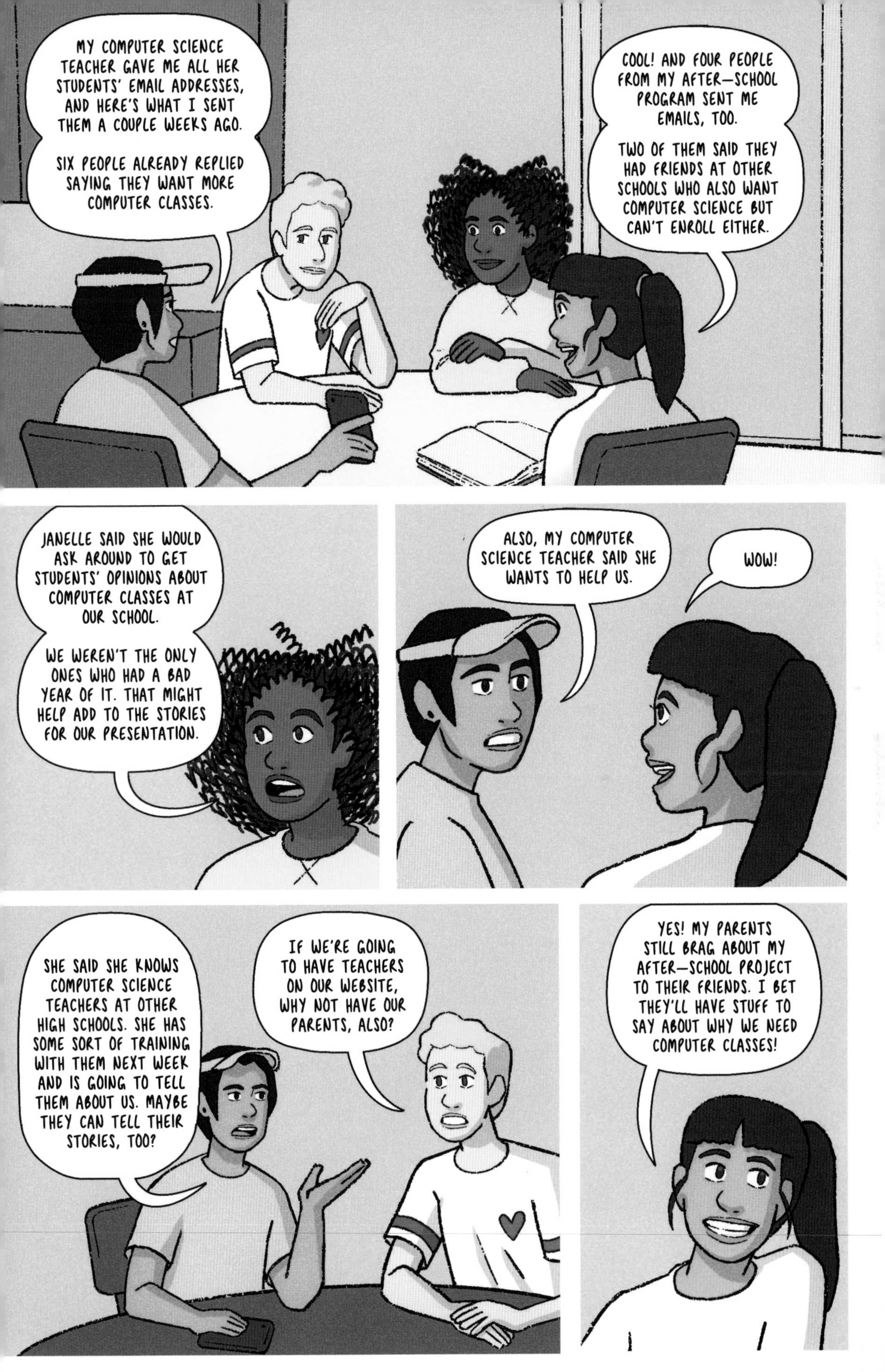
MY COMPUTER SCIENCE TEACHER GAVE ME ALL HER STUDENTS' EMAIL ADDRESSES, AND HERE'S WHAT I SENT THEM A COUPLE WEEKS AGO.
SIX PEOPLE ALREADY REPLIED SAYING THEY WANT MORE COMPUTER CLASSES.
COOL! AND FOUR PEOPLE FROM MY AFTER-SCHOOL PROGRAM SENT ME EMAILS, TOO.
TWO OF THEM SAID THEY HAD FRIENDS AT OTHER SCHOOLS WHO ALSO WANT COMPUTER SCIENCE BUT CAN'T ENROLL EITHER.
JANELLE SAID SHE WOULD ASK AROUND TO GET STUDENTS' OPINIONS ABOUT COMPUTER CLASSES AT OUR SCHOOL.
WE WEREN'T THE ONLY ONES WHO HAD A BAD YEAR OF IT. THAT MIGHT HELP ADD TO THE STORIES FOR OUR PRESENTATION.
ALSO, MY COMPUTER SCIENCE TEACHER SAID SHE WANTS TO HELP US.
WOW!
SHE SAID SHE KNOWS COMPUTER SCIENCE TEACHERS AT OTHER HIGH SCHOOLS. SHE HAS SOME SORT OF TRAINING WITH THEM NEXT WEEK AND IS GOING TO TELL THEM ABOUT US. MAYBE THEY CAN TELL THEIR STORIES, TOO?
IF WE'RE GOING TO HAVE TEACHERS ON OUR WEBSITE, WHY NOT HAVE OUR PARENTS, ALSO?
YES! MY PARENTS STILL BRAG ABOUT MY AFTER-SCHOOL PROJECT TO THEIR FRIENDS. I BET THEY'LL HAVE STUFF TO SAY ABOUT WHY WE NEED COMPUTER CLASSES!

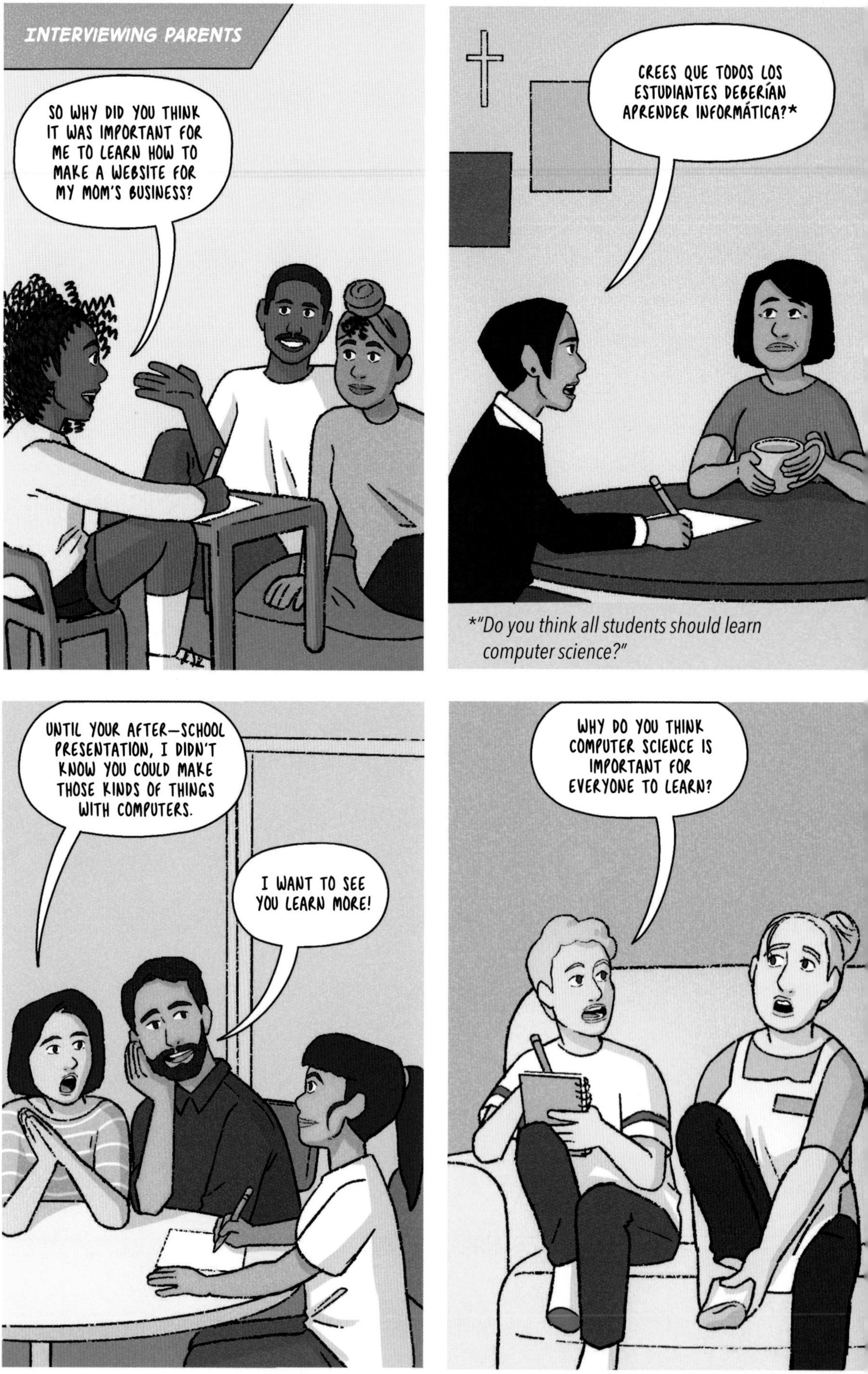
INTERVIEWING PARENTS
SO WHY DID YOU THINK IT WAS IMPORTANT FOR ME TO LEARN HOW TO MAKE A WEBSITE FOR MY MOM'S BUSINESS?
CREES QUE TODOS LOS ESTUDIANTES DEBERÍAN APRENDER INFORMÁTICA?*
UNTIL YOUR AFTER-SCHOOL PRESENTATION, I DIDN'T KNOW YOU COULD MAKE THOSE KINDS OF THINGS WITH COMPUTERS.
I WANT TO SEE YOU LEARN MORE!
WHY DO YOU THINK COMPUTER SCIENCE IS IMPORTANT FOR EVERYONE TO LEARN?

*"Do you think all students should learn computer science?"

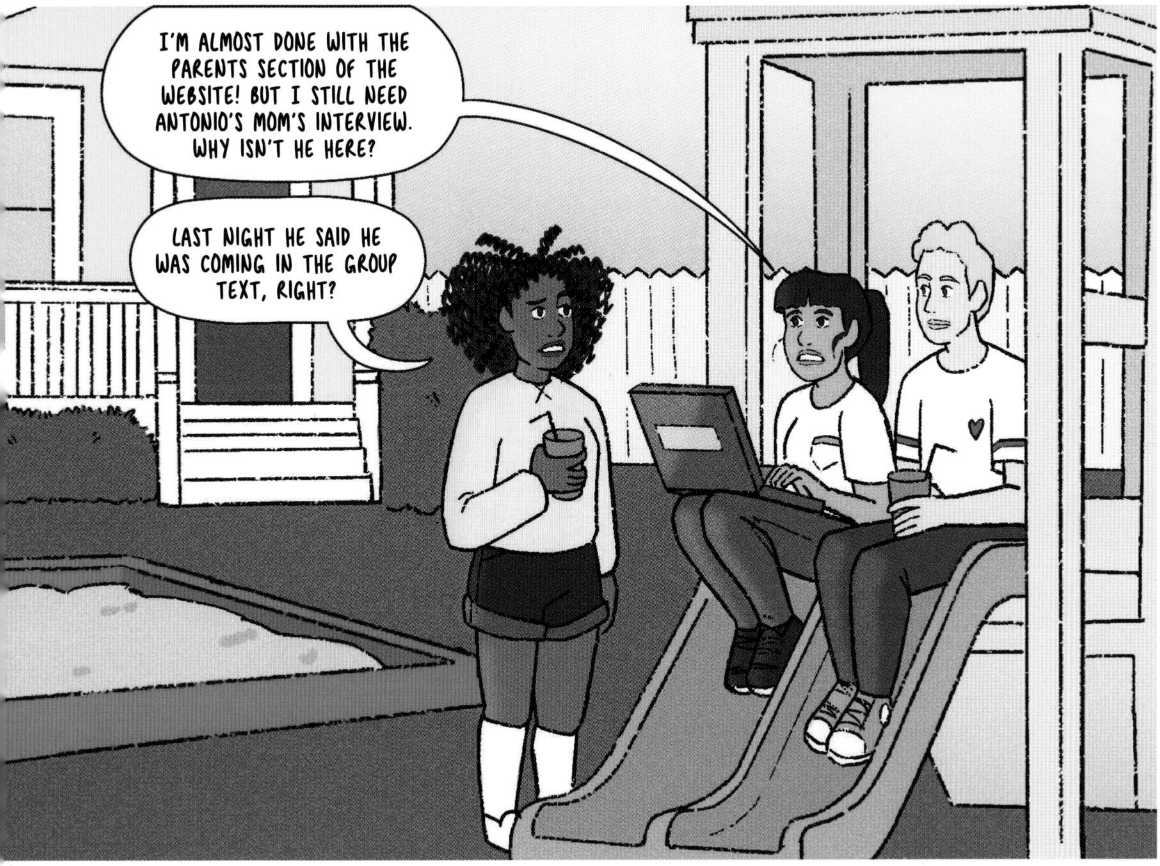
I'M ALMOST DONE WITH THE PARENTS SECTION OF THE WEBSITE! BUT I STILL NEED ANTONIO'S MOM'S INTERVIEW. WHY ISN'T HE HERE?
LAST NIGHT HE SAID HE WAS COMING IN THE GROUP TEXT, RIGHT?

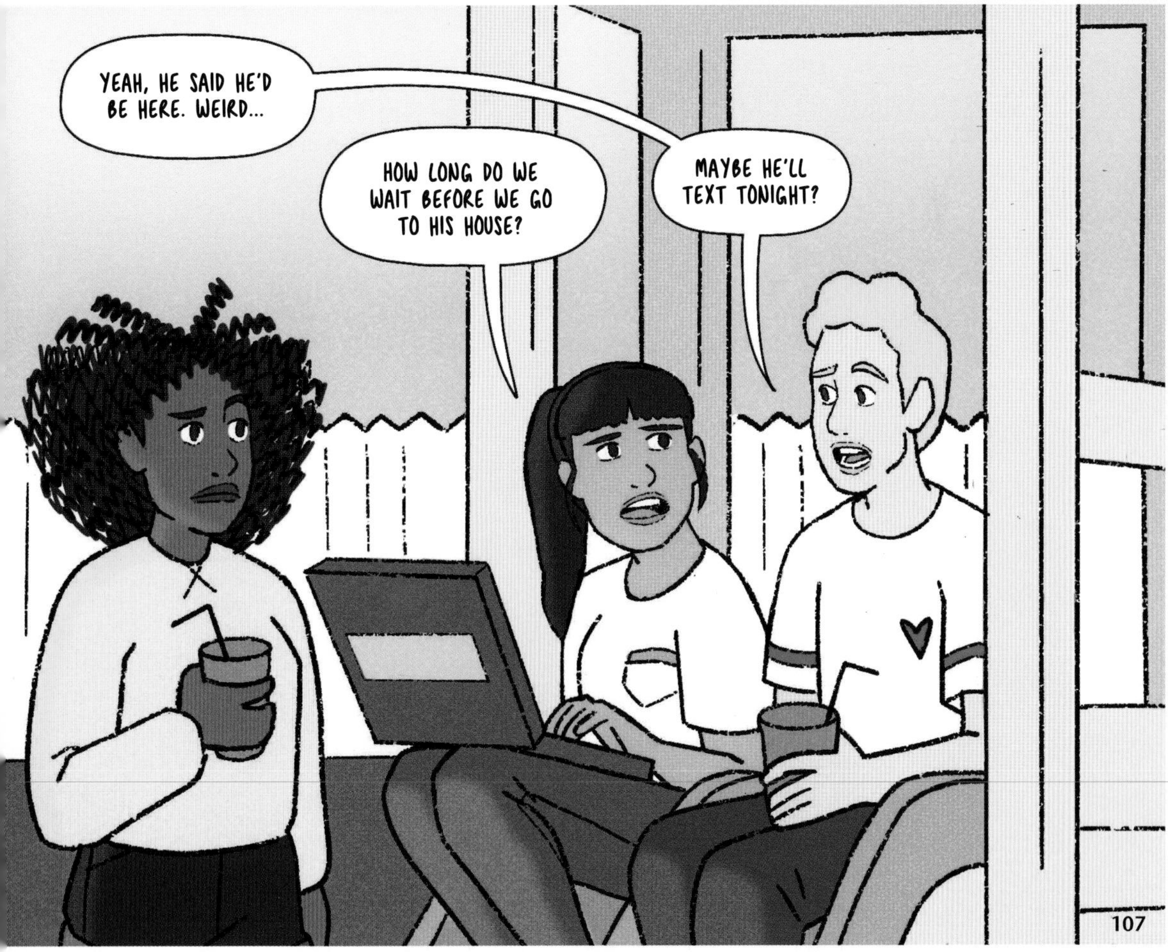
YEAH, HE SAID HE'D BE HERE. WEIRD...
HOW LONG DO WE WAIT BEFORE WE GO TO HIS HOUSE?
MAYBE HE'LL TEXT TONIGHT?

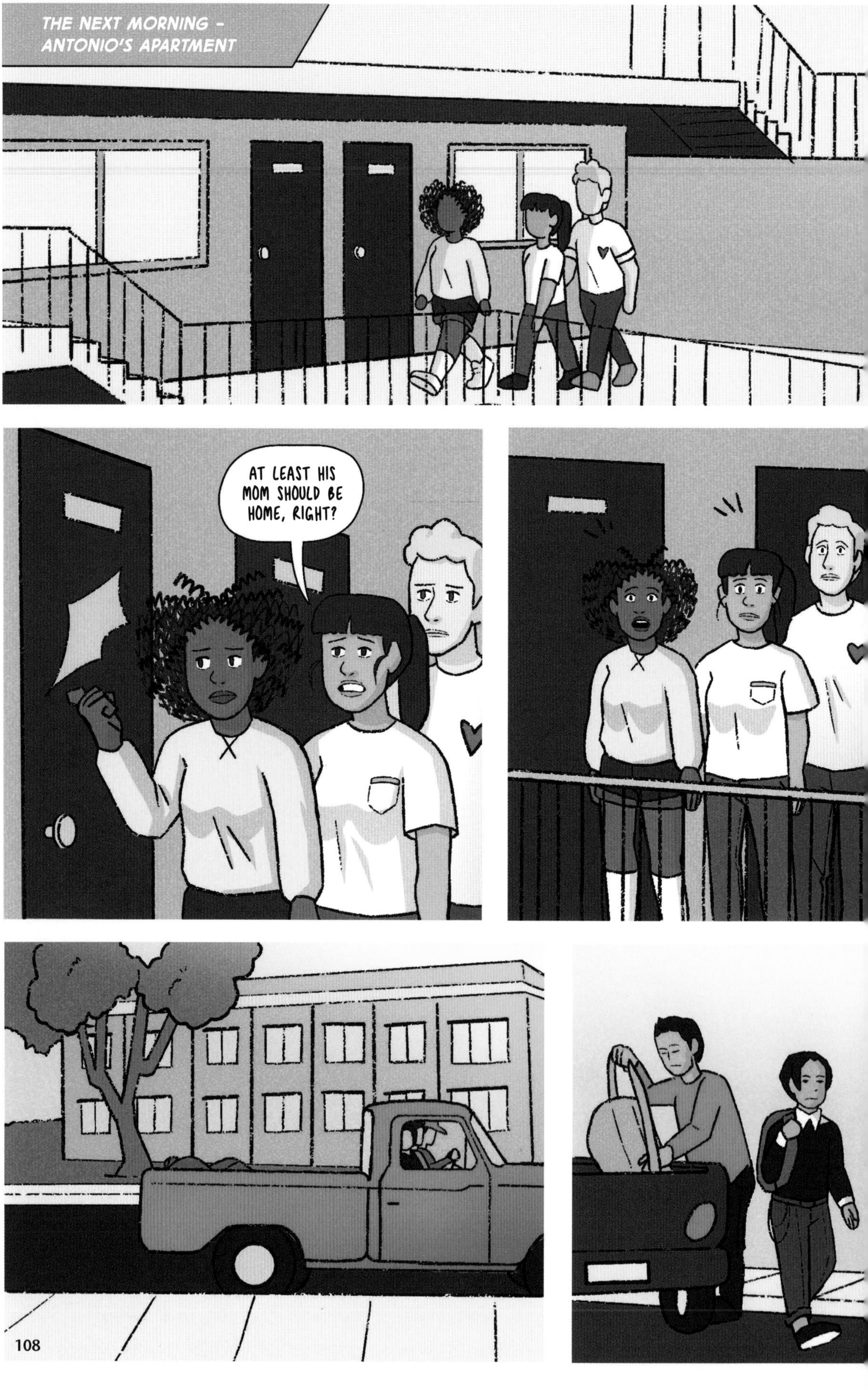
THE NEXT MORNING – ANTONIO'S APARTMENT
AT LEAST HIS MOM SHOULD BE HOME, RIGHT?

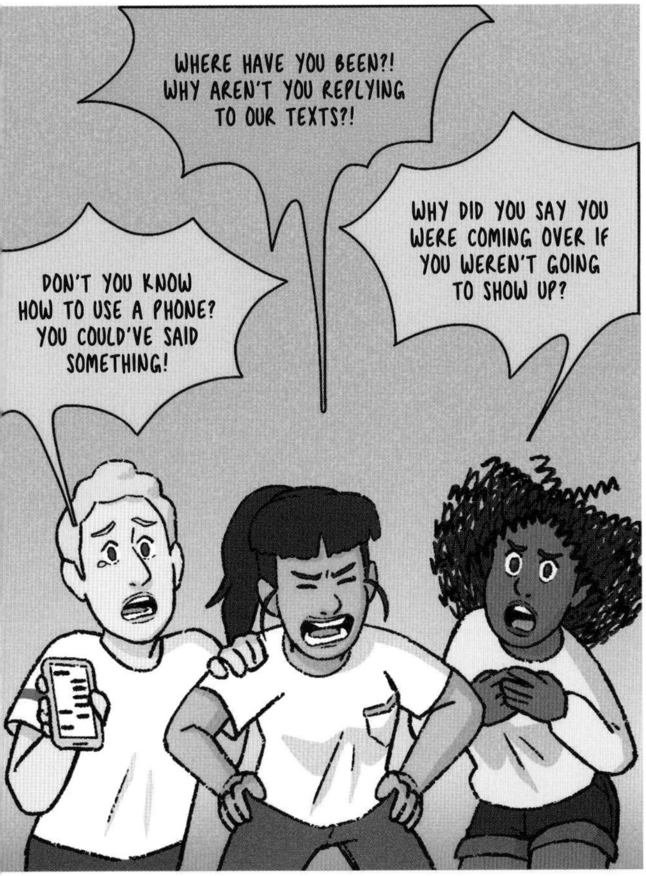
WHERE HAVE YOU BEEN?! WHY AREN'T YOU REPLYING TO OUR TEXTS?!
DON'T YOU KNOW HOW TO USE A PHONE? YOU COULD'VE SAID SOMETHING!
WHY DID YOU SAY YOU WERE COMING OVER IF YOU WEREN'T GOING TO SHOW UP?

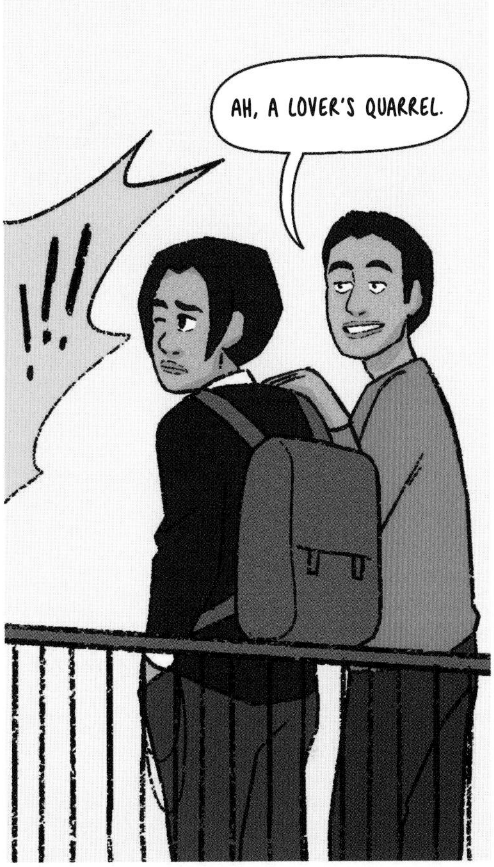
AH, A LOVER'S QUARREL.
!!!

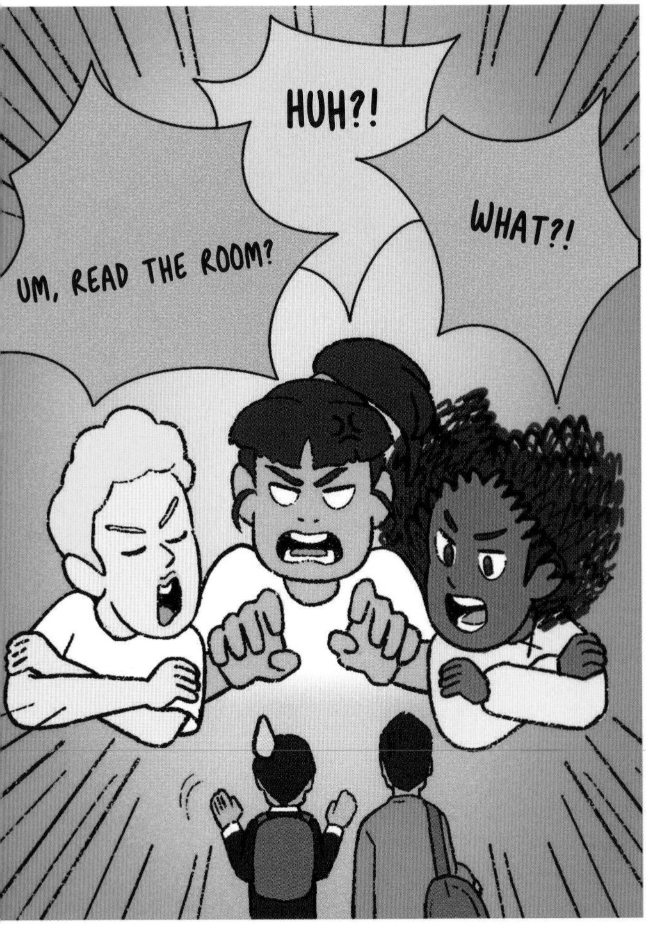
HUH?!
UM, READ THE ROOM?
WHAT?!

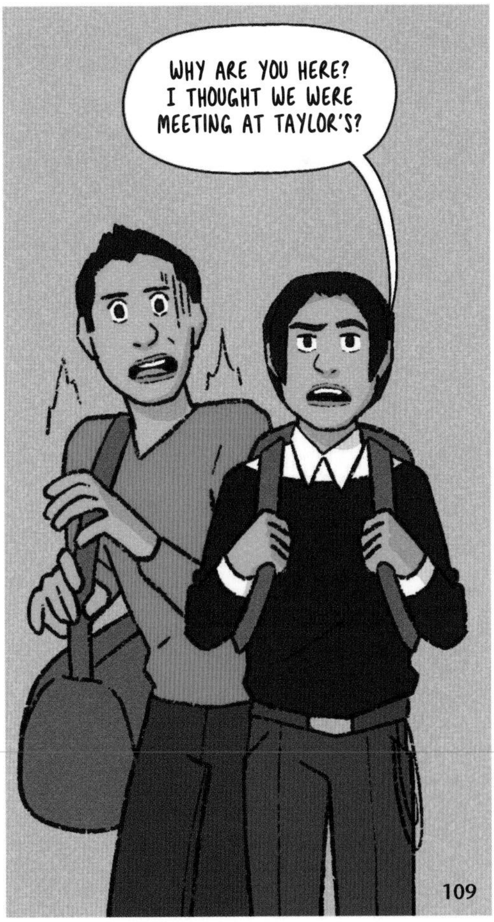
WHY ARE YOU HERE? I THOUGHT WE WERE MEETING AT TAYLOR'S?

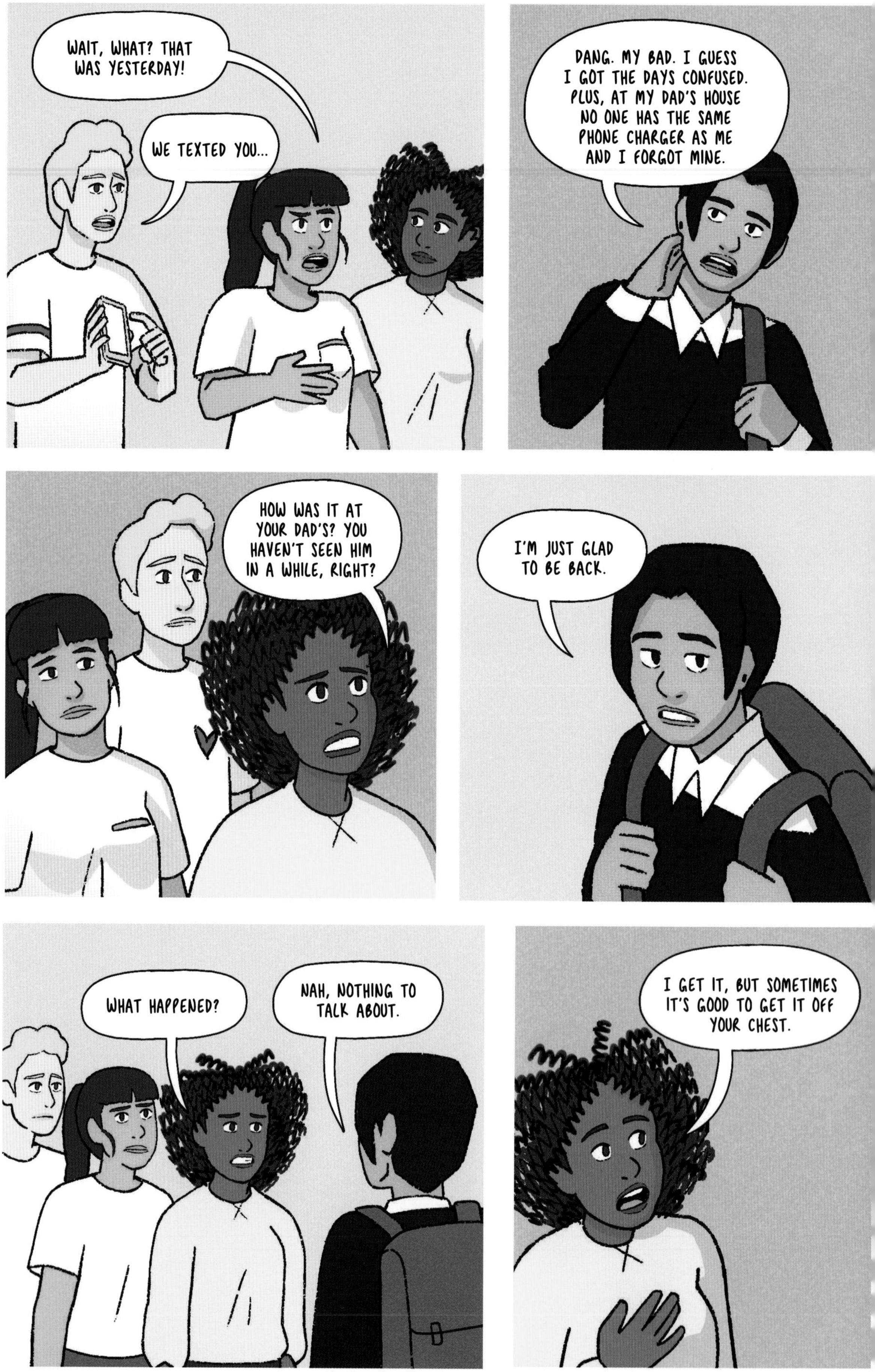
WAIT, WHAT? THAT WAS YESTERDAY!
WE TEXTED YOU...
DANG. MY BAD. I GUESS I GOT THE DAYS CONFUSED. PLUS, AT MY DAD'S HOUSE NO ONE HAS THE SAME PHONE CHARGER AS ME AND I FORGOT MINE.
HOW WAS IT AT YOUR DAD'S? YOU HAVEN'T SEEN HIM IN A WHILE, RIGHT?
I'M JUST GLAD TO BE BACK.
WHAT HAPPENED?
NAH, NOTHING TO TALK ABOUT.
I GET IT, BUT SOMETIMES IT'S GOOD TO GET IT OFF YOUR CHEST.

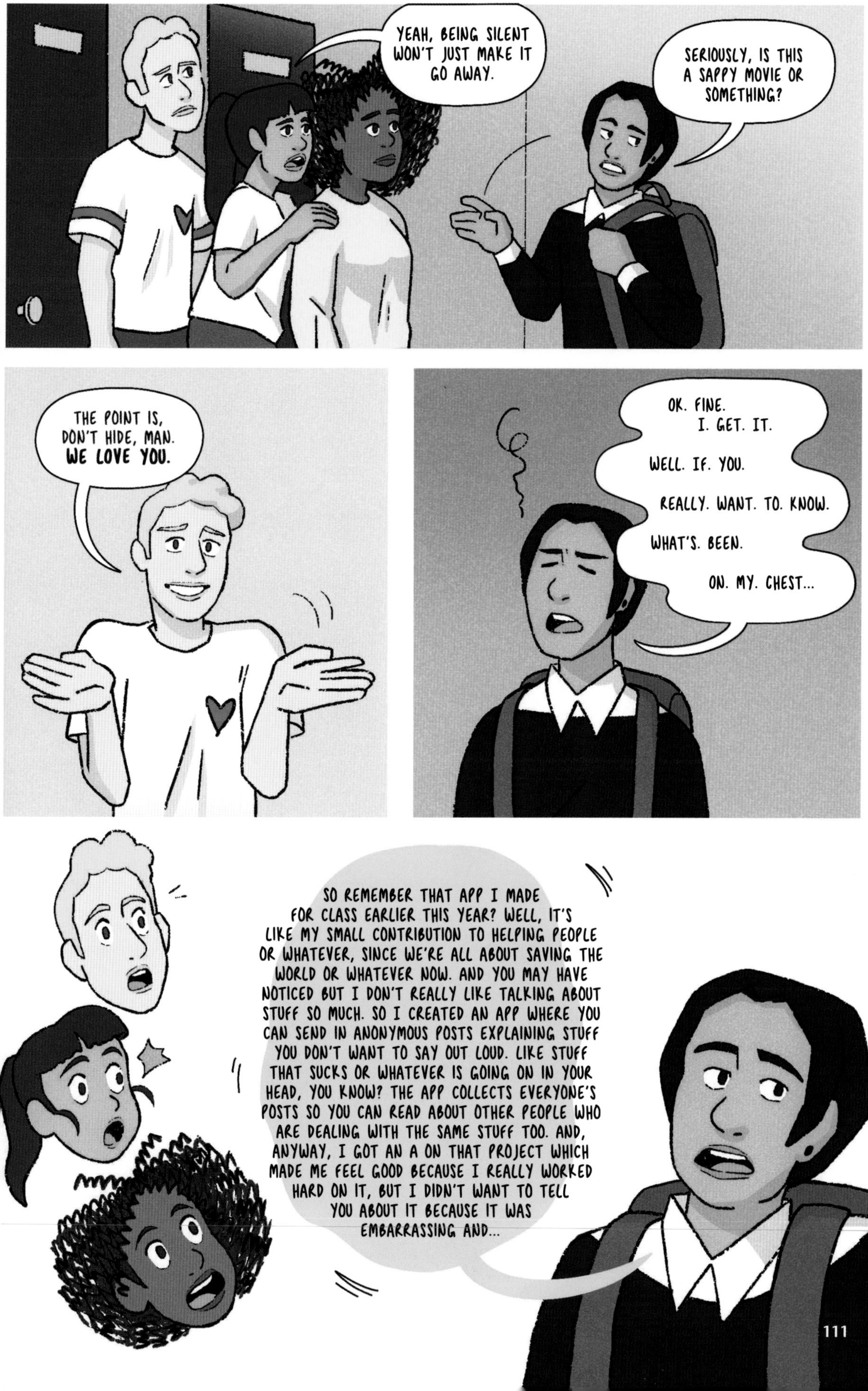
YEAH, BEING SILENT WON'T JUST MAKE IT GO AWAY.
SERIOUSLY, IS THIS A SAPPY MOVIE OR SOMETHING?
THE POINT IS, DON'T HIDE, MAN. **WE LOVE YOU.**
OK. FINE. I. GET. IT. WELL. IF. YOU. REALLY. WANT. TO. KNOW. WHAT'S. BEEN. ON. MY. CHEST...
SO REMEMBER THAT APP I MADE FOR CLASS EARLIER THIS YEAR? WELL, IT'S LIKE MY SMALL CONTRIBUTION TO HELPING PEOPLE OR WHATEVER, SINCE WE'RE ALL ABOUT SAVING THE WORLD OR WHATEVER NOW. AND YOU MAY HAVE NOTICED BUT I DON'T REALLY LIKE TALKING ABOUT STUFF SO MUCH. SO I CREATED AN APP WHERE YOU CAN SEND IN ANONYMOUS POSTS EXPLAINING STUFF YOU DON'T WANT TO SAY OUT LOUD. LIKE STUFF THAT SUCKS OR WHATEVER IS GOING ON IN YOUR HEAD, YOU KNOW? THE APP COLLECTS EVERYONE'S POSTS SO YOU CAN READ ABOUT OTHER PEOPLE WHO ARE DEALING WITH THE SAME STUFF TOO. AND, ANYWAY, I GOT AN A ON THAT PROJECT WHICH MADE ME FEEL GOOD BECAUSE I REALLY WORKED HARD ON IT, BUT I DIDN'T WANT TO TELL YOU ABOUT IT BECAUSE IT WAS EMBARRASSING AND...

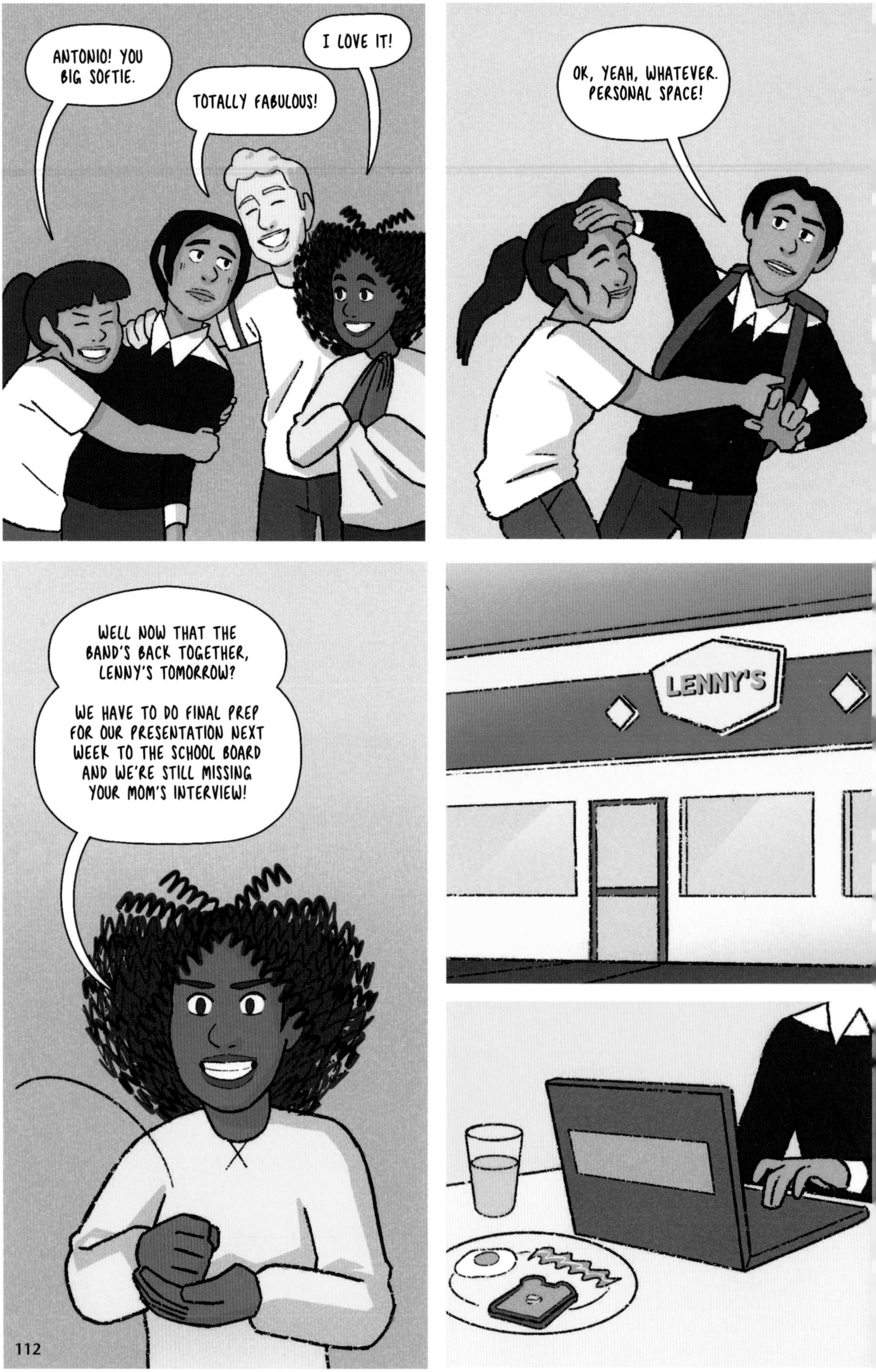
ANTONIO! YOU BIG SOFTIE.
TOTALLY FABULOUS!
I LOVE IT!
OK, YEAH, WHATEVER. PERSONAL SPACE!
WELL NOW THAT THE BAND'S BACK TOGETHER, LENNY'S TOMORROW?
WE HAVE TO DO FINAL PREP FOR OUR PRESENTATION NEXT WEEK TO THE SCHOOL BOARD AND WE'RE STILL MISSING YOUR MOM'S INTERVIEW!
LENNY'S

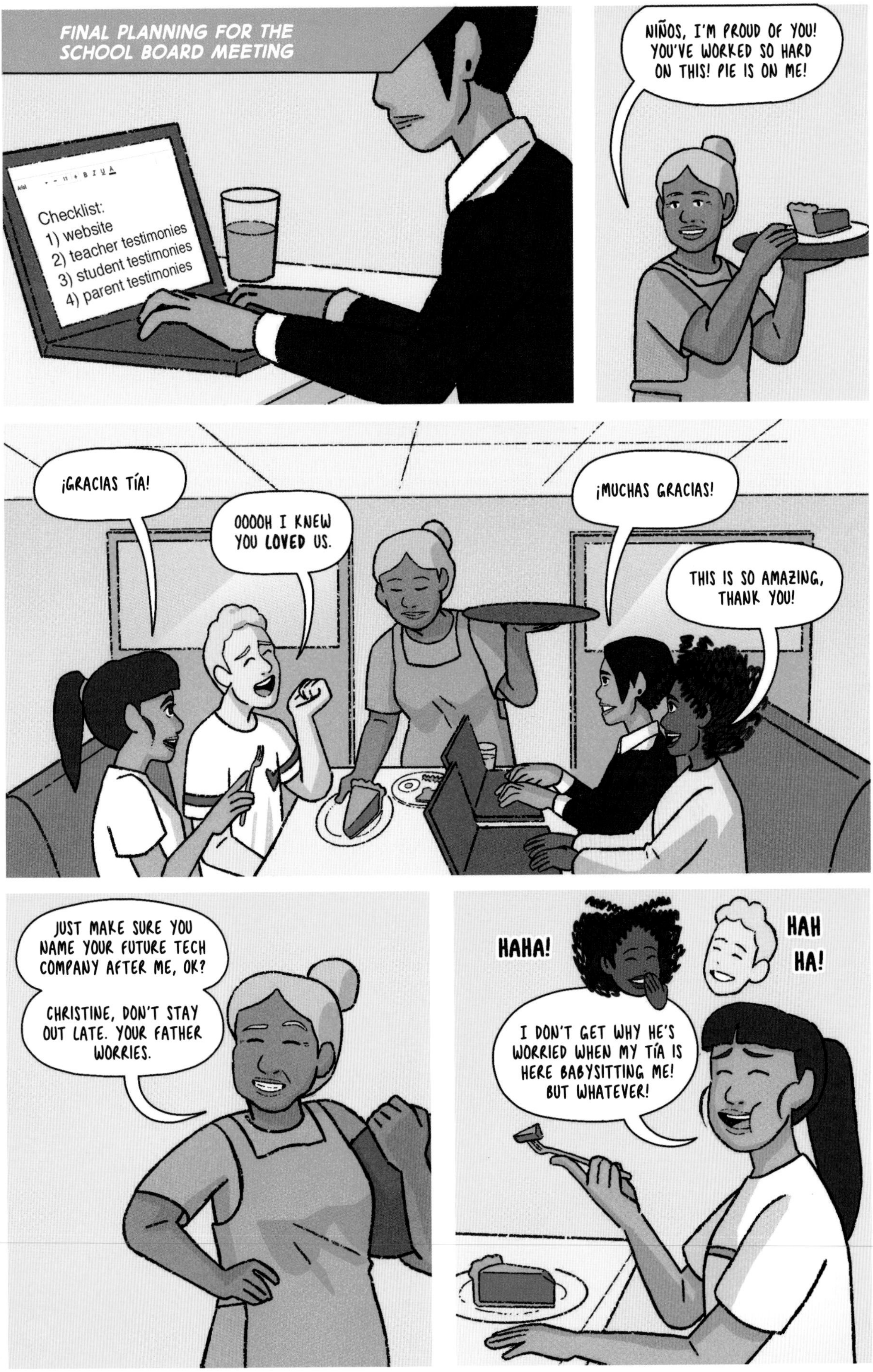
FINAL PLANNING FOR THE SCHOOL BOARD MEETING
Checklist:
1) website
2) teacher testimonies
3) student testimonies
4) parent testimonies
NIÑOS, I'M PROUD OF YOU! YOU'VE WORKED SO HARD ON THIS! PIE IS ON ME!
¡GRACIAS TÍA!
OOOOH I KNEW YOU LOVED US.
¡MUCHAS GRACIAS!
THIS IS SO AMAZING, THANK YOU!
JUST MAKE SURE YOU NAME YOUR FUTURE TECH COMPANY AFTER ME, OK?
CHRISTINE, DON'T STAY OUT LATE. YOUR FATHER WORRIES.
HAHA!
HAH HA!
I DON'T GET WHY HE'S WORRIED WHEN MY TÍA IS HERE BABYSITTING ME! BUT WHATEVER!

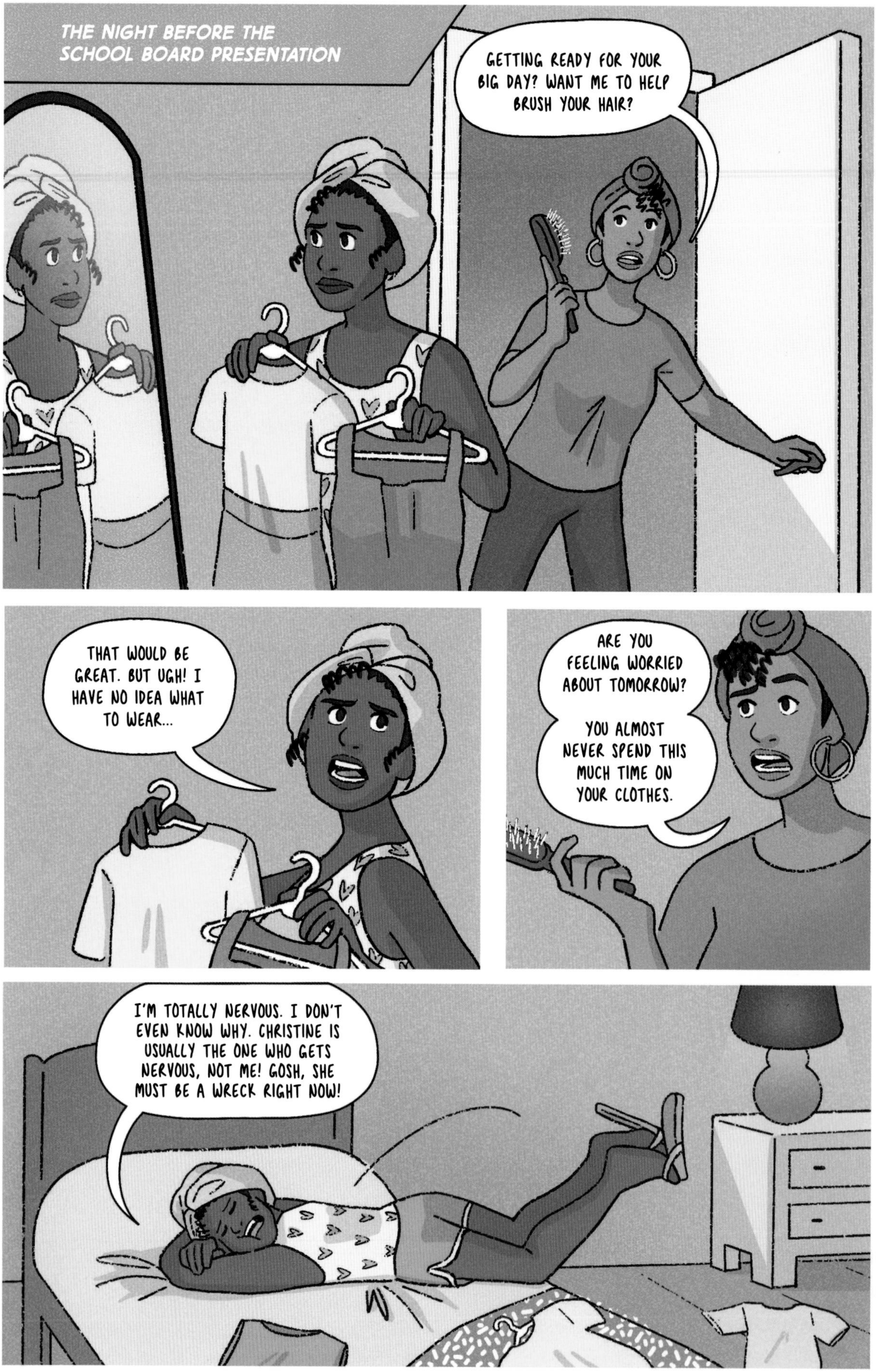
THE NIGHT BEFORE THE SCHOOL BOARD PRESENTATION
GETTING READY FOR YOUR BIG DAY? WANT ME TO HELP BRUSH YOUR HAIR?
THAT WOULD BE GREAT. BUT UGH! I HAVE NO IDEA WHAT TO WEAR...
ARE YOU FEELING WORRIED ABOUT TOMORROW?
YOU ALMOST NEVER SPEND THIS MUCH TIME ON YOUR CLOTHES.
I'M TOTALLY NERVOUS. I DON'T EVEN KNOW WHY. CHRISTINE IS USUALLY THE ONE WHO GETS NERVOUS, NOT ME! GOSH, SHE MUST BE A WRECK RIGHT NOW!

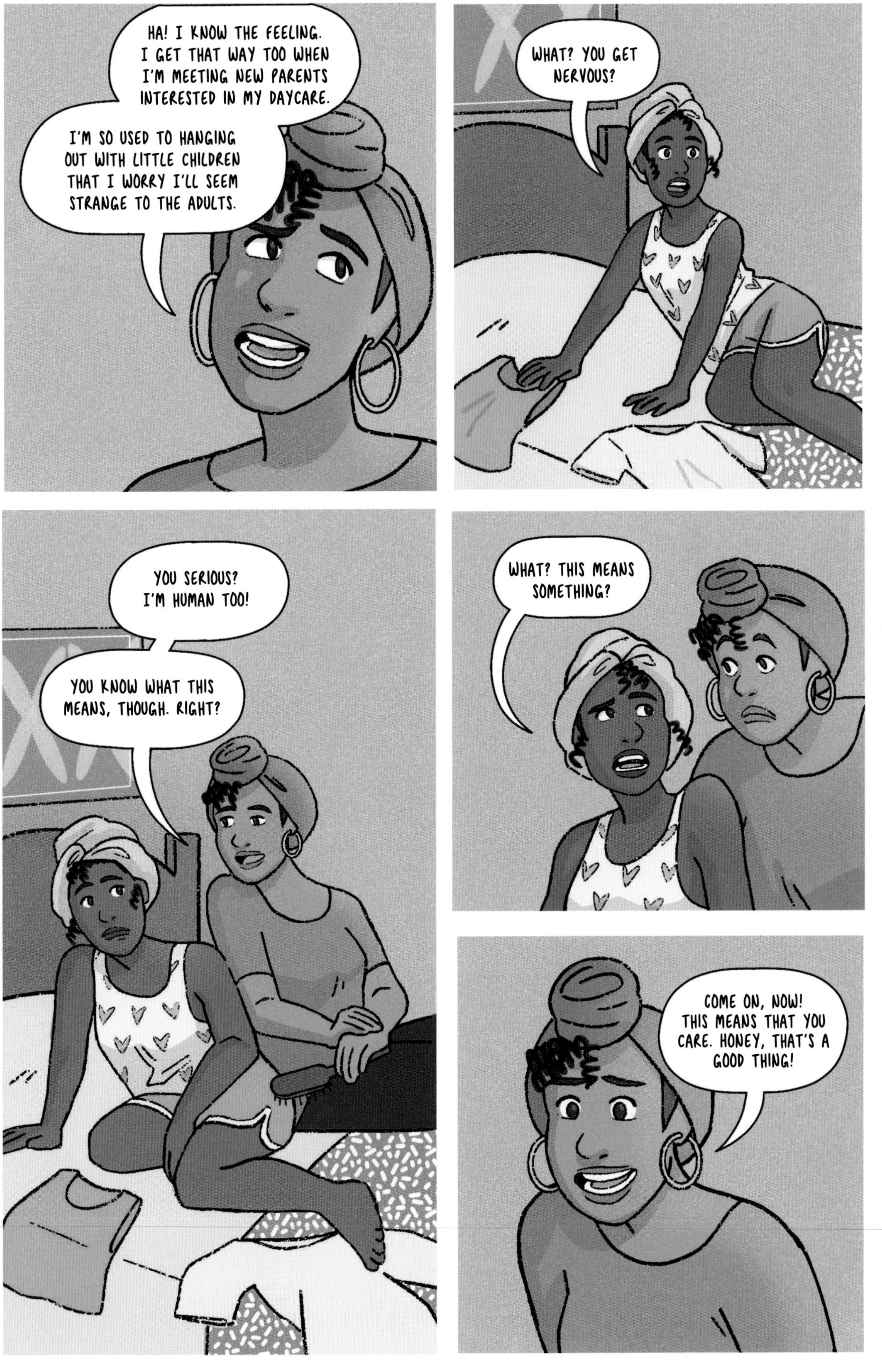
HA! I KNOW THE FEELING. I GET THAT WAY TOO WHEN I'M MEETING NEW PARENTS INTERESTED IN MY DAYCARE.
I'M SO USED TO HANGING OUT WITH LITTLE CHILDREN THAT I WORRY I'LL SEEM STRANGE TO THE ADULTS.
WHAT? YOU GET NERVOUS?
YOU SERIOUS? I'M HUMAN TOO!
YOU KNOW WHAT THIS MEANS, THOUGH. RIGHT?
WHAT? THIS MEANS SOMETHING?
COME ON, NOW! THIS MEANS THAT YOU CARE. HONEY, THAT'S A GOOD THING!

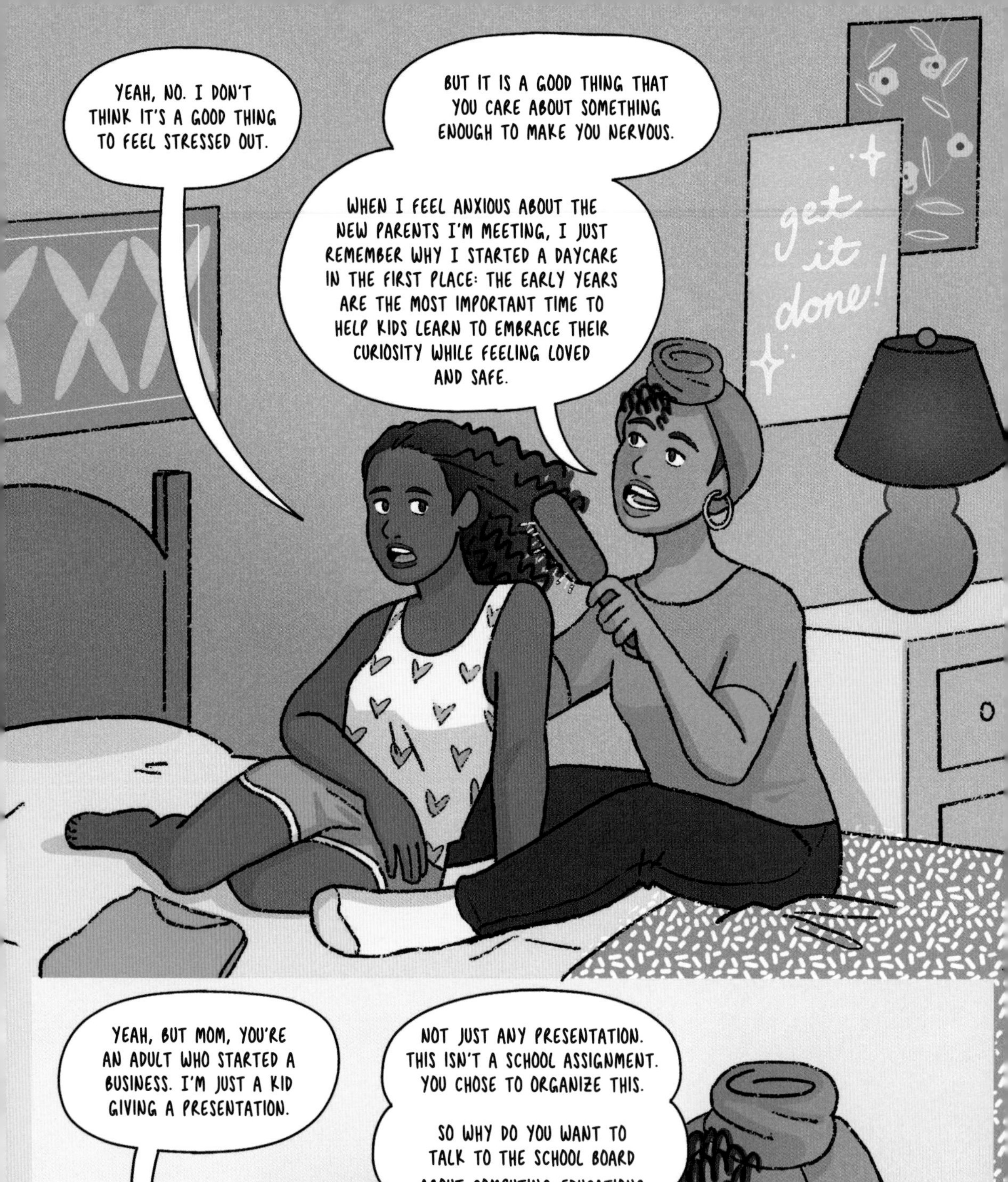
YEAH, NO. I DON'T THINK IT'S A GOOD THING TO FEEL STRESSED OUT.
BUT IT IS A GOOD THING THAT YOU CARE ABOUT SOMETHING ENOUGH TO MAKE YOU NERVOUS.
WHEN I FEEL ANXIOUS ABOUT THE NEW PARENTS I'M MEETING, I JUST REMEMBER WHY I STARTED A DAYCARE IN THE FIRST PLACE: THE EARLY YEARS ARE THE MOST IMPORTANT TIME TO HELP KIDS LEARN TO EMBRACE THEIR CURIOSITY WHILE FEELING LOVED AND SAFE.
get it done!

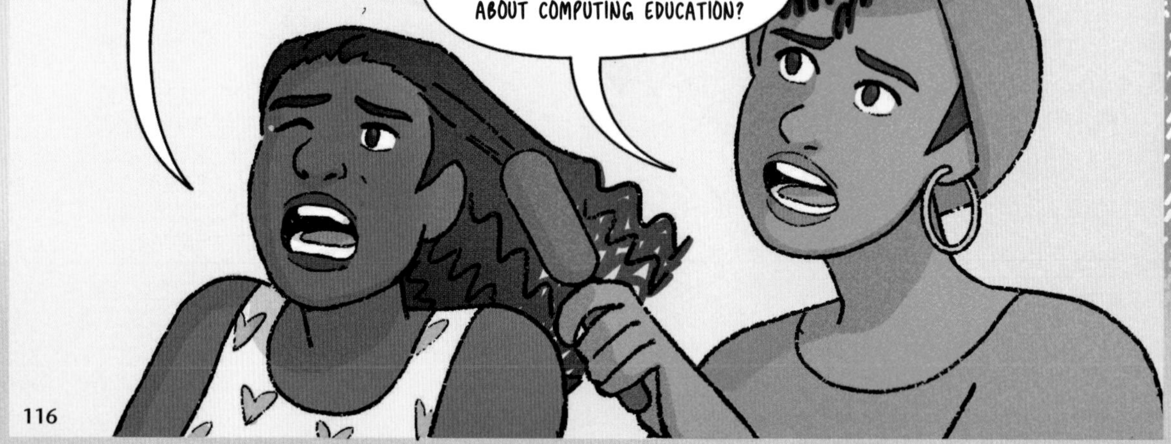
YEAH, BUT MOM, YOU'RE AN ADULT WHO STARTED A BUSINESS. I'M JUST A KID GIVING A PRESENTATION.
NOT JUST ANY PRESENTATION. THIS ISN'T A SCHOOL ASSIGNMENT. YOU CHOSE TO ORGANIZE THIS.
SO WHY DO YOU WANT TO TALK TO THE SCHOOL BOARD ABOUT COMPUTING EDUCATION?

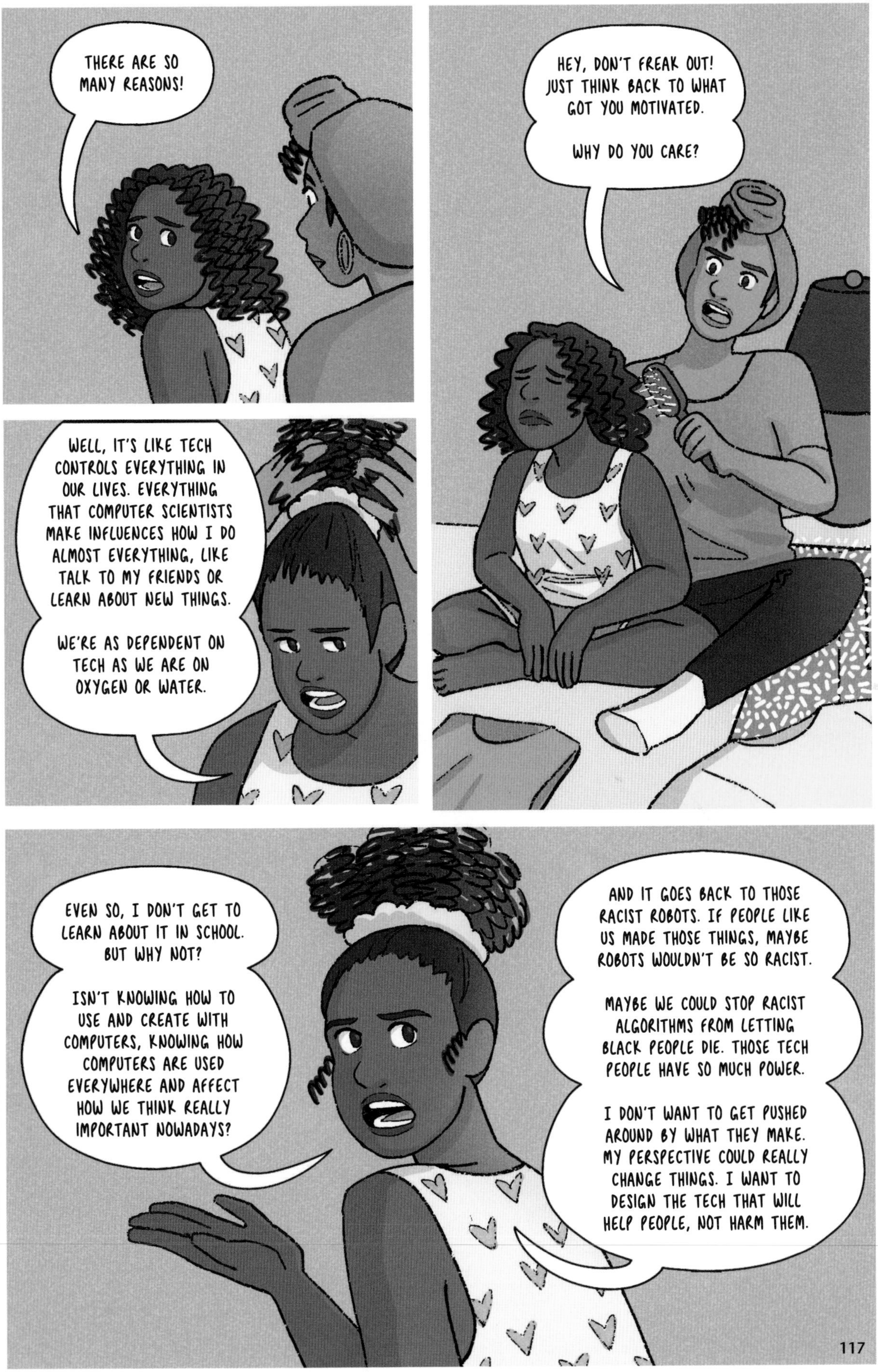

THERE ARE SO MANY REASONS!
HEY, DON'T FREAK OUT! JUST THINK BACK TO WHAT GOT YOU MOTIVATED.
WHY DO YOU CARE?
WELL, IT'S LIKE TECH CONTROLS EVERYTHING IN OUR LIVES. EVERYTHING THAT COMPUTER SCIENTISTS MAKE INFLUENCES HOW I DO ALMOST EVERYTHING, LIKE TALK TO MY FRIENDS OR LEARN ABOUT NEW THINGS.
WE'RE AS DEPENDENT ON TECH AS WE ARE ON OXYGEN OR WATER.
EVEN SO, I DON'T GET TO LEARN ABOUT IT IN SCHOOL. BUT WHY NOT?
ISN'T KNOWING HOW TO USE AND CREATE WITH COMPUTERS, KNOWING HOW COMPUTERS ARE USED EVERYWHERE AND AFFECT HOW WE THINK REALLY IMPORTANT NOWADAYS?
AND IT GOES BACK TO THOSE RACIST ROBOTS. IF PEOPLE LIKE US MADE THOSE THINGS, MAYBE ROBOTS WOULDN'T BE SO RACIST.
MAYBE WE COULD STOP RACIST ALGORITHMS FROM LETTING BLACK PEOPLE DIE. THOSE TECH PEOPLE HAVE SO MUCH POWER.
I DON'T WANT TO GET PUSHED AROUND BY WHAT THEY MAKE. MY PERSPECTIVE COULD REALLY CHANGE THINGS. I WANT TO DESIGN THE TECH THAT WILL HELP PEOPLE, NOT HARM THEM.

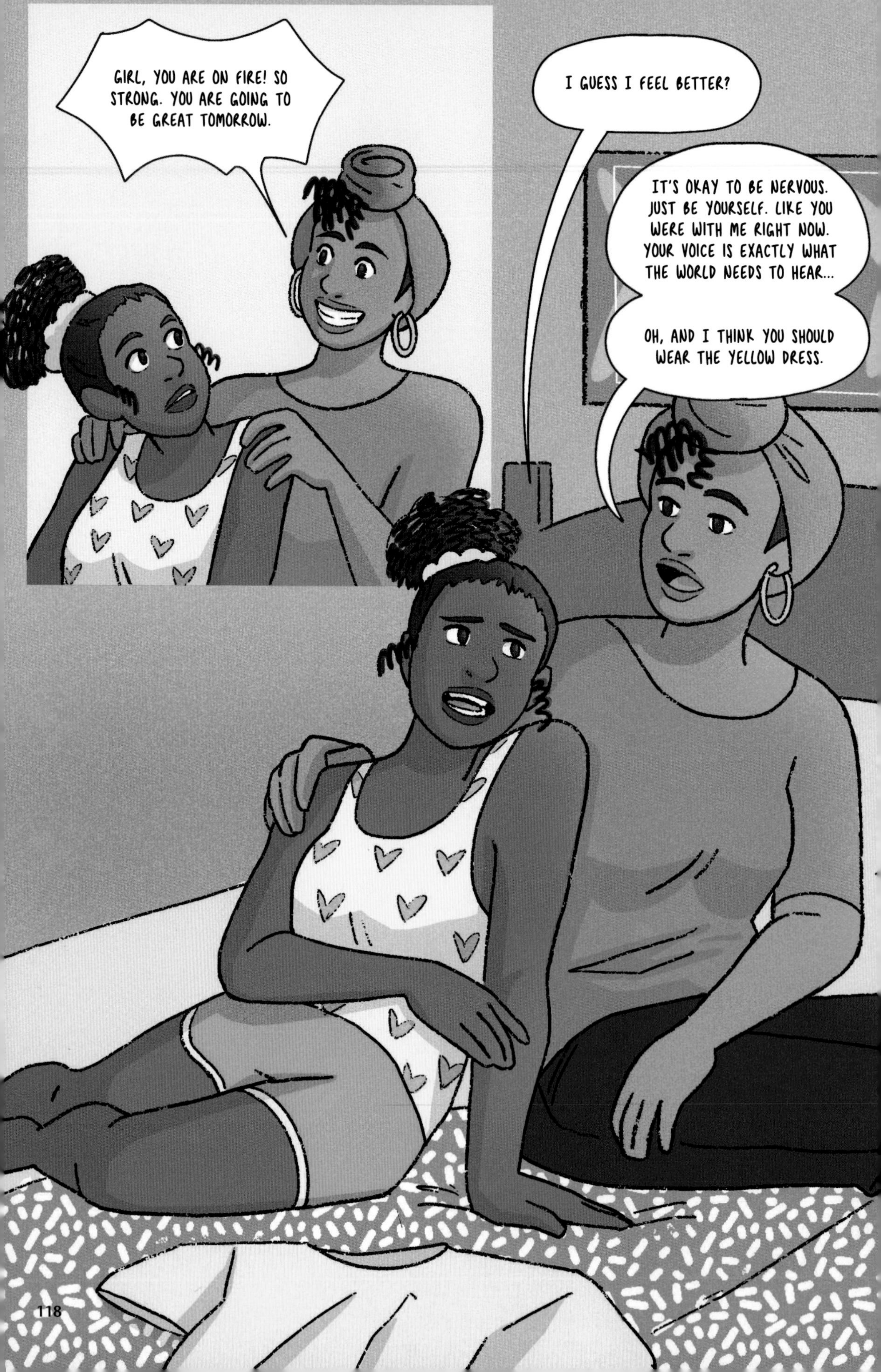
GIRL, YOU ARE ON FIRE! SO STRONG. YOU ARE GOING TO BE GREAT TOMORROW.
I GUESS I FEEL BETTER?
IT'S OKAY TO BE NERVOUS. JUST BE YOURSELF. LIKE YOU WERE WITH ME RIGHT NOW. YOUR VOICE IS EXACTLY WHAT THE WORLD NEEDS TO HEAR...
OH, AND I THINK YOU SHOULD WEAR THE YELLOW DRESS.

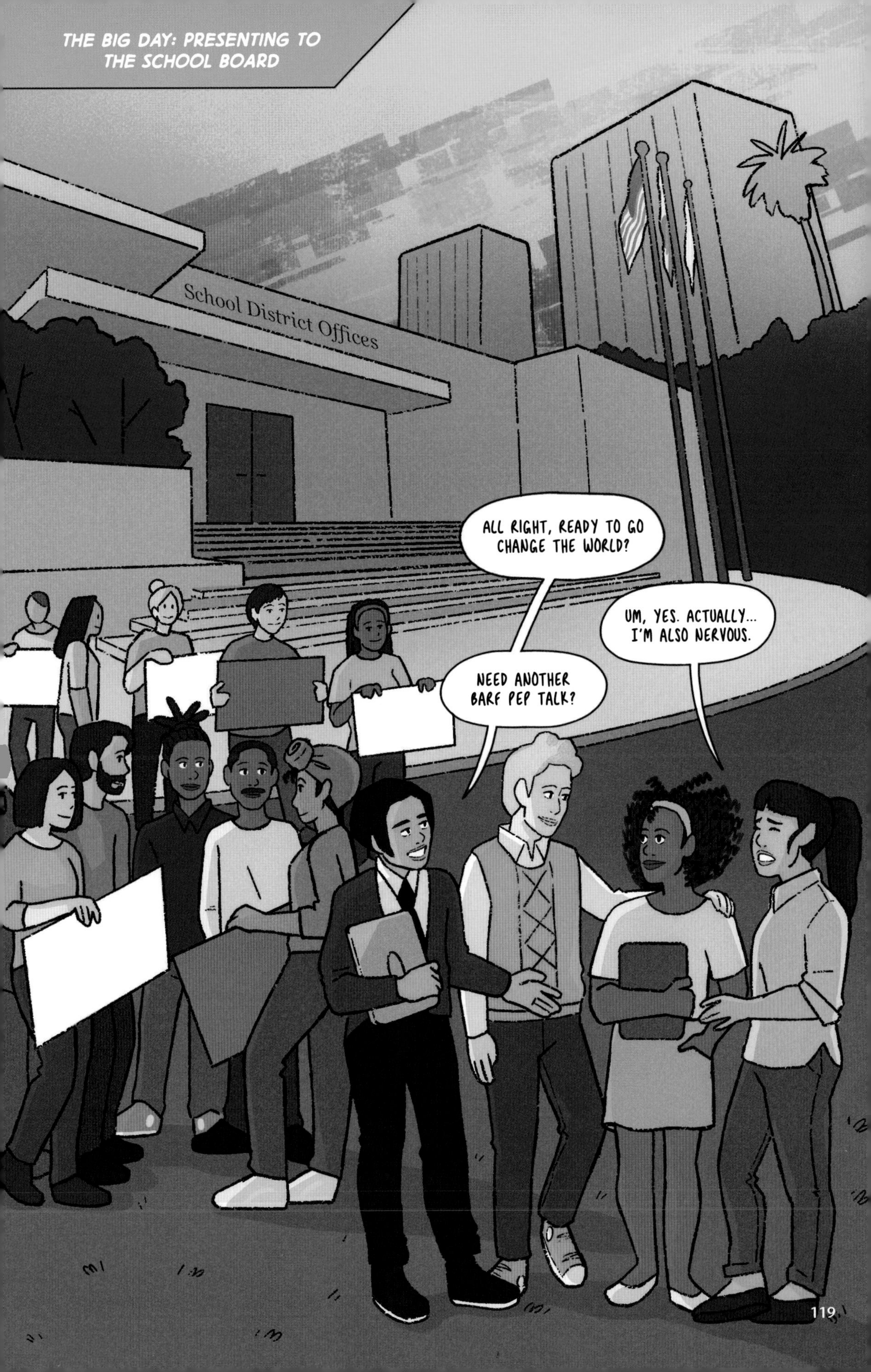
THE BIG DAY: PRESENTING TO THE SCHOOL BOARD
School District Offices
ALL RIGHT, READY TO GO CHANGE THE WORLD?
UM, YES. ACTUALLY... I'M ALSO NERVOUS.
NEED ANOTHER BARF PEP TALK?

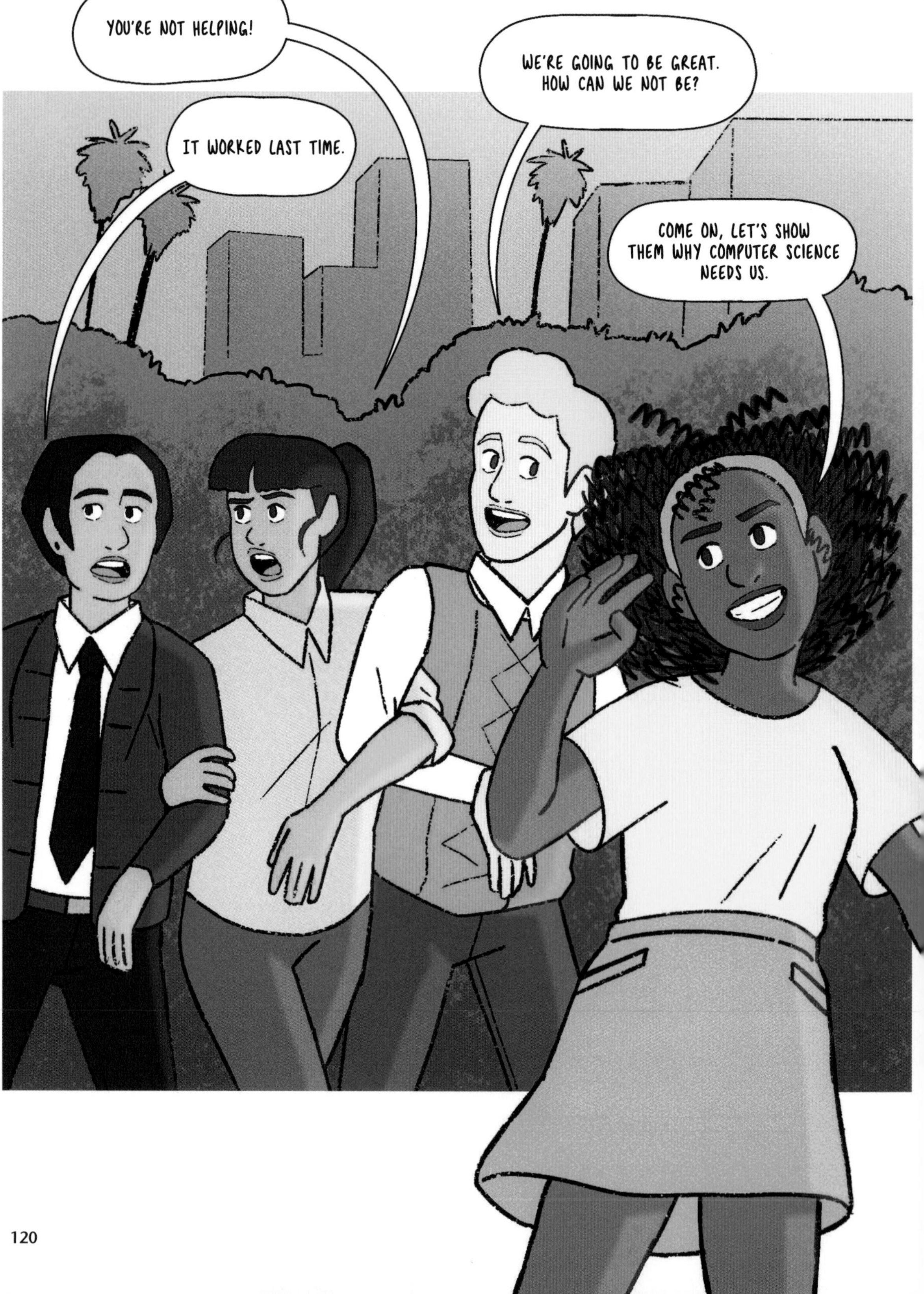
YOU'RE NOT HELPING!
IT WORKED LAST TIME.
WE'RE GOING TO BE GREAT. HOW CAN WE NOT BE?
COME ON, LET'S SHOW THEM WHY COMPUTER SCIENCE NEEDS US.

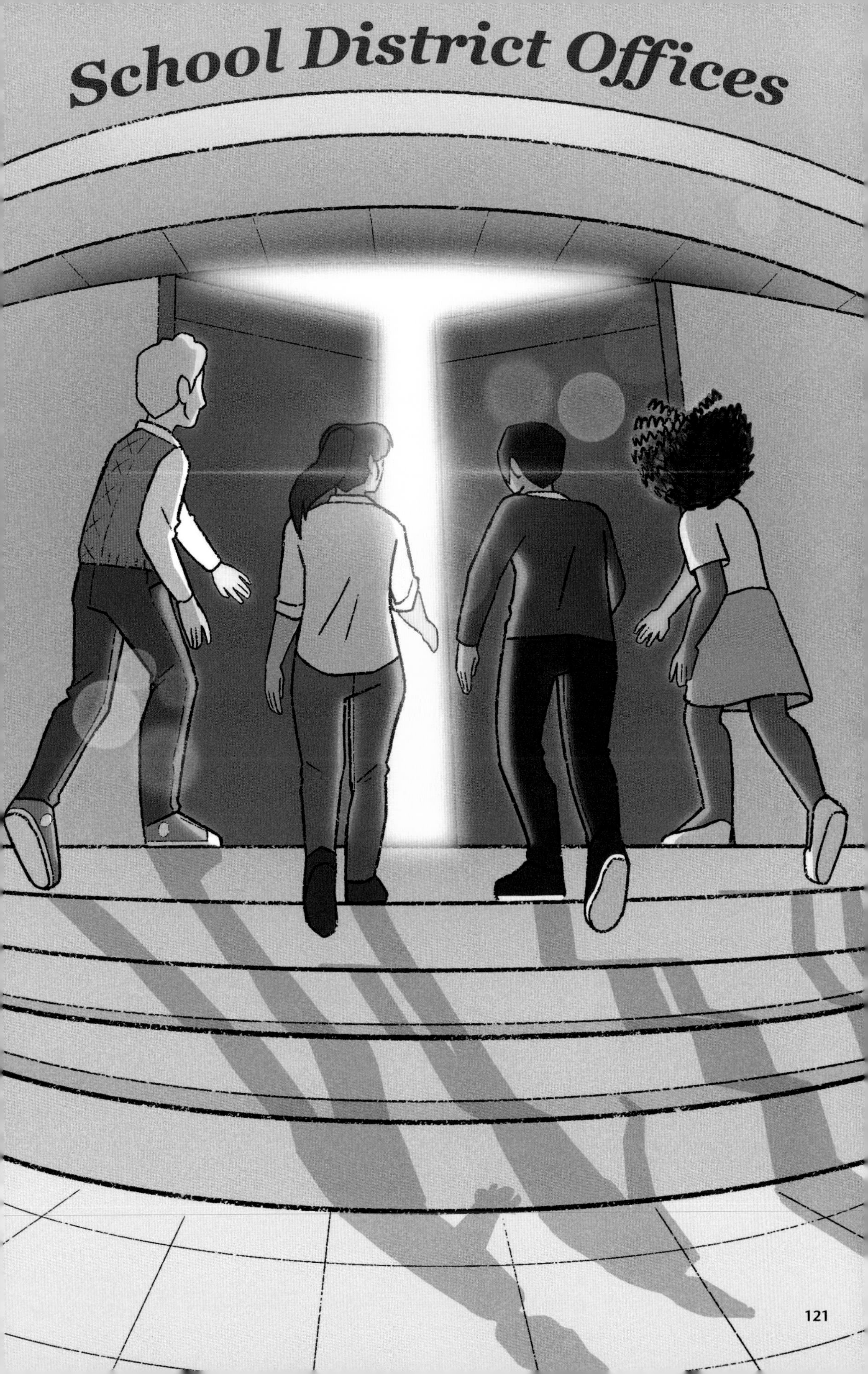
School District Offices

Authors' Statement

Hello Dear Readers!

We hope you enjoyed *Power On!* and will share it with a friend. The characters were inspired by real high school students whom we have had the privilege of working with in Los Angeles and rural Mississippi. Much of the story is based on experiences we've witnessed and learned of through our research about issues of race, gender, and inequality in computer science education. But why did we decide to write a graphic novel for youth, when we usually write books and articles for adults? What we really hope is that this graphic novel sparks new questions and conversations for you, about the way computing impacts our world and why your voice and perspective are needed to shape the technology-driven future for the better of all our communities. Adults may hold a lot of decision-making power, but we believe that young people are often the ones who ask the critical questions and make important observations that are needed for positive innovation and transformation. As Civil Rights activist and math educator Robert Moses once wrote, "We believe the kind of systemic change necessary to prepare our young people for the demands of the twenty-first century requires young people to take the lead in changing it."

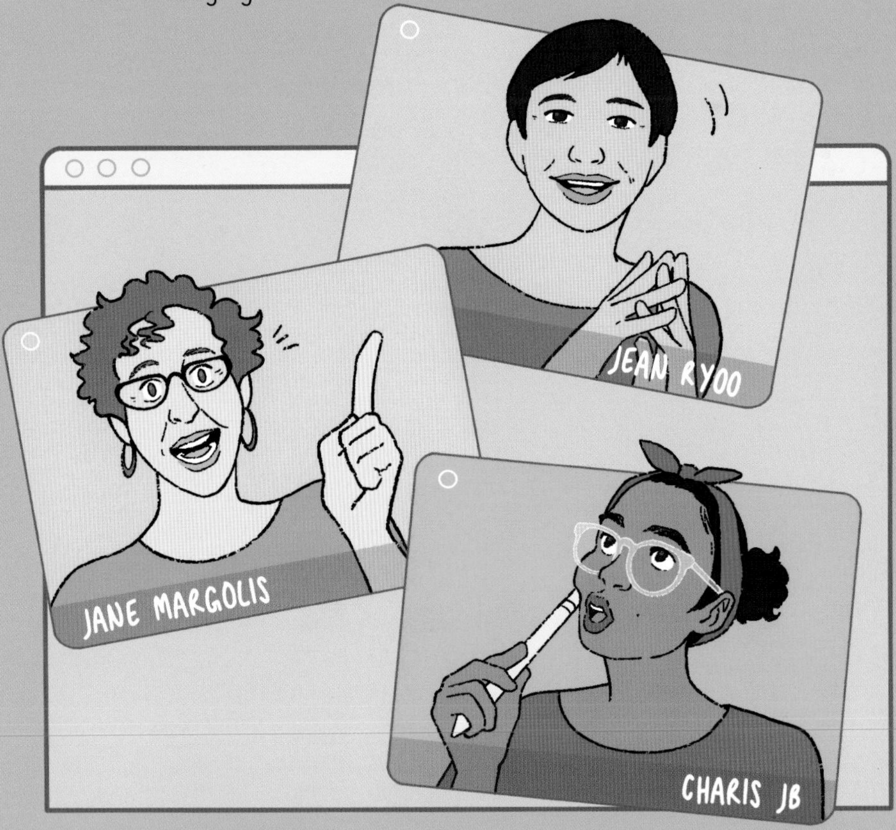
JEAN RYOO
JANE MARGOLIS
CHARIS JB

ACKNOWLEDGMENTS

Thanks to all you dear readers for taking the time to read our graphic novel! We would also like to thank the youth advisory board who offered feedback as we wrote the novel (Brian Arroyo, Journey Clark, Kyla Finney, Natalia Gopar, Gregory Griffin, Rocio Hernández, Stellaluna Lopez-Ramirez, Atani Mone't Nelson, Justice Pankey-Thompson, Markesha Smith, and Axel Tirado); the adult advisory board who shared their input on our book (Brittany Cohen, Lien Diaz, Joanna Goode, Alicia Morris, Solomon Russell, Shana White); our wonderful critical-friend and editor at the MIT Press (Katie Helke) and the entire team of folks there who made this book possible (including but not limited to Judith Feldmann, Yasuyo Iguchi, Jay Martsi, Laura Keeler, Molly Grote, Jessica Pellien, and Bill Smith); our funders from the Bill & Melinda Gates Foundation and National Science Foundation (#1743336 and #2030935); Bridget Bilbo who supported the coloring of pages; the co-authors of *Stuck in the Shallow End: Education, Race, and Computing* (MIT Press, 2008) who helped build the foundation for this work (including Rachel Estrella, Joanna Goode, Jennifer Jellison Holme, and Kimberly Nao); both past and current research team members (Stephanie Bundle, Cynthia Estrada, Je'Monda Roy, and Tiera Tanksley); our project partners (folks named above as well as Shelly Hollis, John Landa, Vic Pacheco, Natascha Woods, and the LAUSD Instructional Technology Initiative); our UCLA team (Julie Flapan, Roxana Hadad, Michelle Choi, and Nina Kasuya); our dear colleagues and partners working tirelessly to center equity and justice in the CS for All community; friends who offered feedback and advice during this process (including Lissa Soep, Cliff Lee, Nicki Washington, and the late and beloved Mike Rose); and, of course, our loving and supportive families and chosen families.

NOTES

CHAPTER 1

1. *Encyclopaedia Britannica*, "Artificial Intelligence," accessed November 5, 2020, https://www.britannica.com/technology/artificial-intelligence.
2. *Oxford English Dictionary*, "Algorithm," accessed November 5, 2020, https://www.lexico.com/en/definition/algorithm.
3. See http://beauty.ai; Jordan Pearson, "Why an AI-Judged Beauty Contest Picked Nearly All White Winners," *Vice*, September 5, 2016, https://www.vice.com/en_us/article/78k-7de/why-an-ai-judged-beauty-contest-picked-nearly-all-white-winners; Ruha Benjamin, *Race after Technology* (Cambridge: Polity, 2019); and Sam Levin, "A Beauty Contest Was Judged by AI and the Robots Didn't Like Dark Skin," *Guardian*, September 8, 2016, https://www.theguardian.com/technology/2016/sep/08/artificial-intelligence-beauty-con-test-doesnt-like-black-people.
4. See Oscar Schwartz, "In 2016, Microsoft's Racist Chatbot Revealed the Dangers of Online Conversation," *IEEE Spectrum*, November 25, 2019, https://spectrum.ieee.org/tech-talk/artificial-intelligence/machine-learning/in-2016-microsofts-racist-chatbot-revealed-the-dangers-of-online-conversation.
5. See Cade Metz, "There Is a Racial Divide in Speech-Recognition Systems, Researchers Say," *New York Times*, March 23, 2020, https://www.nytimes.com/2020/03/23/technology/speech-recognition-bias-apple-amazon-google.html.
6. See also Heidi Ledford, "Millions of Black People Affected by Racial Bias in Health-Care Algorithms," *Nature*, October 24, 2019, https://www.nature.com/articles/d41586-019-03228-6.
7. Joy Buolamwini, "How I'm Fighting Bias in Algorithms," video filmed November 2016 at TEDxBeaconStreet, Brookline, MA. Video, 8:36. https://www.ted.com/talks/joy_buolamwini_how_i_m_fighting_bias_in_algorithms.
8. Data given on this page comes from: National Center for Women and Information Technology, "By the Numbers," April 21, 2020, https://www.ncwit.org/resources/numbers; and Allison Scott, Sonia Koshy, Meghana Rao, Laura Hinton, Julie Flapan, Alexis Martin, and Frieda McAlear, *Computer Science in California's Schools: An Analysis of Access Enrollment, and Equity* (Oakland, CA: Kapor Center, 2019), https://mk0kaporcenter5ld71a.kinstacdn.com/wp-content/uploads/2019/06/Computer-Science-in-California-Schools.pdf.

CHAPTER 3

1. Data on this page reported by GLSEN in Joseph G. Kosciw, Caitlin M. Clark, Nhan L. Truong, and Adrian D. Zongrone, *The 2019 National School Climate Survey: The Experiences of Lesbian, Gay, Bisexual, Transgender, and Queer Youth in Our Nation's Schools* (New York: GLSEN, 2020); reported in Robert R. Redfield, Anne Schuchat, Leslie Dauphin, et al., *Youth Risk Behavior Surveillance–United States, 2017* (Washington, DC: US Department of Health and Human Services, Centers for Disease Control and Prevention, 2017); and reported in the Human Rights Campaign Foundation, *2019 Black and African American LGBTQ Youth Report* (Washington, DC: Human Rights Campaign, 2019).
2. For more information, see Unidos US's "7 Ways Immigrants Enrich Our Economy and Society" fact sheet at https://www.unidosus.org/issues/immigration/resources/facts, and Marshall Fitz, Philip E. Wolgin, and Patrick Oakford, "Immigrants Are Makers, Not Takers," *Center for American Progress–Immigration*, February 8, 2013, https://www.americanprogress.org/issues/immigration/news/2013/02/08/52377/immigrants-are-makers-not-takers/.
3. Jane Margolis with Rachel Estrella, Joanna Goode, Jennifer Jellison Holme, and Kim Nao, *Stuck in the Shallow End: Education, Race, and Computing*, updated ed. (Cambridge, MA: MIT Press, 2017).

CHAPTER 4

1. Ziad Obermeyer, Brian Powers, Christine Vogeli, and Sendhil Mullainathan, "Dissecting Racial Bias in an Algorithm Used to Manage the Health of Populations," *Science 336* (2019): 447–453.
2. Cathy O'Neil, *Weapons of Math Destruction: How Big Data Increases Inequality and Threatens Democracy* (New York: Broadway Books, 2016).
3. Benjamin, *Race after Technology*.
4. Safiya Umoja Noble, *Algorithms of Oppression: How Search Engines Reinforce Racism* (New York: NYU Press, 2018).
5. Virginia Eubanks, *Automating Inequality: How High-Tech Tools Profile, Police, and Punish the Poor* (New York: St. Martin's Press, 2018).

CHAPTER 5

1. Margot Lee Shetterly, *Hidden Figures: The American Dream and the Untold Story of the Black Women Who Helped Win the Space Race* (New York: William Morrow, 2016).